My Re  *C*

A lighthearted Regency romance

Brazen Bluestockings book 1

Shirley Karr

Cover design by Daniela Colleo, StunningBookCovers.com

Paperback ISBN 978-1-955613-11-8

E-Book ISBN 978-1-955613-07-1

First Edition: April 2023

Acknowledgments

My thanks to Geoff Castellucci, whose fabulous vocal performances inspired the "what if..." path that led to this story.

My thanks also to Helen Beseda and Betty Booher, who share my love of music but have a much better understanding of music theory than I do. Any errors are mine.

I'm also indebted to Cheerleader Jessie and the Monday night write-in group from Rose City Romance Writers for holding me accountable and helping me reach my goals. Three cheers for positive peer pressure!

Prologue

Surrey, England
Summer 1801

DAVID HELD HIS HANDS above the keyboard, trying to form the next chord correctly, when he heard a baby crying in the hall. Moments later, his sister Lydia poked her head through the doorway, her eyes closed.

"Are you decent?"

He checked that the blanket on his lap covered his nightshirt and legs, at least as far as he could reach. "Enter," he called loud enough to be heard over the squalling baby.

Lydia shut the music room door behind her and strode directly to David, holding her baby out in front until she thrust the screaming infant into David's arms.

David tucked the baby against his chest and began rocking side to side and uttering soothing nonsense. Within moments Missy began to settle, and soon let David hold her in the crook of his arm.

"Oh, thank heavens," Lydia muttered as soon as the baby quieted. "Keep talking to her, or better yet, sing," she said. "She wouldn't settle for Nurse or me."

David shook his head and frowned at Lydia even as he began to quietly sing a lullaby. Only a few phrases in and Missy relaxed with her chubby cheek against David's chest, one tiny fist clutching his nightshirt.

Lydia tugged the blanket down to cover David's foot, his splinted right leg propped up on the Bath chair. He finished the first verse and began the next, dropping his voice one octave. Lydia sat on the pianoforte stool and swayed as though she were holding the baby.

When he finished the lullaby, Missy gave a tiny yawn and kept her head pillowed on his chest.

Lydia opened her eyes and smiled fondly at her baby. "I noticed how quickly she settled when you held her while we were all singing after dinner."

"I couldn't exactly run away when you handed her to me."

She squeezed his toes. "How much longer did the surgeon say you had to stay off your leg?"

"Another three weeks, at least," he grumbled. "I'll be stuck in here like this the whole rest of the summer."

"Well, at least you won't miss any school. And you have plenty of toys to break up the boredom." Her gesture encompassed the entire room. The family music room held pianoforte and harpsichord, harp, violins, viola and violincellos, Great-Grandfather's viola da gamba, and cupboards with an extensive collection of smaller instruments and music books.

After David broke his leg and was brought to the house, footmen carried him in through the terrace doors and set him on the sofa in here. His mother had since ordered a cot set up and the servants brought some of his belongings and a privacy screen down from his bedchamber while he convalesced in the ground floor room.

"I've heard you, you know," Lydia continued. "When you leave the garden doors open, I can hear you practicing, playing with your voice like it's a new toy. You're getting better at baritone, and when you're playing the pianoforte, I've heard you hit several bass notes."

Missy patted his chest and lifted her head to look at him expectantly. "It's just interesting to see how low I can go now, or how high I can still hit and hold a note." As soon as he began speaking, Missy laid her head down again. He hummed and absently patted her back.

"I'm going to rewrite my latest composition. I knew your voice would keep getting deeper as you mature but didn't realize just how quickly it would change."

"You didn't notice the changes in Philip's voice?" Their older brother had gone from singing tenor to baritone in their family musicales before he left for Oxford two years ago. David had sung soprano at ten, alto at twelve, tenor at fourteen, and now at fifteen could almost do justice to baritone parts. When his voice didn't crack.

"I wasn't trying to make my own voice sound good back then," Lydia said. She took it as a personal insult to have such a limited vocal range—barely one full octave—in a family that sang and played together almost every evening, and often invited friends and neighbors over to join in creating their entertainment.

David grinned. "I *knew* that was why you took up arranging music." Missy made little sounds of pleasure when he spoke. "You snagged a husband, though, so I don't know why you keep doing it."

She gave a soft smile at the mention of her husband, who was currently out of the country on a diplomatic mission. His absence was why she'd come home for an extended visit. "I tangle embroidery threads, and my watercolors are abysmal. But music that I arrange sounds good. Especially if someone more talented than me brings it to life."

Missy was lax in his arms, sound asleep. He stopped patting her. She didn't react. "Going to take her up to the nursery now?"

Lydia wheeled David's Bath chair away from the pianoforte, tugged the stool close to the keyboard, and played a chord. "One more song, to make sure she's sound asleep." She played a familiar tune but in a key that challenged his lower register. His voice was warmed up, though, and he got through it competently if not artistically.

Lydia moved the stool again so he could get close to the pianoforte in his Bath chair before she gently picked up Missy and cradled her. "Thank you. I'll bring her to you tomorrow night if she's fussy."

"No," David said, careful to keep his voice quiet and free of tension. "I am not a nurse. Soothing fussy babies is not my responsibility."

Lydia only smiled as she exited the music room.

The next day, his sister Diana and her family arrived for a visit, to meet Missy. Diana was only six years older than David and two years older than Lydia, but had married a widower with three young children. So far, they'd had two more.

He was not surprised when Diana knocked on the music room door at the children's bedtime and trooped in with her five children, ranging from one to seven years, followed by Lydia carrying Missy.

"They want a lullaby," Lydia said, innocently batting her lashes as she handed him her infant. She rolled his Bath chair away from the pianoforte, pulled up the stool, and began to play.

Diana sat on the sofa with her baby, who was half asleep. Her other children gathered around his chair on the floor. Except for three-year-old Georgia, who climbed onto his lap, careful not to jostle Missy or his injured leg. "Sing, Uncle David," Georgia demanded, pressing her ear against his chest. "Make me shake."

Earlier that afternoon she had snuggled in his lap to press her ear and hand to his chest, and squealed in delight when he had growled like a troll and other scary beasts, intoned the lowest notes he could reach, and practiced scales.

David sang, one arm around Georgia and the other cuddling Missy, even while he stared daggers at Lydia. His friends would never let him live down the ignominy of playing nurse for a half dozen nieces and nephews, even if he did dearly love the little curtain climbers.

An idea formed as he sang the familiar lullaby, a soothing melody with horrific words about a baby in its cradle falling out of a treetop.

By the time he finished, Diana's youngest and Missy were both asleep. "Would you like to hear a bedtime story?" he quietly offered.

Nodding eagerly, the children drew nearer. Lydia and Diana beamed.

David tilted his head back and gave a low, menacing laugh, and then proceeded to warn the children why they should stay indoors after dark and go to bed on time. He described the gathering of ghouls and goblins who came out every night to torment the living with fiendish glee. The hideous creatures would come indoors to hide under the stairs or under the beds of children if the doors were not locked and windows closed. If the children didn't behave, the Bogeyman would get them.

As he spun his yarn he let his voice get quieter and rumble deeper, and finished with another demonic laugh, head tilted back, his teeth bared.

Diana and Lydia looked equal parts horrified and appalled. The children squealed in delight and begged for another.

"Silly Uncle David," Georgia said, patting his cheek. "*You're* the Bogeyman."

Chapter 1

London
March 1816

MISS ASHLEY HAMLIN FOLLOWED her Aunt Eunice and Uncle Edward up the steps into the grand home for her fifth ball of the Season.

They made their way along the receiving line to greet their hosts, Lord and Lady Sedgewick, admiring the sumptuous interior and equally opulent guests. After working at Torquay Academy for Young Ladies for five years, Ashley could perform the social niceties by rote, yet still struggled to not feel like an imposter here in London.

She adjusted her silk shawl, marveling anew at her recent good fortune.

After they were announced at the entrance to the ballroom, Ashley stepped forth into the swirling crowd, feeling like she was heading into battle, flanked by her uncle and aunt.

Lord Sedgewick had engaged a sextet for the event that included a viola and violincello. After so many years of hearing primarily high-pitched feminine voices, and girls who played treble clef instruments like flute and fife, Ashley felt starved for sounds from the bass clef. Dancers had already formed a long double line performing the steps of the polonaise.

"See anyone you like tonight, my dear?" Uncle Edward patted her hand on his arm. "I'll arrange introductions."

"Only for eligible partis," Aunt Eunice said.

"Of course, darling," Uncle said.

Feeling the rhythm of the music resonate within her bosom, Ashley itched to dance. "I'll be sure to let you know." *Not bloody likely.* She pasted a smile on her face. At best, she hoped to hear talented musicians and dance a time or two with some kind gentleman or other who took pity on a spinster. Someone who could suppress his cringe of horror after learning she was a bluestocking.

Three weeks into the Season, the only attention she seemed to draw was from gracious hosts, men doing a good deed, or reprobates interested mainly in the modest dowry Uncle Edward planned to settle on her. Though there was that widower who wanted a mature woman as a mother figure for his brood of eight children. She shuddered.

Her official goal for the Season, the same as for any single young lady, was to secure a husband. Barring some miracle, however, based on the empirical evidence of her social outings so far, she was as likely to jump and land on the moon as get married.

This probable future did not keep her awake at night. She had truly enjoyed her work at the academy. She looked forward to obtaining a position at another school before the Season ended.

They greeted friends as they promenaded the perimeter of the ballroom. Uncle Edward was soon drawn into a discussion with two of his cronies about horses for sale at Tattersall's, and the men drifted toward the card room.

"Miss Hamlin?" came a surprised greeting.

Ashley smiled at the former student of the academy. "Miss Barrow-Smith. How lovely to see you."

Miss Barrow-Smith took a few more moments to recover from the apparent shock of seeing her at a London ball.

Ashley couldn't blame her. The cost of her ecru silk gown, pearl necklace, and other accessories totaled more than double what her annual salary had been at the academy. "May I make you known to my aunt, Mrs. Endicott." She patted her aunt's hand that was tucked in her arm. "Miss Amber Barrow-Smith completed her studies at the academy last year."

The two curtsied and exchanged greetings.

Ashley recognized the looks on their faces—Miss Barrow-Smith calculating the cost of their respective ensembles, Aunt Eunice considering why Miss Barrow-Smith needed a second season on the Marriage Mart to make a good match—and almost laughed.

They parted after exchanging a few more pleasantries, then Miss Barrow-Smith disappeared with other friends and Ashley searched the crowd for a likely dance partner.

"Oh no," she said, stepping behind Aunt Eunice and her purple turban with three ostrich feathers. "*He's* here."

Aunt Eunice followed Ashley's gaze to Sir Rupert Connor. "He has been most assiduous in paying court to you."

Sir Rupert had engaged her in conversation at every event she'd attended. To her regret, she had accepted his dance invitation the first time they had been introduced. She couldn't quite identify what put her off. That he tended to address her bosom when they spoke was not unusual, and other gentlemen might use the same amount of pomade to slick back their hair. Even though they both wore gloves, his touch elicited the feeling that she needed to bathe.

"I'm going to visit the ladies' retiring room." She felt nary a twinge of guilt at using her favorite ruse for escaping unpleasant social situations. "You find a chair and I'll rejoin you soon."

Aunt Eunice sighed. "I'm going to ask Cook if she can concoct something that will help settle your nervous stomach."

Ashley gave her a reassuring smile as she left.

Lord Sedgewick's townhouse was the largest Ashley had been in. She must have taken a wrong turn, as she soon found herself in a quiet hallway. All of these rooms had closed doors, and she hadn't seen a footman since the last turn.

Up ahead she saw a couple in a shadowy alcove. She was about to turn back and give them privacy when she heard a firm, feminine, "No."

Ashley paused.

A male voice spoke, his words indistinguishable but his tone cajoling, followed by a fervent feminine, "No, I mustn't."

The male voice turned angry.

Ashley strode forward. Startled, the couple sprang apart, the young woman looking guilty, the man annoyed. "There you are," Ashley brightly announced, linking her arm through the stunned young woman's and practically towing her back down the hall. "Aunt has been looking *everywhere* for you." She shot a treacly smile over her shoulder at the man. "Do forgive us, but we simply *must* return to my aunt."

"Yes, of course," he said slowly, looking a bit dazed.

The two women walked in silence until they turned the corner. Ashley poked her head in the nearest room, saw that it was blessedly unoccupied, tugged the young woman in, and closed the door behind them. She rested her hands on the girl's shoulders and looked her over in the lamplight. "Are you all right?"

She was dressed in the white muslin of a girl in her first Season. Couldn't be more than seventeen or eighteen. Her strawberry blond curls trembled, her blue eyes wide and bright with unshed tears. She gave a jerky nod. "I am now. Thank you."

Ashley offered a handkerchief from her reticule.

The girl dabbed at her eyes and gave a decidedly indelicate blow of her nose, followed by several deep breaths. She clutched the embroidered linen in one fist. "You must think me a silly gudgeon."

"Not at all." Ashley led them to the sofa before the fireplace and they sat down. "He's handsome and well dressed. I'm sure he was charming. Until he wasn't."

"Exactly!" The young woman tapped Ashley's knee. "I thought he simply wanted to talk, and the music was so loud where we were sitting with my mother."

"You're not the first young woman to be deceived so."

She dabbed her eyes again. "I suppose you're old enough not to fall for such fustian." Her eyes flew open wide. "Oh! I did not mean that as an insult."

Ashley shrugged it off. "This is only my second season, but the first was five years ago."

The girl sat back. "I sense there's an interesting story to go with that statement." She adjusted her embroidered white skirts and plucked a few of what looked like grey cat hairs. "I'm Georgia, by the way."

Stifling a deeply ingrained habit, Ashley did not chastise the girl for being so informal on such short acquaintance. "Ashley." She had nothing to be embarrassed about. Thanks to the largesse of Uncle Edward, her gown, hair, and accessories were first rate. Only her twenty-three-year-old face was out of style.

The clock beside the fireplace chimed the half hour.

"Oh!" Georgia jumped to her feet. "I must return to the ballroom or Mother will send my uncle to hunt me down."

Ashley rose as well. "We'll go together, at least until we get back into the crowd."

"Yes, that's wise." Georgia surprised her by giving her a quick hug. "Thank you so much for pretending to be my friend."

Ashley linked their arms again as they entered the hallway. "Glad I could be of assistance."

Georgia gave her another hug.

Ashley accompanied Georgia back to her mother, who sat near the musicians, and then went to the far side of the room and sat next to Aunt Eunice.

"Feeling better, dear?"

Ashley was about to respond in the affirmative but saw Sir Rupert heading directly for them. She spread her fan in front of her face. "I was."

"Mrs. Endicott, may I say you look more charming each time I see you?" Sir Rupert bowed low, and Aunt Eunice replied with something suitable. He turned to Ashley. Good manners dictated she offer her hand when he reached for it. She tried to disguise her moue of distaste into a smile.

"Miss Hamlin, you look most fetching tonight. I envy that paisley silk shawl the privilege to rest upon your shoulders." He glanced at the musicians, who played the opening notes of the next dance. Sir Rupert opened his mouth to issue an invitation that she could not, would not, let him finish. How often had she taught the students society's rule that once a gentleman requests a dance, one cannot decline unless one is willing to not dance the rest of the evening?

"I find I'm parched," she interjected, to head him off.

He looked taken aback, then quickly regained his composure and gave her an oily smile. "I am your humble servant." He bowed again and left to fetch punch.

"Should we leave now?" Aunt Eunice whispered behind her fan.

Ashley was sorely tempted. But she hadn't had a chance to dance yet. After five years working at a school for girls, she yearned to dance with skilled male partners. How could she rid herself of Sir Rupert and still project her availability to suitable partners? And she still held some small shred of hope she'd find a gentleman who was not put off by her advanced age, advanced level of education, or her unwillingness to simper.

Sir Rupert returned with three cups of punch. He handed the first to Aunt Eunice, then one to Ashley, and took the seat beside her.

She took a sip and grimaced. After such excellent décor and musicians, she thought Lady Sedgewick would serve a better tasting punch.

"Is it not to your liking?" Sir Rupert leaned entirely too close.

"It is delicious," she lied, and took a deep swallow. At least now the song was too far advanced for them to join a square. She continued to sip at the punch, limiting the number of replies she needed to make while still being polite.

Sir Rupert seemed inordinately pleased. Perhaps he really did enjoy her company to stay seated here among the chaperones, wallflowers, and spinsters.

The last few measures of the current song played. Would the pleasure of dancing the next set be ruined if she was partnered by Sir Rupert? The movements of the dance would often separate them.

A wave of fatigue washed over her. It took all of her concentration to remain sitting upright. Her punch cup suddenly felt too heavy to hold. Sir Rupert caught it before it fell from her fingers and set it and his own cup on the tray of a passing footman.

How odd. She'd made certain to get her allotment of eight hours of sleep last night plus a half-hour lie-down this afternoon, to be sure she had energy for tonight's festivities. But suddenly she struggled to keep her eyes open.

David, Earl of Ravencroft, allowed himself to relax when he saw his niece had returned to the ballroom. Where had the scamp gone off to? He'd been about to go search for her. Now, though, he could relax with a cup of punch and pass the time until his sister and niece were ready to leave by evaluating the musicians' performance.

The gentleman beside him at the refreshment table slipped a small glass bottle from a pocket and poured some into a cup of punch ... only one of the three cups he had ladled.

Probably meant nothing. David's friends had amended a cup or two at various events, though Lady Sedgewick's punch tonight was delicious. But he couldn't help watching the gentleman in the green-and-yellow-striped waistcoat deliver the punch to a matron in a purple turban and the young woman seated beside her.

The man gave the cup of altered punch to the young woman.

David stopped slouching against the wall and straightened to his full height.

He stepped to the side when his view became blocked by couples promenading the perimeter of the ballroom. By the time he could set eyes on the trio again, the young woman let out a jaw-cracking yawn without trying to hide it behind her fan, and the cup nearly slipped from her lax hand before her suitor caught it.

Couples were forming two columns for the next song, a contredanse. Striped Waistcoat and the girl headed for the top of the column of dancers ... and kept going, toward the terrace doors.

David ran his tongue across the back of his front teeth, debating. It was none of his business if a couple wanted privacy in the dark garden.

But the girl had probably been unaware her suitor had put something extra in her punch. The man had her arm tightly tucked through his. As they maneuvered through the crowd it looked like he was the main force keeping her upright.

David's niece took her spot at the top of the column just then, opposite some young jackanapes or other who looked fresh from university, both of them shyly smiling.

David would castrate any man who altered her drink.

Who was looking out for the young woman who'd just gone outside? Her companion in the turban was chatting with a matron seated on her other side, oblivious to her charge's whereabouts.

He stepped out onto the terrace.

After the brilliance of the ballroom, it took a moment for his eyes to adjust to the faint light of a waning half-moon. There, at the back of the garden. A flash of pale skirt disappearing into the gazebo.

He hurried down the path, keeping his footsteps light in case he had misread the situation, and peeked into the gazebo.

Hidden in deep shadows, he could barely see the girl, semi-reclining on a bench, her head lolled back, one foot on the floor, one leg stretched out on the bench. Striped Waistcoat had the fall of his breeches unbuttoned and was trying to raise her skirts. She roused a bit at that and feebly batted at his hands. "No. Go 'way," she slurred.

David stepped into the gazebo. "Leave her," he commanded.

Striped Waistcoat dropped the girl's skirt and glared at the intruder. "Get your own bit o' muslin. Bugger off."

"Leave now, under your own power," David said in a conversational tone as he retrieved his dagger from its hidden pocket. He held the blade up, letting moonlight glint off the razor-sharp tip. He dropped his voice two octaves to a rumbling bass. "Or you'll leave as a eunuch."

The man squeaked—really, no other word could describe the high-pitched sound that emerged from his throat—and stumbled from the gazebo, holding up his breeches with one hand, trying to get past David without making contact. With grim satisfaction, David watched him dash down the path until he melted into the shadows near the house, before putting away his knife.

The woman struggled to sit up. "Go 'way," she said. "I'll bite."

"I'd prefer that you didn't." David reached for her but paused. "I'm going to help you stand up." She didn't protest further, so he grasped her wrists and pulled her upright.

She swayed and fell against his chest. "So tired," she mumbled into his cravat, her arms going around him in a loose embrace. The scent of rosewater wafted up, light enough it must be from her soap rather than perfume. "Don't un'stand."

Awkwardly he patted her back, worried about what Striped Waistcoat had given her and its effect on her. "Let's get you back to the ballroom before anyone misses you." He wrapped an arm around her shoulders, got her moving, and steered them out to the path.

They'd gone only a few steps when she wrenched from his grasp. "Sick."

He caught her about the waist in time to keep her from pitching face-first into the rosebushes while she cast up her accounts. He held her silk shawl back and supported most of her weight as she hung over his arm, retching. He hoped she missed his shoes.

She groaned. Coughed and spit. And groaned again.

He winced in sympathy. "Can you walk?"

She needed help to stand upright, but then pushed away from him. She took two steps and her knees buckled.

David caught her and swung her up into his arms.

"Guess not." She patted his shoulder. "Good catch."

"You're welcome." He headed for the terrace, slowing his steps as he realized he could not return her to the ballroom in her present condition. Not unless he wanted to see their engagement announcement published in *The Times* two days hence. How would her companion, the matron in the purple turban, react? Would she be the type to seize any opportunity to marry off her charge to an earl?

He could summon his sister for help. Though Diana was not a gossip, she had never been able to prevaricate in her life. Word would certainly get out if she knew what he'd done, however innocent his actions, how noble his intentions.

After some swift calculations, he swerved off the path, staying in the shadows, and headed around the side of the townhouse. Fortunately Lord Sedgewick's home was at the end of the row, so there was an easy path to the street out front. David paused while he was still fully in the dark. If he stepped out into the light of streetlamps and the half-moon to reach his carriage, the girl's face would be seen.

He propped one foot on a garden bench that no doubt afforded a lovely view of the rosebushes, and rested her weight on his knee. "Please trust that I am trying to help, not make things worse."

She didn't speak. Just patted his shoulder again.

He tugged the delicate silk shawl with its distinctive colors and pattern from her shoulders and stuffed it into his coat pocket. Praying that she didn't have anything more to cast up, he shifted his grip, heaved her up, and settled her over his shoulder, one arm wrapped around the back of her thighs, the other holding her arm over his opposite shoulder.

She made a muffled sound that might have been an indignant protest but sounded suspiciously like a giggle. Her left arm hung down his back, occasionally bumping into him. More than once he would swear she patted his bottom.

Ignoring the stares from passers-by and coachmen, he strode toward his carriage as if carrying a young woman over his shoulder was an everyday occurrence.

"My lord?" Gilroy, his manservant, jumped down from the bench. He and the coachman exchanged worried glances.

"A blackguard put something in her drink." He quickly gave instructions for Gilroy to find the girl's chaperone, a matron in a purple turban with three tall feathers, and tell her the young lady had a headache and was going home with friends. And then convey David's apologies to his sister, as her party would need to find another way home. Several of Diana's friends were in attendance tonight; he was certain she would be annoyed at first but only mildly inconvenienced.

He hoped the woman who was definitely patting his bottom this time did indeed have friends present tonight.

While Gilroy was gone, the coachman helped David climb into the carriage. The miss was as limp as a rag doll, incapable of sitting upright. To keep her from sliding to the floor, he settled her sideways on his lap, holding her head against his shoulder.

She shivered and tried to burrow inside his coat. He mentally slapped himself. "Grab the blanket, if you please."

"Right away, my lord."

Soon they had the carriage blanket draped over her, and she relaxed against David with a sigh.

Gilroy poked his head in the door. "All done as you requested, my lord."

"Thank you." He'd been running through his options of what to do that would have the least consequence for either of them. "Take us to Aunt Constance, please."

Moments later the coach rocked into motion.

She struggled to sit up, frantically looking around the dark interior of the coach. "Can't b'lieve I'm being abducted," she muttered, pushing away from him.

"Appearances to the contrary," David said, tucking her back against him before she overbalanced and ended up on the floor anyway, "this is not an abduction. It's a rescue."

She snorted.

"You'll have to forgive me. I have limited experience at rescuing damsels in distress."

She giggled. "I have lim'ted esper ...exp ... I'm not used to being in dis'ess."

"We'll just have to find our way along together, then." He made sure she was covered with the blanket and wrapped his arms around her more securely as the coach bounced over the cobblestone streets. Though Aunt Connie's neighborhood was respectable, it wasn't as nice as Lord Sedgewick's, the roads not as well maintained.

Her left arm tucked tight against him, her cheek and the back of her hand pressed to his chest, she raised her right arm and twined it around his neck. He was startled to feel her fingers stroking his hair.

Petting him.

He blinked at this unexpected development. Held still while he tried to decide if he should stop her or permit himself to enjoy it. In her altered state of mind she didn't really know what she was doing, did she? Several women had attempted to seduce him after he became the earl, with some of the misses trying to play with his hair.

14

He had leaned out of their reach. His mysterious miss, though, seemed to be touching him for the simple tactile pleasure, like petting a cat. And she was the one purring.

She gave another pleased hum, then shifted her head as she ... sniffed him? With a satisfied "mmm," she pushed his cravat aside and rested her cheek on his chest again.

To distract himself, he explained to her where they were going and what she could expect when they arrived, speaking in the same low, quiet voice he used to soothe his young nieces and nephews.

When her fingers in his hair gradually stilled and her ribcage expanded and contracted in steady, deep breathing, he exhaled in relief. He was enjoying her touch far more than was proper for a gentleman rescuing a damsel in distress. Especially with said damsel, and her enticing curves in all the right places, on his lap, in his arms. He wished he'd paid more attention to what she looked like instead of being distracted by the enormous feathers and purple turban of her companion. He couldn't recall any details of her appearance, not even her hair color.

While she slept, he hummed the last song he'd heard the musicians at the ball playing.

Eventually the coach rocked to a stop and Gilroy opened the door. "Fetch one of Aunt Connie's blankets," David said.

Moments later they switched blankets, making sure nothing of the miss was visible, not a stitch of fabric, slipper, or strand of hair, before he carried her into the townhouse. Neighbors might be nosy but he would give them nothing with which to start rumors.

Other than him carrying in a body, of course. He sighed.

Aunt Connie was not at home.

David groaned.

He summoned the housekeeper as well as a maid to attend the woman. He settled her on a sofa in the front parlor and stepped back to let them slip off her shoes, make sure she was warmly covered with the blanket, set a basin on the floor near her head in case she woke up and was sick again, and a clean cup and pot of tea on the low table before the sofa.

She slept through it all.

The fire popped and crackled in the hearth, the only light in the room. David gave a sigh of resignation, and he and the servants settled in chairs to await Aunt Connie's return.

15

Chapter 2

ASHLEY OPENED HER EYES, stared at the unfamiliar ceiling, and tried to remember where she was. Only jumbled images came to mind.

She remembered going to the ball with her aunt and uncle. Sir Rupert sitting beside her.

Then... things got fuzzy. Cool night air. Dark garden. Uncomfortable bench.

Hands touching her inappropriately.

A low, deep growl, like a large wild animal.

Someone ... a man ... helping her stand. Holding her while she—

Good heavens, holding her up while her supper made a return appearance.

Carrying her over his shoulder like a sack of flour.

Holding her on his lap in a moving carriage.

While she played with his hair. Soft, silky strands. No pomade.

Who was he? Was he here? Where *was* here? She swung her legs to the floor and sat up.

She held her head as the room spun, and fell back against what turned out to be sofa cushions. Gradually she became aware of music quietly being played, a solo string instrument. She sat up straight, searching out the source of the lovely sound.

The music stopped. "Ah, you're awake." The cultured voice came from a woman about her aunt's age, with silver hair and dressed in a maroon ball gown and jewels, who sat in a straight-backed chair by the window. She balanced a soprano viola da gamba on her left knee, bow in her right hand.

After speaking, she rose to put the instrument away in a case, then sat on the comfortable armchair by the hearth, where a blanket was draped over the nearby ottoman. Had she sat with Ashley through the night? A crackling fire blazed. Sunlight peeked through heavy curtains that had been pulled open just far enough to spill light onto the music stand. Carriages rumbled by on the street outside.

Ashley's gaze shot around the nicely appointed room, and discovered she was alone with the silver-haired woman. She glanced down and was relieved to see she was still dressed in what she'd worn to the ball last night—it was only last night, wasn't it?—minus her dancing slippers and paisley silk shawl.

"You likely have a dozen questions. But first I must inquire ... how is your head?"

"My head?" Her voice came out in a raspy croak.

The woman gestured at the teapot and cup on the low table before the sofa. "Help yourself. It has lemon and honey to soothe your throat. Drink up. You need to replenish the fluids you lost."

Ashley felt her cheeks flush as she poured a cup.

She paused with the cup inches from her mouth. The last thing she remembered drinking was a nasty tasting punch.

"You have no reason to trust me, though I assure you you're safe here. This tea has indeed been altered but in a way that will help, not harm."

Ashley took a sip of the cool tea. It felt surprisingly good going down her irritated throat, so she drank deeply. "You seem to know more about what happened to me than I do." She refilled her cup. Her head felt clear with only a hint of leftover headache.

"Not by much." The woman rose and tugged the bellpull. "Do you feel up to eating?"

Ashley's stomach growled.

"I'll take that as a yes." A maid entered and curtsied. "Let Cook know we're ready to break our fast."

"Yes, my lady." She bobbed another curtsy and left.

"Come, child," the silver-haired woman said. "I'll show you to a guest room so you may freshen up."

Ashley stifled an inelegant snort at being referred to as a child but slipped on her shoes and obediently followed. She couldn't help taking note of the furnishings and size of the home. The townhouse seemed at least as large as the one Uncle Edward had rented for the Season, and better appointed.

No family crest hung on the walls to identify the owners, though. The only portrait she saw depicted a young couple dressed from decades ago—a bewigged gentleman playing a lute, his female companion playing a violin. No, on second glance, she played a soprano viola da gamba. The same woman leading Ashley up the staircase, perhaps?

The guest room had a lovely four-poster bed that looked inviting, a cheery fire in the grate, the washbasin on the nightstand held a steaming pitcher of water, and a comb and brush awaited her on the vanity.

"When you feel more the thing, come downstairs. Dining room is the first door on the right at the bottom of the stairs."

"Thank you."

Her hostess shut the door as she left.

Dreading what she might find, Ashley took the opportunity to look herself over thoroughly. With a profound sense of relief, she found no bruises, blood, or other sign of injury, and no rips or tears in her clothing. Not even dark circles under her eyes. She sat down heavily at the vanity and took slow, deep breaths to calm her racing heart. The only physical reminder of the frightening night was her sore stomach muscles. She clasped her hands together to stop their trembling. Her rescuer had arrived just in time.

Had she retched on his shoes? Who was her rescuer? Who was her hostess?

The day was advancing. She'd find out nothing more staying here, no matter how inviting the room. She quickly performed morning ablutions, brushed out her once elaborate but now sadly mussed hairdo, pinned it up in a simple twist, and followed the scent of food to the dining room. At a gesture from her hostess, who had changed into a morning gown and her silver hair combed into a neat chignon, Ashley filled her plate at the sideboard and sat down.

"Who—" she began, but her hostess held up her hand.

"A friend saw that you were in distress last night and brought you here. That is all any of us need to know."

A friend. Whose name she did not know.

Which made two friends she'd apparently made last night, on a first name and a no-name basis. A third friend, if she counted this woman with silver hair and kind face. Madame Zavrina would be appalled at the lack of adherence to Society's rules.

"Once you've eaten, and assuming you feel strong enough, my footman will summon a hackney for you and pay the fare. I suggest you have the driver drop you off a few doors away from your ultimate destination."

At the thought of going home, Ashley panicked. What did Aunt Eunice and Uncle Edward think had happened to her? They must be frantic with worry. "That ... sounds wise."

"I'll give you a cloak I've been meaning to pass along. Keep the hood up until you get indoors." She paused before taking a sip of chocolate. "The woman you were with last night, in the purple turban, was told you went home with friends because you had a headache."

Ashley let out a relieved breath. "That was kind of ... him."

"'He didn't want an alarm raised any more than you would."

Ashley and her hostess shared a small smile, silently acknowledging that her rescuer didn't want to be considered as having compromised her. If no one else knew what happened except her mystery rescuer, this woman, and Sir Rupert, had she actually been compromised?

How would she face Sir Rupert now? Would he dare accost her again?

At least, she thought Sir Rupert was the one who had taken her out to the garden and tried to force himself on her. Her memory after escorting her new friend Georgia to her mother was spotty at best.

Ashley was surprised at how hungry she felt, and helped herself to a second plate and a cup of chocolate. Of course she was hungry. Her stomach was empty because last night she had cast up her accounts. She set her cup down with a thud.

"Laudanum," she whispered, feeling the color drain from her face.

"Hmm?"

"Laudanum. Makes me horribly sick, so I haven't taken any in years. I didn't recognize the taste when Sir R—when an unwanted suitor put some in my punch."

"At a ball in Mayfair." Her hostess shook her head in disgust. "Providence indeed smiled on you last night for my ... for your new friend to realize what was happening." She clucked her tongue and stepped from the room. Ashley heard murmured words exchanged in the hall, then the woman came back to the table and resumed eating.

If Ashley was still in danger, she'd rather deal with it on a full stomach, so she ate the rest of the delicious food on her plate. As she drained the last of the rich chocolate from her cup, a maid entered and bobbed a curtsy. She draped the dark blue cloak on her arm over a chair back and left again just as quickly.

"Don't take this as a hint. I simply want you to feel free to leave whenever you're ready."

"I appreciate your kindness." Her appetite appeased, Ashley began to worry how she was going to fend off questions from Aunt Eunice that she couldn't answer, even if she knew the information.

She rose, and her hostess helped her settle the cloak about her shoulders. Made of a wonderfully soft wool, it undoubtedly had begun life as a costly garment though it was beginning to show signs of wear. They stepped into the hall. When she would have turned for the front door, her hostess steered her toward the back.

"Oh, almost forgot." She retrieved something from a side table drawer and held it out.

Ashley's paisley silk shawl, in red, cream, and blue.

"Keep it hidden until you get home. This cloak looks like hundreds of others, but that shawl is distinctive."

Please trust that I am trying to help, he had said while she perched on his knee, just before he tugged the filmy shawl from her shoulders. Ashley nodded and clutched it in her hand.

"I don't even know your name," Ashley said as they traversed the garden at the back of the townhouse. A hackney was already in the mews, the horse stamping its hooves. "How can I repay you, at least for the coach fare?"

"No need. Help someone else. That is all the repayment I desire."

She remembered Georgia in the darkened hallway. "In that case, perhaps I paid in advance. Or at least a down payment."

"Oh?"

"Earlier at the ball last night, I assisted a young woman whose suitor was trying to steal a kiss against her wishes."

Her benefactress rested her hands on Ashley's shoulders. "Men," she spat the word to the side. Then she smiled and looked deep into Ashley's eyes as she pulled the hood up and over Ashley's head. "We women need to stick together."

That was the feeling among the staff and instructors at the academy, at least until the school had abruptly closed in February. With a pang, Ashley hadn't realized how much she missed their camaraderie. "Agreed."

Moments later she was in the coach, on her way home. She pulled the window shades down and leaned back against the lumpy squabs, clutching her silk shawl to her chest.

She was going to burn this ecru-colored gown she was wearing, or at least give it to her maid with instructions to sell it and pocket the proceeds. Once she took it off, she never wanted to see it again. Sir Rupert had touched it.

The shawl, however... Her rescuer had held it, had saved it for her, had tugged it from her shoulders and tucked it in his pocket so it couldn't be used to identify her, to create a scandal. She buried her face in it.

It smelled different.

Overriding her own barely-there rose-scented soap, she detected... citrus. But sweet. Lemon and honey.

Her rescuer's pocket smelled of lemon and honey?

Not just his pocket. Him. She had sniffed him—her cheeks almost burst into flame remembering how brazen she'd been while on his lap—and recalled being surprised that he did not smell of spice or musk, and instead had a light, sweet citrus scent.

He'd hummed. He'd spoken to her on the carriage ride, though she couldn't recall the words or even the topic. Just that his deep, rumbling voice was soothing and she wanted to stay snuggled on his lap all night, wrapped in his arms and a warm blanket, however inappropriate, and for him to keep humming and talking to her and keep her safe.

She had no idea who he was or even what he looked like. Not his name, his age, certainly not his rank in society.

All she knew was that he was kind, smelled nice, had a deep voice, soft hair, and was strong enough to carry her.

And had scared off her attacker.

Did he know her identity? As they were both attending Lady Sedgewick's ball, it stood to reason they might encounter each other again during the Season. Would they recognize one another? Had they already met?

Had they danced together?

David joined his brother-in-law at his club for luncheon two days after Lord Sedgewick's ball. He had to be back in Parliament later that afternoon for yet another committee meeting but was treating himself to a relaxed meal. The nice thing about dining with Templeton at the club was that they could eat and drink and read the newspaper without engaging in conversation, and no one called them on their boorish manners.

He had just finished his plate of roast beef when Templeton stood to greet newly arrived acquaintances. While his back was turned, David tipped most of his half-glass of claret into Templeton's goblet.

His friends moving on, Templeton sat down and raised his glass. He looked mildly confused when he saw the volume of fluid, then shrugged and drank. "Lydia wants to know if you're coming to dinner tonight at Mansfield's and staying for rehearsal."

David waved over the footman and requested tea and biscuits. "I haven't decided." He had stayed at home each evening, busy with estate business, since leaving the mysterious miss with Aunt Connie. He was uncertain if he wanted to encounter her again, or her attacker. At least there had been nothing about the incident in the newspapers. How would he behave if he saw her? Would he even recognize her? Might she recognize him?

He'd gotten only a glimpse of her here and there in the moonlight, and they had lit no candles in Aunt Connie's parlour. Hadn't really been paying attention to what the miss looked like when they were in the ballroom. Her companion's purple turban with not one but three tall feathers had been distracting.

Templeton let out a belch, a long one, and David realized he was actually trying to sing a bass note. Templeton cut off the sound and took a long drink. "After seventeen years of marriage, you wouldn't think I'd have to court my own wife. But she still wants me to sing to her. And I still don't have your range. I've barely gained two notes in the last decade."

David's singing voice at sixteen had been deeper than Templeton's was now at forty-five and had continued to deepen as he matured. David still entertained his nieces and nephews with it. And had scared off a cad with it. "You sing them with good resonance."

"Bah." Templeton paused while the footman set down the tea things and a plate of biscuits, and ordered a plate of cheese and nuts.

"She's convinced we can win this year's prize at the Catch Club if you join us."

"She well knows I haven't sung in competition since Philip passed. I'm busy. And I'm out of practice." Why couldn't his sisters understand how much time and effort it required to run an earldom? Especially when one had not been trained for the task. David dunked a biscuit in his tea, ate it, and debated if he should have another. Surely, he'd earned two? He took it, then pushed the plate toward Templeton.

"All the more reason to come to rehearsal."

David was about to reply when Sir Rupert settled at the next table over with a friend. He wasn't wearing a green-and-yellow striped waistcoat, but David recognized his voice as belonging to the cad he'd scared off in the gazebo at the Sedgewicks' ball. David snapped open his newspaper, holding it in front of his face. Templeton took the hint.

Nice thing about extended family, they didn't take insults personally. When the footman brought the cheese and nuts, Templeton pushed the plate to the middle of the table so they could share.

David took a bite of cheese, silently chewing, shamelessly eavesdropping on Sir Rupert discussing a plan.

"No laudanum this time," Rupert said. "Got to be direct. No subterfuge."

"With your reputation?" his companion replied. "What chit is going to go off to a darkened alcove with you and let herself be compromised?"

"I'll simply make sure she has no choice but to accept my suit. My creditors won't be put off much longer."

"Whether she spreads her legs for you willingly or not, eh?"

David lowered the newspaper enough to see Sir Rupert give an oily, evil smile.

Rupert withdrew a sheet of paper from his coat pocket. "Here's my list of chits who have a dowry at least as large as I need, and the family not so high in the instep they would reject my suit."

His companion scooted his chair closer so they could both peruse the document. He tapped the paper. "This one is likely to be at Lady Bristol's soiree on Friday. Her mother is friends with the Viscountess."

David could not make a habit of following Sir Rupert around, rescuing young women from his clutches. He also could not let the blackguard force himself on a woman and compel her to the altar just to get his hands on her dowry.

He'd call out the scoundrel, but David's fencing skills were average at best; he only spent time at Henry Angelo's for the exercise. His time at Manton's shooting range was mainly for the satisfaction of blasting paper targets to bits when he was frustrated; his marksmanship was also merely average. He sparred with Gentleman Jackson, enough to know how to protect himself if accosted by footpads.

How could he make sure the blackguard never again forced himself on anyone?

Ashley had now spent two days in her room. After checking on her just after lunch, Aunt Eunice had left Ashley alone in her room for the rest of the day to recover from her "headache," with an arched eyebrow at having friends take her home. Thankfully she did not pry for more details, which left Ashley free to annoy herself, obsessively reliving what had happened at the Sedgewicks' ball, or at least what bits she could recall.

Sally had taken away the ecru gown without comment other than a polite expression of gratitude. Ashley wouldn't allow Sally to freshen the paisley shawl. Instead she wrapped it in tissue and tucked it in a drawer of her wardrobe.

Even when Aunt Eunice dropped hints about how lovely Ashley would look in the two finished gowns that had just arrived from the modiste, Ashley dreaded going out. What if she encountered Sir Rupert? Much of that night was still fuzzy, but she was certain he had drugged her by putting laudanum in her punch, tried to take her against her will, and only the intervention of a stranger had prevented her attacker from succeeding in his wicked plan.

Why had Sir Rupert been so intent on her? The dowry Uncle Edward planned to settle on her was respectable but not large enough to make her the target of fortune-seekers. She had shown Sir Rupert only the barest of courtesies after their first dance together. She shivered anew. Something about him just seemed off.

Then her mood would swing to fury at being in such a vulnerable position in the first place. Society had rules, and she had always strived to follow them. Had taught those rules to hundreds of students in her time at Madame Zavrina's Torquay Academy for Young Ladies, first as a student, and later as a staff member.

Society needed rules, or there would be anarchy.

But why did so many rules conscribe the behavior of women, and not apply to the behavior of men? An unmarried man could visit the bed of dozens of women, perhaps revel in being known as a rake, and still be accepted everywhere, by everyone. An unmarried woman, merely caught kissing a man in a dark hallway, would be forced to wed him or be considered fast at best, wanton and of poor moral character at worst, and her reputation in shreds. Ruined.

She doubted Sir Rupert felt any remorse for what he'd done or what he'd tried to do.

Well, she was done hiding. "I'm going to join my aunt for her at-home today," she informed Sally.

"Yes, miss." They spent a fun hour kitting her out in one of her new gowns, a hairstyle copied from *La Belle Assemblée*, a new silk shawl, and a pearl-studded comb in her hair.

Ashley had just settled on a sofa in the front parlour opposite Aunt Eunice when the first guests arrived. She rose to greet Mrs. Vaughn and her just-out daughter, soon followed by Lady Donkin, a widow aunt's age, and her companion. Conversation was polite and utterly uninteresting to Ashley until the butler announced Lady Diana Mansfield and her daughter, Miss Georgia Aldridge.

Ashley's breath caught when she saw the red-haired young woman in the doorway beside her mother.

The girl she'd rescued at Lady Sedgewick's ball.

Georgia's uncertain expression changed to a broad smile when Ashley rose to greet her. She must not have hidden her own feelings of uncertainty.

"My mother and great-aunt know absolutely everyone in Town, at least their family names," she said quietly as they sat beside each other on the sofa. Georgia's mother took a chair near Aunt Eunice. "I couldn't find you later at the ball. I still wanted to return this to you, and thank you again." She withdrew a handkerchief from her reticule and handed it over.

Ashley's heart pounded at the mention of "later at the ball," but she schooled her expression to one of polite interest. She accepted the handkerchief that she had elaborately embroidered, including her initials in four different styles, one set in each corner. The handkerchief she had given to Georgia when the girl was distraught.

"It looks like something you spent a lot of time working on and might be important to you."

Ashley folded it back up and tucked it under her leg. "Yes, and no. I used it as a sample when I was teaching various stitches to students. It was mainly an exercise in stabbing something five thousand times."

Georgia put her hand over her mouth to stifle a laugh. "I knew you were not the stuffy spinster Great-Aunt Constance said you would be." She sat up abruptly and cleared her throat. "Oh dear. That did not sound right."

After a heartbeat, Ashley decided not to take insult. Georgia was young and seemed to lack malice. "It's true some consider me at my last prayers. I still don't understand why my uncle insisted on giving me another season."

"Aunt Constance recalled that you were presented several years ago but left town abruptly before the end of the season."

Ashley had to look out the window, at the trees in the square just leafing out, evidence of the renewal of life. "My parents died."

Georgia rested her hand on Ashley's forearm. "I am so sorry."

Ashley patted her hand, then forced a bright tone into her voice. "How are you enjoying your season? This is your first, is it not?"

"Other than the other night?" Georgia shuddered. "I must thank you again. I can't believe I was so easily deceived."

"A lesson you won't need to repeat?"

"Certainly not." Georgia gave the clock on the mantel a glance. "I wish to spend more time in your company and become better acquainted. Do you plan to attend Lady Bristol's soiree Friday night?"

"I am uncertain. Aunt has been planning most of our social calendar. She chooses which outings she thinks will give me the best chance to meet an eligible parti."

"My mother, too! It's as if they're showing us off, like we're horses to be auctioned at Tattersall's! I'm surprised none of the gentlemen I've been introduced to have asked to inspect my teeth."

It was Ashley's turn to stifle a giggle. "I think it's a waste of time as far as me making a match, but I do love to dance and hear talented musicians perform."

"Oh! You must come to dinner then," Georgia exclaimed. "Tonight. My Aunt Lydia is coming over with my cousins. It will just be family. No one to be paraded in front of or to whom you must show your teeth. We always play and sing after dinner. Some of us are quite good."

"I wouldn't want to intrude on a family gathering."

"Pish. Friends are always welcome. Back home in Surrey we have neighbors and other guests over more often than not. Our London townhouse music room is not as well stocked as Mansfield Grange or Linford Hall, but we can still make merry noise. Please say you'll come."

Before Ashley could reply, Aunt Eunice spoke up. "We've just been invited to dine tonight with Lord and Lady Mansfield. Isn't that delightful?"

Georgia beamed.

"Yes, delightful." At least her first outing after being attacked by Sir Rupert would not be in public society. Just an intimate family dinner and musical evening with new friends.

Chapter 3

THE "INTIMATE" FAMILY DINNER had as many participants as some of the society events Ashley had attended. Georgia had five siblings and at least as many cousins, plus the requisite parents, aunt, uncle, and spouses of the older cousins and siblings. Ashley gave up trying to remember all the names and was grateful to be seated beside Georgia.

Ashley was accustomed to dining with a large number of female students and teachers but was surprised to see children eating with the family instead of in the nursery. The young man seated next to Aunt Eunice, for example, proudly hanging a spoon from his nose, couldn't be more than ten. The lively conversations and occasional quiet instruction to a child made it clear this was a regular occurrence.

Her heart constricted at the idea of routinely spending time with so many loved ones. At the idea of *having* so many loved ones.

During the second course she felt something soft brush her ankles. Stifling a startled yelp, she glanced down and saw a fluffy cream and brown tail wagging. Georgia slipped her hand down, and the dog gently took the morsel of food. As the meal progressed, the dog stayed, patiently waiting for Georgia to offer more tidbits, the dog's tail swishing across Ashley's ankle. She struggled to maintain decorum and not laugh at being tickled.

"Are you feeling well? You look a little overwhelmed. I admit we can be a boisterous lot at times."

Ashley gave Georgia a reassuring smile. "I am enjoying myself. I am simply not accustomed to large family gatherings."

"Your family is not close?"

"I am an only child, and my aunt and uncle were not blessed with offspring."

"Oh! How sad!" Georgia was quiet for a moment. Then she snapped her fingers. "I'm going to adopt you."

Startled, Ashley dropped her fork to her plate. The conversational buzz at the table was so loud, no one noticed. "I beg your pardon?"

"Adopting you. Claiming you as another sister," she said as easily as one might offer to loan a spare shawl or hair comb. She patted Ashley on the back. "Eat up! You'll need your strength for later."

Ashley choked down a sip of wine. She had longed for siblings, but her mother was lucky to have survived having one babe. The staff and students at the academy were as close as she had come to an extended family, and that had been ripped away from her with Madame Zavrina's passing and the closing of the school two months ago.

The men did not stay at table for port and cigars after the meal. Everyone trooped in ragtag order down the hall to the music room, which was easily large enough to accommodate a modest ball. The dog Georgia had secretly been feeding was a cream and brown Pekingese, missing its front left leg and left eye. It trotted along in Georgia's wake, its fluffy tail coiled over its back, wafting from side to side.

The hubbub of conversation died away as soon as they entered the music room so they could listen to the young woman who stood beside the pianoforte, rehearsing a duet with the gentleman playing for her. She twirled one of her braids as she sang. The pianist wore his hair loose and long enough that it caught on his shirt points, obscuring much of his face.

They paused and repeated stanzas several times, seemingly oblivious to the crowd entering and settling on the various sofas, chairs, and ottomans.

The girl's soprano was tentative but grew more confident with his quiet tenor just beneath, a barely audible support helping her navigate changes in key and pronouncing the Italian lyrics, dropping out when she hit a sustained note.

"My cousin Melissa," Georgia explained as she tugged Ashley down on a sofa beside her. "She'll have her come-out in two years. She's competent with French but finds Italian vexing."

"She has my respect," Ashley said. "I have never even attempted that aria."

Melissa finished the song with a sustained note at the top of her register. Her audience broke into applause. She blushed and glanced around the room as though just now aware they were not alone.

"Missy, I wondered where you had got to," Georgia's Aunt Lydia said. "You weren't hungry?"

"No, Mama. I just wanted a little extra practice."

Aunt Lydia turned her gaze to the gentleman at the keyboard who was now straightening pages of music. "And you were not hungry, either?"

"I arrived late and was drawn in here when I heard Missy." His smile was charming, his mellow baritone speaking voice much lower than his singing voice. Ashley had thought him older because of the grey in his hair but now saw his face was unlined.

"We're lucky he's here at all," Lady Mansfield said, crossing the room to the pianoforte. "Come here," she demanded with a grin. He stood and they embraced, and broke apart only when Aunt Lydia tugged on his arm for her hug.

"Let me introduce you," Georgia said.

Up close, Ashley guessed he was only a few years older than her twenty-three years. Rather than grey hair, he had a single, startling streak of white in his chestnut hair about the width of her pinky, framing the right side of his face.

"Uncle David," Georgia said, drawing his attention.

"Scamp," he replied in greeting, a mischievous smile tilting the corners of his mouth. His hairstyle was old-fashioned, the strands nearly long enough to brush his shoulders, but his clothing was very much *au courant*, perhaps even forward. He wore trousers and a coat of dark blue superfine, emerald green neckcloth, and his pale green silk waistcoat was embroidered with rich green leaves and vines.

"This is my new friend, Miss Ashley Hamlin. Today I discovered she's an orphan so I've decided to adopt her." Georgia turned to Ashley. "My uncle David, Earl of Ravencroft."

Ashley curtsied. "Lord Ravencroft," she murmured.

"Miss Hamlin." His long hair fell forward when he bowed, partially obscuring his face again. Likely he tied it back with a ribbon on formal occasions. He lifted her hand to drop a kiss in the air just above her knuckles. "Welcome to the family."

Something in his rich, deep voice, like rocks tumbling in a river, went straight through her. She suppressed a delicious shiver. "You don't seem the least bit fazed by Georgia's outrageous claim."

"Of adopting you?" He shrugged one shoulder. "Her other adoptees tend to have fur or feathers, but no, I'm not surprised." He bent down to pet the Pekingese, who was leaning against his shin.

Hearing that many words in a row from him, something stirred at the edge of her memory, but she couldn't quite grasp it. "Have we perchance met before, my lord?"

He tilted his head to one side as he straightened. "I would hate to think we had and I'd forgotten it."

"Let's get started warming up," Lady Mansfield called. "Children begin, then ladies, then the men." She pointed a warning finger at the children, who had huddled together, furiously whispering. "If you choose a naughty catch by Henry Purcell again, you will go straight up to the nursery."

That must have been precisely what they'd been planning, because their faces fell. They quickly grinned and huddled and whispered some more.

A few moments later, the boy who'd earlier been using his spoon as a facial fashion accessory announced their choice, "*Three Blind Mice.*"

"Should have warned them nothing gory," Georgia's Aunt Lydia said in a stage whisper to Lady Mansfield.

"What do you expect when your brother regales them with bedtime tales of ghosts and goblins wanting to cut off their heads?" Lord Mansfield interjected.

Georgia chuckled.

Lord Ravencroft had to have heard but he stood by the fireplace, one arm resting on the mantel, showing no reaction save a small smile playing about his mouth as he watched the children prepare. A few people changed seats, and very quickly the ladies were on one side of the room, the children on the other, the men clustered in front of the fireplace. Uncle Edward good-naturedly took a spot beside Lord Mansfield. Ashley couldn't recall if she'd ever heard her uncle sing. Melissa had seemed uncertain where she belonged until her mother waved her over to join the women.

One of the young cousins raised her hand as a signal, and the children started singing.

At the end of the first line, the women began singing. Ashley lent her voice, hidden among a dozen others, and the room swelled with the sweet melody and gory story about a farmer's wife chopping off the tails of mice.

Then the men joined in. Ashley's breath caught in her chest. The men stood so close together she couldn't distinguish which voice was whose. There were at least two tenors, two baritones, and one bass, all underscored by a basso profundo. The hair on her arms stood on end.

Ashley mouthed the words of the age-old song, incapable of producing actual sound, as the catch continued. The children finished, then the women. While the men sang the last line, Ashley felt the low bass notes vibrate in her bones.

Georgia smiled and nudged her in the ribs. "You'll get used to it," she whispered in Ashley's ear.

"I've never heard the like," Ashley whispered back. At the academy, the only male employee had been the groundskeeper who also kept the buildings in repair, and he'd never joined them for music practice. The students and staff all sang soprano or alto, occasionally contralto. Just as she relished the opportunity to dance with men after several years surrounded by women and girls, she loved hearing men sing.

Lady Mansfield directed two more catches, alternating which order the groups sang. Ashley tried to appear nonchalant and join in but lost her power of speech when the men sang.

Satisfied that everyone had warmed up vocally, a brief debate ensued between Lady Templeton, Lady Mansfield, their husbands, and Georgia's older brother Parker as to what should be sung and in what order. Soon Lord Templeton settled at the pianoforte and played a few chords, Parker tuned his violincello, and Melissa played a few scales on her flute. When the musicians were ready, everyone in the room joined in a rousing rendition of *Rule, Britannia!*

They quickly moved on to the next song and then another, with different performers playing a variety of instruments. The Pekingese made the rounds, getting pets and scratches from everyone present. At Ashley's turn, after she rubbed behind his silky ears, he stretched up on his back legs, front paw on the sofa cushion beside her knee, his pink tongue hanging out, tail wagging. She couldn't resist patting her lap. He jumped up and turned around in a circle three times before he settled, half on her leg, half on the sofa, his tail thumping on Georgia's lap.

"Tuffy!" Georgia hissed, putting her hands on him as if to push him to the floor. "I'm so sorry," she whispered to Ashley. "He doesn't usually jump up on company."

"I invited him," she whispered back, stroking the dog. "He's a handsome fellow." She bent down to look him in his one eye. "Aren't you, sweetings?" He licked her face.

She chuckled and straightened, her attention once more on the proceedings, and continued to absently stroke the dog with one hand.

Group songs were interspersed with duets and trios. Melissa, Georgia, and Georgia's older sister Clarissa called on Lord Ravencroft to play the pianoforte again while they sang a Monteverdi aria. This time he sang baritone, a rich accompaniment to their soprano, alto, and contralto, dropping out occasionally to let their voices be the focus.

Mesmerized, Ashley sat perfectly still. Unable to tear her gaze away from Lord Ravencroft, she hardly breathed, barely blinked. Fortunately everyone else was watching the performance as well. She had thought him reasonably handsome when she first got a good look at him, distracted by the streak of white in his otherwise light brown hair. But his voice...

His voice danced over the notes, agile and not the least bit ponderous for its low register, advancing and retreating, always letting his nieces' voices shine through.

That something teased her memory again. Had she heard him sing at a soiree she'd attended? Surely she'd remember a young gentleman with a white streak in his hair, worn long yet loose. Perhaps he'd tied it back? Worn a wig?

She joined in the applause when the quartet finished. Two maids arrived with tea trays, and a governess came to collect the younger children. One of the girls came over to the sofa and patted her chest. Tuffy leaped into her arms, to be carried upstairs.

An hour had passed, seemingly in a blink.

"The two blue pots are hot tea," Georgia explained, retaking her seat on the sofa and brushing dog hairs from her skirts. "The two pots with cabbage roses are cool tea with lemon juice and lots of honey. Very soothing if your throat is irritated or you've been singing a lot."

Ashley froze.

"Something wrong?" Georgia filled her cup from the cabbage rose pot and snagged an apple puff from the tray of a passing maid.

Ashley shook herself and surreptitiously looked at each person in the room again. None of the women had silver hair. "Nothing. It's only the second time I've ever been offered that particular beverage, and the first was two days ago." She selected one of the little cakes and a cup of cool tea.

Georgia shrugged. "We have it often. Someone is always wanting to sing higher or lower or longer than their voice would otherwise allow. And it tastes divine. I could drink it by the jugful."

Conversation buzzed in the room again, and Ashley heard mention of an upcoming competition. "Your family takes singing very seriously. They compete?"

Georgia rose and gestured for Ashley to follow. One of the tall bookcases held folios of music and small instrument cases, like Melissa's flute, but two of the shelves held medals, framed and protected by glass. Georgia reached toward one medal, stopping just short of touching the glass. "On my stepmother's side, my great-grandfather ... or is it great-great-grandfather? ... entertained the court of King George the First, and for his excellent service was made the first Earl of Ravencroft. He was a founding member of the Noblemen and Gentlemen's Catch Club. See these medals? His quartet won several of them for singing performances, as well as he won individually for original compositions. And this shelf has some of my grandfather's medals."

Ashley had heard of the Catch Club, so exclusive and membership numbers so limited that other catch and glee clubs had sprung up, filled with people on the waiting list to get into the original club. "Your stepmother?"

"She's lovely, isn't she? My parents had the three of us. My first mother died when I was a babe. Father married Diana and had three children with her. The governess just took them upstairs. We all look like Father."

"All gingers," Ashley murmured.

Georgia grinned. "And we deserve our reputation for temperament, I assure you." Her face grew more serious as she touched the frame of the last medal. "It quite vexes Diana that Uncle David let the Ravencroft spot in the club lapse instead of taking it up after Grandfather and Uncle Philip died."

"He doesn't like to sing?" *But he has such a beautiful voice.*

"Said he's too busy keeping the earldom running. Rehearsals take up a lot of time." Georgia leaned close and dropped her voice to a conspiratorial whisper. "Mother is hoping that having him here in Town for my Season means she will be able to get him to turn Father's quartet into a quintet, and they'll bring home the next medal. Aunt Lydia is already working on a new arrangement for five voices."

"I hope Lady Mansfield is successful."

They drifted into conversation with other family members, including Georgia's younger cousin, Melissa. With the children gone upstairs, everyone shifted around to enjoy the refreshments. Melissa looked lost again. Ashley patted the sofa cushion beside her. "Come join us. I won't bite."

David carried Thomas, shrieking with laughter, over his shoulder up to the nursery. The group paused for the requisite inspection to see if the Bogeyman was under the stairs—he wasn't, though David tried to imitate him, much to the children's squealing delight—and checked under the beds. Cousins were spending the night so they were all doubling up. Though they no longer needed to be soothed with lullabies, they still demanded a scary bedtime story.

Soon they'd be too old for even that.

But Parker and his wife Deirdre were expecting, and Clarissa would be wed in just a few weeks. Georgia might choose a husband this spring; by next spring she could have a babe. Another generation of babies to sing for.

His fifteen-year-old self would have been horrified at the prospect. His present self just felt old.

Warmed up from singing after dinner, he voiced the scary monster in tonight's story with his deepest tone, and used his highest falsetto to portray a woman describing the frightful beast. Each character got their own voice distinct from the narrator. He tried out a new demonic laugh at the end, and generally played with his voice as though it were a toy. Just as Lydia had accused him of doing all those years ago.

A positive aspect about getting older ... no, getting more *mature* ... is that his voice kept getting deeper, even without regular rehearsal. He had gained a note lower every year for the last several years, and he could still hit the high tenor notes. Most of them even sounded decent. He sang to his horse on his morning rides if they were alone, the only time he felt he could indulge his creative side. The rest of his days were eaten up by endless meetings and overseeing estate business.

Story finished, he exchanged hugs and kisses goodnight, went downstairs, and stopped just outside the music room door to observe Georgia's new friend, Miss Hamlin.

She had indeed seemed familiar when they were introduced, but he couldn't quite place her. Georgia had made many new acquaintances since they'd come to London last month. So many young women on the hunt for husbands attended the events that he often escorted Diana or Lydia and their daughters to, if his brothers-in-law were unavailable.

Miss Hamlin was certainly at the top end of the husband-hunters, age-wise. On the shelf, even. How many seasons had she tried to snag a husband and kept coming back? Why had she not married and given her husband two or three babies by now? She was pleasant enough to look upon, had polite manners, and a passable singing voice. What was wrong with her or her family?

As he watched, Miss Hamlin invited Missy to sit beside her. "I won't bite," she said with a charming smile.

Breath caught in his chest. He knew that voice. *I'll bite.*

His mysterious miss!

He took several steps away from the door and flattened his back to the hallway wall, his heart racing. He waved away a concerned-looking footman.

What he'd done with her after she'd been drugged at Lady Sedgewick's ball, however well-intentioned, was beyond the pale as far as Society was concerned. If she figured out he was the one who had spirited her away in his carriage, she could force him to the altar.

Being married was fine ... for other people. He had no intention of marrying, felt no need to provide an heir to be the next Earl of Ravencroft. He had never wanted to be the earl. He'd put aside his own interests and taken on the responsibilities only because someone had to protect all the tenants, servants, and relatives depending on the estate.

Schooling his expression to one of polite interest, he strolled into the music room. As soon as Diana noticed he'd returned, she sent a maid over to him with a tray. In addition to the light dessert items, there were savory meat pies the size of his palm. He raised a pie in a silent toast to her before he ate. They were well into adulthood, but she still had a tendency to look after him. Little brother missed the evening meal? Get him a hearty snack.

Now he wouldn't have to worry about finding food to sustain him for the task that awaited him later tonight. He patted his waistcoat pocket, making sure the small bottle was still there. He'd been late arriving for dinner because he'd paid a call on the magician who'd entertained at his nephew Thomas's tenth birthday celebration last week. The entertainer had been reluctant to share his secret. David just kept offering more coins until the man handed over what David needed.

He took a deep swallow of the honey and lemon tea as he glanced at everyone in the room, eating, drinking, and chatting away. If Georgia was serious about keeping company with Miss Hamlin, inviting her to family gatherings, he'd have to keep his distance. Avoid speaking to her as much as possible, yet not in a way that would draw attention to the fact he was avoiding her.

What a coil he'd created for himself. And later tonight he would make his life even more complicated. But he couldn't back down. Too much was at stake.

Sir Rupert Connor struggled to wakefulness, roused from his slumber by a deep growl. The growl grew louder and impossibly deeper, and close by. Deeper than any dog, more rumbling than a lion he'd once heard in the Tower Menagerie. Barely daring to breathe, he sat up and darted his gaze around his boardinghouse bedchamber, searching for the source of the unearthly, bone-chilling sound. With the fire burned down to embers, his chamber was shrouded in midnight darkness save for a sliver of moonlight that sliced across the foot of his bed.

Movement at the end of his bed drew his attention. A form separated from the shadows, and the growl resolved into words.

"Rupert Connor." The apparition spoke his name in a gravelly voice so deep it came from the grave. "You have drawn my wrath."

"Who-who are you?" With trembling hands, Rupert held the blanket up to his chin. His emotions swung between anger at the audacity of an intruder in his rented chambers, and terror that this was no mortal burglar.

Rupert heard a faint hiss as the apparition shifted and something, maybe an arm, pointed toward the window. "I am the shadow on the moon at night." The words were uttered slowly, as though dredged up from the depths of hell. The arm swung toward him. "I am what you fear is under your bed."

"What—" Rupert stopped to clear the squeak from his voice. "What do you want?" He could barely hear over the pounding of his heart.

"The women of London are *mine*," the intruder rumbled, his tone dropping so deep on the last word that Rupert felt it vibrate like a massive stone being rolled in front of a tomb. "I curse you to never find a bride until your intentions are honorable."

Rupert whimpered.

"You should leave London." There was another hiss as the figure shifted and his appendage dropped. "Leave England."

Rupert gulped. "Who *are* you?"

The figure took a step forward, becoming somewhat human in appearance as moonlight outlined his black-clad figure. He wore a tricorn hat and black cape that absorbed what little light fell through the gap in the curtains. His face was a pale blur, and where his eyes should be there was only blackness. He tipped his head back and opened his mouth wide, baring teeth, to utter a demonic laugh, rattling Rupert's bones with the subterranean tone.

"I. Am. The Bogeyman." He lunged forward, reaching for Rupert.

Rupert shrieked. Light flashed, blinding him, and Rupert fell back on the bed, senseless.

When he opened his eyes again, the apparition was gone.

Rupert stumbled out of bed, his hands shaking so badly it took several tries to light the candle on his bedside stand. He held the candle high over his head, his gaze frantically darting about the room, searching the chamber for any sign of the intruder. He quickly lit the candles on the mantel, lit every candle and lamp in the chamber, as his gaze flicked over each shadow in the room. Trembling at the prospect of what he might see yet desperately needing to know, he dropped to his knees to look under the bed.

Nothing there but dust.

He stood in the middle of the chamber, his heart pounding, limbs quivering, the only sound his harsh breathing and ticking of the clock. He checked that all the windows and doors were closed and locked, and jammed a chairback under the knob of the door to the hallway.

Clearly, he'd get no more sleep this night. Before he sat in the armchair to keep vigil until dawn with his pistol in hand, however, he needed to change into a clean, dry nightshirt.

Friday evening while preparing to attend Lady Bristol's soiree, Ashley changed her gown no less than four times. Sally, bless her, patiently helped her change and suggested different wraps and slippers for each ensemble.

Her only outing since being drugged and assaulted had been the family dinner with her new friend, Georgia. In fact, Georgia and her parents were coming to collect Ashley and Aunt Eunice in their large coach in, oh dear, less than an hour.

Clad in only her shift, stockings, and stays again, Ashley looked over the gowns in her dressing room.

"May I suggest the cream silk with blue trim? Your red and blue paisley shawl would look a treat with it." Sally poked through the stack of folded shawls. "Though I don't know where it's got to. It's not here with your others."

"No!" Ashley held her hand to her chest to calm the pounding. "That is, perhaps the yellow sarcenet will do after all. And the dark blue wrap."

"Yes, miss."

She hated the paisley shawl because Sir Rupert had touched it. And loved it because her mysterious rescuer had kept it safe for her. Would she see him tonight? Either man.

Would she be able to maintain her composure if she saw Sir Rupert? Should she behave as though nothing had happened? Give him the cut direct? Slap him?

Ooh, that would feel good. So, so satisfying. She could almost hear the crack of her palm on his face, feel the sting in her hand, see his cheek turning red.

Everyone would stare.

People would want to know why she'd done such a thing. Behaved so outrageously.

"Miss?"

"Hmm? Oh!" Ashley unclenched her fists so Sally could slip her arms into the sleeves of the gown.

What really fried her curls is that if word got out that Sir Rupert had tried to get under her skirts, she'd have to marry him or be considered ruined. Society would consider *his* actions to be *her* fault.

He wouldn't survive their wedding night. At least not with his manhood intact.

Madame Zavrina had made sure her instructors and staff knew what behavior was acceptable and what wasn't, had taught them ways to avoid unwanted attention from the fathers and brothers who came to the school dropping off and picking up the students. Some of the instructors had shared additional techniques that Madame Zavrina would have frowned upon had she known the bloodthirsty nature of the defense tactics.

One of the teachers had been dismissed last year because she'd resisted a visitor's advances. Sabrina was the one with a torn gown and mussed hair, but the visiting lord had insisted *she* had assaulted *him*. When it came to the word of a penniless spinster or a wealthy gentleman, neither Sabrina nor Madame Zavrina had stood a chance.

As vexing as some men could be, there were other men who restored her faith. Like Uncle Edward, who'd returned from Jamaica two months ago, newly rich and insisting on treating her to a Season.

And like her mysterious rescuer.

What would she do if she encountered him? Thank him? Apologize for casting up her accounts practically on his shoes?

Would he accept that her forward behavior—*she had toyed with his hair!*—had been due to the influence of the drug?

She went still. Would he think she would try to trap *him* into marriage? Oh, dear. They'd been alone in his carriage. In some ways, he'd taken more liberties with her person than Sir Rupert had. Carrying her. Holding her on his lap.

But his intentions had been honorable. He had been gentle and caring. Respectful. *Please trust that I am trying to help.* Not licentious or lustful. He'd gone to great lengths to preserve her reputation.

He'd also gone to great lengths to remain anonymous.

The more she considered the events from her rescuer's point of view, the more it seemed likely he would want to put it behind him as much as she did.

Perhaps she should not try to identify him. Trust that if they were meant to meet, they would encounter each other again. London society wasn't that large, after all. No need to acknowledge their first encounter.

Yes, that was for the best.

Chapter 4

LOGIC SATISFIED, ASHLEY WAS FIRM IN HER RESOLVE to not try to identify her mysterious rescuer. Didn't stop butterflies from trying to take flight in her midsection, though, as she descended the stairs and joined Aunt Eunice moments before Georgia and her parents arrived to take them to tonight's entertainment.

After exchanging polite greetings and compliments, the five of them settled in the carriage for the short drive to Lord and Lady Bristol's home.

The butterflies were still fluttering madly as Ashley surveyed the other guests in the drawing room. At least three dozen people were already present, and more still arriving. Two sisters stood at the pianoforte, singing to the accompaniment of their mother. Ashley had been introduced to them a week or two ago and had already forgotten their names.

"Do you see him?" Aunt Eunice whispered behind her fan.

It took all of Ashley's strength of will to remain calm. "Not yet."

"Who are you looking for?" Georgia whispered, leaning close.

"Sir Rupert," Aunt Eunice replied, still holding her fan in front of her lower face.

"He won't be here tonight," assured a feminine voice behind them.

The three women turned to see the new speaker.

Miss Valerie Kenyon, a miss in her second Season whom Ashley had exchanged pleasantries with before, stood just behind Georgia. "Or any night in the near future. My maid has a brother who works as a footman at a boarding house on Jermyn Street, and he said the owner was complaining that one of her tenants left abruptly yesterday morning. Still owed her a fortnight's rent."

"Sir Rupert?" Georgia began to ply her fan as well.

Miss Kenyon nodded. "My maid's brother overheard Sir Rupert tell the jarvey to take him to the docks. Planned to sail on the next available ship. Said it didn't matter where it was going."

Ashley locked her knees to keep them from buckling. "He's gone." She wouldn't get to slap him, but wouldn't have to face him, either. An unexpected mix of relief, disappointment, and anger flooded through her.

Georgia tapped her arm. "Were you hoping to make a match with him?"

"Heavens, no!"

"He did seem to be paying court to you," Aunt Eunice said. "He was most assiduous in his attentions. He didn't give you any indication he was leaving on a journey?"

"I don't think his trip was planned," Miss Kenyon interjected. "He took only one portmanteau, and the footman said he looked frightened. Kept looking over his shoulder, his eyes wide as saucers, as though he was being pursued."

"Pursued by debt collectors, perhaps," Georgia said.

The group turned to look at her. "My uncle and father warned me off him should Sir Rupert seek an introduction," she explained. "They said the man is a scoundrel and is only seeking a wife for her dowry."

"When?" Ashley wished someone had shared this information with her a few weeks ago, before she'd accepted that first dance invitation from Sir Rupert.

Georgia tapped her bottom lip with her index finger while she thought. "Yesterday. Or possibly the day before. I don't believe I'd even heard his name before Uncle David mentioned him."

Lady Bristol gestured for everyone to hush, and they quickly took seats. The sisters had finished their song, and now Amber Barrow-Smith stood at the pianoforte nervously adjusting her gloves and shawl. Eager to hear a former student, Ashley gave the girl her full attention.

Amber was tentative at first, her voice growing stronger the further she went along, singing about her one true love. Her accompanist struck a few wrong notes but Amber seemed not to notice.

"Oh, dear," Lady Mansfield muttered, looking between Amber and someone in the audience.

Ashley craned her neck and finally saw who Amber seemed to be singing to—a young man in a bright jonquil coat and floral print neckcloth. His expression could only be described as rapturous, clearly just as smitten with Amber.

"Is he not a suitable match?"

Lady Mansfield gave a tight shake of her head. "Her parents have already rejected his suit. Though it appears neither of them are deterred. It doesn't appear her chaperone, Mrs. Driscoll, is having any better luck."

Their true love, Amber sang, was so strong that the thwarted lovers would live together or perish together. "Oh dear, indeed," Ashley muttered.

Amber finished her song and blushed while curtsying to the applause, and she and Mrs. Driscoll took seats in the audience.

Another duo sang, then a trio playing flute, harp, and lyre. All were young women showing off their accomplishments in a typical Marriage Mart activity. Perhaps Ashley would be perceived as less of a bluestocking, and have a better chance at making a match, if she were to polish a song to sing or play, and find an opportunity like tonight's event to show off her talent, just like these women.

Did she have a song fit to perform in such a setting? Did she even want to put herself on display in such a manner? Could she attract someone other than reprobates like Rupert, or widowers? Her aunt and uncle hoped she would make a match, of course, as had Ashley at the start of the Season. After several men expressed distaste for her recent history working at the academy—they said they wanted a biddable wife, not a bluestocking—she had changed goals.

Now her first priority, after securing a position at another school, for which she'd already sent out inquiries, was simply to dance. Nearly on the shelf, after years at school where she performed the man's part so the students could learn the steps, she just wanted to dance the lady's part. With men. So many of the country's young men had gone off to war, many of the smaller towns and villages were desperately short on dance partners of the male variety. Even when Ashley accompanied the older girls to assemblies in Torquay, she usually had to be one of the women wearing a sash that indicated her willingness and ability to dance the man's part.

Everyone at Madame Zavrina's academy participated in music lessons. The teachers and staff had to lead by example, to display every attribute and skill the students were required to learn and develop. The townhouse Uncle Edward had rented for the Season had a well-tuned pianoforte in the drawing room, and Ashley had occupied many hours playing it with competence if not great artistry.

Polite applause brought Ashley back to the present. The latest trio to sing and play took their seats, and Lady Bristol waved over two men, one in his mid-fifties, the other in his late twenties, who bore a strong family resemblance.

"It is not just the young ladies who are going to show off their talents for us tonight," Lady Bristol said. "I have a special treat for us." She introduced the father-son pair, and they began to sing without any accompaniment.

Ashley tried not to wince when the father's baritone was often flat, and the son sang overly loud tenor with more enthusiasm than actual skill. They were trying, though, so she listened with polite interest.

"Mr. Grantham is looking for wife number three," Lady Mansfield leaned over to whisper to Ashley. "Six thousand a year, and he has his heir here plus two spares at home, so I don't think he's looking to have more children. I can arrange an introduction if you like."

He wasn't an appropriate match for Georgia. Ashley chose to view Lady Mansfield's willingness to pass him on to her daughter's friend as a kind gesture rather than a comment on Ashley's impending spinsterhood. She was spared having to reply as Lord Mansfield leaned over to his wife to quietly complain that Lord Templeton had not arrived yet.

The duo blessedly finished their song, bowed, and sat back down. Lady Bristol looked expectantly at Lord Mansfield. He shook his head.

His refusal seemed to throw Lady Bristol off-kilter, but she quickly rallied and invited up a quartet of young men. As they took up positions, their apparent leader, a handsome gentleman with romantic black curls and piercing blue eyes, looked at each woman in the audience. His gaze lingered over the young misses, and he seemed to delight in being the center of their attention.

"Lord Leighton," Lady Mansfield leaned over to whisper to Ashley and Georgia. "Don't be taken in by his looks and charm. His father bankrupted the estate. He hasn't a feather to fly with."

Suitably warned, Ashley sat back and enjoyed the performance—the preening as well as the singing, for clearly all four men were trying to appeal to the fairer sex.

After another shake of Lord Mansfield's head, Lady Bristol made a small hand gesture, and a footman passed a message through to the next room. Four gentlemen, led by Lord Bristol and all wearing matching red neckcloths, soon entered the drawing room. He settled on the bench at the pianoforte and arranged a sheaf of music.

"I have the privilege of listening to their rehearsals, and tonight I share with you the winners of last year's top singing prize at the Noblemen's and Gentlemen's Catch Club." With a nod to her husband, Lady Bristol sat down and the men began.

After a small commotion at the back of the room, Lord Mansfield kissed his wife on the cheek and left.

Lord Bristol played the introductory stanza, then began to sing as he accompanied himself. Ashley was transfixed by his lovely baritone voice, joined on the next stanza by the bass and two tenors standing beside him. With wonderful harmony they sang of valor in battle. After the second verse, they encouraged the audience to join in on the chorus. Sharing a grin with Georgia, Ashley sang the familiar words, goosebumps raising on her arms as she felt the room swell with the sound of voices raised in unison. At the end of the song, the audience erupted in applause and subtle foot stomps.

Lady Bristol poked her head in the next room, then withdrew and gestured at her husband to keep going. He began playing and singing *To Anacreon in Heaven* as a solo. When it came time to repeat the last two lines of the first verse, the tenors and bass joined him.

"No wonder they won last year," Ashley whispered to Georgia.

Georgia's only reply was a soft *harrumpf*. Ashley didn't have time to puzzle out her friend's reaction, as her own body was buzzing from the joy of hearing talented male voices.

The entire quartet sang the second verse, and when they repeated the last two lines, it seemed all the men in the room joined in.

"And long may the sons of Anacreon intwine the Myrtle of Venus with Bacchus's Vine."

At the end no one raised their glass in a toast, though Ashley had heard the men often did so when they sang this song at the beginning of Catch Club meetings.

Lady Bristol gave her husband a nod, and he and the other members of his quartet bowed amidst the applause and *huzzahs!* before taking seats in the audience.

The door from the other room opened and in walked Lord Mansfield, Lord Templeton, a gentleman Ashley had never seen before, and Lord Ravencroft, who carried a violincello. All wore matching neckcloths of dark blue.

Georgia grabbed Ashley's hand and squeezed. "*Now* you'll get to hear talent," she said, practically vibrating with excitement.

On the opposite side of the room from the pianoforte, Georgia's father, uncles, and the other gentleman clustered around the chair where Lord Ravencroft was settling with the violincello. The unknown man handed the bow to Ravencroft. Under cover of checking its strings, Ravencroft stared at Lady Mansfield and slowly drew the bow in a slashing motion across his throat, one eyebrow arched, the other lowered.

Shocked, Ashley checked Lady Mansfield's reaction. She had one hand to her bosom, a look of total innocence on her face ... until she erupted into quiet laughter, hidden behind her fan. Ravencroft's severe expression eased to a hint of a smile.

"My brother Parker was supposed to play tonight," Georgia whispered. "But he cut his finger on his penknife this morning. I'm glad Mother and Uncle Stanley were able to persuade Uncle David to come after all."

"Who is the fourth gentleman?"

"Mr. Westbrook. I call him Uncle Liam. He and Uncle David have been close friends as far back as I can recall."

"It is my pleasure to introduce the quartet that may very well offer the best challenge to my husband's group at this year's competition next month," Lady Bristol announced, and sat down.

Mr. Westbrook began singing, a warm baritone. He dropped out after a short stanza and Lord Templeton sang the next phrase, a tenor. Lord Mansfield sang the next phrase, a bass. On the fourth phrase, all four men sang in unison and Ravencroft began to play the violincello. The powerful, deep sound of the instrument and low male voices resonated right through Ashley until her whole body seemed to vibrate.

Ravencroft turned his head to watch his bow on the strings and his hair fell forward, concealing much of his face. As if he didn't want to see the audience. Or perhaps he didn't want them to see him? The men's voices danced along the melody, someone going up into high tenor while another went down to basso profundo, in a glorious harmony that had Ashley's heart pounding, her breath shallow.

Lady Barbour, a matron sitting two chairs over and one row ahead of Ashley, began fluttering her fan furiously, her cheeks flushed.

The words and tune were familiar but Ashley had never heard this arrangement before. All but one voice would drop out for a phrase, then the others return, highlighting each voice in turn, the plural voices always underscored by the deep tone of the violincello. In all the previous performances of this song Ashley had heard, a tenor sang lead all the way through, accompanied by pianoforte. Hearing it performed by a deeper instrument and deep voices made it an altogether different experience.

Lord Mansfield stayed in basso profundo, his heavy and slow voice filling out the bottom of the tune. At one point he winked at his wife. Ashley heard Georgia snort. Lady Mansfield had a beatific smile, a slight flush on her cheeks.

The men finished with one incredibly long sustained note held in perfect harmony, then bowed amidst applause.

Lady Bristol quickly thanked those who had performed and reminded everyone refreshments were now served.

"Lord Ravencroft acquitted himself well for filling in at the last minute," Ashley said. Their seats were on the far side of the room from the refreshment table. Given the crowd size, it would be a few minutes before she could fetch herself and Aunt Eunice a cup of punch.

"Of course he did," Georgia replied absently. "It's his arrangement." She scanned the crowd, who had all stood and started mingling as footmen moved chairs to the edges of the room. "I've heard him play it better, though." She grabbed Ashley's elbow and tugged. "Come," she said. "Something juicy is afoot!"

Processing the information that Lord Ravencroft could sing *and* arrange music *and* play at least two instruments, Ashley allowed herself to be towed along until they reached Miss Kenyon, who was chatting with Miss Amber Barrow-Smith.

"How romantic," Miss Kenyon gushed.

"Isn't it just?" Amber replied, one palm over her heart.

"Tell me!" Georgia demanded, leaning close to them, her voice hushed but urgent.

"But you can't tell anyone else!" Amber admonished. She glanced at Ashley, who shook her head in a mute promise to keep quiet.

With a look around to see if anyone else was paying attention—her chaperone was over by the refreshment table—Amber lowered her voice. All four women leaned in close. "On Sunday morning I will have a headache and need to stay home. We're going to elope while Mama and Papa and Mrs. Driscoll are at church. By the time they realize I'm not in my bed, we'll be hours ahead on the road north." She glanced over Miss Kenyon's shoulder, where her beau stood with a glass of punch. He blew a kiss to her. Amber tittered.

Oh, dear. Ashley had given her promise; what could she do?

Another friend walked up to their group, and Miss Kenyon and Georgia greeted the newcomer. Ashley stepped closer so she could whisper in Amber's ear. "What do you think Madame Zavrina would say?"

Amber looked stricken for a moment, but only a moment. She threw her shoulders back and looked as mulish as when she'd refused to acknowledge she'd incorrectly conjugated a French verb. "I don't care." Her voice rose with her passion, to a normal conversational level. "I love Sir Peyton and he loves me, and we're going to be married over the anvil by Tuesday night. My parents will accept him once they see how happy we are together."

David had tucked his violincello away in its case and was working his way through the crowd to speak with his sister when he heard the young woman declare her love for Sir Peyton. He paused, his back to the group so they wouldn't notice him eavesdropping. Seemed Peyton was up to his old tricks. Poor, foolish girl. Stubborn girl, as she resisted Miss Hamlin's entreaties for a calm head and to take more time to ponder her actions.

Georgia and another friend joined them, and they turned the conversation to their plans to attend the masquerade ball the following night, and the costume each planned to wear.

Grantham walked up to the group then, accompanied by Lady Bristol.

"My dear Miss Hamlin," Grantham said once the introductions were done and Lady Bristol moved on to other guests. "May I fetch you a glass of punch?"

David's heart stuttered as Miss Hamlin took a beat too long to answer. "Thank you, that's very kind. But ... I'm not thirsty."

From the corner of his eye, David saw Grantham recoil in surprise. Fetching punch and receiving the cup was a major part of the Marriage Mart mating rituals. No miss refused a glass, even if she just held it and didn't drink it.

David found his emotions mixed. Glad the chit was refusing punch from strange men, and also sad that she now felt the need to protect herself this way.

"Please excuse me," Miss Hamlin said. "My aunt is signaling me."

Grantham's jaw worked like a landed fish as he watched her go.

A few minutes later the crowd around the refreshment table thinned, and David ladled a cup of punch for himself. Miss Hamlin stood beside him, an empty cup in hand, patiently waiting for the ladle. Confident she had seen him fill it, he handed her his cup.

Their bare fingers brushed, startling him. He hadn't put gloves back on after his performance, and hers were poking out from her reticule. Under the bright chandelier, he noted her light brown eyes were the color of sherry, and sparkled like the small diamond earbobs and necklace she wore. Unlike when she conversed with Grantham, she appeared relaxed. With a little teasing he was sure he could coax a smile from her, were he inclined to strike up a flirtation. Which he reminded himself he had no intention of doing.

"Thank you." She immediately took a sip, and set down the empty cup she'd been holding.

He filled another cup for himself and stepped back so some swain could fetch two cups.

Miss Hamlin followed him. "May I compliment you on your performance?"

He froze in mid-step.

"Georgia said that was your arrangement. Very clever how it featured the deeper voices so well."

He started breathing again. "Mansfield wanted something so he could impress Diana on their tenth wedding anniversary. Was a simple matter of shuffling parts. Pitch them down an octave." He was supposed to keep his distance, not speak to Miss Hamlin, but David found himself oddly reluctant to leave her company.

"Simple for you, perhaps. I cannot imagine trying to—"

"Sorry to interrupt," Mansfield said. "Diana wants to tuck in the little ones, and Miss Hamlin, your aunt asked to make a night of it as well."

"Of course." She put her cup on the table. David couldn't resist raising her hand to kiss it, and wished her a good night before she accepted Mansfield's arm and walked away.

Saturday evening, Amber Barrow-Smith walked arm in arm with Mrs. Driscoll. As the weather had remained fine, even though no moon shone tonight, she had followed through with her plan to walk to the masquerade ball hosted by Lord and Lady Waldon. Their home was only one square over from her own. What could go wrong?

Mrs. Driscoll let out a quiet shriek as a cat darted out from the gate they were passing and dashed across the road. Mrs. Driscoll halted, her hand over her chest.

"Do you need your smelling salts?" Amber inquired, struggling to be patient. This widowed chaperone her parents had hired for the Season was great to play cards or chess with when they were short on social engagements, but jumped at every shadow.

"I ... I shall be fine. The cat was not black." She adjusted the bright blue cape she wore over her Grecian costume. Amber had persuaded her to dress as Hera, goddess of marriage, matching Amber, who'd chosen to be Athena, goddess of wisdom and reason.

They each carried their silk half-mask in a reticule. Sir Peyton knew what Amber was wearing. He was to be dressed as Eros, with wings and a bow and quiver of arrows. They intended to sneak away to the garden for a few moments during the masquerade to finalize plans for Sunday morning.

After a few deep breaths, Mrs. Driscoll began walking again. They were about ten steps from the corner. "There is no reason to be nervous," she said, patting Amber's hand. "This is a perfectly lovely—"

A large figure jumped out from the alley, dressed all in black, holding a walking stick with a gleaming silver handle, and blocked the path in front of them.

Mrs. Driscoll shrieked.

Amber clutched Mrs. Driscoll's hand. She heard a low, breathy growl that gradually increased in volume until the unearthly sound resolved into words.

"Amber Barrow-Smith," the figure intoned in the deepest, most gravelly voice she had ever heard, a tortured, slow sound dredged up from the bowels of the earth. He—it?—raised the walking stick to chest height, its hand holding the stick halfway up like it was a weapon.

She gulped. In the light from the streetlamps, she could just make out a tricorn hat, a black cape lined with blood-red silk, and the walking stick topped with a gleaming silver skull. The figure's face was a pale blur except where there should be eyes, she saw only blackness.

She trembled.

"Amber, you have made a poor choice," the creature continued. Its voice was so low it seemed to come from the depths of the grave, barely audible over the pounding of her heart. She felt the rumble more than she heard each slow syllable. "I do not like it when my minions are disobedient, so I have come to warn you."

Mrs. Driscoll shuddered and dug her fingers into Amber's arm, but Amber stood tall and drew her shoulders back, chin up. "What poor choice?"

"Sir Peyton." Derision infused the breathy growl.

"What about him?"

Its slow voice seemed to come from a long way away, from the bottom of the ocean. "Before you pledge yourself to him, ask him about ... Janet."

Amber finally looked past the silver skull and up toward the creature's face, trying to read its expression. "J- Janet?"

Mrs. Driscoll whimpered.

"Who—who are you?" Amber's tiny store of courage was rapidly eroding.

The creature tipped its head back, opened its mouth, and emitted a demonic laugh that seemed to come straight from the bowels of hell. Amber shook. Lamplight glinted on its sharp teeth. "You do not recognize me, my dear?"

Amber gulped. She and Mrs. Driscoll clutched each other.

"I..." It took one step toward Amber. "Am." Another step. "The Bogeyman." He lunged forward, one outstretched hand reaching for Amber, and there was a blinding flash of light.

Mrs. Driscoll screamed and fainted. Amber tried to catch her but only managed to slow her companion's descent to the ground. By the time she looked up again, the creature was gone.

Chapter 5

ASHLEY ENTERED THE MASQUERADE with Aunt Eunice, a flutter of excitement in her belly. Musicians played, dancers glided across the dance floor, and everywhere revelers mingled. There were devils and angels, Greek and Roman gods and goddesses, court jesters and royalty in scarlet robes, everyone wearing at least a half-mask. And of course there were those in a simple hooded domino like Ashley. Madame Chantel had offered to create a more elaborate costume, but Ashley felt guilty about how much money Uncle Edward had already spent on her wardrobe. She'd chosen a domino in a rich sapphire blue silk, a color she would never otherwise be able to wear unless she was married or prepared to fully declare herself a spinster.

She pushed the hood back, as the room was warm with so many people, careful to make sure her half-mask was still firmly tied in place. Like other revelers, she removed her gloves and tucked them in her reticule.

Over the buzz of conversation and the music, they heard a commotion down the hall.

"A demon, I tell you!" came an anguished feminine cry in a voice that seemed familiar.

Ashley exchanged glances with her aunt, and they pushed their way through the swirling crowd toward the source. Inside a small salon, two Greek goddesses sat on a sofa, one trying to console the other, as others stood by, discussing the scene the goddesses were making. Ashley recognized the voice of the calm one.

"Amber?"

Amber Barrow-Smith stood up. "Miss Hamlin?" She sounded near tears. Ashley opened her arms and Amber fell against her and wrapped her arms around her waist in a suffocating hug, her breath coming in harsh pants.

Ashley rubbed her hand up and down the girl's back and made soothing noises. "Whatever has happened?"

"It was a demon!" Ashley recognized the voice of Amber's companion, who sat on the sofa. "A demon accosted us, and no one will believe me!" Mrs. Driscoll held the back of her hand to her forehead and swooned against the sofa cushions.

The crowd shifted and their hostess Lady Waldon entered, accompanied by a maid carrying a silver vinaigrette.

While Aunt Eunice and the other ladies attended to the companion, Ashley turned her attention to Amber. "A demon?"

"Yes! No. Well, probably not." Amber straightened, took a step toward the fireplace, and inhaled several calming breaths. "He said he was... the Bogeyman."

Ashley fought hard to keep her expression and voice neutral. "The Bogeyman."

Amber shrugged. "It sounds fantastical, but that's who he claimed to be." She went on to describe the apparition that had confronted them a few steps from Lady Waldon's home. He was shrouded head to toe in black except for the blood-red lining of his black cape that hissed when he moved, like snakes. Walking stick with a silver skull for a handle. Pale blur where a face should be. "And black holes where his eyes should have been. It seemed like you could see all the way to hell." She shuddered.

"And fangs!" Mrs. Driscoll added. She visibly shivered. " As long as I live I shall never forget the sight of his fangs, or the sound of his evil laugh!"

Ashley glanced from the sofa back to Amber. "Did he say anything else? Give any reason for his, ah, visit?"

Amber stared down at her fingers, where she was fidgeting with her handkerchief. "He called me by name and said..."

"Yes? What did he say?"

Her voice was barely audible. "He said I had made a poor choice."

Lady Waldon ushered people out of the room. As soon as she was gone, Miss Kenyon and Georgia entered, Sir Peyton at their heels.

Amber took a deep breath. "You!" she shouted, stretching out one arm and pointing her finger at Sir Peyton.

He jumped and glanced behind himself to see if she was angry with the person behind him. No one else was there.

Amber advanced on him, speaking one sharp syllable with each step. "Who. Is. Janet?"

Sir Peyton's mouth moved but no sound came out.

Ashley gestured for Georgia and Miss Kenyon to exit the room with her. Given that Amber and Sir Peyton were still chaperoned, Ashley shut the door. They heard Amber's muffled voice, throbbing with anger, interspersed with Sir Peyton's placating tone.

Ashley ushered the two girls down the hall until they caught up with Georgia's mother, who told them she'd heard about the commotion from Aunt Constance, who'd arrived just before them.

"Mother, who is Janet to Sir Peyton?"

Lady Mansfield beckoned them to a quiet alcove. "A cautionary tale." She draped one arm around Georgia and the other around Miss Kenyon, and made sure Ashley was also listening. "Last year, Sir Peyton courted Janet. You don't need to know her family name. Suffice to say, the situation was much the same as with Miss Barrow-Smith. The young lovers were determined despite her parents rejecting his suit. He told her they were eloping and they left in the dead of night. But he is a scoundrel. Instead of taking her to Scotland and marrying her, rumor has it he took her to some out of the way inn and demanded a large sum of money from her parents for her safe return."

Miss Kenyon gasped.

"Some say she joined a convent. Others say she married a vicar in a small village somewhere. And she has not been seen in Town since."

Ashley digested the information. "She has not been seen, yet Sir Peyton is still received in society."

Lady Mansfield slowly nodded. "I'm afraid that's the way it is."

"But he is a cad!" Miss Kenyon said.

"And he planned to do the same thing with Amber!" Georgia stomped one foot. "Ooh, he should be horsewhipped!"

"I tried to persuade her against following through with their plans when we spoke last night," Ashley said. "Given her anger I saw just now, it would seem the ... ah, Bogeyman ... succeeded where I could not." It felt strange to feel gratitude toward a, well, demon. Whatever he or it was, the Bogeyman had definitely not been a figment of Amber's imagination. And she was grateful Amber had been spared Janet's fate.

They joined the crowd in the ballroom just as the musicians struck up a waltz. Miss Kenyon accepted an invitation from a jester, and Georgia danced away on the arm of a pirate. Ashley planned to chat with Lady Mansfield, but a gentleman in a blue and gold domino and matching half-mask bowed over her hand and silently led her out to dance. By the copper-red hair flecked with strands of silver, she felt fairly confident it was Lord Mansfield.

Before Ashley could feel left out or awkward and go in search of her aunt, a man dressed all in black save for his white cravat, scarlet cape, and matching scarlet half-mask approached and bowed. He held out his ungloved hand, palm-up, in a silent invitation to dance.

She hesitated. Would she be opening herself up to another potential predator like Sir Rupert? Then she recognized Lord Ravencroft by the streak of white in his chestnut hair. Butterflies rioting in her stomach, she placed her hand in his and they joined the other dancers.

He danced divinely. Of course someone skilled as a musician and singer would understand the rhythms of dance and move gracefully. She sighed with pleasure. Not once did he tread on her toes.

She was acutely aware of the warmth of his large right hand on the small of her back, applying just enough pressure to guide her, avoiding collisions with other couples on the crowded dance floor. Good thing he was leading because she was oblivious to anyone else in the room. No silk or kid leather separated the skin of her right hand securely tucked in his left, his fingers curled around hers so that she felt the calluses on his fingertips. She'd lived at a school for girls too long. Holding hands with a man this way felt scandalous. Naughty.

And yet, so right. She was a traveler in the desert finally reaching an oasis.

Surprised at her own daring, she slipped her left hand under his cape instead of on top, to rest on his shoulder that was so broad her hand barely curved over it. The black velvet lining caressed the top of her hand when his cape slid to one side as they turned, the scarlet silk top layer whispering as it shifted. The soft black superfine of his jacket and trousers absorbed all the light. If not for his cravat and cape, he could melt into the shadows. Be a figment of her imagination.

He hummed along with the music, barely audible over the instruments, but she felt it.

Something teased at the edge of her memory.

She swept her gaze from their joined hands up his chest, past the ruby stick pin winking in the folds of his snowy white cravat against the black muslin shirt, past his strong jaw, his full lips curved in a hint of a smile, to his eyes.

He stopped humming but kept dancing. Kept that hint of a smile.

On their first meeting she had thought his eyes to be brown. This close she realized they were hazel, with flecks of mossy green and dark amber, like aged brandy. His lashes were darker, longer, and thicker than she recalled, as if he'd enhanced them with cosmetics. Probably just an illusion, the result of his eyes being isolated from the rest of his face by the scarlet half-mask.

She'd get to see all of his face at midnight, at the unmasking. She'd never been in such a hurry for midnight to arrive.

She realized she'd been staring, and that he was staring right back at her. The bemused look on his face, the sparkle in his eyes, was as if he silently asked if she liked what she saw.

Yes, indeed.

Did he like what he saw? What little of her was visible. She'd wanted to attend the masquerade despite knowing some people stretched and even broke the rules of decorum. Her first Season had ended so quickly, she'd never had the chance to attend one before. She'd deliberately chosen the domino because it concealed her from head to ankle with the hood up. Though she was of average height there were still plenty of men tall enough to look down her cleavage even with a modest neckline on her gowns, as had already happened numerous times with previous dance partners.

Realizing the tune was more than half over and they'd not exchanged a single syllable, she inhaled and opened her mouth to say something.

He gave a subtle shake of his head.

She closed her mouth.

He pulled her a tiny bit closer on the next turn and kept her there. He already held her closer than any other dance partner ever had. She felt the heat from his body. He wore no cologne; he smelled of fresh air and a hint of something sharper, that reminded her of gunpowder. Perhaps he had visited a shooting range before coming to the ball.

Another couple, staring into each other's eyes, came dangerously close to colliding with them. Ravencroft easily guided Ashley out of their way without breaking the rhythm of the waltz. His breath stirred the hair at her temple, and she felt the sudden urge to lay her head against his shoulder and wrap her arms around his waist. Have him wrap his arms around her.

How odd.

She wasn't tired. Was she so starved for male attention, so desirous of physical intimacy, that she'd fling herself at the first man who caught her fancy?

Perhaps she shouldn't have stayed at the Torquay Academy for Young Ladies so long.

Perhaps she needed to get back to a school for ladies and learn more self-control.

Hmm.

Later she would ponder it. Right now she was enjoying being held in a handsome man's arms, as they moved in unison to lovely music.

When the song ended, he kept her hand tucked in his and led her toward the edge of the dance floor, unerringly back to where she'd been standing before the music started. As the crowd thinned, he shifted her hand to tuck it in the crook of his arm, just before Lady Mansfield and Georgia became visible. He bowed over her hand, kissed her knuckles—his lips were soft and warm—and departed.

All without uttering a syllable.

She wanted to examine and relive every moment in Ravencroft's arms, but Henry the Eighth asked her to dance the Roger de Coverley just then. As long as she did not accept any drinks and stayed in the crowded ballroom, she felt safe enough to enjoy herself.

One dance led to another, each with a different partner. Even though every other song was a waltz and she had a partner for each one, none seemed as intimate as the silent dance with Ravencroft. Finally she saw him again when he helped Lord Mansfield bring drinks to her, Georgia, her mother, and Aunt Eunice while the musicians were taking a break.

During the pause in music, several of the conversations audible in the room drifted back to Mrs. Driscoll's claims about seeing a demon, and the ensuing argument between Amber Barrow-Smith and Sir Peyton. All three of them had left the masquerade, the former two in Lord Waldon's coach with an escort of three extra footmen and Lord Waldon himself. Armed.

Having delivered the drinks, Ravencroft started walking away again. A gent in a solid black domino with a cream silk half-mask joined him.

"Fangs?" asked the voice she recognized as Mr. Westbrook.

The two friends exchanged glances. Ravencroft shrugged.

Break over, the musicians struck up another waltz. Ashley was old for a debutante, but her skill made her a popular partner while everyone was masked. Though she looked for him, Ravencroft proved elusive, and much to her disappointment he did not ask her to dance again. As a minor sop to her ego, she did not see him dancing with anyone else, either.

At last the clock struck midnight. The musicians stopped playing, more candles in the chandeliers were lit, and everyone removed their mask. Amid laughter and gasps, the buzz of conversation grew louder.

But no Ravencroft.

When Ashley came back from dancing the next polonaise, Aunt Eunice asked to make a night of it. Ashley's feet ached, one toe might be broken from having been stepped on, and she may have actually danced a hole through the soles of her slippers. With Ravencroft absent, she readily agreed to go home.

Sunday offered a much-needed day of rest. By Monday Ashley was eager to see her new friend Georgia again. She and Aunt Eunice were welcomed into the Mansfield townhouse and joined Georgia and her mother in the front parlor for their at-home. On the other side of the wall was the music room. Ashley quickly became distracted by memories of the first time she'd heard Ravencroft sing and play.

Miss Kenyon's arrival startled Ashley out of her reverie. While her mother went to join Lady Mansfield and Ashley's aunt in conversation, Miss Kenyon selected a chair and pulled it close to the sofa where Ashley and Georgia sat.

Miss Kenyon leaned her elbows on her knees, practically vibrating with excitement. "My maid has heard from her brother again," she said. "Now that word is going around town that Amber and Mrs. Driscoll saw the Bogeyman, her brother added another detail to Sir Rupert's abrupt departure."

Georgia and Ashley both glanced to make sure the older ladies were uninterested in their conversation. Georgia made an impatient hand gesture.

"Remember how he said Sir Rupert kept looking over his shoulder, as though he was being pursued?"

"By debt collectors," Georgia said.

Miss Kenyon shook her head. Her blonde curls quivered with her exhilaration. "By the Bogeyman!"

"What?" Ashley said at the same moment Georgia exclaimed "No!"

Miss Kenyon glowed with the joy of being the one to share such a juicy tidbit of gossip. "It seems Sir Rupert was visited by the Bogeyman ... in the middle of the night!"

Ashley and Georgia glanced at each other, wearing identical expressions of surprise.

"Why did your maid's brother not say so before?" Georgia said.

"Can you imagine being the first to claim such a thing? Consider how everyone looked at Mrs. Driscoll and Miss Barrow-Smith on Saturday night."

"Like they were less than sane," Ashley said softly.

Georgia silently tapped her bottom lip with her index finger.

"But now there are three witnesses," Miss Kenyon said.

"If we accept that someone calling himself the Bogeyman is real and not a demon nor a figment of imagination," Georgia said slowly, "I have to wonder why he appeared to Amber and to Sir Rupert."

"Well, he did warn Amber not to elope with Sir Peyton, in a roundabout way," Miss Kenyon said.

"What a cad," Georgia said, with a theatrical shudder. "Can you imagine planning to ruin an innocent girl?"

Ashley felt the blood drain from her face.

Georgia rested her hand on Ashley's knee. "What is it? You look as if you've just seen a ghost!"

Ashley silently debated. The burden of keeping the secret to herself, of not being able to discuss it with anyone, had weighed heavily on her. "I wasn't going to tell anyone. And you must swear on your honor not to share this with anyone else. Ever."

Georgia and Miss Kenyon leaned in close, both drawing an X over their heart. "I solemnly swear." Miss Kenyon nodded.

"I would never betray a sister," Georgia fervently added.

Ashley squeezed Georgia's hand in gratitude. After a quick glance to make sure the other ladies in the room were still paying them no attention, she took a deep breath. "Sir Rupert tried to ... ruin me." Her heart was pounding. She had never said the words aloud to anyone, not even to herself.

Miss Kenyon drew her brows together in puzzlement. "You planned to elope with him?"

"Good heavens, no!" Ashley shuddered. "He put something in my drink while we were at a ball. My memory is fuzzy after that, but I remember being in the dark garden with him, in the gazebo. He attempted to... take liberties."

Georgia's eyes grew round. Miss Kenyon gasped.

"Did he... Were you able to fend him off?" Georgia sounded appalled.

"I tried, without much success. He'd given me too much laudanum. Fortunately, another man—a true gentleman—intervened and sent Sir Rupert away before he could ... could do what he planned." Ashley smoothed her skirt, wishing her hands would stop shaking. She had tried not to think about that night. The uncertainty of being in a dark carriage with a strange man, in an intimate position with her mysterious rescuer while she was so vulnerable. Waking in the home of a kind but unknown lady. And she was still so horrified by what Sir Rupert had intended to do to her, she shied away from thinking about that part of the night altogether. Her stomach knotted again at reliving the memory.

"But how did the Bogeyman find out? Do you think your gentleman rescuer told him?" Georgia said.

"Perhaps they are friends."

Both Georgia and Ashley gaped at Miss Kenyon.

"Well, we don't *really* think the Bogeyman is a demon from hell, do we? So it stands to reason that he is human. Perhaps even a member of London society."

Georgia spoke slowly. "Perhaps he's a gentleman himself."

"With fangs?" Ashley shook her head. "That would be hard to disguise."

Miss Kenyon snapped her fingers. "That's it! The fangs are simply part of his disguise!"

The three pondered that idea while a maid entered with the tea tray. Several minutes passed before they sat back again with cups of tea and little plates of delicate pastries.

"Who could he be?" Miss Kenyon popped a tea cake in her mouth.

"Someone who knew about Sir Peyton's plan to elope with Amber," Georgia said. "And Sir Rupert's plan to, ah, compromise Ashley."

Ashley suppressed a shudder. Her appetite gone, she put the pastry back on her plate. "Gentlemen discuss things at their clubs," she said slowly, remembering some of the conversations Uncle Edward had mentioned. "Perhaps he overheard one or both men bragging to a friend about their plans."

"Father says men gossip as much or more than women." Georgia took a sip. "He's overheard all sorts of things at his club, including which music Lord Fairfax's group is planning to perform at the next Catch Club competition. But what I don't understand is, what would make a gentleman respond to hearing about such abhorrent plans by dressing up and impersonating a demon?"

"Why didn't he simply call them out? Fight a duel?" Miss Kenyon ate another pastry.

"The fact that dueling is illegal may have deterred him." The raspberry filling and lemon icing looked delicious. Ashley decided to try a tea cake after all.

"And," Georgia gestured with a biscuit, "generally a man throwing down the gauntlet is defending a lady's honor. He would need to have some connection to Amber and Ashley in order to fight duels on their behalf."

Miss Kenyon refilled her cup. "Do you share anything in common with Amber?"

"She was a student at the ladies' academy where I worked." Ashley selected another pastry and popped it into her mouth. Ah, yes, lovely. "But she left to be presented at court last year at the start of the Season, and the academy closed in February this year."

Miss Kenyon's mother rose from her chair, collected her daughter, and they departed. Ashley was startled to realize she had stayed well past the twenty minutes that was polite for a morning call. When she made to rise as well, Georgia tugged on Ashley's hand. "Please say you'll come for dinner tonight," she said quietly.

Aunt Eunice rose also and joined Ashley by the sofa. "We're leaving now, my dear, but coming back for dinner," she said with a smile.

Georgia let out a quiet squeal of delight. Ashley squeezed her hand in farewell, and she left to continue paying morning calls with Aunt Eunice.

They were removing their wraps in the entry hall at home when Aunt Eunice checked the silver salver for the day's mail. She set all but one aside and immediately broke the wax seal.

Ashley was preparing to go upstairs when Aunt Eunice gave out a small sound of distress. "Is something wrong?"

Aunt Eunice's brow furrowed as she scanned the letter again. "It's from my old music teacher, Mrs. O'Keefe. We've been corresponding these thirty years or more. She writes that she's had an accident and is confined to bed. I have been meaning to visit her while I'm living only two hours away."

"This seems like an excellent time to go, while you're in England."

"It's rather late in the day to set out on a visit." Aunt Eunice glanced down the hall toward her husband's study, then back at Ashley. She patted Ashley on the shoulder and marched into the study, calling her husband's name.

Ashley went up to her room, freshened up, and was debating whether to have a lie-down or request a light meal, when Aunt Eunice knocked on her door.

"I have decided to go visit Mrs. O'Keefe this afternoon, and stay the night. "

"Of course you must go to your friend. It's a long journey. I would be happy to keep you company."

She shook her head. "Edward is going to tear himself away from his work and come with me, so that won't be necessary."

Ashley felt a measure of disappointment. Naturally her aunt should visit her friend. But with both her aunt and uncle gone, that meant Ashley could not visit Georgia tonight and have dinner with her friend's large, boisterous family.

"But I don't want to leave you here alone."

"There are a dozen servants in the house, Aunt. I won't be alone."

"All of whom came highly recommended. But none have worked for us for longer than six weeks. I would not feel comfortable leaving you here alone with just the servants."

Ashley gritted her teeth. She was an adult, a woman of twenty-three years. She should be able to spend an evening at home by herself, with or without servants.

"I've had a better idea." Aunt's eyes twinkled with merriment. "I don't wish to interfere in your plans. You should spend time with your young friends. To that end, I have exchanged notes with Lady Mansfield." She gave Ashley's shoulders a squeeze. "Lord Mansfield is going to send his coach for you. Not only will you get to have dinner with your friend, you are to stay the night with Georgia. Is that not marvelous?"

Ashley's first reaction was irritation. She was not a child who needed a governess or nurse to look after her. But then she thought how much fun it would be to spend the night with Georgia. They could laugh and be silly until all hours, just as students had often done at the academy. It had been more than a decade since she'd last spent the night at a friend's home.

"Thank you, Aunt. That is very thoughtful of you."

Aunt Eunice pulled her in for a quick hug. "You don't have much time before the coach will be here." They kissed each other on the cheek in farewell. Aunt left for her room to pack, and Ashley rang the bell so Sally could help her pack.

She had barely snapped the valise closed when a footman knocked on her door to let her know Lord Mansfield's coach had arrived.

Soon she was ushered into the Mansfield townhouse entry hall, her bonnet, cloak, and gloves taken by the butler, a footman disappearing upstairs with her valise and her maid, and Georgia pulled her into a hug.

"I feel bad for your aunt's friend, but we're going to have ever so much fun!" She tucked her arm through Ashley's and began to lead her toward the staircase. "You can help me pick out what to wear for dinner. You'll get to meet Great-Aunt Constance tonight. I think Uncle Liam is already here."

Strains of music had been drifting into the hall. The singing and playing abruptly cut off and voices rose in tense conversation. Ashley cocked her head to listen.

"Ooh, it sounds like they're arguing again," Georgia said, obviously delighted. "Let's go watch!" She held one finger over her lips. They tiptoed into the music room and sat on two of the straight-backed chairs lined up along the back wall, behind the large sofa where Georgia's sister-in-law, Deirdre, was asleep, her embroidery hoop and threads abandoned on the cushion beside her.

Lord Mansfield sat at the pianoforte, with Lord Templeton and Georgia's oldest brother, Parker, standing just behind him so they could look over his shoulder at the music. Mr. Westbrook was off to one side with a mandolin on his lap. Completing the circle, Lord Ravencroft sat with his back to Ashley, holding a violincello. Lady Templeton stood near the fireplace in front of a large slate mounted on a frame, similar to those used in classrooms at the academy. Several bars of music had been written on the slate. Lady Templeton waved a sheet of paper with one hand and held a piece of chalk in the other.

"That's not the way I wrote it!" She stabbed the slate with her chalk. "Go up to the C and then step down to the F sharp."

"But it sounds better this way!" Ravencroft gestured with his bow as he spoke.

Ashley felt something tickle her lower leg, and with a huff of annoyance, bent down to retie her garter.

"Why don't we ask our audience which version they prefer?" Lord Mansfield said.

"I only arrived in time to hear the argument," Georgia said sweetly. "I'll need to hear the music."

Ashley retied her other garter for good measure, adjusted her skirt, and sat back up.

Lady Templeton blew out a puff of air that lifted strands of hair from her forehead. "Very well. From the beginning, shall we? My version first." She raised her hand, and the quintet began.

The five voices were barely strong enough to not be drowned out by the three instruments. Except Ashley could only distinguish four voices.

After a few measures, Lady Templeton waved her hand to cut them off. "David, why aren't you singing?"

"You don't need my voice. I'm only here because Parker can't play for another week or two."

As if on cue, Parker glanced at the bandages on the index and middle finger of his left hand. "Three weeks."

"And by then he won't have enough time to become proficient with this piece before the competition." Lady Templeton softened her tone. "We have a better chance of besting Lord Bristol if you join us." She sauntered close to Ravencroft. "And I know you'd enjoy beating Lord Fairfax."

Ravencroft tapped her shoulder with the tip of his bow. "You're not playing fair."

Lady Templeton leaned closer and lowered her voice even further, a teasing smile in her tone. "Dear, sweet, little brother. When have I ever played fair?"

Ravencroft's shoulders rose and fell in a sigh. Instead of replying with words, he played the opening four notes of Beethoven's *Fifth Symphony*, dramatically drawing out the last note.

As she walked back to the fireplace, Ravencroft, Lord Mansfield, and Mr. Westbrook played the next four notes. Parker and Lord Templeton joined in by singing, "*dun dun dun dunnnn.*"

"Boys!"

Ashley and Georgia both smothered a laugh. "Are they always like this?" Ashley whispered.

"Sometimes they're even more childish," Georgia replied, her quiet voice quavering with barely contained laughter.

"We have less than an hour before Diana will expect us in the dining room," Lady Templeton said. "Please concentrate." She tapped the chalkboard and gestured for them to begin.

They played both versions, and Ashley agreed Ravencroft's version was more melodious. Georgia didn't even have to voice her opinion, because Lady Templeton wadded up a sheet of music and tossed it at Ravencroft. He batted it aside with his bow.

"You're right. I'll recopy the music tonight. Let's work on the other piece. David, please help Parker out on the high tenor line."

Lady Templeton started them off. Parker's voice grew stronger, and the men's voices were no longer in danger of being overwhelmed by the instruments. Ashley was puzzled, because now it sounded like she heard a violin. With two strong voices singing the high tenor line, a slightly lower tenor, plus the bright tone of the violin, the song seemed top-heavy, despite Lord Mansfield's bass.

They made it all the way through once. Lady Templeton held the heel of her hand to her forehead, her eyes squeezed shut. "Mansfield, you sound like a bullfrog."

Ashley was shocked to hear Lady Templeton speak to her brother-in-law this way, but he merely said, "Again?" and shook his head.

"Open up your embouchure to get more warmth in your tone. David, why don't you sing the bass line with him this time? I'm not sure where we need your voice most."

Ravencroft saluted his sister with his bow. This time when they played, the bright violin was gone and the deep tone of the violincello was back, and Ashley realized Ravencroft was playing a seven-string viola da gamba, not a violoncello.

The song sounded much better with the deeper tones, more balanced, though Ashley conceded she was partial to low voices.

Only a few measures into it, Parker struggled on the high tenor again. Ravencroft finished the verse with him. On the next verse, Ravencroft sang the low tenor part with Templeton. On the chorus he was back to bass with Mansfield, and on the third verse he sang baritone with Westbrook. For the final chorus he went back to bass, dropping down yet another octave to basso profundo for the first word in each phrase.

At no point did he sound like a bullfrog.

Through it all Ashley sat perfectly still, hardly daring to breathe, her heart pounding madly.

That voice! She'd heard that voice before! The mellow tenor, the warm, comforting baritone. The basso profundo that had terrified Sir Rupert into fleeing the gazebo.

Could it be? Her mysterious rescuer was Ravencroft?

Chapter 6

"HE'S DOING THAT TO ANNOY AUNT LYDIA," Georgia whispered. "It quite vexes her that he has a range of nearly five octaves even without rehearsing regularly, and she can barely reach one full octave no matter how much she practices."

Ashley tore her gaze from Ravencroft's profile, and noted Lady Templeton's brow furrowed, her eyes narrowed. When the song ended, she cut them off with an abrupt gesture. "Enough of that. Let's move on to *The Last Rose of Summer*."

Georgia grabbed Ashley's elbow. "Come! We barely have time to dress for dinner!"

Ashley followed her up the stairs, still in a daze of whirling thoughts at her realization of Ravencroft being her secret rescuer.

"You can have your own guest chamber, of course," Georgia said as they reached the first-floor landing, looking shy and uncertain. "But I hoped you might want to stay in my room instead."

At the top of the stairs, Ashley impetuously pulled her in for a quick hug. The close friends she'd had as a child and young adolescent were long married and had families of their own, but once upon a time she had spent a night here and there nestled under the blankets with a friend, whispering and giggling until the wee hours. "Of course! We'll have fun tonight, long after everyone else has gone to sleep."

Georgia let out a quiet whoop. Arm in arm they entered her bedchamber, summoned their maids, and quickly dressed for dinner.

Ashley had no time to ponder her revelation about Ravencroft. When she and Georgia entered the drawing room where the family gathered before going into dinner, she was nearly overwhelmed. So many people! She couldn't imagine having so many relatives. Georgia's parents, aunt, and uncle greeted her warmly. She had previously been introduced to Georgia's older siblings and this time recalled their names—Parker and his wife Deirdre, and sister Clarissa and her fiancé, Lawrence Norcross.

Mr. Westbrook was introduced as another friend of the family. His smile reached his brown eyes that twinkled with humor, and his thick, curly brown hair was combed forward, à la Brutus. Ashley found him charming.

Before Mr. Westbrook could engage her in light flirtation, Georgia tugged on her arm. "Come, you must meet Great-Aunt Constance. She is the reason I was able to return your handkerchief."

Ashley took two steps ... and froze at the sight of the elegant matron with silver hair.

Great-Aunt Constance was the kind hostess who had fed her breakfast, gave her a cloak, and sent her home in a hackney.

On what could have been one of the worst nights of her life, Ravencroft rescued Ashley from being attacked and took her to his aunt for safekeeping.

Georgia formally introduced her as Lady Bedford. "Pleased to make your acquaintance, Miss Hamlin," the *grande dame* said. The tilt of her head and direct eye contact told Ashley not to contradict her.

Ashley opened her mouth to speak, closed it, and dipped into a curtsy. "I am happy to make your acquaintance as well, my lady."

Melissa was the youngest present tonight, as the younger children were not included. A footman circulated with a tray of aperitifs. Ashley selected a glass of sherry and listened to the conversation between Lord and Lady Templeton, Lord Mansfield, and Parker. She didn't feel guilty about eavesdropping, as it was a spirited discussion about the music they'd practiced earlier and further changes they wanted to make to the composition.

"I understand my niece borrowed your handkerchief," Lady Bedford said softly, standing shoulder to shoulder beside Ashley. "Lucky you had embroidered your initials on it."

"I am grateful she made the effort to return it," Ashley said just as quietly. "In the short time we've been acquainted, she has become a dear friend."

"She did not reveal how she came to be in possession of it."

Ashley debated how much to tell and how much to keep private. "I was nearby when she found herself in distress and needed the help of a friend."

Lady Bedford smiled and gently clasped Ashley's shoulder, then turned her head to converse with Melissa.

As Ashley took another sip of sherry, she noticed Ravencroft standing by the fireplace watching her and Lady Bedford together with what she could only think of as a panicked expression. As little as two hours ago, she would have been confused. Now, however, she gave him an innocent smile, as though recalling their waltz together. As though she hadn't figured out his secret.

His expression relaxed, and he was soon drawn into the conversation with his sister, nephew, and brothers-in-law about the composition.

The butler announced dinner was ready. While Ashley was mildly disappointed that she was seated too far away to converse with Ravencroft or Lady Bedford, Georgia, Parker, and Parker's wife Deirdre were delightful dinner companions. They were having a lively conversation about the operas they had each seen at Covent Garden when the fish course was brought out. Deirdre turned her head aside, her mouth tightly pursed.

"Please take it away," Parker said to the footman.

"Are you unwell?" Ashley inquired.

"I will be fine," Deirdre said between deep breaths. "Normally I adore cod with lemon butter sauce, but these days all I seem to want are potatoes with pearl onions."

Lady Mansfield, seated on the far side of Deirdre, waved over the footman and quietly spoke to him. Moments later he returned with another generous serving of the potatoes with pearl onions that had accompanied the roast beef. Deirdre gave him a dazzling smile and dug in as though a woman starved. Parker gave her an adoring smile and a kiss on her cheek.

"They were married at the end of last Season," Georgia whispered as an aside to Ashley. "You'd think they would stay in the country while they still can't keep their hands off each other." She let out a little giggle.

Parker tossed a pearl onion across the table at Georgia. She threw it back.

Lady Mansfield cleared her throat ominously, glaring at the siblings.

Suitably chastened, they returned the topic of conversation to the current theater and opera offerings. Ashley participated in the discussion, as she had been to the theater several times in the past few weeks, but a small part of her wistfully thought that no one had ever thrown food at her. What an odd thing to miss.

At the conclusion of the meal, once again instead of the men staying at the table for port and cigars, everyone went directly to the music room. The chairs and sofas had been arranged around the harpsichord and pianoforte in a circle large enough to accommodate everyone present, with music stands in front of several of the straight-backed chairs. People got out instruments in a flurry of activity.

While Lord Mansfield and Lord Templeton debated which of them should be seated at the pianoforte, Georgia slipped in and took the bench, settling the matter with a grin as she played a chromatic scale. Her fluffy dog went around the room to be petted by everyone, then curled up at her feet.

Lady Mansfield held a violincello, Mr. Westbrook had his mandolin, Ravencroft the viola da gamba, Melissa her flute, and Lady Templeton a lyre. Deirdre held a violin, and Parker stood behind her chair.

Ashley was feeling uncertain until Lady Bedford tugged her down onto the sofa beside her. Deprived of the keyboard at least momentarily, Lord Templeton sat down on her other side. Georgia's older sister Clarissa sat close to her fiancé, Lawrence, on the other sofa. Lord Mansfield gestured for them to separate and sat between them. Ashley ducked her head to hide her smile when she caught Clarissa rolling her eyes.

"Time to warm up!" Lady Mansfield called. The noise level had already risen as people started to chat and play, but now it became a cacophony as everyone played something different.

Beneath it all she heard the deep tones of the viola da gamba. She watched Ravencroft bow the instrument slowly and deliberately, staying on the lower strings, his eyes closed. Suddenly he began playing the higher strings in a lively tune, and she recognized Pachelbel's *Canon in D*, a piece her vicar in Torquay had often played on the church organ. Ravencroft's brow furrowed in concentration, his eyes still closed as though trying to see the music in his mind. There were no sheets of music on his stand. She wasn't sure if the notes he missed were because he was out of practice or couldn't see the music, but he would shake his head and repeat the passage.

Long before he'd played as much as Ashley wanted to hear, Lady Templeton tapped on her music stand and suggested the first piece for them to play and sing together as a group warm-up. With Lord Templeton and Lady Bedford singing beside her, Ashley joined in the familiar tune.

They played and sang two more songs, then Lord Mansfield stood up and announced tonight was a Challenge Night. The group greeted the news with equal parts laughter and good-natured groans. "Norcross," he said, "please choose a number between ...?" He trailed off as he consulted with his wife, who was perusing a sheet of paper.

"Ten and forty-five," she said.

"Twenty-two," Norcross replied.

Lady Mansfield ran her finger down the list in her hand, then set it aside and pulled the appropriate sheets of music from folders in a cupboard. She handed half the stack to the person on her left, the other half to the person on her right, and the papers went around the room until everyone had a copy.

Ashley was surprised to see the children's nursery rhyme, *Frère Jacques*. First they played and sang it in English as *Brother John*, then a second time with the French lyrics.

"Count off by fives so we can sing it as a catch," Lady Templeton directed. She pointed to herself and said "One." She looked at the person to her left who counted two, the next person three, and so on around the room. With fourteen people present, Ashley discovered she and Ravencroft were the only fives.

To add to the delightful confusion of sound when they sang it as a catch, some of the groups sang French lyrics and some chose English. She and Ravencroft were the last voices to join in. She wasn't sure which she was going to sing until she saw his lips form the letter *F*. She heard his confident baritone with a lovely French accent, distinctly different from Mr. Westbrook's baritone and Lord Mansfield's bass. As the last group to sing the last phrase, she and Ravencroft sang a duet for the sound of the bells. Instead of singing words with her, though, he imitated the sound of a bell with a rich *"bom bom bom."*

Ashley had to pinch the skin beside her knee to keep from grinning with pleasure like an idiot.

"First challenge," Lady Templeton said. "Turn the music upside down and play it again."

There was much laughter as the musicians complied. The music was delightful and unexpected, with only a few discordant notes.

"Second challenge," Parker said, "same music, played in the correct order ... with your other hand."

Westbrook, Ravencroft, Deirdre, Lady Mansfield, and Lady Templeton switched their bow or instrument to their other hand, and Melissa held her flute out to her left. Georgia held her hands on her lap instead of on the keyboard.

They began to play and it was ... not awful, but nowhere near the skill level they had previously exhibited. More like first-year students. They laughed at themselves as well as each other, and no one seemed to have hurt feelings.

Lord Templeton issued the next challenge. "Everyone, move two seats to your left. Instruments stay where they are."

More laughter and grumbling as everyone shuffled to their next seat. Ashley was confident she could acquit herself at the pianoforte as she often played the simple song for a warmup.

"No cheating, Lydia," Ravencroft called to his sister, who was struggling to balance the viola da gamba and held the bow overhand, as one would for a violin.

She blew out a huff of air and pointed the tip of the bow at him. "Then come show me how you hold this ancient thing. It was old when Purcell wrote his last song."

Ravencroft got up from his new seat on the sofa and helped his sister adjust her feet—heels together, toes out—to balance the large instrument on her calves and hold the bow underhanded. Lady Templeton drew the bow across all seven strings, one at a time, and screeched twice. Ravencroft gave an exaggerated flinch at each screech.

"Go sit down, you oaf," she muttered.

Ravencroft sat down again, the left side of his mouth tilted up in a smile.

At last they played again, and Ashley was pleased she got through it without stumbling, even though it had been months since she'd practiced this song. Not everyone could play the instrument they found themselves at, though everyone certainly made noise. Lady Templeton only played about a third of the notes on the viola da gamba.

Two maids entered with tea trays on rolling carts, including two blue teapots with hot tea, and two cabbage rose teapots with the cool honey-lemon tea. In addition to the expected little pastries, there were cheeses, nuts, and fruits to sustain one for the arduous entertainment. Family members teased each other about their musical talents—or lack thereof—as everyone sorted out getting drinks and filling a plate.

Ashley soaked it all in, cherishing the feeling of being part of a large family, however temporary, however illusionary. She would store up this feeling of belonging, to have it to pull out and remember when she was alone, wrinkled and graying. A spinster.

Lady Bedford issued the next challenge after everyone had fortified themselves. "Play it," she commanded, "but without any instruments at all."

How could one play without an instrument? All of the musicians sat back in their seats, hands on their knees, instruments set aside.

Moments later Ashley had her answer. Westbrook and Lord Mansfield whistled, Ravencroft made his voice sound like he was plucking a double bass, Georgia and Melissa sang wordlessly, like an opera aria; and several others were humming.

Just as they finished, a redheaded boy of about six wearing a nightshirt appeared in the music room doorway, his breathless governess skidding to a halt behind him a few seconds later.

"What is it, Matthew?" Lady Mansfield said.

"Uncle David is here, but he hasn't come up to say good night yet."

"My most humble apologies, lad," Ravencroft said, rising from his chair. "I quite lost track of the time." He strode across the room as Lady Templeton and Lady Mansfield discussed what the next challenge should be.

Ashley followed his dignified progress, and smothered a chuckle when he suddenly ran the last three steps, bent low, and with a deep growl, slung young Matthew over his shoulder and kept on running. Matthew squealed in surprise and giggled madly. Ravencroft's footsteps thundered down the hall, up the stairs, and faded away, the governess's lighter steps trailing behind.

After the next challenge—everyone moved another two seats to their left, and Ashley discovered she still couldn't cleanly finger just one string at a time on a violin—she excused herself to use the retiring room. She was just coming back out to the hall when she heard a short, shrill scream from upstairs.

No one else seemed to have heard it. No servants came running.

She glanced up and down the hall, debating what to do, then tiptoed up the stairs. She stopped when she was high enough up the staircase to lean forward, hands on a stair tread above, and peek around the balustrade to look down the hallway, her head just above the floorboards.

Lord Ravencroft sat on the floor next to an open doorway, his legs folded tailor style. He cuddled a red-haired girl of about four on his lap, his other arm around Matthew, who sat on the floor beside him. Two girls, about eight and twelve, sat on the floor a few feet away in front of him. Seated on the footman's bench outside the bedchamber doorway, a girl of about fourteen patted the governess's shoulder, comforting her. All of the children were dressed for bed. Only two candle sconces were lit, leaving eerie shadows flickering in the hall.

"And then what?" the little girl on Ravencroft's lap demanded.

"Then the troll said," Ravencroft replied in his normal speaking voice, then dropped at least two octaves, "if you want to cross the bridge, you must pay the toll."

"But what if I don't have money for the toll?" Matthew asked.

"Then I will eat you for dinner!" Ravencroft replied in a gravelly, breathy growl. He tipped his head back and let out a demonic laugh. The candlelight and shadows fell across his face and open mouth in a way that made his teeth seem more prominent, especially his canines.

Fangs.

The younger girls screamed in mock horror. The governess made the sign of the cross. Matthew chuckled.

Ashley held her hand to her pounding heart. Well, fangs only if one were in a fanciful mood. Or being confronted by what one thought was a demon, on a dark street.

"The moral of the story," Ravencroft continued in his speaking voice, "is—"

"Always carry toll money!" the children shouted in unison.

"Very good." He gave the child on his lap a squeeze and a kiss on her cheek. The little girl twisted to give him a hug and a kiss in return, then clambered to her feet. After a flurry of hugs and kisses and wishes for sweet dreams, the governess and older girls ushered the children into their rooms.

Ashley quickly retreated down the stairs and back to the music room, her mind racing even faster than her feet as she took her seat.

Georgia was playing Deirdre's violin, as everyone had shifted seats again while Ashley was gone, and she was now expected to take a turn playing the lyre.

There were too many people present to discuss what she'd just seen. But did she want to share what she'd just seen, even with Georgia?

As she tried to play the lyre, Ashley held her new knowledge about Ravencroft's secret to herself, like hugging a warm blanket on a cold winter's night.

David waited until everyone was in their room before he awkwardly climbed to his feet and dusted himself off. Diana would ring a peal over him if the new governess quit. He'd forgotten the previous one had returned to Berkshire to tend an ailing relative, and this one was so new she had never heard any of his bedtime stories before. He hoped she hadn't soiled herself when she screamed.

He retrieved a honey and lemon pastille from the snuffbox he carried in his coat pocket and popped it in his mouth to soothe his irritated throat. The growls and falsetto notes were the most taxing. The bedtime tale, on top of the singing he'd done in rehearsal and after dinner, was far more voice work than he'd done in years. He was definitely out of practice.

Downstairs, everyone else was putting away their instruments and music, so he started to tuck his great-grandfather's viola da gamba in its case.

"Aunt Connie," he heard Parker say, "would you mind dropping off Deirdre and me on your way home?"

"You're not riding with Ravencroft?"

David could feel his aunt's eyes on him. He stayed studiously busy with the straps to secure the bow in the case and did not look up.

"He and Uncle Liam rode their horses over, but he's not staying at the Ravencroft townhouse. He's letting us have it to ourselves for the Season. A first anniversary gift, he said."

"Surely the house is sufficiently large enough that all three of you could stay there and not see or hear each other if you chose."

Parker coughed. From the corner of his eye, David saw Deirdre blush. He closed the instrument case and stored it in the cupboard.

Parker's voice was barely audible. "You know he still hasn't set foot inside since ... since he inherited."

Aunt Connie let out an exasperated sigh. "Yes, I had just hoped that by now, he... never mind. Come along, dear child, and we'll get you home." Aunt Connie held her arm out for Deirdre, and the three of them said their good nights and left the music room.

David made sure the other instruments were secure before looking for Liam to see if he was ready to leave. His friend stood in a cluster around the tea tray, chatting with Georgia, Clarissa, Norcross, and Miss Hamlin.

Her gaze drifted from Norcross—who was yammering on about the banns having been read for him and Clarissa for the first time yesterday—across the room and rested on him. He could tell the moment she realized he was looking back, as twin spots of color bloomed on her cheeks.

Pray tell, what about him caused her to blush? Was she remembering the moments they sang together, just the two of them, as though alone in the room? It had only lasted a few seconds, just two measures, but those seconds and sounds were imprinted on him forever. How their voices had blended in perfect harmony.

She lowered her gaze, the corners of her mouth tilting up the tiniest bit as though she were repressing a smile. Why would she hold back a smile from him? He wanted to see her smile, to know that she felt confident and safe. That she had no lingering fears from her encounter with Sir Rupert. That his efforts had been worthwhile.

A footman entered to inform him and Liam that their horses were ready.

David joined the group by the tea tray. "Miss Hamlin, is your uncle coming to fetch you, or is Mansfield escorting you home?"

Before she could reply, Georgia tucked her arm through Miss Hamlin's in a possessive grip. "Neither!" Georgia declared with the giddiness of a child at Christmas. "She is to be my guest for the night, and we're going to have ever so much fun!"

Miss Hamlin appeared a little less giddy than Georgia but happy nonetheless.

"Then I bid you good evening." David raised Miss Hamlin's hand and kissed her knuckles. He had to shake his head a little to get the hair from his eyes when he straightened, and after he had done so realized that she was looking directly at him. Not at their still joined hands, nor a coy glance and then look away. Extended eye to eye contact as though she could see right through him. It could have been unnerving, except she appeared pleased by what she saw.

He returned her smile with an intimate one of his own, and let go of her hand before they drew attention to themselves. He and Liam bid everyone else good night and departed.

Upstairs in Georgia's bedchamber, Ashley quietly checked with her maid that she'd been given comfortable accommodations for the night.

"Yes, miss," Sally replied just as quietly. "It's as nice as my room at Mr. Endicott's house."

Georgia sailed into the room on the heels of her maid, who was bearing a tray with covered dishes and a pitcher of lemonade. "If you'll help me with my dress," Georgia said, "I'll help you with yours, and we can dismiss our maids and let them have a little fun tonight, too."

Ashley readily agreed. Both maids curtsied and left with a covered dish of their own.

"Oh, I almost forgot to feed Robin," Georgia said, taking a paper twist off the tray. She pulled the stool from the dressing table over in front of the window, hiked up her skirts, and climbed up.

Only now did Ashley notice the large birdcage suspended on a chain from the ceiling, dangling well back from the window. As she watched, Georgia opened the cage and withdrew a wriggling worm from the twist of paper.

"Look, Robin!" she cooed, dangling the worm in front of a robin sitting on one of several perches. "John Footman found you a nice, juicy worm tonight!"

The bird chirped and fluttered its wings, and flew down to eat the worm Georgia set in a dish. While the bird was eating, Georgia refilled a little bowl of water before adjusting some of the branches that led up to perches.

"Eat up, my sweet," she murmured, stroking the bird's head with one fingertip, before she closed the cage and moved the stool back to the dressing table.

The bird chirped several times and hopped up one of the branches before settling on another perch. From this angle, Ashley now saw the bird had only one wing. The other was a tiny stump.

Her chore done, Georgia and Ashley quickly changed into their night rails and wrappers.

Realizing they were alone except for the bird, Ashley asked, "Does your dog sleep in your room?"

"Tuffy prefers to spend nights in the nursery, guarding the children. He thinks he's a Mastiff." She chuckled.

Ashley reached to pull the pins from her hair but stopped when she saw the wistful look on Georgia's face. "What is it?"

"You will think me silly, but..."

"But what?"

Georgia bit her bottom lip, and then blurted out, "Clarissa and I used to brush out each other's hair every night before she became betrothed, and ... and I miss it. I was wondering if you would mind if..."

"No, you're not silly, and I would not mind at all." Ashley tried not to get choked up at this latest example of Georgia treating her like a sister. "Shall I brush yours first?"

Georgia gave her a slight push until Ashley sat on the stool in front of the dressing table mirror. "I guess I have my answer." She and Georgia shared a smile in the mirror. Georgia removed the pins and strand of pearls from Ashley's hair and began to brush.

"My mother used to brush my hair on some nights." Ashley let her head fall forward, relaxing under Georgia's ministrations. The younger girl wielded the brush in long, gentle strokes, careful not to pull when she encountered knots. "Often it was because she wanted to have an awkward conversation with me."

"About your changing body?" Georgia grinned at her in the mirror. "About not kissing boys under the apple tree? About what makes a gentleman suitor suitable or not?"

Ashley chuckled. "Lakeside folly for me. No apple trees close by."

"Well, no awkward conversations tonight." Georgia separated Ashley's hair into three sections and began plaiting into one long braid down her back.

"I've only recently become used to having a maid again to dress my hair. It feels different when someone else does it." And it felt different again being done by someone who was not a servant. She almost felt like purring.

Georgia's brows rose in surprise. "What did you do before?"

"Dressed it myself, of course. All of the staff at the academy did their own hair. Madame Zavrina considered it very important that we set a good example for our students, and not put on airs." Ashley couldn't recall anyone helping her with her hair when she was there as a student. She didn't have siblings, and had only caught snatches of conversations with students discussing what went on between sisters.

Georgia indicated her own hair with a glance upward. "I am very thankful I've always had a maid or sister to help me tame this riot." She tied Ashley's plait with a ribbon, and they switched places on the stool.

"Why did you decide to become a teacher?" Georgia closed her eyes as Ashley removed the pins and her hair tumbled down.

"I did not choose it." She reached for Georgia's hairbrush.

Georgia's eyes popped open. "Then how...?"

"We were barely a month into the Season when my parents perished in a carriage accident." She began drawing the brush through Georgia's hair, trying to focus on the red-gold waves rather than painful memories. "My cousin Niles was disappointed at how little he inherited beyond the barony. His wife suggested they could dismiss their governess as a way to economize, since I was there to help take care of their children." Ashley quickly discovered the curls in Georgia's hair owed nothing to curling tongs. "At first my friends came to visit, but no one seemed to know what to say beyond offering condolences. Soon they stopped coming."

Georgia reached over her shoulder to give Ashley's hand a gentle squeeze.

"Madame Zavrina, the headmistress of the school I had attended for four years, read about the accident in the newspapers and sent a note of condolence. I wrote back, and in a complete loss of decorum, poured out my grief and frustration upon the pages of my letter. Within a fortnight she came in her carriage and made a place for me at the academy as part of her staff."

"But what about your uncle and aunt? Wouldn't they take you in?"

Ashley divided the hair into three sections. "Just a few weeks before the accident, they had set sail to Jamaica to take possession of a sugar plantation Uncle Edward unexpectedly inherited. By the time a letter could reach them, I was already settled at the academy." Her braid was not nearly as neat as the one Georgia had created. Fortunately no one else would see it.

"But you left the academy this year."

"Because it closed. Madame Zavrina died in an accident, and her brother ... made changes."

"Horrible changes?"

"He turned the school into a brothel."

Georgia giggled, then covered her mouth with her hand. "I'm sorry. That's not an appropriate source of amusement."

Ashley shrugged. "I am fortunate that fate provided for me once again. My uncle got his plantation operating the way he liked it and came back to England for a visit this spring. His timely arrival meant I did not have to rely on my cousin's hospitality again."

Uncle Edward had appeared like a fairy godfather, waving his bank account balance instead of a magic wand, providing a dowry and all the essentials to enjoy a London Season so she could find a husband. And like Cinderella's coach turning back into a pumpkin at midnight, he was returning to Jamaica in May so that he and Eunice would not be at sea during hurricane season. Ashley had until they left to find a husband or employment, or have to go live with her cousin Niles, his wife, and their many children.

She tied off the braid and steered the conversation to lighter topics. She tried not to be envious of Georgia and Clarissa's bond if they did this sort of thing regularly. Chatting about their day. Laughing about the music challenges after dinner. Ashley's first attempt at playing a lyre. Trying not to screech like a cat being stepped on when she bowed a few notes on the violin.

"I do love it when I can beat my father and uncles to the pianoforte," Georgia confessed with an impish grin.

They had just settled on pillows on the floor near the hearth, with slices of bread and cheese from the covered plates, plus toasting sticks that were leaning against the fireplace bricks, when they heard a soft tap and Clarissa poked her head around the door. "I'm hiding from Mother."

Grinning, Georgia waved her in.

Before Clarissa shut the door, a fluffy grey cat ran between her feet and into the room. The cat skidded to a stop and put one paw on Georgia's bent leg, then paused to stare suspiciously at Ashley through its left eye. The right eye was gone, the tip of its right ear a jagged half-circle instead of a sharp point, and halfway down its tail bent sideways.

Clarissa joined them before the fireplace. "I can't bear to review the guest list or the seating chart for the breakfast, again." She settled on a cushion. "She's said 'just one more time' at least twice already."

Ashley and Georgia made sympathetic noises. Georgia snuggled the cat to her chest. "Smokey, dear sir," Georgia said to the cat, "this is my friend, Ashley."

"Pleased to make your acquaintance, Smokey," Ashley said, glancing at the cat and then away. She broke off a morsel of cheese and offered it on her open palm. She and Clarissa exchanged greetings, studiously looking at each other and not the cat, other than quick glances. Clarissa was similarly dressed in a night rail, wrapper, and slippers, with her red hair in a long braid down her back.

After a moment the cat deigned to leave Georgia, sniffed at Ashley's hand, and daintily ate the proffered cheese. He graciously allowed Ashley to pet him and meowed for another piece.

As there were only two toasting forks, they took turns until everyone had toasted cheese on toasted bread. Smokey took care of any crumbs before returning to Georgia's lap for more cuddling.

Between snacks, the cat circled the floor beneath the bird cage. It sat on its haunches and stared up at the cage, then at the nearby furniture and windowsill as though calculating distances and angles.

"You're not getting up there, you naughty boy," Georgia called to the cat, patting her leg. "Come sit with me."

Tail twitching, Smokey returned to her lap.

"You must have a hundred things to do if you are getting married in three weeks," Ashley said, arranging cheese on her toast.

"True, though I think Mother is enjoying the planning more than I. She didn't have much say in Parker's wedding breakfast last spring."

"You could have been married last autumn if Lawrence was a faster learner, or a better musician." Georgia poured each of them a glass of lemonade.

Clarissa shrugged one shoulder. "At least now I can be sure that he genuinely cares for me," she said. "And he learned he has to take me seriously."

Ashley's confusion must have been evident.

"It's a Linford family tradition," Georgia explained. "Going back at least five generations, the Linfords have only married those who share their affinity for music. Prospective spouses don't have to be talented singers or musicians but they do have to make an effort. Diana would not agree to marry our father until he serenaded her. "

"Every now and then he sings and plays the same song for her again." Clarissa offered a bit of her toasted cheese and bread to the cat. "And then they inevitably disappear up the stairs for a few hours, hand in hand."

Georgia waved away the image her sister's words conjured of her amorous parents. "I don't care about a suitor's title or wealth," she said, "but I won't accept any offer unless he can sing or play for me, too."

Clarissa turned to Ashley. "Do you have any similar requirements for a suitor?"

Ashley sipped lemonade while she collected her thoughts. "I doubt anyone will offer for me, other than perhaps a widower seeking a mother for his children."

Clarissa and Georgia exchanged glances. "It seems to have worked out for Diana and our father," Georgia said.

"I meant no offense," Ashley quickly said. She stroked the cat. "The men who so far have sought an introduction to me are unsuitable." She winced as an image of Sir Rupert's face flashed across her mind. Georgia gave her hand a reassuring squeeze. "Or much older. I don't think a suitable man with less than forty years in his dish has even spared a glance for me."

"Deirdre caught herself a young husband," Georgia said. "And she is at least as old as you."

Ashley forced herself not to wince at the reminder of her advanced age for a woman on the Marriage Mart, since she had been the one to bring up the subject.

"Not the same circumstances at all." Clarissa skewered another piece of cheese and held it over a coal. "Parker has been in love with Deirdre since he was fifteen and she was nineteen. He was devastated when her parents arranged for her to marry a viscount three times her age."

"But her husband obligingly stuck his spoon in the wall two years ago," Georgia added. "Parker sent her a note of condolence, they continued corresponding, and they were married one year and one month after the viscount was put to bed with a shovel." She stroked Smokey, who had curled up on her lap, his crooked tail lazily swishing back and forth. "If you want to be like Deirdre, we can help you search for a suitor who is, what, twenty? Twenty-one?"

Ashley let out a self-conscious laugh. "No, thank you. I don't see marriage in my future. I am determined to enjoy the Season but I intend to find another position at a ladies' academy before the end of May, when my aunt and uncle return to his plantation. I have already sent out several employment inquiries."

"As you say."

Ashley gave Georgia a curious glance. Georgia was busy scratching under the cat's chin.

They chatted a little longer, until Clarissa yawned and bade them good night.

Ashley and Georgia finished getting ready for bed, blew out all the candles except one, and climbed into the enormous tester bed. Smokey jumped up, turned in a circle, and curled up at their feet. The down mattress was even more comfortable than Ashley's bed at Uncle Edward's townhouse. She indulged in a luxurious long stretch and tucked the blanket under her chin.

"I can think of at least one suitable gentleman who has spared a glance for you." Georgia blew out the candle on the bedside table. "Someone who is not a widower, and who is under forty." She counted on her fingers. "He's thirty, to be exact." She plumped her pillow. "As much as I like having you for an adopted sister, I think I would like having you for an aunt even better."

Chapter 7

REFUSING TO TOSS AND TURN any longer, David got out of bed, tied the sash on his banyan, and lit a candle before opening the cover on the clavichord. Being such a quiet instrument, it seemed the least likely of those available to disturb anyone.

He warmed up with a few scales and tried to play Pachelbel's *Canon in D*. It had been too long; he'd forgotten too much. He lit more candles and dug through the music folders until he found the sheets he wanted. Now with the music, he was able to play the entire piece through, albeit slowly.

He was still rusty, so he started again. He faltered when the door opened but kept going, and soon a violin joined him. As the last chord died away, he put his hands on his lap. "I thought this would be quiet enough it would not wake you."

Liam set down his violin and bow. "I was not sleepy. I'm actually glad you're awake because I didn't want to disturb *your* slumber." He began shuffling through the music folders. "Although I do owe you retribution for the way you disturbed my sleep last week. Scared five years off my life with that menacing growl in the middle of the night, and that frightful makeup and costume."

"I needed to rehearse."

"Lucky me, letting you sleep in my music room so I was close at hand as your test audience."

"You do have your uses."

Liam grinned and pulled out a different sheet of music. "How about this one? Because I assume we are not going to discuss what is keeping you awake. Though I can guess her name."

"What makes you think... Never mind."

They played Beethoven's *Für Elise* as a duet, starting over again from the beginning as soon as they had finished because David was still hitting too many wrong notes. The second time through was more satisfying.

"If it's of any help, she seems as enamored of you as you are of her. Should you decide to court her, I don't believe she'd turn you away."

David patted his right knee. "You know I have no intention of marrying."

Liam dragged David's cot away from the wall to reach into a different cupboard and pulled out music books. "Perhaps I will pay her court. She has a lovely alto voice. And unlike so many of the younger misses on the Marriage Mart, she doesn't seem to be silly."

David scowled but was unwilling to ponder why the idea of Liam courting Miss Hamlin annoyed him. "Play something else. The violin is too sweet for my mood just now."

"Then *you* should play something more appropriate." Liam pointed at the violoncello on a stand in the corner. "Like that."

Having made his selection, Liam took David's seat at the clavichord. David set up a chair and the violoncello where he could see the music propped above the keyboard.

"Did you see her talking to Aunt Connie?" David played a minor scale to warm up and adjusted the tuning of two strings. "Wonder what they had to discuss."

"With Miss Hamlin formally meeting Aunt Connie, as a woman of reasonable intelligence, you must know she's going to figure out it was you who rescued her from Rupert. If she hasn't already."

David froze in mid-note. Had she? Is that what that knowing smile tonight was about, that blush?

Liam played a dramatic chord. "I would be willing to wager she has." He played three more chords in rapid succession. "The question is, what is she going to do with her new knowledge?"

David played an arpeggio. "Now you know why I am awake at this ungodly hour."

Aunt? Georgia could not mean what Ashley thought. "I- I beg your pardon?"

"I did not stutter." Ashley heard the laughter in Georgia's voice. She turned on her side to face Ashley and propped her head in her hand. "I saw you dancing together at the masquerade. You looked like you were in alt. And Uncle David never dances, at least not in public."

"No?" Ashley's heart raced even faster.

"Mother and Aunt Lydia often coaxed him into helping with our dance lessons before he inherited the title. But he did not like to dance for long, and hasn't done so at all since he became the earl. Until you."

Did she dare let her thoughts go down this path?

Ravencroft didn't know her at all when he'd rescued her from Rupert. When they'd been introduced at Lady Mansfield's home, he didn't appear to recognize Ashley as the woman he'd rescued. Had he hidden his recognition? And been so smitten with her that he dressed up two nights later as a frightening creature from folklore, invaded Rupert's lodgings, and scared him away lest the blackguard try to hurt her again?

Yes, smitten with a woman who cast up her accounts in front of him on first acquaintance, and nearly on his shoes. Ashley almost snorted.

A few nights later, he had dressed up again to scare Amber Barrow-Smith away from eloping with Sir Peyton. His theatrical performances had protected her and Amber from predatory men. As far as she knew, Ravencroft did not have any connection to Amber. Nor to Ashley, other than having rescued her.

So why *had* he done it? Was he simply a gentleman using his unique vocal talents to protect women, in a way that was no more significant than another man might use his strength and quick reflexes to pull someone out of the way of a runaway horse and carriage?

"We did not exchange a single word during that dance." Perhaps he *did* recognize her but hadn't wanted her to recognize his voice. Recognize *him*. He'd gone to great lengths to protect his reputation as well as hers that first night, to keep his identity secret.

She'd dashed his plans by making friends with his niece, which led to meeting his aunt, which led to her discovering his secret identity. And even though he'd kissed her hand rather than the air above her knuckles, she'd exchanged more words in conversation with his friend Mr. Westbrook than with Ravencroft.

He was holding back from her.

He likely did not know she had been at rehearsal tonight. The only time he might have seen her she had been bent down, tying her garters. If he had seen her and knew she was the miss he'd rescued, he probably would not have used his distinctive voice so freely.

Which left her puzzled as to why he danced with her. Perhaps he had *not* recognized her? Unlike his hair, her dark blonde locks were quite ordinary, as was the domino she'd been wearing. Had he danced with her because he finally felt like waltzing in public and decided she'd do as well as any other partner? Like the dozen or so anonymous men who had asked her to dance while everyone was masked?

A deflating thought.

And this whole line of thinking—she knew he was her rescuer but didn't know if he knew she was the miss he'd rescued—was making her head spin.

No, she did not want to go down this path. If Ravencroft was interested in courting her, he would not be holding back. At the very least he would take advantage of opportunities to converse with her, not keep quiet.

"If he is seeking a wife—and I've seen no indication that he is—as an earl, he can look much higher for a bride than someone like me. Someone younger, with a larger dowry."

Georgia's immediate reply was a simple, "*Hmm.*" She plumped her pillow. "Let us change the subject, then. I said we'll have no awkward conversation tonight, and I don't wish to discomfit you. What do you think of Lord Leighton? I think the reports of his father bankrupting the estate have been exaggerated. His countenance is quite handsome."

Ashley turned on her side to mirror Georgia's position, and they proceeded to discuss the gentlemen bachelors of the *ton* well into the night.

"You shouldn't be the least bit surprised Georgia befriended her." Liam chose a different song for them to play. "How many injured cats, orphaned puppies, and humans down on their luck has she taken under her wing? Even in her debut Season, of course she'd find a miss with a sad story and want to make her better."

David carefully kept his voice only mildly curious. "What sad story?"

"Miss Hamlin's parents died a month into her first Season. The cheeseparing cousin who inherited her father's title not only refused to pay for another Season when their mourning ended, he spent her dowry on his pile of bricks in the country."

David was thinking of a suitable comment about Liam and society gossip when his friend continued.

"My sisters discussed and dissected the poor girl's situation at great length. Heaven help anyone who might deprive them of *their* Season and a chance at making a good match. I think my father and brothers may have even changed their wills as a result."

"Yet here she is, attending all the entertainments, behaving like any other young woman hunting matrimonial prey."

Liam rearranged the music above the keyboard. "You remember the stir a few years ago when a plantation owner in Jamaica freed his slaves and then hired them as paid workers?"

"Vaguely."

"That was Mr. Endicott. He did not lose his fortune, as many predicted. Quite the opposite. Came home to England for a visit this spring and is feeling annoyed with his wife's pinchpenny nephew, and generous toward her niece, Miss Hamlin."

"This news was also gleaned from your sisters?"

"Lord Sedgewick supports the abolitionist movement. Emily made certain Lady Sedgewick knew of Mr. Endicott's unusual business model, ensuring the Endicotts and their niece received an invitation to the Sedgewicks' ball, which opened more doors for them."

David grunted. "Your sister Emily has almost as soft a heart as Georgia. Too bad Lady Sedgewick also invited Sir Rupert."

"Thanks to you, though, he no longer poses a danger to any of the ladies of London."

They both cocked their heads at an unexpected sound—a scratch on the outer door to the hall.

"Expecting late-night visitors?"

Liam grabbed a candle and went through the sitting room to the apartment door. David trailed after with another lit candle. In the pool of light, they saw a folded sheet of foolscap that had been slid under the door. They stood close together, holding their candles aloft, while Liam read the note.

"It seems one of my neighbors is fond of Mozart. He is requesting we play something from the *Magic Flute* or *The Marriage of Figaro.*"

"Someone else with insomnia."

Liam shrugged. They went back to the music room and he began searching through his collection of music. David idly strummed the mandolin until Liam looked at him with his eyes squinted, wincing in pain.

David put down the mandolin. He'd always been better with vertical strings than horizontal. "We established why I'm awake at an unusual hour. What is keeping *you* awake?"

Liam took so long to respond David began to think he hadn't heard or was going to ignore the question. "I may have to start charging you rent," he said, barely audible.

"Oh?"

"I think I've lost my patron. I, ah, may have offended him. "

David sat in the chair. "One, I find that hard to believe and two, surely the stipend he pays you won't have much impact on your budget if it is true."

Liam slumped on the bench, staring at his feet. "I haven't paid my coal merchant in two years. Nor my tailor."

David knew his friend to be an honorable person. He raised his brows in silent query.

"Each time I try to make payment, the bill has already been settled. Even my account with the greengrocer and the coffeehouse next door have a generous credit each month." He studied the fingernails of his left hand. "The merchants will only tell me my benefactor wishes to remain anonymous."

David chose his words carefully. "Sounds like he is paying for more than private music lessons."

"He is lonely. He has stories to tell, fascinating tales after two decades in the army. But his daughters don't want to hear them, his wife is dead, and his son lives in Northumberland. I enjoy hearing them." Liam let out a gusty sigh. "We have been meeting once a week for over two years. We've always held his lessons at the pianoforte in his drawing room. Two weeks ago we had just begun when he suggested that we move the lesson... to his bed." Liam rubbed his temples with the heels of his hands. "I never thought he would expect me to be an *eromenos* to his *erastes*."

David dredged up what he could recall of ancient Greek social structure. "Since you are the teacher, wouldn't those roles be reversed?"

Liam looked at him askance. "I told him that it is possible to hold someone in great esteem and affection without wanting to share one's body with them."

"Or their bed."

Liam gave a ghost of a grin. "Unless the headmaster is being stingy with the coal and trying to freeze us to death."

Reminded at how some nights the Eton dormitory had been so frigid they could see their breath, David threw another scoop of coal on the fire. He and Liam had often doubled up in the winter to share their blankets. "How can you be certain the relationship has ended?"

Liam put away some sheets of music and got out others. "He sent a note to cancel our next lesson, and I have not heard from him since. The knocker is gone from his door."

David fetched a decanter and two glasses from the sitting room. He poured two fingers' worth of whisky in Liam's glass, and half that for himself.

Liam held his glass up in a silent toast before he downed it in one go. "Now you know why I helped Diana persuade you to join us for this year's competition. I need a share of the prize money."

David took a sip. "*You're* the one who persuaded her to bring the viola da gamba to London." The precious instrument had not left the music room at Linford Hall in years.

"It had its own private coach and a full complement of outriders. You would have thought the crown jewels were inside." Liam poured himself another whisky. "And now you can play it every evening after spending your days fulfilling your responsibilities in Parliament and with your steward."

It was not that simple. "You don't need me. The four of you sound fine even if Parker doesn't play. Besides, I'm out of practice. I don't have *time* to practice. I have too many obligations as it is."

"Your voice is not currently in top form, true, but even so it's better than many singers can hope for. And I know you practice in the mornings. It wouldn't take you long to get ready for competition if you determined to do so."

"Morning practice? I don't know to what you're referring."

Liam glanced at him sideways. "Oh, please. Half the village knows you serenade your horse."

"I do not sing to my horse," David said indignantly. He stared into the amber liquid in his glass. "She simply does not mind the sound when I sing on our morning rides." He had to set aside frivolous music when he took up the burdens of the title, but couldn't bear to leave it behind completely.

Liam moved the silver skull-handled walking stick so he could reach into a different drawer with music folders. "You know we have a better chance against Bristol and Fairfax with you," he continued. "Mansfield can hit the basso profundo notes, but they drop like rocks in a pond. Whereas your voice is light and agile, hopping from one lily pad to another, even on the lowest notes."

David narrowed his eyes. "Did you just call me a frog?"

Liam continued as though David had not spoken. "While I can hit a few bass notes, I can't lounge about in that register all day like you can. There is something about the bass voice that affects the judges—even male judges—almost as much as it affects women."

"Affects?" He took another sip.

Liam's melancholy expression vanished, replaced by a knowing grin. "Don't tell me you haven't noticed. At Lady Bristol's soiree last week, at least two matrons in the audience had all the telltale signs. Flushed cheeks, rapid breathing, fanning themselves..." He mimed fanning himself. "Lady Barbour practically swooned when she heard you sing. If you had crooked your finger, she would have followed you anywhere, done anything you wanted." He lowered his chin and raised his eyebrows, giving David a suggestive look. "Anything."

David tried to recall Lady Barbour. Or any of the ladies in the audience. He'd been so busy avoiding looking at Miss Hamlin, he hadn't noticed.

"Helping us beat Fairfax and Bristol is what a good brother-in-law, and good friend, would do. Like when I carried you home after you broke your leg."

"We're going to be eighty, bald, and toothless, and you're still going to hold that over me, aren't you?"

Liam ruffled his full head of hair. "Who says I'm ever going to be bald?"

David gave an impatient snort. "Magic or marriage?"

Liam found the sheets he'd been searching for and held them aloft with a flourish. "Figaro!"

As they played the overture to *The Marriage of Figaro*, David concentrated on playing the correct notes, refusing to think about Miss Hamlin and her reaction when she heard him sing.

Ashley awoke when daylight first peeked through the curtains, to the sound of birds just outside the window and the robin in the room cheerily welcoming the sunrise. Though she and Georgia had stayed up late, talking and giggling like schoolgirls, she never had been able to sleep well in unfamiliar places. Careful not to disturb Georgia, she arose and dressed. She didn't know the household's morning routine—if they dined in their rooms, or at the table as a group, or something else entirely—and didn't want to be a nuisance.

The haunting refrain of the music Ravencroft had played last night as a warmup came back to her. She finished her morning ablutions and hurried downstairs. No one else was about as she entered the music room. She found the right cupboard with the music folders, blessed Lady Mansfield's careful cataloguing of her collection, and soon sat at the pianoforte with the music she wanted.

Dare she?

She shut the door to the hall, then sat on the bench again. She closed her eyes, picturing Ravencroft last night as he played, tried to hear the sounds he'd made on the antique viola da gamba, and set her hands on the keys.

Music flowed from her fingers as it never had before.

It ebbed and flowed, crescendo and pianissimo, glorious even when she stumbled over some of the sixteenth note runs. She kept going, losing herself in the centuries-old melody, the perfectly tuned instrument making her effort sound better than the mediocre pianoforte at the academy ever had, even better than the one in her uncle's rented townhouse.

She was halfway through before she realized it was not Ravencroft in her head she was hearing, but an actual violincello.

Lady Mansfield had joined her and was playing with her eyes closed, lost in the music she was creating in what had become their duet. She alternated between the violincello's traditional eight-note part and the melody that was usually played by the violin.

Ashley's pulse pounded but she kept going until the final chord.

Not until the last note faded away did Lady Mansfield open her eyes. She smiled at Ashley fondly. "Good morning. How did you know that's one of my favorite tunes?"

Ashley allowed herself to relax. "Lovely, is it not?" She smoothed her palms on her lap. "I did not wish to disturb anyone. Georgia was still asleep…"

"And the music called to you." Lady Mansfield set the violincello and bow in its holder and got out her lyre. "I completely understand." She plucked a few notes on her instrument. "Would you like to play some more together? Or would you prefer to practice alone?"

"I would be honored, my lady. Though you may regret your offer. My skill pales in comparison to yours.'

Lady Mansfield smiled. "There is only one way to improve. What shall we play next?"

After a lovely morning in the music room with Lady Mansfield and a raucous breakfast with the family in the dining room, Ashley was almost disappointed when her uncle's carriage came to collect her shortly after noon. She said her goodbyes as Sally and a footman carried their valises out to the carriage.

Georgia pulled her in for another hug and squeezed Ashley's hands before she would let go. "Please promise me we will do this again."

Ashley blinked back tears. Georgia had truly made her feel like a sister last night. "That would be most pleasing." As long as Georgia didn't discuss her matchmaking plans for her uncle and Ashley. Such a union was completely out of the realm of possibilities. Ashley was going back to working at an academy when the Season ended.

Once home, Ashley inquired about her aunt's friend.

"Oh, la, she is so lonely," Aunt Eunice said. "Tomorrow I'm going back and plan to stay for two days."

Ashley tried to keep her expression neutral. Much as she adored Georgia, she could not stay the night with her young friend again so soon. Georgia needed time to transfer her attention to some other topic. Finding her own suitor, for example.

"But I could not miss Lady Calvert's musicale tonight," Aunt Eunice said as they walked along the hall to her bedchamber. "I know how much you enjoy the music. Lady Calvert is friends with Lady Bristol, and they made special arrangements for tonight. Instead of listening to young misses who are looking to catch a husband, we'll hear several of the groups who will compete at the Noblemen and Gentlemen's Catch Club." Aunt Eunice held her hand over her heart. "How I do love a talented male quartet, don't you?"

"Couldn't agree more."

Lady Calvert's ballroom had rows of chairs for the audience, set well back from the stage area where there was a pianoforte, harpsichord, and an elegant harp at least as tall as Ashley, mingled with straight-backed chairs and music stands for the musicians. Uncle Edward had made sure they arrived at just the right time. Only a few people had sat down so far, mostly gray-haired matrons and their escorts. The other guests mingled, chatting and sizing up each other.

One of the seated matrons turned her head, and Ashley recognized Lady Bedford. Their eyes met and Lady Bedford gave her a small smile and a wink before turning back to her companion, an army major in full uniform.

Good thing Lady Calvert's ballroom was so large. Within the hour it seemed everyone Ashley had met in London was present.

David helped himself to a cup of punch and scanned Lady Calvert's ballroom, looking for familiar faces. Lord Bristol had not been jesting when he said tonight would be a preview of this year's competition at the Catch Club. Lord Ferguson and his group in black neckcloths clustered near the pianoforte, quietly warming up. Several side rooms had been set aside for just such a purpose, but there was only one pianoforte. Lord Bristol chatted with his wife, and David saw other members of his group in their matching red neckcloths circulating among the guests. Mansfield and Templeton and their entourage entered the ballroom. Liam had arrived with David and gone to greet other friends. That just left—

"Evening, Ravencroft."

David deliberately took a sip before turning to greet the newcomer with a nod. "Fairfax." The viscount no longer outranked David, but Fairfax still stood a good four inches taller than him.

"Could have knocked me over with a feather when Sutcliff said he heard from Westbrook that you were singing again. But here you are."

"You know how persuasive my sisters can be." David gave a negligent shrug. He was searching for a different topic of conversation when he heard Fairfax's sharp intake of breath.

Fairfax had one hand over his heart, the other on David's shoulder, staring at Liam. "Who is the new filly Westbrook is flirting with? I haven't seen her before."

David had to lean to the side to see around Fairfax, and was transfixed himself at the sight of Miss Hamlin holding court. She looked poised and elegant in a pale blue gown that shimmered in the light from the chandelier. Diamonds in her hair combs sparkled almost as much as her smile. Whatever could Liam be saying that was so funny? Her gentle peal of laughter reached him. All other women in the room ceased to exist. Feeling a tight squeeze in his chest, David was startled to realize *he* wanted to be the one to make her smile with such delight.

"Miss Hamlin," he whispered.

Fairfax looked at him sharply. "You know her?"

David exhaled. "I could introduce you if you like," he said with the same degree of enthusiasm as if presented with a plate of raw liver and onions for breakfast.

Fairfax clapped David's shoulder and gave him a push.

Ashley thought she was laughing entirely too much and should probably hide her lower face with her fan, but Mr. Westbrook's childhood tale involving a frog and two of his sisters was most entertaining. When Ravencroft approached with another gentleman, she took a sudden deep breath and composed herself.

"Miss Hamlin," Ravencroft said in his silky deep voice, raising her hand and dropping a kiss on her knuckles as he bowed.

Warmth suffused her at hearing him speak her name. Watching the tiny shake of his head to get his hair from his eyes as he straightened, she almost forgot to curtsy. "Lord Ravencroft. It is good to see you again."

His companion elbowed him, a slight frown marring his handsome features, his intelligent brown eyes looking upon her with blatant admiration and expectation.

"Vincent, Viscount Fairfax, may I present Miss Ashley Hamlin." Ravencroft turned to Fairfax. "Georgia recently adopted Miss Hamlin." He turned back to Ashley. "We—" he indicated himself, Westbrook, and Fairfax, "—have been friends since we attended Eton."

Lord Fairfax also took her hand and raised it to his full lips for a kiss as he bowed over it. "Enchanted to make your acquaintance, Miss Hamlin. Miss Georgia's adoptees usually have three legs and a tail." He chuckled as he straightened, giving a slight shake to get his hair out of his eyes, the same gesture she'd seen Ravencroft make. Fairfax wore his hair longer than Ravencroft, the glossy black strands brushing his shoulders. No white streak, though.

His deep bass voice, even lower than Ravencroft's, rumbled and washed over her. Ashley almost shuddered. It took her far too long to remember to curtsy. "Lord Fairfax," she finally managed to choke out.

Being the sole focus of three handsome gentlemen was a novel experience. Georgia and Miss Kenyon had been here just moments ago but seemed to have melted into the crowd to greet other friends. Ashley was glad she'd let Sally experiment with a fancy hairstyle copied from *La Belle Assemblée* tonight, and worn the periwinkle blue satin dress Madame Chantel had sent over just this morning, which the modiste had assured her was in the first stare of fashion.

"I can see why Ravencroft was reluctant to introduce us," Fairfax said, still holding her hand. Ravencroft scowled at his friend. "I would be reluctant to let any other man meet you, too. Where have you been all my life, *cara*?"

She almost laughed when both Ravencroft and Westbrook rolled their eyes at the Italian endearment. "Living in Torquay, my lord. Where have *you* been?"

Fairfax laughed, a rich rumble that vibrated right through her.

She was spared the indecision of retrieving her hand or not by their hostess announcing they were ready to begin and requesting everyone take their seats.

Fairfax kissed her hand again before releasing it. "I hope to see you again later, Miss Hamlin, and further our acquaintance."

"That would be agreeable, my lord," she said.

Westbrook and Ravencroft took their leave as well, and Ashley walked in a daze through the crowd to the seat that Aunt Eunice had saved for her.

"Three gentlemen suitors!" Aunt Eunice said with barely restrained excitement. "*Three!*" She patted Ashley's knee, beaming.

Ashley shook her head. "Lord Ravencroft is my friend Georgia's uncle. Westbrook and Fairfax are his friends. They were merely being polite."

"As you say." Aunt patted her knee again. "You know it is my fondest wish to see you happily settled before we return to Jamaica."

The two matrons seated on Ashley's other side left to go sit with other friends, and Georgia and Miss Kenyon took their places. They exchanged hushed greetings as everyone in the room settled.

The assembled crowd quieted as Lord Bristol and the three other members of his group, again wearing matching red neckcloths, took their place around the pianoforte. They sang the same song about valor in battle, though this time she was more aware of the bass singer. He wore a red neckcloth like his companions, but unlike their neatly shorn locks, his dark blonde hair reached past his sharply defined jawline. Was there some rule of fashion that all bass singers must have long hair?

As before, they finished the first song, then included the crowd in performing *Anacreon in Heaven*, and took their bows and their seats.

Lord Fairfax and three companions, wearing matching green neckcloths, sang next. They each stood an arm's reach apart, no instruments accompanying them. As the song progressed, an Italian aria, it became apparent they had arranged themselves in order from highest to lowest voice. The tenor on the far left had the face and voice of an angel, his clear tone reaching higher than she thought possible for a man past adolescence. He looked young enough to still be a university student. The other tenor and baritone were in their thirties to mid-forties, and then Fairfax singing bass. They each stayed in the range she expected of them as the song progressed, with Fairfax sometimes hitting notes lower than seemed humanly possible, a rumble that seemed to make the floor shake.

He didn't give her goosebumps though, the way Ravencroft did. The timbre of his voice was different. Plenty of women in the room, and more than a few men, did seem deeply affected. Several ladies were vigorously plying their fans, their cheeks flushed. Some of the reaction may have been from his blatant flirting—smiling at certain women, a wink here and there. When he directed one at Ashley, Aunt Eunice squeezed Ashley's knee. She thought she heard an indignant snort from Georgia.

They finished the first song and performed a second, each singer getting a chance to solo on the melody at some point while the others provided background harmony.

Many in the audience cheered *Huzzah!* when they finished in addition to applauding.

"They're good," Ashley whispered to Georgia.

"They're technically proficient," she replied with a dismissive sniff.

Ashley quickly returned her attention to the stage, where Lord Fairfax's group had left and the next group was getting ready to perform—Lords Templeton, Mansfield, Ravencroft, Mr. Westbrook, and Georgia's brother, Parker.

"The blue neckcloths were Mother's idea," Georgia confided as the men prepared.

Lord Mansfield seated himself at the pianoforte, Parker and Templeton standing behind him, while Westbrook settled with a mandolin on his lap and Ravencroft balanced the viola da gamba on his calves, and they began to play.

Ashley recognized the opening lyrics of a Thomas Moore song, "*The Last Rose of Summer.*" This arrangement made the most of the deeper tones of the instruments and the men's voices, as if Moore had arranged the tune for baritone and bass voices rather than harp and tenors. Each singer had a solo for a stanza before the others joined back in. Her breath caught as she finally heard Ravencroft sing by himself. His magnificent bass voice slid in a smooth glissando up to tenor before settling back to baritone. Several audience members gasped. The fine hairs beside her face stirred with so many fans in the room madly fluttering.

Of course. It had to be Ravencroft's arrangement. She stared transfixed at him, giving free rein to her expression of delight at the beautiful music.

Unlike at Lady Bristol's soirée, tonight Ravencroft was not trying to hide. His glances took in his fellow performers as well as the audience and the instrument he was playing. He looked directly at Ashley as he sang the line, "*I'll not leave thee, thou lone one, to pine on the stem.*"

She couldn't breathe.

It wasn't until Westbrook took over the lead in his sweet baritone and Ravencroft checked the placement of his bow on the strings that she could draw air again. She should probably fan herself but she still couldn't move, even when Aunt Eunice and Georgia briefly stared at her before turning their attention back to the quintet.

They finished the song, paused for the applause, and then played the song she'd heard them rehearsing at Lord Mansfield's townhouse. Ravencroft's version of the arrangement, not Lady Templeton's.

Lovely as it was, her mind kept going back to the line he'd sung to her, "*I'll not leave thee.*"

No, he hadn't been singing to her. It was just a line in a song, written by another man years ago. Purely coincidental that Ravencroft had looked at her while singing those words.

Ashley was oblivious to the other groups who followed them, her mind replaying the two songs Ravencroft had performed, trying to recall every facial expression, every note, every nuance. Eventually Lord Calvert stood up to thank everyone who had generously shared their talents tonight.

Ashley wanted to linger near the refreshment table, to speak with Ravencroft even as he and Lord Fairfax critiqued each other's performance. She came crashing back to reality when Aunt Eunice touched her elbow.

"Our carriage is here, my dear," she said.

With great reluctance, Ashley bid good night to her friends, knowing she would not see them for at least two days while her aunt visited her former music teacher. Ravencroft was conversing with Mansfield, Fairfax, and Westbrook. Even though his back was turned, his deep voice carried clearly beneath the din of conversation. Lord Fairfax, facing her, raised his cup of punch in farewell to her.

A rainstorm moved in overnight. Rain was still falling when Ashley went downstairs to breakfast the next morning. As soon as they'd finished eating, Uncle Edward and Aunt Eunice prepared to depart.

"Are you certain you do not wish to come with us?" Aunt Eunice cast a worried glance at servants attending to their duties farther down the hall. "I hesitated to leave you for one night, and now here I am leaving you alone for two."

Ashley tied the ribbon on her aunt's bonnet. "I shall be fine. As I already told you, I have a great deal of correspondence to catch up with. I have been remiss in keeping up with some of my friends from the academy. And I could use the rest of a quiet day or two."

As lies went it was a tiny one, considering most of the correspondence she planned to engage in related to finding a position at another academy.

They exchanged hugs and farewells, and as soon as her uncle's carriage was out of sight, Ashley hurried to the desk in her room, the latest newspapers with job postings tucked under one arm, and got to work.

By midday, her hand was cramping and her stomach rumbling, but she had several letters ready to drop in the tray for the outgoing post, and the sun was shining. Remembering the treat Madame Zavrina would offer the students and staff at least once per term after a storm, as soon as she was done eating she informed the butler and housekeeper she was giving the staff a half-day off.

"Enjoy the sunny afternoon," she told them when they looked uncertain. "We can all have a late supper when you get back."

Delighted at the bonus time off, they went to spread the news to the rest of the staff.

Upon returning to her room, Ashley debated whether to lie down for a nap or actually write letters to friends from the academy. The sun shining in her window drew her gaze to the garden in back of the house. Such a lovely spring day, everything fresh and washed clean from the rain.

"Sally, would you mind going for a walk with me before you leave?"

The maid paused in the act of tidying the dressing table. She glanced out the window, and a smile spread across her face. "That sounds lovely, miss."

Soon they were both dressed appropriately for the mud they were likely to encounter on their walk, and with a last glance to be sure no other clouds loomed on the horizon, they set out.

Chapter 8

DAVID HURRIED ALONG BOND STREET, enjoying the sun breaking through after the morning's rain shower. Later this afternoon he had a meeting at the House of Lords, but first needed to meet with his steward. Liam had taken on new students and was giving lessons in his apartment at the Albany, so David was on his way to his steward's hotel.

He paused to sniff appreciatively at the scents emanating from Mr. Jamuna's Bakery, decided not to go in to buy any of the sweet Indian pastries, and kept walking. As he neared the butcher shop, he heard a commotion in the alley—a male voice raised in anger, punctuated by a female's pleas for mercy. Her cry of terror struck him. He darted around the corner and saw a man dressed in cast-off finery standing over a woman who knelt at his feet. The brute shouted another curse and struck the woman across her cheek so hard she fell backward into the mud.

"Here now! Stop that!" David strode toward the pair. Other people had already gathered in the alley, street vendors and shoppers alike, but no one else tried to put a stop to the spectacle.

"This ain't none of yer affair," the man growled. His outdated and worn clothes were filthy. When the woman at his feet tried to move away, he grabbed a handful of hair that had fallen from her once-neat bun. Tears coursed down her cheeks, smearing her face powder and rouge. One eye was already swelling closed. Her red silk dress, cut too low for daytime wear, had muddy skirts and was ripped at the shoulder.

David searched the crowd again. Would no one protect her from this brute? "I'm choosing to make it my affair." The brute was about three inches taller and three stone heavier than David, but David had sparred with Gentleman Jackson just last week. "Does it make you feel like more of a man to beat on a woman?"

The crowd let out a collective, *"Ooh!"*

Brute let go the woman's hair and turned to face David, drawing to his full height. "I do what I 'ave to, t' keep me girls in line."

The woman in the red dress scrambled backwards until she huddled against the wall of the butcher shop. Street urchins began to circulate through the still-growing crowd, probably picking pockets.

"Damaging the merchandise does not seem like a wise business decision."

Brute took a step toward David, his fists clenching and unclenching. "You calling me stupid?"

The crowd behaved as though they were watching a sporting match, their gaze swiveling from David to the brute and back, keeping away from them in a semi-circle. Another glance at the terrified woman strengthened his resolve to not back down, despite the dwindling possibility of settling this with words.

"I would never impugn the intelligence of a businessman. I would, however, say that a pimp who beats his whores is stupid and a coward."

With a roar, Brute swung his huge right fist toward David's jaw. David ducked. His hat fell off and rolled, and was picked up by an urchin. David slammed his fist into the brute's midriff. As the pimp doubled over, David shoved his other fist upward beneath Brute's chin, snapping his head backwards.

His jaw was much harder than the practice dummy at Gentleman Jackson's. David shook out his stinging hands and stepped to the side, rethinking every decision in his life that had brought him to this moment.

On his way to straightening up, Brute grabbed David at his waist, swung him high, and slammed him into the ground.

Stunned, David lay motionless in the cold mud, the breath knocked from his chest. Brute turned to acknowledge a man's cheer for showing the gent what-for. David rolled to his knees, ignored how the ground was spinning, and with the side of his hand clipped Brute behind his knees. He climbed to his feet just as the pimp crashed to the muddy ground. Gasping for air, David tried to step backward, and ran into a human wall of muscle and bone.

Oh hell. The pimp had a friend.

The second attacker yanked David's coat from his shoulders halfway down his arms, pinning him. David abruptly shoved his head backwards but the giant holding him was so tall, he only impacted the man's collarbone. Despite the sun in the sky, stars floated across David's vision.

Brute climbed to his feet. His lips twisted in a snarl and his hands curled into massive fists as he advanced.

From the corner of his eye, David saw the woman in the red dress cowering against the building, crying and watching him in open-mouthed horror.

"Run!" he yelled at her. If he was going to end up with bruises or a bloody nose over this, he at least wanted to know she was safe. For today, at any rate. Still pinned by the giant holding him from behind, David stiffened his arms and jumped up to slam both feet into the pimp's chest.

All three of them fell to the mud, which had an odd red-brown tinge David didn't want to contemplate. He finished shrugging out of his coat as he stood, freeing his arms just in time to block a punch thrown by Brute. He was too slow to avoid the right cross from Giant to his jaw but he spun with the punch and used his momentum to smash his fist into the pimp's nose. Blood sprayed.

Still struggling to draw air, David shook his head to get his hair out of his eyes and clear his vision.

Breathing hard, Brute bent over, hands on his knees while blood trickled from his nose.

David hoped that was the end of it. He'd recently dressed up in a crazy costume to protect two other women, even broke into a man's lodgings in the dead of night to do so, and escaped unscathed. Yet here in daylight, he was going to be black and blue if he wasn't careful.

Giant punched him in the back, a quick one-two below his ribs. David kicked backwards, and heard a satisfying *crunch* and gasp of pain. He staggered forward to catch his balance just as Brute straightened, and barely registered sunlight glinting off a knife blade the pimp had pulled from his boot. David raised his arm in time to block a slashing blow aimed at his throat.

Someone screamed. He hoped that high-pitched sound came from a woman in the crowd and not himself. Fire raced up his forearm and blood soaked his torn sleeve. He felt hot and cold at the same time, and it was getting difficult to tell which way was up. His own knife was in a pocket of his coat ... several feet away, crumpled in a mud puddle.

The pimp wore a feral grin as he tossed the knife from one hand to the other, a bright red smear of blood clinging to the silver blade. David's blood. Brute advanced and David retreated, trying to keep an eye on the pimp and also figure out where Giant had got to.

Someone new stepped into the alley from the back door of the butcher shop. "What the 'ell is going on 'ere?"

As David turned to look at the mountain of a man in a bloodstained apron, the Giant's fist crashed into David's cheek, and the world went black.

Ashley decided to skip walking in the park in favor of heading to the shops just a few blocks over. "You can help me pick out a better color of ribbon," she said, touching the white satin bow beneath her chin that held on her chip-straw bonnet.

"I know just the shade of yellow ribbon you need, miss," Sally said with a conspiratorial smile.

They headed for the linen drapers past the bakery rather than walking all the way to Madame Chantel's modiste shop without a footman. They were almost there when a commotion behind the butcher shop drew their attention.

Ashley peered around the corner, trying to see through the crowd that was egging on combatants in a fight. Three men? That didn't seem fair, two against one.

"Are you sure about this, miss?" Sally whispered as Ashley moved closer.

Ashley had broken up her share of fights, all of them between female students. She had heard of men fighting, but the alley seemed an odd place for a boxing match. And weren't boxing matches always and only between two men at a time, not three? Some of the men in the crowd were placing bets with each other.

The butcher stepped out of the back door and roared to demand what was going on.

One of the fighters turned to look at the distraction. The taller of the other two took the opportunity to plant him a facer, and he went down like a sack of turnips. He didn't move.

Despite the mud and blood spattered on all three men, Ashley saw the streak of white in the unconscious man's shoulder-length hair.

What in Hades was Ravencroft doing, fighting two men?

The butcher took off running, chasing the other two down the alley.

Without thinking, Ashley dashed forward, shoving her way through the crowd. She didn't see Westbrook or anyone else she thought was a companion or servant of the earl. Who would come to his aid?

Two street urchins darted in and stole his shoes right off his feet. Somebody else snatched his coat that was crumpled in the mud a few feet away. All three disappeared into the crowd that was now quickly dispersing.

She dropped to her knees beside Ravencroft's inert form and pushed on his shoulder to roll him from his side to his back, and brushed the hair from his face so she could assess his injuries.

Blood was pooling beneath his right forearm at an alarming rate.

A woman came out of the shop, wearing a bloodstained apron. "What's going on 'ere?"

Ashley pulled her handkerchief out of her reticule, and quickly realized it was woefully inadequate. So much blood! She held Ravencroft's wrist up to let the blood drip freely through his slashed shirtsleeve. "Sally, hold up his arm."

Sally leaned over and took Ravencroft's wrist, holding him with only two fingers and her thumb, while Ashley dug her penknife out of her reticule and cut away his sleeve at the shoulder. Too filthy to use as a bandage, she used it to wipe away some of the mud, then tossed it aside and untied his cravat. There had to be some clean sections in the folds.

As she cradled his head in one hand to slide the linen free, hoping the damp on her fingers matting his hair was just mud and not blood from a head injury, his eyes opened.

So many words came to mind at once, none would come to her mouth.

He squinted and blinked, as though trying to bring her into focus. His left eye was already red and swelling, and would probably be swollen shut by nightfall. Blood trickled from his nose. He brought his free hand toward her cheek.

She leaned forward to hear him as he tried to raise his head.

"I'll not leave thee," he whispered.

Her breath hitched as she recognized the line from the song last night.

His eyes rolled back and his hand fell to his chest, and his head was heavy in her hand again.

The woman beside her in the bloody apron, whose presence Ashley had forgotten, clucked her tongue. "Yer man certainly ain't leaving you." She slapped his cheeks, so vigorously Ashley winced, then shook her head. "Be awhile 'afore 'e comes 'round again, though." She looked up as her husband returned.

The butcher rested his hands on his knees when he got close. "Bast— ah, blighters got away," he said between gasps. Beads of sweat rolled down his temples, his cheeks flushed.

"Where's yer carriage, my lady?" the butcher's wife asked Ashley. "I'll 'ave me boys 'elp yer servants carry yer 'usband. Poor gent, 'e won't be walkin' any time soon."

Ravencroft's cravat in her hand, Ashley froze. "Oh, he's not, uh, we're, uh..." She cast a panicked look at Sally, whose eyes were wide.

"We walked," Sally whispered.

Ashley nodded slowly, her mind spinning. "It was so nice when the sun came out, we decided to walk."

The woman pointed to her husband. "Sam, go get the cart. And put down fresh straw."

"Yes, dear," said Sam, the big man in a bloodstained apron. He walked away, bellowing for the boys peeking out of the shop door to come help.

The woman patted Ashley's shoulder. "I'll be right back."

Sally's hand trembled, which made Ravencroft's arm shake as Ashley tried to wind his cravat around his forearm, to slow the bleeding. Sally looked even paler than the white linen.

"I don't have a vinaigrette in my reticule," Ashley said.

"I'll be fine, miss, uh, my lady." Sally raised her gaze to rooftop level and took several deep breaths.

By the time the butcher arrived with his horse and cart, Ashley had done all she could for Ravencroft with the supplies at hand, on the ground in the alley. A smaller boy came out from the shop and held the horse's head collar while Sam and his two biggest sons loaded Ravencroft into the cart. He didn't even moan at being jostled.

The butcher offered Ashley a hand to climb up to the driver's seat. Instead of sitting on the bench, she tucked up her skirts and climbed into the back. She settled on the straw to cradle Ravencroft's head on her lap, carefully resting his injured arm across his stomach, while one of the boys assisted Sally into the back of the cart.

Where should they go? She didn't know where the earl resided and wasn't confident she could find Lady Bedford's home. Her thoughts still in turmoil, clear only about the urgency of treating Ravencroft's injuries, Ashley gave Sam directions to the mews behind Uncle Edward's townhouse.

The butcher's wife came running out of the shop with two bundles tied in paper and string. "Here, my lady," she said, reaching over the cart's side rail to hand the smaller one to Ashley. "Put this on 'is eye. Will 'elp ease the swelling." She handed the other bundle to Sally. "There's more for later. Or for his supper. You decide what's best."

Ashley unwrapped the chilled, raw beefsteak and placed it over Ravencroft's left eye. "Thank you. You've been most kind."

She shook her head. "My Sam's chased that pimp and 'is girls away before. They keep coming back 'cuz there's always gents what go to the bakery next door and are 'ungry for a different kind of tart." She made an impatient *tsk* sound. "He ain't nice to 'is girls. Yer 'usband is the first I ever seen stand up fer one of 'em."

Ashley glanced down at Ravencroft's still form and brushed a lock of hair away from his face. "He's a good man." She wanted to say more, but no words would come.

"Giddy up," Sam called to the horse, and the cart started rolling. Two boys sat on the bench beside their father, and the youngest hopped up into the cart to sit beside Sally.

Soon they arrived at the stables, empty because Uncle Edward and Aunt Eunice had taken their only carriage and team of horses. With the half-day off Ashley had given everyone else, the rest of the staff wasn't due back for several more hours.

The boy beside Sally jumped down and assisted the maid to the ground.

"Please run ahead and put a clean sheet on top of m- our bed," Ashley said, giving her a significant look.

Sally dipped her chin in acknowledgment, bobbed a curtsy, and scurried away.

After Ashley grabbed the beefsteak, Sam and his boys carried Ravencroft through the garden and into the house. She discreetly tossed the dirty steak into a bush for the neighborhood dogs to dispose of, and directed Sam to the back stairs, the shortest distance to her bedchamber. When they reached the narrow space, Sam slung Ravencroft over his shoulder and climbed the stairs as though the earl weighed no more than a sack of potatoes. Ashley sincerely hoped he didn't have any broken ribs.

Sally was waiting for them at the open doorway, having spread a Holland cover over Ashley's bed.

Sam's boys trooped in after him, and they laid Ravencroft out on the bed with more gentleness than Ashley expected.

"I feel right terrible," Sam said, tugging his apron back into place. "Yer man was doing fine 'til I opened me big mouth and distracted 'im, and that big cur got in a lucky punch."

They both looked down at Ravencroft, who still hadn't moved or made a sound.

"One of me boys can run to fetch a surgeon, if you like."

Ashley patted the butcher on the shoulder and gently steered him toward the door. "You and your boys have done more than enough, kind sir. Indeed, your whole family. I'll have one of my footmen fetch the surgeon."

Sam gave a last glance at Ravencroft on the bed. "If you're sure..."

"I'm positive." She gave a nod to Sally, who escorted the men from the room and down the stairs.

Ashley closed the door, tossed the package of steak onto the dressing table, and set about getting the supplies to clean Ravencroft and better assess his injuries.

Careful of his bruised knuckles, she had washed away some of the mud and blood from his face and hands by the time Sally returned, carrying an armload of towels, washcloths, and other linens.

"We'll need more water," Ashley said. "Lots of warm water." She'd already used most of the fresh water in the ewer, and now the basin was full of filthy brown water.

Sally flung open the window and unceremoniously emptied the basin onto the flower bed below. She soon had buckets of water heating before the fireplace, while Ashley sat on the edge of the bed and used a light-colored cloth to wipe the mud from Ravencroft's hair. When it came away mud brown instead of blood red, she tossed the cloth aside with a sigh of relief. As soon as the water was warm, she continued washing him. There was so much of the red-brown muck, it seemed as if he'd dropped and rolled in it.

"We need to see if he has any injuries besides the knife wound on his arm," she said, looking him up and down. She gulped. "We have to get these filthy garments off him." Her hands shook as she reached for the buttons on his waistcoat.

Sally lingered near the foot of the bed. "Should I go fetch a surgeon?"

Ashley stood up to stare at the man on her bed, her hands propped on her hips to hide their trembling. She'd been acting purely on instinct since seeing Ravencroft go down in the fight. She'd been too flummoxed to correct the assumption of the butcher or his wife about her relationship with Ravencroft, and now it was finally sinking in that she was an unmarried woman with a man in her bed.

Ravencroft taking her away in his carriage after Lord and Lady Sedgewick's ball was a turn about the park compared to this compromising situation. And she'd brought it on herself.

She took a fortifying breath. "First we'll see how badly he's hurt. I often assisted in the infirmary at the academy. Perhaps I can treat his injuries without anyone else needing to know he was here." She'd clean him up and stop the bleeding, and soon he'd wake up and be able to leave. Perhaps even before the servants came back from their half-day off.

That seemed to ease Sally's mind. She began to remove Ravencroft's muddy stockings while Ashley unbuttoned his waistcoat. As the shirt was ruined anyway, she got a pair of scissors and cut it down the front so she could pull it aside. Red marks were already forming on his chest and abdomen where he'd have bruises.

She couldn't help but take a moment to admire his physique. Though she'd seen farm laborers out in the fields during harvest stripped to the waist, this was her first view of a man's naked torso up close.

Sally had reached under his trouser legs to untie the garters and peel off his stockings. She gestured vaguely at his waist. "Should we... Do you think we ought to..."

Ashley finished tugging his shirt from the waistband and peeled back the soft wool of his trousers a little bit. She took a deep breath in relief. Thank goodness he was wearing drawers.

"Yes. Not only do we need to see if his legs are injured, his trousers are filthy."

Together they soon had him stripped to his drawers and lying atop a clean sheet over the coverlet. The muddy Holland cover was consigned to a corner with the other dirty laundry.

She'd never seen this much bare skin on an adult male.

He was stunning.

Still, she tried not to stare, to give him the same dignity she would want were their situations reversed. Ashley quickly and efficiently conducted her examination. No bones seemed to be broken and his nose had finally stopped bleeding. That left only the knife wound on his forearm that required immediate attention. He needed stitches. She wrapped a towel around the cravat she'd previously applied as a bandage, to sop up the blood that was soaking through.

She covered him with a blanket so he wouldn't get chilled. "I'm going to check downstairs and see if we have the supplies on hand that I need."

"Yes, miss," Sally said. "Or should I keep calling you 'my lady'?"

Ashley gave her a grim smile. "That won't be necessary."

A quick perusal of the stillroom left Ashley frustrated and hurrying back upstairs after raiding the liquor stock in the cellar. "For a furnished rental house, there is woefully little in the stillroom," she said, putting the bottles of gin and whisky on the bedside table. "I hope the cook is careful with her knives because I didn't find so much as sticking plaster." She pulled paper from her desk and sat down to make a list of things she'd need to buy. A moment later she slapped her palms on the desk in frustration. "We can't leave him here alone," she said, "and I can't go to the shops on my own." She blew a puff of air to dislodge a loose strand of hair that had fallen into her eyes. "I am so sorry, Sally. I need you to go on this errand for me instead of getting your afternoon off. I promise to make it up to you another time."

Sally paused in the act of sorting Ravencroft's clothes into a basket separate from Ashley's dirty laundry. "I don't mind, miss. This is the most interesting day I've had in years."

Ashley began writing. "You shouldn't need to go far. We passed an apothecary before we got to Mr. Jamuna's bakery, and the linen drapers is just a little bit further past the butcher shop." A few moments later she showed the list to Sally. "For the moldy bread, I mean it should have green or white fuzz, not just be stale. The fuzzier, the better."

Sally's eyebrows rose but she nodded.

"We can't use Aunt Eunice's sheets for bandages, so get plain sheets from the linen draper, or better yet, just lengths of muslin. The apothecary might try to talk you into buying a fancy marble mortar and pestle. A simple oak one will do. They should have the arnica, yarrow, and other herbs in stock." Ashley tapped the quill between her fingers. "The only shop I'm not sure about is where to buy the whisky and gin to replace Uncle Edward's stock. I don't want him to worry that I've suddenly begun tippling heavily."

"Or that the staff is drinking it." They shared a quick grin. "Don't worry, miss. I know where to buy the liquor. My papa used to enjoy a nip before bed every night."

Ashley patted Sally's shoulder in relief. "Get two bottles each of whisky and gin."

Sally made note of the labels on the liquor bottles, and peered at the shopping list in her hand. "Is laudanum on the list? He's going to be right sore when he wakes up."

"That's what the whisky is for. There is a bottle of laudanum in the stillroom, but I don't want to dose him with it unless he's awake enough to say that's what he prefers." After having laudanum forced on her, Ashley couldn't bring herself to give it to anyone who hadn't first requested it.

While Sally studied the list, Ashley dug into her trunk to retrieve the miser's purse that had belonged to her father. Uncle Edward granted her a generous allowance for pin money, but the amount she had left for the month wasn't enough to purchase all the items on the shopping list. Fortunately she 'd saved much of her salary from the academy. While most of it was invested, she kept emergency funds on hand, stashed in her father's purse and a few other hiding spots. She counted out the coins that she thought Sally would need, added a few more just in case, and poured them into the coin purse from her reticule, save for one.

"This should be enough to buy everything on the list," she said, handing the purse to Sally. She held up the extra coin. "Buy yourself a treat. Some ribbon for your own bonnet, or perhaps a pastry while you're in the bakery. Whatever catches your fancy."

Sally opened her mouth to protest, shut it, and slipped the coin and purse into her apron pocket. "Thank you, miss."

Ashley pulled her sewing kit from the mending basket and set it on the bedside table. Sally took one look at Ravencroft's bloody forearm Ashley lifted out from under the blanket, turned pale, and barely bobbed a curtsy before running from the room.

"It appears she's squeamish," Ashley said to Ravencroft.

He didn't reply.

It was just as well he was still unconscious for this step. It would hurt like the devil. She made sure she had everything handy that she expected to need, then unwrapped the bloody makeshift bandage. Her own stomach twisted at the sight of the injured flesh.

The slash went nearly from his elbow to his wrist on the underside, as if his arm had been raised when it was cut. She washed her hands with gin, then held his arm over the basin and let the alcohol dribble into the wound and surrounding flesh. Half the bottle was empty before she was satisfied the dirt had rinsed away, and she started stitching.

The cut was long but didn't appear to be deep. With any luck, no tendons or other important flesh had been permanently damaged.

Sally returned just as Ashley cut the thread on the last stitch. "Here you go, mi—"

Ashley caught her and the large shopping basket before the maid crumpled to the floor, and helped her sit beside the bed, her back against the bedpost. "Take deep breaths."

"I'm right sorry, miss."

"Clearly there's a good reason you chose to work as a maid rather than assistant to a surgeon."

Sally gave her a sheepish grin.

"Stay there until you no longer feel lightheaded." Turning her writing desk into a stillroom worktable, Ashley unpacked the basket. She melted beeswax and mixed together a small batch of medicinal ointment. The bread would take more time to prepare so she set it aside.

From her seat on the floor, Sally ripped muslin into lengths for bandages.

Ashley sprinkled basilicum and yarrow powder over Ravencroft's stitches, noting the bleeding had stopped. How much blood had he lost? His cravat and the towel had been soaked. She spread a thick layer of the healing ointment on a piece of muslin as a wound dressing, then wrapped muslin strips around Ravencroft's arm. She sat on the edge of the bed, holding his hand to make sure his fingers stayed warm. If they turned cold or changed color, the bandage was too tight.

She wished his fingers would curl around hers. That he would speak to her so she could hear his rumbling, resonant voice. Open his eyes so she could see the flecks of amber and moss green. But he was going to be in a lot of pain when he woke up; he was better off if he stayed unconscious awhile longer.

He suddenly groaned and sat up, his left hand to his mouth, his breath coming in harsh pants. His eyes opened, revealing a mix of panic and confusion as he locked gazes with her. She grabbed the basin and guided him to it, and listened helplessly as he violently lost everything he'd recently had to eat or drink.

At the sound of Ravencroft heaving, Sally rushed to the window and threw it open, leaned out so far Ashley feared she would fall, and vomited.

"Good thing we're on the garden side and not the street side," Ashley muttered, long inured to such sights and sounds from assisting in the academy's infirmary.

Ravencroft moaned and collapsed, his head and left arm hanging over the edge of the bed.

"My lord?"

He was still.

She knelt on the floor to see his face, which was pale, his eyes closed.

She pushed on his shoulder and upper chest to roll him over onto his back again. Sally was no help, as she still had her head out the window, taking deep breaths.

"Open the hall door," Ashley instructed, "and swing it open and shut several times."

Her hand to her mouth, head tilted back, Sally hurried to do as asked, pointedly looking anywhere but near the bed. Fresh air began to waft through the room.

Ashley tipped the basin out the window, rinsed it, and flung that water farther onto the shrubs below. "Probably good as fertilizer," she said looking down, hoping rain would disperse everything before the gardener noticed anything unusual.

Back at the bed, she stared down at her patient. Was there anything else she could do to speed his healing or ease his pain? She grabbed the tin of ointment she'd made and set about gently massaging it into each bruise that was beginning to bloom, starting with his cheek. By tomorrow he'd be lucky if he could open his eye at all.

Sally closed the door and came to stand beside her as Ashley pulled the blanket down low enough to expose Ravencroft's naked torso.

"He's a handsome gent, ain't he?" she said reverently. "Not so big he's scary. Not scrawny, neither."

Holy Hannah, Ashley couldn't agree more. Muscles indicated by the planes and curves of his arms and chest, even at rest, proved Ravencroft often engaged in activities more physically strenuous than playing musical instruments.

"There weren't no padding in his stockings. Some of the gents me brother has worked for wear trousers so they don't have to pad their calves to look good in breeches."

Come to think on it, Ashley had never seen Ravencroft in breeches. He'd worn the matching neckcloth when he performed, but was the only one in the quintet to wear trousers.

Not trusting herself to comment, Ashley dipped her fingers into the ointment and spread it on a bruise on his abdomen—his flat, taut abdomen—and noticed another bruise forming on his right shoulder that wrapped around toward his back. "Help me roll him onto his side," she said.

One pushed, the other pulled, and together they eased him onto his left side, resting his injured arm on a small pillow. The heavyweight linen of his drawers covered him from his waist to just below his knees, and Ashley couldn't resist a quick glance of confirmation. No, indeed, Ravencroft's calves would not need padding to look good in breeches.

SHIRLEY KARR

Sally took a deep breath of the pungent aroma before she moved the tin closer to Ashley's reach. "Smells like the stuff me mam used to make," she said with a smile. "Every cut or scrape or bruise, out would come her little tin."

Ashley treated the bruised shoulder and upper back, massaging it into his skin. "An army surgeon was kind enough to share his recipe with me. I hope I got the proportions correct. I used to make much larger batches at the academy."

"You followed the drum, miss?"

Ashley shook her head. "His daughter was one of our students. He brought her back after Christmas break and quarantined with us for a fortnight because we had an outbreak of influenza."

Realizing she was stroking Ravencroft's shoulder just because it felt nice, she shifted her gaze to check for other injuries. She winced in commiseration when she saw the bruises forming on his lower back, including two fist-sized marks just above his waistband. "That's close to the kidneys, I think," she said softly.

Sally swore. "That's dirty fighting, is what that is," she said. "Those buggers are lucky Sam the butcher didn't catch up to them."

With Ravencroft cleaned, bandaged, and ointment applied to all the bruises they could see—she was *not* removing his drawers unless she saw blood soaking through or a bone at an unnatural angle—they got him under the blankets proper and his head and shoulders propped up with extra pillows. "Raising his head will help the blood drain and lessen the bruising on his face," Ashley explained. She prepared a compress with cool water and witch hazel, dabbed it on his cheek and along his jaw, then settled it over his left eye, careful not to cover his right in case he woke up.

No, for *when* he woke up. He was definitely going to wake up. Any time now.

"Too bad it's not winter. Ice would help reduce the swelling better." Ashley stretched, her hands braced in the small of her aching back. "I think that's all we can do for him, at least for now."

"Right then, time to take care of you, miss." Sally came around to the same side of the bed. "I might can save this dress, but I need to get it soaking right away."

Ashley held out her mud- and blood-stained skirts with a grimace. She hadn't considered how dirty she was getting or even thought to put on an apron, as she used to do at the academy.

119

When Sally reached up to undo a button, Ashley stepped out of her reach. "Let's go into the dressing room first."

Sally glanced at Ravencroft and grinned. "Yes, miss."

As they passed the window, Sally gasped. "Oh my stars, I completely forgot!" She peered out into the garden.

"What is it?" Ashley also looked out the window, checking for anything out of the ordinary.

"When I came back from the shops, I met someone hiding in the stables. Asked if she could sleep in the hayloft tonight."

"She?"

Sally nodded. "The wh-, er, the tart his lordship was fighting over. Says she can't go home. They'll hurt her."

Ashley stared at Sally. "Well, we can't allow that. Help me change my dress and then go bring her here."

"Here, miss? In the house?"

"Here in my room. It's not safe for her in the stables, either."

They quickly got Ashley into a clean gown. "The blood on my dress doesn't bother you?" Ashley asked as Sally clucked over the various spots and splatters and sank it into a bucket of water to soak.

"On fabric? No, miss. I deal with that every month. It's when it's from, uh..." she trailed off, staring at Ravencroft.

"Fresh from the source. Understandable." She glanced out the window. "Go get her, if she's still here."

Chapter 9

ASHLEY WAS WRINGING OUT the compress for Ravencroft's face when Sally returned, the prostitute at her heels.

Her mud-stained scarlet silk dress was torn at the shoulder, her disheveled long blond hair hung down in tangles, and tears had left tracks in her face powder and rouge. She clutched a small valise with both hands as she tiptoed toward the bed, staring at Ravencroft.

Ashley replaced the compress on the earl's eye and straightened. "Who are you?"

"*Je suis Marguerite*," the prostitute said, in the worst fake French accent Ashley had ever heard.

"Try again." Ashley put her hands on her hips. It felt good to use her Teacher voice.

Her shoulders slumped. "Me mam and da named me Maggie, but Big Bob said customers like a girl with a French name better." She sidled closer to the bed. Her hand went to her cheek, the same side that was injured on Ravencroft. "Is he hurt bad?" Tears welled up in her eyes and she sank to her knees, one hand clutching the edge of the blanket. "He stuck up for me when Big Bob was mad. I can't remember the last time anyone stuck up for me. And I never even boffed him!"

Sally gasped. Ashley grabbed a washcloth and handed it to Maggie, and steered her toward the fireplace and buckets of water warming on the hearth. "Wash your face and tidy up. Do you have something else you can wear?" Ashley pointed at the valise.

Maggie sniffed. "All me dresses are like this." She pointed at her low neckline. "When I heard Big Bob stomping up the stairs, I only had time to grab me flannel night rail and a few things before I climbed out the window."

The years seem to fall away as Maggie washed off her cosmetics, leaving her looking much younger than Ashley had originally thought. The girl should still be in the schoolroom. Her bottom lip was split and swollen, and the left side of her face showed signs of bruising, her left eye nearly swollen shut.

"Why did you come here?"

Still clutching a wrung-out washcloth, Maggie walked toward the bed and gestured with one arm as though to stroke Ravencroft, still several feet away. "He's kind. I could see it in his eyes. And then I saw how gentle you was taking care of him. I was hiding but heard you tell Sam where you lived." She squeezed the washcloth so tight a few drops of water fell to the floor. Her voice dropped to a whisper. "The last time Big Bob got mad at me like this, he beat me so bad I couldn't work for almost a month. Near starved."

She faced Ashley, her head bowed. "I wanted to see how badly they hurt his lordship. Hoped maybe I could do some sort of work and you'd let me sleep in the hayloft in exchange. Let me help take care of him." She choked back a sob. "I feel terrible he got hurt on account of me. And I can't go back to Big Bob and Little Lenny. They'll kill me for sure this time. They was spitting mad that his lordship hurt Little Lenny. Busted up his knee."

Sally handed her a dry cloth, Maggie wiped her eyes and blew her nose, and Ashley wondered how Ravencroft had injured a man's knee in a fistfight.

"We'll figure something out. Meanwhile, let's take care of your face and find something more appropriate for you to wear." Ashley sat Maggie at the writing table while she applied ointment to her bruises. "Are you injured ... ah, anywhere else?" she quietly asked.

"No, my lady," Maggie answered just as quietly.

Ashley breathed a sigh of relief. While Maggie applied the ointment to her split lip, Ashley freshened the compress on Ravencroft's face. They moved to the dressing room and Ashley searched through her dresses. She and Maggie were of similar height, though Maggie had a slighter build. Perhaps one of the dresses she used to wear working in the academy's garden would fit close enough, at least temporarily. She pulled out a tan dress in sprigged cotton that she liked because the floral pattern helped conceal dirt stains. She held it up to Maggie to check the fit.

Standing so close, there was no missing the loud rumble from Maggie's stomach.

"When was the last time you ate?"

Maggie took a moment to ponder. "Last night, a customer let me have the last bites of his steak and kidney pie."

Ooh, steak. Ashley's mouth watered. She glanced at the clock. The cook and the rest of the staff weren't due back for another two hours. "Sally, can you cook the beefsteak Sam's wife gave us?"

Sally looked stricken. "I'm so sorry, miss. I could fry you up some eggs, but I know nothing about cooking steak."

Ashley patted her on the shoulder. "Fortunately, I do. At least I think I remember." She handed her the dress. "You two make Maggie more presentable, and I'll go fetch us some food." Ashley grabbed the wrapped steaks from her dressing table on her way out.

The kitchen was smaller than the one back at the academy where she had often assisted if the cook or undercook was ill, and did not have a closed stove, which was good because neither did the academy. She built the fire back up and set to work.

Luckily, the larder was much better stocked than the stillroom. She found plenty of fresh butter, rosemary, and thyme, and even lemons to make a pitcher of lemonade while the steaks and diced potatoes cooked. She longingly eyed the bag of dried apple slices. Had she more time, she'd make a pie or tart. It had taken a lot of practice to get the crust just right, and she hadn't made a pie since Christmas.

Ashley was breathing hard and her arms aching by the time she climbed the stairs with the laden tray and set it on her dressing table. Ravencroft hadn't stirred. Two maids bobbed a curtsy as she entered.

"I remembered I saw a trunk in one of the attic rooms," Sally said, "full of uniforms and livery."

Maggie's black dress had been made for someone shorter and with a more robust figure, and consequently showed several inches of black stockings above her ankles, but was a vast improvement over the immodest gown she'd been wearing. Her cheeks flushed red as Ashley looked her up and down. "Good thinking, Sally," Ashley said. "Maggie, is this more to your liking?"

She dipped another curtsy, bowing her head and showing that her hair was neatly coiled into a bun, tucked under a mob cap. "Yes, my lady, thank you."

"Good. Now that's settled, let's eat!" Ashley set aside one-fourth of the food and put it on the hearth to keep warm under a cover, filled her plate and cup of lemonade, and sat on the sofa before the fire. She'd eaten two bites before she realized neither woman had moved.

She set down her fork. "You don't like it?"

They glanced at each other and then back at her.

"Come. We passed proper behavior when I got down on my knees in the muddy alley. Fill your plates and eat with me."

"Don't have to tell me twice," Maggie said. They served themselves, then knelt by the hearth instead of sitting on the sofa with her.

Fair enough. No need to break *all* of society's rules in one afternoon.

Maggie wolfed down her first few bites as though afraid the food would be taken away, then slowed down. She moaned with delight. "I don't think I've ever had steak before. Thank you, my lady."

Ashley and Sally shared a glance. "We are hiding you here," Ashley said when she'd cleaned her plate. "And happy to keep you safe from Big Bob. But you're not my only secret."

Maggie set aside her fork and empty plate, giving Ashley her full attention.

"The butcher's wife misunderstood." Ashley vaguely gestured at the bed, where Ravencroft slept. "We, ah..."

"They ain't married," Sally interjected when words refused to come. "The gent don't live here."

Maggie said nothing, though her eyes grew round as she glanced between the two of them and the bed.

"I'm properly addressed as Miss, not my lady. I'm not sure where Ra— where his lordship resides. We are acquainted, and he recently rescued me from a difficult situation. When I saw that he was injured, I..."

Maggie nodded. "I knew he was kind. And you wanted to help him."

"Exactly!" Ashley finished off her lemonade.

Sally got up and refilled their cups. "Oh!" She set the pitcher on the bedside table. "I almost forgot!" She pulled a wrapped packet from her apron pocket and resumed her spot by the hearth, untying the string. She opened the packet to reveal a half dozen biscuits. "I got these at the bakery for us to share." She offered them to Ashley, then to Maggie, before biting into one herself.

"Until we decide on a long-term solution, should anyone ask, we can say that I hired you," Ashley said to Maggie. She wouldn't need Sally after she found work at another academy, never mind *two* maids, but she could offer gainful employment to both women until then. "What skills do you possess?"

Maggie considered while she chewed her biscuit. "I know ten ways to make a man spill his seed."

Ashley choked.

"Truly?" Sally said. "I only know of four, and two of those are considered indecent even between husband and wife."

Ready to count on her fingers, Maggie drew breath. "Well, there's—

"I meant, more socially accepted skills," Ashley interrupted. "Do you cook, or sew, or...?"

Maggie pleated her skirt, staring at her nails. "I couldn't even learn to pick a man's purse from his pocket without him noticing." She raised her chin. "But I'm willing to learn something else. I don't want to go back to ... to what I was doing this morning."

Ashley addressed Sally. "It appears you have an under-maid, at least for now."

Sally sat up straighter and a smile spread across her face. "Cor blimey, I've never had one before!" She cleared her throat. "I mean, ah, thank you, miss."

Maggie beamed.

Letting Sally and Maggie take care of the dirty dishes, and only half-hearing their plans for tackling the unexpected laundry as they carried it all downstairs, Ashley went to check on Ravencroft.

His chest still rose and fell regularly, and his forehead felt cool to the touch. His eyes moved beneath his lids and his left arm twitched. Was he dreaming about the fight? Or were his dreams filled with something more pleasant, like the music he'd performed?

She sat on the edge of the bed, tin of ointment in hand, when he suddenly opened his eyes and stared wildly around the room. He struggled to move his arms out from under the blankets and swore, his breathing ragged. One of the milder oaths she'd heard from the farmhands working near the academy, but something she'd never heard from a gentleman.

She rested her hand on his chest, in a spot with no bruise. "You're safe, my lord. You're safe here."

He turned his gaze on her and stopped struggling. He squinted at her, lines of pain tightening around his eyes.

"I know you're hurting. I can offer you laudanum or whisky. Which would you prefer?"

He squeezed his eyes shut and winced, immediately relaxing his face as he discovered the soreness around his left eye. After a few deep breaths, he focused his gaze on her once more. He pursed his lips as though trying to say a "w," but no word emerged before another wave of pain washed over him and he let out a deep moan, his breath coming in harsh pants.

He must have been trying to say whisky. She quickly poured some into a glass—two fingers' worth, just as her uncle took it—and lifted Ravencroft's head as she held the glass to his lips. He coughed several times but eventually drank it all, and she let his head relax back down to the pillow.

"Are you—"

His eyes rolled back in his head. He was unconscious once more.

Well. Probably for the best. As much as she would like to have talked with him, to hear his voice, sleep was the best and fastest way for him to heal.

She applied ointment to his injuries again. This time she noticed the split in his bottom lip, which was beginning to swell. She warmed a bit of the ointment between her thumb and forefinger before stroking her fingertip across his lips.

She'd never touched a man's lips before.

What would they feel like against her own? She had watched them, rapt, as he sang and spoke, studying his full lower lip, the perfect Cupid's bow on his upper lip, while his smooth, rumbling voice sent tingles down her spine.

His long brown lashes rested against his cheeks. At the masquerade ball, seen through his half-mask, they had definitely been black.

His costume as the Bogeyman must have included cosmetics to disguise his face. Amber had described him as having black holes where his eyes should be. Squinting through blackened lashes, with kohl brushed around his eyes and lids, might give that appearance.

When she had waltzed with him, his red silk cape had been lined with black velvet. He could have worn it reversed when he scared Mrs. Driscoll and convinced Amber to abandon her improper suitor.

Twice Ravencroft had dressed up as a frightening character at night to protect a woman, with no one the wiser, and received no injury. Today he'd stepped in to protect another woman, dressed as a gentleman, in the middle of the day. "And look what that got you," Ashley whispered.

She smoothed back a lock of his long hair from his forehead. The strands felt gritty instead of soft, and his streak looked more grey than white. Later she'd try to brush out more of the dirt now that the mud was drying.

Much as she wanted to sit here all evening, admiring him, she dragged herself away. Time to prepare the moldy bread. A quick trip to the kitchen—she could hear Maggie and Sally working in the laundry room, chatting about the most effective methods for getting mud and bloodstains out of different types of fabrics—yielded the right size bowl. Back upstairs, she tore the fuzzy bread into small chunks, sprinkled enough water to make it all damp, covered it with a scrap of muslin, and set the bowl in a warm spot on the hearth. With any luck she would not need it, but she wanted to be ready.

She mixed up another tin of ointment, then tidied up all trace of her apothecary activities. The rest of the staff was due to return any time. She tried to put away, hide, or remove any evidence of the earl's presence or the things she used to treat him, save the man himself asleep in her bed. She even closed the bed curtains on three sides, leaving open only the side facing the fireplace.

Ashley had just sat on the sofa, about to read the journal with her notes from helping in the infirmary, when she heard a scratch on the door. "Come in," she called.

Mrs. Gillespie stepped in. "Just letting you know everyone is back, miss, and how much we appreciated the afternoon off. Is there anything we can get for you? Would you like some tea or supper?"

Ashley marked her place with her finger. "Supper and tea would be lovely, thank you."

"Right away, miss."

She'd forgotten to ask Sally to wash their dirty dishes. Perhaps the cook wouldn't notice.

Alone again, Ashley knelt on the sofa, resting her chin on her hands on the back of the sofa, and stared at Ravencroft's profile.

What had she got herself into?

Even if he woke up in the next little while, in full possession of his faculties and typical energy level, he couldn't leave. His shoes, coat, hat, even his shirt, were unavailable. His few remaining garments wouldn't be clean and dry until tomorrow, if Sally could make them presentable at all. And he was much too tall and slender for her to raid Uncle Edward's wardrobe for him.

She had spent the last decade strictly following all of society's rules. Always properly behaved, groomed, and dressed. Always said the exact proper thing, or remained quiet. She set a good example for the students at the academy, wanting to never give Madame Zavrina cause to regret giving Ashley refuge after her parents died. She'd worked hard to keep her reputation spotless.

And now, by her own doing, she had a half-naked man asleep in her bed.

With no clothes for him to wear when he woke up.

How was she going to get him out of the house without creating a scandal?

Why, oh why, hadn't she directed the butcher to take them to Lady Mansfield's home? While she had no clue where Ravencroft resided and doubted she could find Lady Bedford's home again, she'd been to Georgia's home twice. Probably could have found it. That would have been the logical thing to do. The proper thing.

But then she'd have to explain to the butcher and Georgia and everyone else that she'd dropped to her knees in the mud to minister aid to a man she'd been formally introduced to only a week ago. And then let Ravencroft's sister and her family take care of him.

Someone else care for him. Not her.

Footsteps approached in the hall. Ashley quickly closed the last panel of the bed curtain, after checking that Ravencroft was indeed still asleep, and opened her door. "Put it on my desk, please," she said to the maid bearing a tray.

The maid set down the tray and withdrew a letter from her apron pocket. "This just came for you, miss."

Ashley accepted the letter but waited until after the maid closed the door on her way out to look at it. Georgia had written to tell her how dreadfully dull her day had been, the only entertainment coming when Smokey made the cook scream by bringing her a gift of a not-quite-dead rat, one that Tuffy had tried to play with, too. She invited Ashley to go for a walk in the park tomorrow afternoon.

"After what happened on today's walk, I'm not sure I'm up for another one so soon," she told Ravencroft's still form.

She freshened the compress and rested it on his face while she ate everything the maid had brought except for an orange. How had she missed those in the larder? She'd resumed her seat on the sofa with her journal and a cup of tea when Sally and Maggie returned, carrying a basket of damp clothes.

"I figured as how we can't hang his lordship's clothes to dry on the line in the garden," Sally said, "but we can hang them in here on a rack by the fire."

"Good thinking." Ashley let them deal with the wet clothes while she scoured her journal. Had she forgotten or missed any recipes from the surgeon or Mrs. Rafferty, the school's healer? She opened one of her trunks in the dressing room and dug out her copy of Culpeper's *The Complete Herbal*. Were there any herbs, oils, or other remedies that would help Ravencroft heal faster?

She was yawning by the time Maggie and Sally built up the fire again.

"If it's all right with you, miss," Sally said, "we were thinking Maggie could sleep in my room. There's a spare cot in the room that has the trunk of uniforms. We can just move it across the hall into my room."

"You don't mind sharing?" Ashley glanced between the two young women.

"No, miss," they replied, practically in unison. "I'm used to having to share a bed with other maids at my previous posts," Sally added.

"There's a lot for me to learn, being in this kind of household," Maggie said. Sally nodded.

"Agreed." Ashley tried to hide a yawn behind her hand.

"If it's not too impertinent to ask," Sally said, "should we bring a cot down here to your room?" They all glanced over at the bed. As large as Ravencroft was, there was still plenty of room for someone to stretch out beside him.

"I'm going to sleep here." Ashley patted the sofa cushion, ducking her head so they wouldn't see her flaming cheeks.

She prepared for bed, donning her flannel night rail and wrapper. When Sally would have taken the dishes with leftover food down to the kitchen, Ashley instead had her move them to the bedside table. She still hoped Ravencroft would wake up soon, and he would likely be hungry.

She gave Maggie her own tin of ointment with instructions to apply it to her bruises at least three times a day, then dismissed Sally and Maggie for the night after they fetched her an extra blanket and pillow. She made sure the bed curtain facing the fireplace was open so she could see Ravencroft if she sat up, blew out all the candles save one, and lay down on the sofa, so tired she was asleep as soon as her head hit the pillow.

David opened his eyes. At least, he thought both eyes were open. He patted his cheeks and discovered the left side of his face was puffy, his bottom lip tender to the touch. His right arm hurt like the devil, throbbing in time with every heartbeat, and his whole body felt like he'd been run over by a coach and four. He sat up anyway and swung his legs over the side of the bed, and gripped the mattress while the room spun. He was in a strange bedchamber, well-appointed from what he could see in the dim light from the fire and the lone candle on the bedside table, and apparently alone.

The chamber had all the expected accoutrements in the expected places, and he quickly took care of his most pressing need. As he retied the tape on his drawers, he became aware of a pungent aroma in the room. Rosemary? Lavender? He swiped his hand over his chest—his *bare* chest—and realized the scent came from himself. Someone had stripped him to his drawers and smeared something on his chest and right shoulder. The slick substance was also around his left eye and on his cheek.

Who had done this to him? Where was he?

The last thing he clearly remembered was the giant's fist slamming into his face as the butcher came out into the alley. Night sky was visible through a gap in the window curtains. How long had he been here? Wherever *here* was.

Flickering candlelight reflected on a covered dish on the bedside table. He lifted the lid and discovered steak and fried potatoes. Cold, of course. He was too hungry to care. The scent of rosemary in the ointment with so prevalent, he even tasted it in the food. Still good, the meat tender. He washed it down with lemonade from the pitcher beside the covered dish, awkwardly poured with his left hand because it hurt too much to move his right arm. A thick bandage wound around his right arm from elbow to wrist. The more he looked at it, remembering the searing flash of pain when the pimp sliced his arm, the more it throbbed.

For once he wished he had something stronger available to drink.

A bottle on the floor caught his eye, tucked behind the table, mostly hidden by the bed curtain.

Whisky.

He'd never been so glad to see spirits. He squeezed the bottle between his thighs to open it one-handed and took a deep drink. Coughing, throat burning and his eyes watering, he sealed it and put it back in its hiding spot.

He had questions and wanted to explore his surroundings, but he suddenly felt chilled at the same time the warmth of the alcohol spread through him. A wave of exhaustion slammed into him so strong, he barely had the strength to limp back to the bed and pull the blankets up to his chin before he passed out again.

Ashley sat on the edge of the bed the next morning, applying ointment to Ravencroft's bare chest. She'd already tended to his face and applied a fresh compress to his eye. "I like how the bruises aren't as deep as one might expect at this point, and the swelling is coming down," she said to Sally, "but I'm concerned that he hasn't woken up yet."

"Oh, he's been awake. Out of bed, too," Maggie said, throwing a scoop of coal on the fire. "At least for a little while."

Ashley and Sally both stared at her.

Maggie pointed at the privacy screen in the corner, which concealed the chamber pot and close stool. "I emptied it this morning. It had definitely been used."

Ashley felt her cheeks flush. "Was there... Was his water bloody?"

"The bruises by his kidneys," Sally murmured. Ashley glanced at her and nodded.

"No, miss."

"Oh! And he was hungry," Sally chimed in. "Unless you ate the last of the steak during the night. And the pitcher of lemonade was empty."

"He got up, and I slept through it?" Ashley shook her head, annoyed at herself. That had to be a good sign, though, that he'd been awake and had something to eat and drink.

"Shall I take this downstairs with your tray?" Maggie held up the bowl from the hearth.

Ashley set down the tin of ointment and went to check. "No, this stays here where it's warm." She stirred the contents. "Lovely." Coming right along, the whole mixture was turning a mushy, fuzzy grey-green. She covered it again and set it back on the hearth.

Ravencroft seemed just as unconscious as he had been yesterday afternoon. "Help me turn him." She pulled the blankets down to his waist and the three of them made easy work of rolling him onto his side, again cushioning his injured arm on a small pillow. She had just finished smoothing ointment on the rest of his bruises when they heard a scratch on the hall door.

All three of them froze.

Sally recovered first and went to open the door a crack. "Yes?"

"This just came for Miss Hamlin," the upstairs maid said, and handed over a letter.

Sally shut the door and brought the letter.

Ashley sat at her desk to read it. Another note from Georgia. Oh dear, she had forgotten to reply to last night's note. This one was a little more frantic in tone. Mother and Aunt Lydia were in a tizzy because Uncle David had not come to rehearsal last night and had not even had the courtesy to send a note with Uncle Liam, who had offered no explanation as to Uncle David's whereabouts.

Blast. She had been so worried about how she could get a half-naked earl out of her home without causing a scandal, she had forgotten to consider how his disappearance would affect his friends and family. Ashley tapped the letter on her desk, her thoughts racing.

She did not know where Ravencroft resided, but surely Mr. Westbrook did.

She quickly wrote two notes. In the first she asked Mr. Westbrook to join her in a turn about the square this afternoon. In the second note, she apologized to Georgia for her delay in responding, and commiserated with the cook about the unexpected gift from the kitty as well as Lady Mansfield's frustration regarding Lord Ravencroft's absence. In the last paragraph, she asked Georgia to get the enclosed note to Mr. Westbrook so she could ask him a question about his mandolin. With a twinge of conscience at her lie, Ashley folded the note closed and asked Sally to deliver it right away.

"You can go along too," she said to Maggie, "if you feel it's safe for you to be seen in this neighborhood."

"Ain't no one I know going to recognize me dressed like this," she replied, spreading her black skirt. Sleeves extended past her elbows, and the high but loose neckline was augmented with a tucked-in white fichu.

Ashley considered the ill-fitting uniform the girl was wearing. "We need to get you something that fits better." And that blended in. Only the housekeeper here wore black; the other maids in Uncle Edward's employ wore dark green, as did the footmen.

"The linen draper keeps used clothes in the back," Sally offered. "We might could find something there."

Before Ashley could reach for her reticule, Sally retrieved the purse from her apron pocket. "I didn't spend it all yesterday." She shook the purse. Coins jingled.

"Off you both go, then."

Alone with Ravencroft, Ashley eased him onto his back. Seemingly of their own accord, her hands lingered on his warm bare skin. Yes, lovely and warm. Too warm? She pulled the blankets up to his chin, sat on the edge of the bed, and held the back of her fingers to his forehead. He definitely felt warmer than he had yesterday.

While she pondered if his temperature was high enough to be considered a fever, he opened his eyes.

"Good morning," she offered, quickly withdrawing her hand to her lap.

He blinked, glanced around the room, and closed his eyes. Just when she thought he'd fallen asleep again, he looked at her. "Not dreaming?" His normally deep voice sounded especially rough, like boulders tumbling down a ravine.

She shook her head.

"Coach and four run over me?"

The bed and even the floor at her feet seemed to vibrate when he spoke. She gave a tiny shake of her head. "You ran afoul of two pimps, Big Bob and Little Lenny. Apparently you injured Lenny's knee."

He raised his eyebrows in surprise before he squinted his eyes shut, grimacing in pain, his breathing becoming rapid and shallow.

She retrieved the whisky bottle from its hiding place and poured two fingers' worth into a glass. "Here, this will help." She lifted his head and held the glass to his mouth while he drank.

"Ow, ow, ow," he muttered, and probed his split lip with his tongue.

She forgot to breathe for a moment, staring at the tip of his tongue, then shook herself. "I have something that will help." She grabbed the smaller of the tins she'd mixed. "This formula has more beeswax in it and will help protect the cut." She warmed it between her thumb and forefinger as before and applied it to his split lip. He stayed perfectly still, his hazel gaze riveted to her face as she brazenly caressed his lips with her fingertip.

She cleared her throat as she wiped her fingers on her apron.

"Oh," he said, more of a moan than a word, and seemed to relax farther into the pillows. The lines of pain on his forehead eased.

Ah, good. The whisky was taking effect.

He gave a slow blink. "How..."

"How did you end up here?"

He raised his chin in a brief nod. She explained about her stumbling into the alley at the end of the fight, the misunderstanding with the butcher and his wife, the household staff being gone for the afternoon. "And now not only am I hiding you in my bedchamber, the girl you fought to protect is hiding here as well."

He watched her intently as she spoke, not saying anything, only his facial expressions responding to her tale, as though it took too much effort for him to comment. He was slower and slower opening his eyes after each blink, and by the time she finished her explanation, he was asleep again.

"I will chalk that up to the pain and whisky rather than a negative reflection on my story-telling abilities," she said softly.

With squeamish Sally being gone, now was a good time to change the dressing on his arm. Ashley unwrapped the muslin bandage and checked the stitches. Only a little spotting from fresh blood, no more than expected, but the edges of the cut were a brighter, angrier shade of red than she'd hoped for.

He flinched when she dribbled gin over the wound and let it drip into the basin, but didn't fully wake up. She sprinkled a generous amount of basilicum powder and dried, crushed lavender all along the line of sutures before applying a fresh dressing and bandage to his arm.

The old bandage was burning in the fireplace by the time Maggie and Sally returned. "The Mansfield butler said he would get the note directly to your friend," Sally said. "And Mrs. Gillespie asks if you're going to have lunch downstairs or would prefer a tray in your room."

Ashley glanced at Ravencroft. "I'll go downstairs. I need to keep to a normal schedule and keep other servants out of here as much as possible. Any luck at the linen drapers?"

Maggie triumphantly retrieved a paper-wrapped package from the shopping basket. "Just needs a little nip and tuck."

Lunch was delicious. Ashley passed her compliments along to the cook and requested an extra serving of almost everything. When the footman wasn't looking, she tucked the buttered rolls, nuts, cheese, and other dry foods into a napkin which she concealed in the folds of her skirt as she returned to her room.

She set her bounty on the bedside table beside the orange from last night. "I may have to send you out to buy food from a street vendor," she said to Sally. "The other servants will get suspicious if I regularly start consuming enough food for a grown man." She glanced at the clock. "We'll buy our guest a pasty or something after I'm done speaking with his friend."

She accepted her bonnet, shawl, and gloves from Sally. "You need to come with me," she said to Sally as she tied her bonnet ribbons. She turned to address Maggie, who was seated in the chair, sewing by the window. "If he wakes while I'm gone, try to get him to eat and drink."

Maggie bobbed a curtsy, and Ashley left the house to meet Mr. Westbrook in the park, to have possibly one of the most awkward conversations in her life.

Chapter 10

RELUCTANT TO LEAVE THE COCOON OF SLEEP, David tried to find a more comfortable position, gave up with a gasp of pain when he bumped his arm, and opened his eyes. His body ached all over, he felt hot and cold at the same time, his right arm throbbed, and his head hurt with the type of headache that came from not eating. But at least Miss Hamlin would be nearby. He struggled to sit up.

"Oh good, you're awake, my lord."

David didn't recognize the voice. He risked turning his head to look around the sunlit room. A young maid approached the bed.

"The Miss said I was to try to get you to eat or drink. May I help you with a pillow?"

Before he could respond, she arranged the pillows so that he was sitting up more comfortably. He rested his arms atop the blankets, pulled halfway up his torso. He could swear the maid licked her lips before she raised her gaze to his face.

"She said she was going to get you a meat pasty after her walk. Until then we've got some cheese, an orange, and other foods. I'll fix you a tray."

While David was still adjusting to sitting more or less upright, the maid filled a plate and set the tray across his lap. "Thank you." He picked at the bread and cheese. He had no desire for food. He only wanted to consume enough to stop the demented carpenter hammering away in his head.

"Oh! I almost forgot!" The maid poured from a teapot warming on the hearth, added a generous splash of whisky, and set the cup on the tray. "The Miss said willow bark tea might help you feel better."

David choked down a few more bites and washed it down with the tea. The maid was still staring at his naked chest and shoulders. "That will be all." He gestured for her to take away the tray.

She came right back and continued to stare at him. Self-conscious, David tugged the blankets high enough to cover his chest. "What?"

"I just..." She bowed her head and twined her fingers together. "I can't thank you enough for your kindness yesterday."

Yesterday?

"I thought for sure Big Bob was going to kill me. Then you shouted at him, and he stopped beating on me and started beating on you instead." Her voice cracked on the last few words. "I could scarce believe that a rich toff like you would stand up for a whore like me."

Ah, now he recognized her, but only by her words. This tidy young woman in a modest maid's uniform looked at least a decade younger than the disheveled prostitute he'd seen in the alley. "Please don't cry. I don't have a handkerchief to offer you."

His lame attempt at levity had the desired effect, and she gave him a faint smile and sniffed back her tears.

"I want to show my appreciation," she said, coming closer to the bed. "I can make you feel good." Her voice turned low and sultry, and she pulled the scarf out from the neckline of her dress. "Make you feel real good, I can."

"That's not necessary. I would have done the same for any woman ... anyone ... I saw being attacked."

She leaned forward, giving him a look down the front of her loose-fitting dress, and raised one hand to his chest. With the lightest of touches she began to stroke her fingertips downward, from his bare sternum to his blanket-covered belly. "You just lie there, relax, and I'll do all the work. Make you feel fine as fivepence in no time."

Before she could reach lower or pull back the blankets, David grabbed her wrist and lifted it away from him. "While I appreciate the offer," he cleared his throat, "that kind of thanks is entirely unnecessary." For heaven's sake, she looked younger than his niece Missy, who was still too young to have her come-out.

"But—" she backed away from the bed a step and bowed her head again. "Now I've ruined everything," she said so quietly David barely heard her. "I'm ever so sorry, my lord."

"Nothing is ruined." The pounding in his head was easing, and his body felt less heavy. He was going to float away at any moment.

Only his throbbing arm kept him anchored to the bed. "Tuck your scarf back in."

"Yes, my lord." She grabbed the scrap of lace and did as asked.

"The Miss was correct," he said when the silence began to grow awkward, what with the young woman still standing beside the bed, staring at him as if he were a banquet and she hadn't eaten in days. "The tea is helping."

What did one call a prostitute dressed as a maid? Whatever she was, she leapt into action, refilling his cup with the tea and a splash of whisky, and handed it to him with great reverence.

"Thank you... what is your name?"

"I'm Maggie now." She dropped into a deep curtsy. "Sally is teaching me how to be a maid, and the Miss was kind enough to let me hide here. Big Bob and Little Lenny are ever so mad that you hurt Lenny's knee."

David glanced at his hands. The knuckles were sore and discolored, but he didn't recall striking anyone in the knee with his fist.

"Not with your hands," Maggie said. "With your foot, when Lenny grabbed you from behind and you kicked him."

He did recall being grabbed from behind. He switched the cup to his right hand and felt along the back of his head with his left. Ow. Yes, he had a big goose egg, apparently earned when he'd slammed his head back, hoping to break the other fellow's nose, and hit the man's collarbone instead because he was so tall. "*Little* Lenny?"

Ashley and Sally had walked around the park in the square three times. Just as she was going to give up and go back upstairs, thinking the note had not been delivered to Mr. Westbrook or that he'd decided not to respond, a rider dismounted, tied his horse to a post, and looked about the park. Seeing the two women, he headed down the path toward them.

The fashionably dressed gentleman fell into step beside her, and Sally dropped back.

"What a pleasant afternoon for a stroll," Westbrook said.

Ashley struggled to find a way to broach the subject of the purpose of their meeting, and could not even produce polite chatter.

Just as she'd finally hit upon the brilliant conversational volley of, "good afternoon," Westbrook cleared his throat.

"Your note was intriguing, if a little vague. You wish to discuss a mutual friend?"

Oh, good. Polite chatter was unnecessary. "Ravencroft."

He tilted his head to look at her sideways. "You have spoken to him directly on numerous occasions and are good friends with his niece Georgia. What do you hope to learn from me?"

"It's about his location."

Westbrook's step faltered. "As it happens, I do not know his present location."

"I do."

He stopped to face her, one eyebrow raised. "You know where he is?"

She glanced up and down the path and at the patch of grass in the center of the square, confirming that the governess and her two charges who had been playing nearby earlier had left, leaving just her, Westbrook, and Sally in the square. She raised her gaze high, all the way up to look Westbrook directly in the eye. "In my bed."

Westbrook's mouth opened, but no sound came out. He closed it, scratched his jaw, then clasped his hands behind his back. "He missed two appointments yesterday as well as rehearsal last night. Most unusual behavior for him." He gave her a quick glance head to toe and shrugged. "But you are both adults. If—"

"Unconscious."

"—you and he... He's what?"

"He's injured." She forced her fingers to untangle from each other. She started walking again, and Westbrook kept pace beside her. As they followed the path around the square, she gave an abbreviated account of yesterday's events. "So even when he becomes awake and alert enough to leave, he can't. I was hoping you know where he lives and could somehow get some of his things. Clothes. Shoes. A hat."

Westbrook had made odd choking noises at certain points as she told her tale, and now she could only stand and stare, open-mouthed, as he doubled over with laughter.

She planted her fists on her hips. How rude! His friend was injured, had been set upon by thieves, and Westbrook found this a source of amusement? She brought out her Teacher voice. "If you are quite finished..."

"I do apologize, Miss Hamlin." Westbrook wiped his eyes with a handkerchief and tucked it back in a pocket. He offered his arm, and they began strolling again. "He's been staying with me, in my bachelor quarters at the Albany. He has been sleeping in my music room since coming to Town. Did you say he is in your music room, too?" He chuckled again.

Ashley frowned. Why would an earl, especially one with such a large family who seemed to all like each other, stay with a friend and not with family or in his own townhouse? "The butcher thought we were husband and wife, so he is in my bedchamber." She glanced up at the sky, noting how much of the day had passed. "My aunt and uncle will return tomorrow. But even if you get his things to me before they arrive home and we contrive a way for him to sneak past the servants, I fear he may not be able to leave for a while yet. He has awakened for only a few moments at a time before he passes out again. And his wound is showing signs of infection, despite my best efforts." She squeezed her eyes shut. "There was so much blood. And mud."

Westbrook grew serious. "Please tell me again about his injuries. I fear I was distracted earlier."

They walked and talked and came up with a plan. It depended on Ravencroft, of course, and how quickly he recovered. They finished another circuit of the park and stopped when they came to where Westbrook had tethered his horse.

He retrieved a purse from his pocket and held out a large handful of coins. "This is not payment for your services, for I know you would not accept that, but to reimburse you for your expenses in caring for him."

Ashley had indeed been about to refuse. At Westbrook's quirked brow and hint of a smile, she graciously accepted the money and tucked it in her reticule.

"Should you need more, or indeed anything else, have your maid tell David's manservant Gilroy, and he'll pass on word to me. I know where David keeps a stash of blunt. He can pay for his own upkeep."

They shared a brief smile. Westbrook raised her hand and dropped a light kiss on her gloved knuckles. "Take good care of him, Miss Hamlin," he said quietly. "He's very dear to me."

Ashley choked up at his unexpected display of serious emotion, and could only nod and curtsy.

Westbrook rode away in one direction, and Ashley and Sally walked the opposite way, toward the street where there were always vendors selling oranges, meat pies, and other ready-to-eat foods.

Back in her room, Ashley went straight to the bed to check on Ravencroft, barely acknowledging Sally collecting her outdoor wear to put away.

Maggie set aside her sewing and came to stand beside her. "He woke up for a bit, miss. Ate a little bread and cheese, and drank two cups of the willow bark tea."

"Two? The girls at the academy hated the taste. Getting them to drink even one was a struggle." Ashley held up the meat pies in their grease-stained paper wrapping. "These will taste much better warm than cold." She bit her bottom lip. Should she wake him, or let him sleep? She pressed the back of her hand to his forehead. Definitely warm enough now to be considered a fever. "Blast," she murmured. She handed the pies to Maggie, who wrapped them in a towel and set them on the hearth.

Had she made a mistake, not just in bringing him here but in keeping his presence a secret? Should she have summoned a surgeon? There must be several surgeons in London experienced at treating the kind of injury Ravencroft had sustained.

Then she recalled Captain Blackthorn's stories about the aftermath of battles, as surgeons worked frantically to save lives. Often the course of treatment for bullet and bayonet wounds alike was amputation. Better to lose a limb than a life.

But if Ravencroft's arm was amputated at the elbow, he'd never be able to play the viola da gamba again.

He can't play anything if he's dead.

His life was more important than either of their reputations, or his ability to play instruments. If his condition continued to deteriorate and his wound did not respond to her treatments, she would send for a surgeon.

She washed her hands with gin and sat on the edge of the bed to treat his bruises. When she applied the balm to his split lip, she noted how soft his skin was, especially compared to how rough the razor stubble was on his cheek and jaw. Rarely had she seen a man with this much stubble, up close.

Soon Sally tied on her bonnet to go meet with Gilroy, Ravencroft's manservant. "You go, too," Ashley said to Maggie. "I might need to send you by yourself at some point."

As Ashley could do nothing more for Ravencroft at the moment, she removed her shoes, lay down on the sofa, and rested her eyes. If his fever continued to rise, the night ahead could be a long one.

She must have dozed off, as she sat up in time to see Ravencroft walking back to bed.

Limping.

"Oh no!" She jumped up.

At her startled exclamation, he stumbled the last step and barely turned in time to sit on the edge of the bed instead of falling to the floor. He tried to pull the blankets over his lap as she knelt before him.

"I was worried your legs might be hurt but I didn't see any blood." She lifted each foot in turn, rotated the ankle, and felt along his calves.

He again tried to pull the blanket over his lap. "That's not necessary, Miss Hamlin. My legs are not injured."

She barely registered his low, gravelly voice. "Nonsense. Why else would you be limping?" She pushed his linen drawers above his knees, and froze.

They didn't line up.

His knees didn't match up, because one leg was shorter than the other. Smaller.

She finally looked up at his face, which was flushed red. Anger or embarrassment, she wasn't sure which. Probably a combination of both. Her cheeks began to feel hot as well.

Slowly she became aware that she still had her hands on his bare knees. He was sitting on the edge of her bed wearing only a bandage on his right forearm and the drawers that she was touching, a man's most intimate, most personal garment.

His long hair was dirty and disheveled, his jaw unshaven, bruises discolored his face and torso, and his bare chest and shoulder glistened with ointment she had applied with her bare fingers.

He was magnificent.

One knee beneath her hand twitched.

She glanced down. She should probably move her hands. Keep them to herself. Instead she realized her thumbs were stroking him. "Have... Have they always been this way?"

He flipped the blanket over his lap. She took the hint and sat back on her heels, her hands resting on her own thighs.

"No." He looked away, out the window.

She ached to smooth the lines from his forehead, the creases at the corners of his eyes from pain. "Does it hurt?"

His shoulders slumped. He dropped his chin but still wouldn't look at her. "Not when I wear my shoes. Unless I have to walk a long distance. Or spend long periods standing."

"This is why you don't dance," she murmured, thinking of what Georgia had said. "But you waltzed with me. At the masquerade ball."

Slowly he turned his head, as though reluctant to look at her. He cupped her cheek with his left hand. "I wanted to hold you in my arms," he said, barely audible. "Just once."

She might have been insulted he found her an unpleasant dance partner, except for the look of yearning on his face. He caressed her cheek with his thumb.

Abruptly he dropped his hand.

She cleared her throat. "Your shoes!" She stood up and shook out her skirts. "I'm afraid thieves made off with them in the alley."

He gave a harsh bark of laughter. "Joke's on them. No one else will be able to wear them comfortably." At her raised brow, he continued. "I have a talented cobbler who can make up for the difference in leg length. One shoe has a thicker sole on the inside."

"That's why you always wear trousers instead of breeches, even though—" she cut herself off before she could finish the comment about how good his muscular calves would look if he wore breeches. She busied herself pouring a cup of willow bark tea so he wouldn't see her blush at the direction of her thoughts.

"My sisters are always trying to get me to dress more fashionably. Wear my hair in a more current style."

She thought he shuddered in horror, but it was a shiver. He got into bed properly, propped up by pillows, and pulled the blankets up, wincing as he moved his right arm.

She held out the cup of tea. "This will help with the pain and your fever."

He took a sip, grimaced, and tried to give back the cup.

"I thought you liked it. Maggie said you drank two cups."

"Maggie added whisky."

Ashley raised her brows. "She did? Well, it's time for you to have more anyway." She poured some into the cup. He still held it out, so she added another splash.

He grimaced as he drank, and soon emptied the cup. She took it from him before he dropped it on his stomach. She prepared the cool water and witch hazel mixture for the compress. "Tell me if this makes you chilled." She set the cloth over his left eye. "I can get you another blanket."

His only response was to let out a deep breath, asleep again.

The candle on the bedside table had burned down to a stub when Ashley awakened at the sound of the bed creaking as Ravencroft lay back down. He'd flung the blankets back before getting up, and did not cover himself.

Ashley shrugged into her wrapper and tied the belt as she went to check on him. Sweat glistened on his face and torso. She lit a candle and held it high.

He winced and turned away from the light, but not before she saw his fever-bright eyes and flushed cheeks. She set down the candle and held the back of her hand to his forehead.

"You're burning up."

He grunted in reply but didn't shy from her touch.

She added another scoop of coal to the fire and checked the clock. Time for another dose. She was generous with the splash of whisky in the willow bark tea and helped him sit up enough to choke it down. She wrung out the cloth in the water and witch hazel mixture and gently wiped his face, careful of the bruises on his cheek, and began working her way down his neck to his shoulders, stopping often to rinse and wring out the cloth before continuing.

As before, she could tell the moment the alcohol hit him, as he relaxed and let out a little sigh. He let her lift his left arm to stroke

145

the damp cloth all the way to his fingers and back up, under his arm, and down the side of his torso, lazily watching her the entire time.

She tried to remember how dispassionately Mrs. Rafferty had treated their patients at the academy infirmary, and not make it a caress as she wiped the cooling cloth across the earl's naked, sweaty chest.

"Not even my mother knew."

Ashley faltered in reaching toward his right shoulder. "I beg your pardon?"

Ravencroft slid his feet up on the bed, bending his knees, one leg slightly shorter than the other. His drawers bunched up, exposing more of his muscular thighs, and revealed a jagged scar on his right thigh. "She thought my limp was just from having broken my leg, months after it healed." He tapped his knee. "My tailor recognized the problem. Brought in his brother, a cobbler. They helped hide my defect."

Defect? "That's a harsh word."

"Would you prefer deformity? Disability?"

Uncertain how to respond, she rinsed out the cloth and stroked his right arm to the edge of the bandage. A lock of her loose hair fell forward as she leaned over him.

He twined the fingers of his left hand in the lock, stroking it and loosely twisting it around one finger. "Tell me, my dear Miss Hamlin, how does society view those who are different? Even the brave, wounded war heroes, as they came home on crutches or missing body parts such as eyes. Arms." He tapped his knee. "A leg or two."

She wiped the fingers of his right hand, careful not to jostle his arm. "Not well at all," she whispered.

She recalled how difficult it had been when the daughter of a marquess enrolled at the academy. All her father's wealth and the exhortations from the teachers and staff could not ease the way for the other students to accept the girl with a club foot. She withdrew after only one term.

Just last week Ashley had been walking down Bond Street with Sally when she saw two gentlemen walking toward their club, one with his empty right sleeve tucked into his coat pocket, his companion wearing an eye patch. A long scar curved from above his eyebrow to his upper lip. Other gentlemen exiting the club darted out of their way and cast furtive glances, as though afraid their conditions were catching.

Beads of perspiration were forming again at his temples. "Ravencroft, I—"

"Don't call me that."

She swished the cloth in the basin. "Beg your pardon?"

"Ravencroft was my father. Was supposed to be my older brother Philip after Father died. Years and years from now. Never me. I'm just David Amadeus Linford. A plain mister. The spare, not the heir."

Ashley squeezed out the cloth and stroked his face. "You would prefer that I address you as Mr. Linford?"

He flung his arms out to the side and dropped his legs back to the bed, pushing the blankets farther away with his bare feet. "Under the circumstances, formal address seems ridiculous, don't you think?"

He lay there, naked and exposed except for his drawers. She wore her night rail and wrapper, and not a stitch else. She'd dismissed Maggie and Sally hours ago because Mrs. Gillespie did a bed check of the female servants. The darkened bedchamber was lit only from the firelight, partially blocked by a rack with his drying clothes, and the candle on the bedside table.

"Then it seems only fair, David. You may address me as Ashley."

He reached up to stroke her hair again, his full lips faintly curved in a smile. "Ashley."

Her stomach did an odd flip hearing his rumbling voice speak her given name. At last she understood the desire to swoon, or at least grin like an idiot.

"I can't quite tell the color." He lifted more of her hair and let it slide through his fingers. "It's like old gold. Or old honey."

A frisson of pleasure at the sensation of him playing with her long, loose hair crept down her scalp and spine. "Using the word 'old' in any description of me is ungallant of you," she said, struggling to maintain her equilibrium.

"My humble apologies, Ashley."

She held her hand to her heart at hearing him say her name again. Unfortunately it was the same hand with the wet cloth, and now she had a large wet spot in the middle of her chest.

He grinned, entirely aware that he had discomfited her, his gaze directed at the damp spot as though he could see through to her bare skin.

She glanced down. As thin as the pale blue fabric was, he very well could from his angle. "Wretch."

His answering grin was unrepentant.

She began sponging him down again. "It was distinctly blonde when I was a child, quite fair. Especially if I'd been out in the sun without my bonnet. It became darker as I—" she was about to say 'got older' but reconsidered "—matured." It seemed appropriate that her hair was not quite blonde yet also not quite brown. She was in Society yet didn't quite belong.

When she lifted his arm, he toyed with her hair again instead of being completely passive as he had before.

She could do this all night, stroking his fevered body over and over, letting him play with her hair. She cleared her throat. "The willow bark tea helps treat the symptoms of your fever, but Captain Blackthorn had a treatment to get at the underlying cause of the fever. The infection itself."

He let go of her hair. "Who?"

"An Army surgeon who stayed with us at the academy during an influenza outbreak. He was most generous in sharing his knowledge with me and Mrs. Rafferty."

"So you could be his assistants?"

"Mrs. Rafferty was the matron of our stillroom and in charge of the herbal garden. She was very knowledgeable as a healer. She and the captain often disagreed on the best approach based on their different experiences, but they shared the same goal of helping patients heal."

Ashley retrieved the bowl from the hearth and gathered everything necessary to change the bandage on Ravencroft's ... no, on *David's* arm. She washed her hands with gin and unwound the stained muslin from his forearm.

He grimaced as he stared at the angry red swelling along the stitches. "Skin is not supposed to be that color."

She shook her head. "Captain Blackthorn developed a treatment protocol in India during the war, after comparing notes with some local surgeons. Many people ridiculed him for what he did, yet the mortality rate among his patients dropped significantly, as well as a reduction in the number of amputations he had to perform because of gangrene."

David's face paled. "Green?"

She made sure the basin was in the correct spot on the floor and held his arm over it, bottle of gin in her other hand, and met his gaze. "This is going to sting."

Chapter 11

DAVID LICKED HIS LIPS. "How about another splash of whisky, without the tea?"

Ashley poured two fingers' worth in a glass and helped him sit up enough to drink it, and encouraged him to eat one of the meat pies. "You probably don't feel much like eating, but food will help you heal faster."

After eating and drinking, he lay back with a deep sigh of resignation. "Do your worst. Or best." He gestured with his left hand. "Whatever it is I'm supposed to wish on you."

While she fussed with capping the bottle of whisky and switching back to the bottle of gin, then uncovering and stirring the bread mixture, the alcohol had time to spread through him. He hissed as she dribbled the gin on his arm, and she winced in sympathy. This was so much easier when the patient was unconscious. She patted dry his arm and hand, staying away from the wound itself.

When she pulled out the first handful of the mixture from the bowl, he opened his eyes and scrunched his nose. "That smells like moldy bread."

"Because it is." She worked the mixture between her fingers, making sure it had broken down to the consistency of gruel, and began to spread a thick layer of it along the line of stitches. A quick glance at his face revealed that he was trying to be stoic, but the rapid, shallow rise and fall of his chest and fluttering pulse at his neck gave away that he was in pain.

"Tell me how you broke your leg," she said to distract him.

"I was fifteen and foolish."

She bent his arm back, resting his hand on the mattress by his ear, and applied more of the mush poultice. "Everyone who reaches adulthood has been fifteen and foolish. Not everyone breaks their leg."

"Was a hot day. Went swimming with friends. Jumped off the bridge into the river, like I had a hundred times before." He squeezed his eyes shut and exhaled sharply. "Water was lower than usual. A boulder was closer to the surface than usual." He hissed again as he watched her apply more of the mixture to his arm.

"And?" she prompted.

He squeezed his eyes shut again. "My so-called friends ran off when they saw I was hurt. Except Liam. Even then he was bigger than me, though we were born only weeks apart. Carried me to the house until servants heard his shouts and came to help."

One more scoop should be enough. "They took you to the music room rather than your bedchamber?"

He gave a tight nod. "Mother thought it made sense to keep me in a room on the ground floor while I healed. And I'd have access to all the instruments to ease my boredom while I was confined to bed. Or a Bath chair."

She wiped her hands on a towel, got him to hold his arm up, and began wrapping a fresh dressing and bandage around his forearm.

"Thought I was quiet and brave about it, until the surgeon arrived and explained what he was going to do. Only then did I see the edge of the broken bone sticking out. Liam says I screamed and fainted." He watched her reaction to his admission.

Ashley paused, her heart aching for the injured boy. "Probably best that you were unconscious for what the surgeon had to do."

He'd been clutching and releasing the sheet with his left hand as he spoke, but now he pointed at his forehead. "My hair was solid brown until then. White streak started growing in after that day."

She tied off the bandage, which included more layers than previous bandages to absorb the moisture from the poultice, and rested his arm on his stomach. "I have heard of people's hair turning white after they suffer a shock or trauma. Yours is the first I have seen in person."

He shuddered. He stretched out his left hand, the blankets just out of reach. "Cover me, Ashley," he said so quietly she barely heard him. He shuddered again, and she realized he was shivering.

Quickly she pulled the blankets back up to his chin and tucked them over his bare shoulders. "Oh! I almost forgot." She grabbed the garment that had been draped over the foot of the bed, and held up a bottle green silk banyan, trimmed in dark blue. "Next time you get up, you have this to put on. Mr. Westbrook sent it over."

"Liam?" He squinted in confusion.

"Since thieves took your coat, hat, and shoes, and your shirt was ruined, even if you are feeling well enough, you can't leave. I arranged with Mr. Westbrook to get some of your things." She pointed at a package on the dressing table. "He had your manservant Gilroy pack your shaving gear and other toiletry items, and, ah, changes of linen." At the last item she felt her cheeks heat.

His lips moved though she heard no words.

"It had also occurred to me that your sisters might be worried by your absence. At least now Mr. Westbrook knows where you are and why. I left it up to him to explain why you missed rehearsal."

She sat on the edge of the bed, a clean dry cloth in her hand, and sponged the sweat from his brow. "The night we met, you abducted me in order to rescue me." She hadn't ever intended to tell him. Looking at him in her bed, she now had a deeper understanding why the young ladies at the academy were strongly admonished to never be in a darkened room with a handsome man. Shadows lent themselves to temptation.

The left side of his mouth lifted in a faint smile. "Liam said you'd figure it out." His words seemed to come from a long way away. His voice became so quiet, she had to lean close to hear him.

She dipped her head in acknowledgment. "Yesterday, in trying to rescue you, it seems I inadvertently abducted you."

He shivered. "What are you asking for ransom?"

She folded her arms and tapped one finger on her chin. "I think a peer of the realm should be worth at least ten thousand pounds, don't you?" She grinned at her silliness.

He smiled and gave a slow blink in response.

She wiped his face again. "Try to sleep, David."

After what seemed only minutes of sleep, Sally roused her to get dressed and go downstairs to keep to her morning routine. Ashley noted David's fever seemed unchanged, and his sleep restless. He let out little sounds now and then, less than a moan but more than a sigh.

"He must ache abominably," Sally said, as they stood side by side staring at him. "I had a fever last winter. For a week I felt like I'd tumbled down two flights of stairs."

Ashley went down to the dining room to have her usual cup of chocolate, toast, and today asked for soft boiled eggs. Starting the day by reading the newspaper while eating was a habit leftover from the academy, when she needed to be well versed in what was going on in the world. The staff would also look to see if any of their former students had been mentioned in the society columns—hopefully for having made an advantageous match and not because of scandal. Since coming to London, Ashley had been paying more attention to the Help Wanted advertisements.

"This morning's mail, miss," the butler said, setting a silver salver on the table.

"Thank you, Farnham." She waited until he left the room to excitedly break the seal on the first letter addressed to her. *Thank you for your inquiry. We regret to inform you the position has already been filled.* "Blast. Well, I didn't want to move to Liverpool anyway," she muttered. She had another sip of chocolate, a bite of toast, and opened the next letter. *Thank you for your inquiry. After careful consideration, we have decided your qualifications do not meet the high standards required of our teaching staff. Best of luck, etc.*

The third and final letter began, *We regret to inform you...* She wadded it up and drew her arm back to fling it across the room, then decided it would be more satisfying to watch all three letters burn in her fireplace. At least she still had three more queries that she'd sent out earlier this month, plus those she'd sent out this week.

She sat back in her chair, refusing to let her shoulders slump because poor posture would prove the author of the second rejection letter was correct. "Manchester isn't any better than Liverpool."

"Beg pardon, miss?"

Ashley almost dropped her cup. "Nothing, Farnham, just thinking out loud." She hadn't heard him return, and only now noticed he was carrying a package.

"This just arrived. Would you like to open it here, or shall I have one of the footmen deliver it to your bedchamber?"

"Here, please."

After he set it on the table, she resisted looking at it until a maid had delivered her soft-boiled eggs and she was alone again. She untied the string and opened the paper wrapping, revealing a beautiful rectangular wooden case with a carrying handle. Inside was a ten-string lyre and a note from Lady Mansfield. *Perhaps we can play a duet again soon, on instruments that are easier to transport.*

Ashley lifted out the instrument and admired it from all angles. Nestled in the bottom of the case was a sheaf of music, from beginner to more advanced compositions. "How thoughtful," she murmured, grinning with delight.

As she put it all back together and tied the string, she noticed another letter.

Uncle David is no longer in Mother's black books, Georgia wrote. *Well, he is partially, as he is still missing rehearsals. Uncle Liam told us the Ravencroft steward notified him of some emergency at the estate in Surrey, and left town so quickly he didn't even say goodbye. Liam didn't see the note until yesterday afternoon. Did he answer your question about mandolins?*

As soon as Ashley finished her chocolate and toast, she dropped an egg in each pocket of her skirt, gathered up her letters, package, and a spoon, and went upstairs. Watching the letters of rejection curl up, burst into flames, and be reduced to ashes in the fireplace did indeed feel satisfying. She set down her things on her writing desk and with only a tiny sigh, jotted updates in the journal in which she tracked her employment search efforts.

David still slept, fitfully.

She washed her hands, treated the bruises she could reach on his face and chest, and then called Maggie and Sally over to help turn him on his side. She'd neglected the bruises on his back last night, and noted these bruises were healing more slowly than those she'd anointed more often.

"You just want to look at my bum," he mumbled, startling all three women.

Sally tittered.

"It is a nice one," Maggie solemnly agreed.

Ashley covered her mouth to muffle her chuckle. And yes, it was. She cleared her throat as she sat on the edge of the bed behind him. "This is the only way I can treat the bruises on your back." With a damp cloth she wiped away the sheen of perspiration coating his skin, and gently smoothed on the ointment.

"Right," he said, drawing out the word. "You already patted my bum. The night we met."

Ashley dropped the tin. She couldn't look at Maggie or Sally, though from the corner of her eye saw they were staring at her, mouths agape. Hazy memories stirred, of being carried over his shoulder, one arm hanging down, her hand—acting completely on its own volition—intrigued by the soft wool of his trousers and the firm muscles of his buttocks as he walked. She cleared her throat. "How ungallant of you to mention something I may or may not have done while under the influence of an intoxicating substance."

His face half buried in the pillow, he chuckled, a delicious rough rumble of sound that went right through her.

Picking up the tin, she noticed how the pillowcase was dirty from the dried mud in his hair, and the difference in color of the sheet where he'd been laying. She patted his shoulder. "You can roll back now." While he did, with a muffled moan and his eyes still closed, she turned to Sally. "Please fetch clean linens. These are damp."

He squinted at her with one eye. "Haven't wet the bed since I was in leading strings."

She pulled the blankets up and brushed a lank lock of hair from his sweaty forehead, and showed him her glistening fingertips. "Perspiration."

Wearing his banyan, David settled in a chair by the window, drinking a cup of willow bark tea with whisky and was about to eat the second soft-boiled egg, when Sally returned.

She shut the door and leaned against it as though blocking barbarians from without, clutching bed linens to her chest, her face pale. "It's Gretchen's day to dust, miss." She glanced over her shoulder, as though she could see through the door at the upstairs maid marching their way. "She's nearly done with Mrs. Endicott's chamber."

Ashley glanced from Ravencroft sitting by the window, to her bed with its heavy velvet bed curtains. He stared back at her, shrugged, and started to rise.

"It's the third week of the month, so she also beats the curtains and drapes."

Maggie gasped. "We can't let her in!"

"Yes, we can. We must if we are to avoid raising suspicions. It's already odd that you two are fetching the water *and* the coal instead of letting the footmen bring it in." Ashley grabbed her blanket and pillow from the sofa and waved David over. "She doesn't dust in the dressing room, so you'll have to hide in here until she's done."

She quickly got him settled as comfortably as possible under the circumstances, then raced with Maggie and Sally to remove all traces of an injured person's presence from her room, hiding many of her supplies in the dressing room.

By the time Gretchen scratched at the door a few minutes later, Ashley was seated at her writing desk trying to pen a thank you note to Lady Mansfield for the lyre, while Maggie and Sally started changing the bed linens.

David tried to get comfortable, seated on the floor, partially hidden by Ashley's gowns hanging from hooks. He didn't think he'd ever seen a woman's dress from this angle before. He finished off the whisky-laced tea in the cup he'd brought in with him. This was all part of a feverish dream, right? Or an alcohol-induced hallucination. But the bruises on his back and the goose egg on his skull that made it uncomfortable to lean against the wall argued otherwise.

His stomach rumbled. He wished he'd had a chance to eat the egg. Or dared eat the apple that was here somewhere, among the supplies they'd cleared off the bedside table. The maids were chatting as they worked, but he didn't want to risk drawing attention by making crunching sounds.

There should be some cheese in here, and a roll that might not be stale. Somewhere. Without thought, he reached his right arm out to find it in the semi-darkness of the dressing room, and bumped his injured, infected forearm on a leg of the clothes drying rack. He clenched his fist to stifle an oath as pain jolted through his entire body, reverberating with his suddenly accelerated heart rate. He let his head fall back against the wall, breathing hard, counting to one hundred, alternating numbers in Greek and Latin.

Gretchen flung the window open wide and beat the heavy velvet window curtains. Sally came around to the side of the bed nearest Ashley as the maid continued to instruct Maggie in the proper way to make a bed, when Ashley heard the distinctive sound of glass on wood.

They'd forgotten to hide the whisky bottle.

Without missing a beat in her instructions, Sally used one foot to slide the bottle further around the bedpost, tucking it between the bed and the wall.

By the time Gretchen left, Ashley was a bundle of nerves, her note to Lady Mansfield illegible. She crumpled it into a ball and tossed it in the fireplace on her way to the dressing room and flung open the door.

His right arm held cradled to his chest with his left, Ravencroft had slid sideways until his head rested on the floor, his legs still folded, eyes closed.

"That can't be comfortable," Ashley murmured. She crouched beside him and gently shook his shoulder. "My lord?"

He gave a slight moan.

"David?" She gently patted his uninjured cheek, two days of razor stubble prickling her palm. "Wake up. You need to get back in bed." She shook him a little more firmly, and he finally roused enough to climb to his feet. He leaned on her, one arm slung over her shoulder, as they walked to the bed. She instinctively wrapped her arm around his waist, wincing in empathy as she felt him shiver.

He looked vaguely confused as to what he should do once they stood beside the bed, his cheeks flushed, hazel eyes bright with fever. When he made no move to untie the belt on his banyan, Ashley untied it and brazenly reached up to slip the silk garment from his shoulders. He shifted his grip on her shoulders, turning so she could undress him. As she tossed the banyan toward the foot of the bed, he wrapped his arms around her in a full embrace, resting his chin on her shoulder, leaning some of his weight against her, and let out a contented sigh.

His heart beat next to hers. Her arms were full of his bare skin. She was half tempted to pat his bum, just to see his reaction and because she didn't really remember what it felt like when she did it before. If indeed she had actually done so.

This hug was heavenly. He seemed to think so too, as he ran one hand up and down her spine, mumbling a barely audible, "Mmm."

Heavenly, except for the fact that he was feverish, shivering, and Maggie and Sally were doing their best not to watch but failing miserably.

"You need—" Ashley's voice cracked. "You need to get into bed."

He dropped his arms and straightened, his expression hopeful. "Coming with me?"

Before Ashley could do more than blink in astonishment, her mouth gaping, he toppled backwards.

He landed on the bed, arms flung out to the side. Asleep.

Sally held her hands clasped together over her heart, a look of utter delight on her face.

"I'd go with 'im." Maggie propped her hands on her hips. "Wouldn't 'ave to ask me twice."

Ashley flapped her hands, trying to get her brain functioning again. "Help me get him the rest of the way into bed."

They lifted his legs and pushed and tugged until he was properly situated on the bed and covered up. As she positioned his injured arm, Ashley noticed the bandage was damp. "The poultice is soaking through. I'm going to need more muslin so I can wrap the bandage with more layers."

As they retrieved the items they had so hastily hidden in the dressing room and put them back where she needed them, Ashley assessed her supplies. "We also need more whisky, and gin, and..." She sighed as she glanced at the clock. "I'll make a list. You can visit the shops after your meeting with Gilroy. "

Sally and Maggie quickly retrieved their cloaks and bonnets, and Ashley handed over the shopping list as well as the note to be passed to Westbrook, with the promised update on Ravencroft's condition.

"Are these more of the same things I bought before, miss?"

Ashley looked over Sally's shoulder and skimmed the list. "More or less. This time you'll be getting willow bark tea and witch hazel from the apothecary but no essential oils. And you might need to go to a second or even third bakery to find enough moldy bread." She pulled money out of her reticule. "There's enough here for a hackney so you don't have to walk. Please hurry. I'd like you to be back before Uncle Edward and Aunt Eunice return. I expect they'll be home well before dark."

Maggie's eyes opened wide. "A hackney just for us, miss?"

Ashley nodded. "Courtesy of our guest. These are his funds."

They both muffled a squeal of delight and curtsied toward the bed. "Thank you, my lord," they said to David's unconscious form, grabbed the shopping basket, and left.

Alone, Ashley touched David's face—checking his fever, definitely not a caress—and rested her palm on his chest to check his breathing. His fever didn't seem any worse, though he had to be delirious to have hugged her like that and invite her to bed.

Perhaps it was the whisky. She had heard that some men were prone to making inappropriate propositions when foxed. He hadn't had much but given his nearly empty stomach perhaps the whisky affected him more strongly. With his inhibitions loosened by the alcohol, he might desire her as a bed companion. And what girl hadn't dreamed of a handsome man falling madly in love with her? But Ashley knew from her years at the academy that earls married higher than the daughter of a baron of modest means.

Dismissing youthful fantasies, she sat at her desk and composed the thank-you letter to Lady Mansfield and a note to Georgia. Yes, Mr. Westbrook had been most helpful in her research on mandolins, she wrote. She expressed her hope that the emergency at Ravencroft's estate was not too serious and he would soon return, appease his sisters, and participate in rehearsals again. She looked forward to hearing the quintet sing again.

Letters folded and ready to drop in the outgoing tray downstairs, Ashley sat on the edge of the bed and mopped David's brow. The swelling around his left eye was barely noticeable, and only a thin red line marked the split in his bottom lip. The bruises, while still purple, were already turning green at the edges.

"I had the strangest dream," he murmured. "I was wearing a dress. Pink. With ruffles." He stared up at the bed canopy. "Don't think I've ever worn pink."

"There is a pink gown in my dressing room." She rinsed the cloth and placed it over his left eye and cheek. "It has ruffles at the bottom."

He briefly opened his right eye. "Doubt it would fit me."

She tried to picture him in a pink gown. Yes, his long hair could be styled effeminately, but with his chiseled jaw, pronounced Adam's apple, and deep voice, no one would ever mistake him for a woman. "Perhaps you'll get one tailored to fit, in case you tire of your Bogeyman costume."

He laughed. A full-throated, deep, warm sound that went right through her.

"Why did you do it?" She fussed with the cloth over his face. "You could have been hurt." They shared a wry grin. "Before this."

"When I saw Rupert practically carrying you from the ballroom, I knew what he intended. If any man tried to force himself on Georgia, or any of my nieces or sisters, I'd castrate him." He shrugged one shoulder. "You didn't seem to have anyone around to protect you."

"My uncle thought we would be safe in the ballroom, so he went to the card room with friends soon after we arrived."

David's stomach growled. "Mansfield, Templeton, or I always accompany the girls at night. No matter where their entertainment takes them. Always armed with at least a knife."

Ashley quickly peeled the orange and set it on a dish with the last of the cheese and a roll, tossed the cloth that was on his face into the basin, and helped rearrange the pillows so he could sit up to eat. "But breaking into Rupert's chamber, in costume, to scare him? That seems terribly dangerous."

"I had a pistol and a dagger with me, to appease Liam. But I knew I wouldn't need them. Rupert's a bully. Like most bullies, he turned coward when confronted." He ate an orange segment. Given his rapturous expression, it must taste like ambrosia.

Realizing she was staring, thinking about other things he could do with his mouth, she cleared her throat. "But why did you dress up and scare him, after you scared him away the first time?"

He stared at her so long, she began to think he wouldn't respond. "I overheard him planning to do it again, targeting a different woman." He gave a negligent shrug. "I don't have time for a new hobby of preventing him from forcing a bride to the altar."

Ashley clutched her hands together so David wouldn't see them shaking. She had come so close to being coerced into an intolerable position. "And Amber?"

He took a bite from another orange wedge, then dropped his hand to his lap. "Peyton is a calculating bastard, not a bully. Amber was puffed up in her own pride, too stubborn to take advice. She needed a nudge to ask Peyton the right question. Come to her own conclusion."

The door to the hall opened just then. Sally and Maggie rushed in and quietly but quickly closed the door behind them. "Beg pardon, my lord, miss," Sally said. "But we could hear you out in the hall."

"Hear you talking, my lord," Maggie added. "Could feel it right down to me toes."

Ashley jumped up from the bed, her heart pounding. "Did anyone else hear?"

Sally shook her head. "No, miss. Most of the other servants are down in the kitchen or servants hall. Your meal will be ready in a few minutes."

"Here, we brought you this." Maggie held out a meat pasty to Ravencroft. Steam was still escaping from the paper wrapping.

He opened his mouth to speak, closed it, then silently mouthed, "Thank you," as he accepted it.

Maggie curtsied, her cheeks flushing pink, and she and Sally unpacked the shopping basket while David ate. In addition to fetching the items on her list, they had also bought another orange to go with the pasty, and collected a white linen cravat folded in tissue paper. Westbrook and Gilroy had not sent over a nightshirt, though. Perhaps David didn't normally wear one? As she tucked his cravat into a drawer with her shawls, she felt her cheeks heat at the thought of him sleeping entirely nude.

Evidence of his appetite was good to see, but the lines of pain around his eyes and the tightening around his mouth was returning. Ashley brought him a cup of willow bark tea with a generous splash of whisky. Now that they knew his voice carried down the hall, they certainly didn't need him moaning or groaning because of pain. They needed to set up a regular schedule to dose him.

She got more of the moldy bread brewing, wrote out the schedule of when to give him whisky and willow bark tea every four hours when he was awake—he'd already fallen asleep again—and explained it to Sally and Maggie, then took the letters downstairs to put in the outgoing tray on her way to the dining room for her midday meal.

The afternoon passed quietly. Maggie and Sally took care of the laundry, washing the dirty sheets themselves instead of giving them to the laundress, and worked on the alterations to Maggie's uniform. Ashley treated David's injuries, noting the edges of the wound were still bright red with infection but hadn't gotten any worse. She was updating her journal with notes on his condition when someone knocked on the hall door.

"We're home!" Aunt Eunice called.

Chapter 12

ASHLEY MADLY GESTURED for Maggie and her sewing to go to the dressing room, and Sally and Ashley whipped the bed curtains closed. "Come in!" she replied, sitting down at her writing desk.

Aunt Eunice sailed in and Ashley rose to greet her with a hug. She gently guided her aunt to the sofa before the fireplace where their backs would be to the bed.

"How is your friend? You must tell me all about your journey."

"Oh, la, it is much too fatiguing to discuss all that has happened the last two days."

You have no idea.

"Suffice it to say Mrs. O'Keefe will soon be back on her feet, though I may go visit her again, soon. I want to spend more time with her before we return to Jamaica. Such a dear heart. So supportive when I was young. All the girls at my school seemed to have a natural talent for music except me. I don't understand keys at all. If the composer wants a note played or sung as a B flat, I ask you, why don't they just write it on the staff as a B flat?"

Ashley joined her aunt in chuckling. She forced her smile to remain in place when she noticed the bag containing Ravencroft's shaving gear was sitting in plain sight on her dressing table.

"And you, my dear?" Aunt Eunice patted her cheek. "You look quite burnt to the socket. You didn't go out dancing on your own, did you?"

"No, of course not. I confess I stayed up too late last night. Reading," Ashley said with a twinge of conscience. "I kept meaning to stop after just one more page, but I had to find out what happened next."

Aunt Eunice chuckled again. "I've done that myself a time or two." She rose and shook out her skirts. "I'm going to have a lie-down before dinner. Perhaps we can play cards tonight after we eat, and you can tell me about the book. Perhaps I've read it, too. Or will want to read it."

They hugged again. Ashley leaned against the door after she closed it behind her aunt, breathing deep to bring her heart rate down. She opened the bed curtain on the side towards the fireplace, noting that David still appeared to be sound asleep. Then she grabbed the bag with his shaving gear and went to the dressing room door. "You may come out now."

Maggie exited, wearing her newly finished uniform. The dark green fabric looked similar to that worn by the other staff, and with the white apron tied on, she'd blend right in with the rest of the household maids. She turned in a circle so Sally and Ashley could inspect it.

"Much better." Ashley stashed Ravencroft's shaving kit in a drawer of her wardrobe.

"We'll wash the other one and put it back in the trunk in the attic," Sally said.

"We'll still need to find or buy another uniform, so you can have a change of clothes."

"Thank you, miss."

Ashley absentmindedly waved acknowledgment as she opened her trunk of things she'd brought from the academy. Knowing her stay in London would be brief, she hadn't unpacked much. Now she brought out her small collection of books and made space for them on the bookcase near her writing desk. She pushed aside her fan, vinaigrette, and other trinkets like the seashell from a long-ago holiday in Brighton with her parents. She took a moment to touch their small, framed portrait, and organized the books as well as her journals.

Feeling a touch of defiance, she also brought her apothecary supplies out of hiding and arranged them on the shelves. As quickly as she was using up her hand cream, to offset the drying effect of washing with gin, she would need to make a new batch soon.

By the time she went down to dinner, she had chosen one of the novels she'd read enough times to remember the plot in detail— *Sense and Sensibility*—in case Aunt Eunice really did want to discuss it.

When David awoke, the bedchamber was quiet and semi-dark, lit by a candle on the bedside table on one side and a candle on Ashley's writing desk on the other. When he limped back to the bed, he noticed the book she'd left open on her desk. Tired of lounging in bed, he shrugged into his banyan and sat down at the desk to read.

As much as she delighted in Uncle Edward and Aunt Eunice's company, Ashley didn't need to feign yawning after playing only a few hands of cards.

"I'm going to turn in," Uncle Edward said after Ashley's second yawn in as many minutes. "Have a lot to do tomorrow to catch up after being gone."

Aunt Eunice agreed, and they all trooped upstairs and said good night in the hallway.

Sally and Maggie efficiently helped Ashley get ready for bed. While Sally took care of her clothing and arranged her blanket and pillow on the sofa, Maggie brushed out her hair and plaited it. When Ashley went back to working at a school, she was really going to miss this luxury of having someone else do her hair.

"He ate a little something while you was downstairs," Maggie said so softly Ashley barely heard her. "And drank another cup of tea and whisky."

Ashley looked at her in the mirror. "Thank you."

After she dismissed her maids for the night—and how strange to think that she had maids, *plural*—Ashley glanced with longing at the comfy sofa and soft blanket. But she needed to change the poultice before she could give in to her exhaustion.

She got everything ready and sat on the edge of the bed. Ravencroft appeared to be sound asleep. Her heart sped up, just a little, as it did every time she prepared to touch his naked skin. Trying not to wake him, she treated his face, then eased the blankets down a little so she could treat the bruises on his torso. She froze when she saw he'd fallen asleep with his left hand holding a book.

One of her journals.

She gently slid it from his lax grasp. Which one had he read?

"My apologies," he softly rumbled.

Startled, she met his gaze.

"I confess to a vain curiosity to know if you had written about me." His voice was so quiet she barely heard him, even as close as she was. "I would have stopped reading before prying further into your private thoughts. But it's not a diary."

She glanced at the journal in her hand, the one where she kept notes from working in the infirmary. Patients, illnesses and injuries, treatments and outcomes, lessons learned from the Army surgeon and Mrs. Rafferty, instructions and recipes from apothecaries.

"Guessing I'm Patient DL?"

Numbly, she nodded.

"Just what did you teach at the academy?" He gestured at the bookcase. "One journal has recipes and instructions for preparing meals for a large group. Another has notes on experiments to increase yields in the kitchen garden. Which herbs to grow for medicinal as well as culinary uses." His hand dropped to the blanket. "Another was all about advertisements to attract students and how effective each was. Experiments about ratios of students to teachers for the best academic outcome. Exactly what subject did you teach, Ashley?"

"I was not a teacher." Her throat was so dry, the words came out as a rasp.

He raised both brows. "What, then?"

"A charity case." She wanted to run, to snuff out the candles, to curl up on the sofa where he couldn't see her. He must have sensed it, as he rested his hand on her leg. Not on her knee, but halfway up her thigh. She stared at his hand. He gave her an encouraging squeeze.

This man lay in her bed, stripped to his drawers. She had repeatedly run her hands on his naked skin to treat his bruises. He was essentially her prisoner, though she'd had the most innocent of intentions in bringing him here. Even if he had the strength to get up and walk out, he had no shirt, no shoes, no coat. He'd have to rummage through her dressing room to find his trousers and waistcoat.

His question made her feel as bare and vulnerable as he must. She owed him an explanation. She licked her dry lips and stared at

SHIRLEY KARR

his big hand resting on her upper thigh. "Madame Zavrina took me in when I did not appreciate my cousin's ... hospitality ... after my parents died."

"Unpaid governess."

She gasped.

"Liam has sisters. They talk. Sometimes he listens." One side of his mouth quirked in a smile. "And *he* talks."

How many other people knew? How mortifying! A ghost of her resentment at Niles and his odious wife surfaced. She firmly tamped it down. "Madame Zavrina made a place for me at the academy, where I had recently been a student. I was not qualified to teach any subject. I felt the need to justify my presence there, on the staff."

"Economies in the kitchen? Serving in the infirmary?"

"I tried to find ways to save the school money, to pay her back for my room and board. She even paid me a salary!"

He turned over his hand. Hesitantly, she rested her palm on his. He curled his fingers, holding her snug. She felt as if he'd put his arms around her in a comforting embrace.

"The first time I received wages, I remember feeling overwhelming gratitude, of being unworthy. I vowed to save every penny I could, so I would never be dependent on my cousin's so-called kindness again. And I made myself as useful as possible so Madame Zavrina would never have cause to regret taking me in."

His brow furrowed in confusion. "Georgia said you taught embroidery."

"I often assisted the teachers. Or filled in if someone was ill or otherwise unavailable to lead their class."

"Aha! So you *did* teach!" He squeezed her hand.

As much as she enjoyed the gesture, she didn't miss his subtle wince of pain. With great reluctance, she gently disentangled their fingers and bent his arm back to unwind the bandage from his forearm.

He was being stoic again, pretending he wasn't hurting as she exposed the infected wound and wiped off the poultice. But he couldn't hide his racing pulse fluttering at his neck. After she tossed the old bandage into the fire, she poured another cup of tea and whisky and offered it.

"That concoction stinks." He downed half the cup in one go. He could have been referring to the willow bark tea, but his head tilted

167

toward his arm, where she was smearing on a thick layer of the gruel-like moldy bread.

"Yes, but it's effective. See how the flesh is not such an angry shade of red?" She held the candle over it for a closer look. It truly did look improved.

He faced the bookcase and swallowed the rest of the tea. "Rather not see it at all."

"Understandable." She tucked his hand under her arm, as she'd previously done when she'd changed the bandage, and began wrapping the muslin strip around his forearm. This was the most efficient way to hold his arm up and she thought nothing of it ... until she realized he was staring.

At where his hand disappeared in the folds of her night rail. Beside her breast.

He'd been asleep or unconscious when she'd done this before. Now his hazel eyes tracked her every movement.

She swallowed hard. "Folklore has many frightful creatures. Why did you choose the Bogeyman?"

"I didn't."

She paused her wrapping to look at his face, her brows raised.

"Georgia has been calling me the Bogeyman since she was little."

Georgia? Ashley thought back to the conversation she'd had with Georgia and Valerie Kenyon, when they tried to identify the Bogeyman. Had Georgia deceived her, and known her uncle's secret identity all along?

Her thoughts still racing, she resumed winding the muslin, trying to get the tension just right.

"Lydia and Diana came home for a visit when my leg was healing, their little children in tow. Missy stopped fussing when I held her and sang. Poor babe, had a new tooth coming in." He covered his eyes with his left forearm. "The next night my sisters brought all their children to the music room at bedtime and expected me to sing them a lullaby. I didn't want them to make a habit of it. So I sang the requested lullaby, and then asked the children if they'd like a bedtime story. Diana and Lydia looked so pleased." He smiled at the memory, though there was an edge to his grin.

She'd heard that little brothers could be mischievous. "And what delightful tale did you tell those young, impressionable nieces and nephews to send them off to slumber?"

His grin was decidedly feral. "The scariest story I could think of, complete with demonic voices and an evil laugh. Diana and Lydia were appalled." His smile faded. "But the little buggers were delighted. Demanded another. And instead of worrying about the Bogeyman being under her bed, Georgia assured me *I* was the Bogeyman."

Ashley couldn't help a small smile. "And you've been telling them scary bedtime stories, complete with scary voices, ever since." She finished tying off the bandage and rested his arm on his stomach. "I heard their governess scream the other night. You do have the most horrifying, evil laugh. I would have been quite frightened myself if I'd heard it alone in a dark room, instead of peering around the corner from the staircase. "

He lifted his arm from his face. Understanding dawned in his eyes.

"And I had only just figured out that you were my mysterious rescuer when I heard you sing at rehearsal earlier that evening. That must vex the other gentlemen at times, knowing you can sing anyone's part, in any register." She pulled the blankets up to his chin, making sure his bare shoulders were covered, and began tidying up.

"Not *everyone's* part." His words were coming further apart, his eyes blinking more slowly. "Can't hit soprano since I started needing to shave."

She chuckled. "I'm sure that's a great comfort to Liam, Parker, and your brothers-in-law. Not to mention those competing against you, like Lord Fairfax."

"A pox on Fairfax," he mumbled, his eyes closed.

There was no heat in his voice. Given the steady rise and fall of his chest, she realized he'd fallen asleep. "But Fairfax has such a nice voice."

She updated her journal and the paper with the dosing schedule so Sally and Maggie would know when he'd last been given whisky, and blew out the bedside candle.

Sally shook her shoulder. "Mrs. Gillespie has the water heating for your bath, miss. What shall we do?"

Ashley blinked, struggling to wake up after what felt like only a few minutes of sleep. "Bath?" She sat up and leaned her head on the back of the sofa. "Blast. It's Saturday already?" With a groan she got up, tied on her wrapper, and went to check on Ravencroft.

He was sound asleep, not restless at all. She held the back of her hand to his forehead. Warm, not hot. She cupped the side of his neck, his whiskers scratching her thumb. Also warm. And his skin was dry, rather than damp with perspiration.

"His fever broke," she said, almost to herself.

"Praise be," Maggie said, opening the window curtains.

"Shall I tell them not to bring the bath?" Sally twisted her apron in her hands.

Ashley bit her bottom lip. One of her favorite indulgences since coming to live with her aunt and uncle was a weekly up-to-her-neck soak in a tub of hot water. She leaned toward Ravencroft. "My lord?" she whispered.

His breathing did not alter.

Ashley stood. "We'll close the bed curtains and carry on as usual so no one thinks anything is out of the ordinary." She glanced at the earl. "And pray he stays asleep."

Within minutes they'd pushed the sofa to the side and put her blanket and pillow away, just before a footman scratched at the door. He carried the tub over one shoulder and placed it before the fireplace, and other footmen marched in behind him carrying buckets of steaming water to fill the tub, with more buckets staying warm on the hearth for rinsing.

With a furtive glance at the closed bed curtains, Ashley slipped off her night rail and sank into bliss.

David woke to the sound of water pouring, and an accompanying need to relieve himself. No candlelight or sunlight penetrated the gloom. Was it morning or night? He stretched out his hand and encountered heavy velvet. Why had the bed curtains been drawn?

The hall door closed.

He risked sitting up and pushed aside the curtain enough to peer through a tiny gap.

In time to see Ashley sit down in the tub.

Her long, dark blonde hair hung loose over her bare shoulders and back. She leaned back with a deep sigh of contentment, resting her head against the tub's edge.

His heart beat faster. Blood rushed through his veins. He tried to slow his breathing. Surely in thirty years he had seen more tempting sights than a woman stepping into her bath, heard more arousing sounds than her soft moan of pleasure. Yet he couldn't stop staring.

Until he heard movement and other voices, and realized her two maids were there, quietly offering a choice of soaps and scented bath oils.

He lay back, slowly so as not to make the bed creak.

Which scent had she chosen? She'd repeatedly slathered so much healing ointment on his bruises, all he could smell was rosemary and a hint of lavender. What did she smell like?

What did *he* smell like? He'd been sweating like a pig for days with this fever. But he no longer felt feverish. Gone, finally, were the chills that had him alternately huddling under the blankets and kicking them off.

He was still exhausted and felt like he'd been pummeled—because he *had* been pummeled—but at least he now felt confident he'd heal. His right forearm no longer felt on fire, though it still throbbed with every heartbeat and he had to bite back an oath every time he bumped it and pain went searing up his arm, flaring through his entire body.

The hall door opened and closed, and he heard the gentle slosh of water. He peered through the curtain again. He didn't see or hear the maids.

"If you promise not to peek," Ashley quietly said, her gaze directed at the fireplace, "I will promise the same. But you only have a few moments before Sally and Maggie return."

David sat up and swung his legs over the side of the bed, paused to make sure the floor and ceiling stayed in their proper places, then shrugged into his banyan on his way to answer the call of nature behind the privacy screen.

On his way back to bed, he couldn't resist turning his head for a quick look. Ashley leaned forward in the tub, exposing the long sleek line of her naked back, her cheek resting on her drawn-up knees, her glistening arms wrapped around her shins ... looking right back at him.

So much for not peeking.

They shared a grin, and turned in unison when they heard footsteps in the hall. David rushed the remaining steps and barely twitched the bed curtain back into place before the door opened.

He lay motionless, half listening to Sally instructing the younger girl on the proper way to wait on a lady in her bath, such as having a towel ready for her body as well as one for her wet hair, and Maggie comparing it with her experiences attending to customers in their bath. She seemed to delight in shocking the other two women with her nonchalant descriptions in graphic detail.

David had never thought about men wanting to be bathed by their bed partners, especially paid companions. For him, getting clean had always been simply a perfunctory, impersonal task. Yet now he could see the appeal, especially if Ashley were the one washing him.

Fuzzy memories came to mind, of Ashley bathing his fevered brow, and her soft hands gently washing his naked torso with a cool damp cloth before massaging ointment into his skin with her bare fingers. He wished he'd felt well enough to truly appreciate the experience at the time. But if he'd been well, there would have been no reason for her to touch him in such an intimate manner.

Exhausted, he yearned for sleep that wouldn't come, tortured by images conjured from the sounds coming from the other side of the curtain. Ashley rising from her bath like Venus from the sea, water sluicing over her silky skin, stepping naked from the tub to stand before the crackling fire, her skin softly scented and warm. The desire for *him* to be the one toweling her off and brushing her hair caught him by surprise.

Propinquity. That's all it was. Continual nearness to each other. The unexpectedly intimate nature of their relationship the last few days would go back to societal norms when he was well enough to leave. As soon as he was strong enough to walk down the stairs and out the door to a waiting carriage without collapsing, he would go. She would return to being an intriguing woman, his niece's latest rescue. Miss Hamlin.

Not Ashley.

Not the woman who had knelt at his feet, agony in her eyes, worried that he was in pain from his mismatched legs. Upset that she had missed something in tending his wounds.

The woman who risked her reputation to care for him when he was injured.

He must have dozed off, as David found himself blinking in surprise when the bed curtain opened, sunlight temporarily blinding him.

Ashley reached a hand to his forehead. He stilled, letting her touch him all she wanted, while he drank in the sight of her leaning over him, dressed in a simple light green gown, her hair hanging down, loose and damp.

"Definitely gone," she muttered to herself. She withdrew her hand, much to his regret. "The breakfast tray has been brought up. Do you want to sit at the table, or would you prefer a tray across your lap?"

"Table." He sat up, vaguely surprised to note he was still wearing his banyan, though the belt had come untied. The small table by the window with two straight-backed chairs couldn't have been more than six steps away, yet he felt like he'd walked six miles by the time he sat down.

Ashley sat across from him and pushed the tray closer to him. "Have whatever you'd like, as much as you feel up to."

The tray had a cup of steaming chocolate, two soft-boiled eggs, toast, and a small jar of marmalade. Definitely a lady's breakfast. As he reached for a spoon and the first of the eggs, he realized she had nothing except a newspaper. "You're not eating?"

"You need to build up your strength. Sally will sneak me something from the kitchen later." She resumed reading the paper. Not the front page or the Society news, which she set within his reach, but the Employment Opportunity advertisements. Was she planning to hire even more maids?

Not only did it feel awkward to be the only one eating, it took just a few bites using his right arm to realize that while his fever may be gone, the pain from his wound was not. He switched to using his left hand and cradled the right in his lap.

Ashley tossed aside the paper. "Oh, how foolish of me!" She muttered more words as she went to fuss with something at the fireplace, and barely glanced over when the hall door opened.

Her two maids entered, one of them carrying an armload of linens, and they quickly began changing the bed.

Everything and everyone was fresh, except him. He hadn't shaved or washed in days, except for Ashley's sponge baths, and his uncombed hair had to be sticking up at odd angles where it wasn't matted to his skull.

The younger maid, the prostitute he'd defended, kept sneaking glances at him.

He refused to reach up and finger comb his hair but he did use the napkin to make sure there was no food on his face. At least his chest was not naked this time.

Ashley brought him a teacup half-full of willow bark tea. "This will help you feel better. Maggie, can you reach the whisky?"

The maid bobbed a curtsy and retrieved a bottle on the floor that had been hidden by the bed curtains. "May I say how pleased I am you're on the mend, my lord?" She poured enough whisky to fill the cup to the brim.

"Um," was all he could manage. The cup seemed to weigh ten pounds as he raised it to his mouth and drank deeply. Hating the taste as much as ever, he choked it down so it would dull his throbbing aches. He was still hungry after he finished one egg and a piece of toast slathered with marmalade, but he barely had the strength to hold his head up, never mind lift his hand to his mouth. He tried to rise before he passed out in the chair.

Ashley was there, a hand under his elbow helping him to stand, her arm around his waist, letting him lean on her as he traversed the vast distance to the bed.

"Rest now, David," she said softly as he let her strip him of his banyan before he slid under the covers. Some of her hair fell forward as she leaned over to pull the blanket up.

Resting his left elbow on the bed, he slid his fingers through a handful of strands. "So soft." He could play with her hair for hours ... as he felt himself floating away.

Confident that Ravencroft was asleep and Sally in her room to keep an eye on him, Ashley went about her day as Aunt Eunice expected. Shopping for a new fan because Eunice had left her previous one with Mrs. O'Keefe who had sighed in pleasure at seeing the tropical scene painted on it, paying morning calls on Aunt's friends, and a stroll together in St. James Park.

"It's the hour to see and be seen," Aunt Eunice said, tucking her arm through Ashley's while a footman followed them at a discreet distance. "Oh my, so many handsome gentlemen are out today!"

Oblivious to the many men on horseback and on foot and instead thinking of the handsome gentleman in her bed, Ashley murmured an appropriate response.

"Look, there's Mr. Westbrook. Do you think we'll see his friend Ravencroft, too?" Aunt Eunice raised her hand in a subtle wave, a large enough gesture to get the gentleman's attention without seeming crass.

Soon Mr. Westbrook and his two companions, who turned out to be Lord Fairfax and Mr. Huntley, the tenor with the angelic voice, caught up with them on the path and everyone exchanged polite greetings.

"Such a beautiful day," Lord Fairfax said, doffing his hat as he bowed and raised Ashley's hand for a kiss. "Made even more lovely by encountering two beautiful ladies." Aunt Eunice let out a girlish giggle, and Fairfax gave his head a slight shake to get his long hair from his eyes as he straightened.

His bass voice didn't rumble as much outdoors with no walls or furniture to bounce the sound off of, but Ashley saw Aunt Eunice fluttering her lashes at him like a schoolgirl, still affected by his rich tone.

Feeling bold, Ashley offered her hand to Westbrook. "I'm glad the weather is no longer hot," she said, looking him directly in the eye.

He paused, ever so briefly, before he straightened and let go of her. "It *was* too hot, wasn't it?"

She nodded. "But not any longer."

He gave her a relieved smile.

"If you ask me, I thought the weather has been chilly," said Mr. Huntley, looking slightly puzzled by their exchange. Aunt Eunice agreed.

Fortunately they moved on to some other inane but polite and appropriate topic of conversation, and then to the entertainments planned for tonight, and who was going to be at which event. Ashley barely paid attention, distracted as her stomach growled. How hungry was Ravencroft? Had Sally brought him any food? How could she get enough food for him without arousing suspicion? Now that his fever had broken, his appetite should return. He needed to eat in order to regain his strength.

A cluster of young ladies strolling with their chaperone caught Lord Fairfax's attention, and soon Ashley and her aunt were walking alone again. "If you are hungry, why didn't you simply say so?" Aunt Eunice took Ashley's arm and they headed toward the park's exit nearest their home.

Ashley's cheeks heated and she placed her hand over her stomach. "Do you think they heard me?"

"I'm sure all three are too much of a gentleman to acknowledge it if they did, my dear."

Chapter 13

BACK AT THE TOWNHOUSE, Aunt Eunice beamed at her when Ashley asked for a second helping of everything. "Have to keep your strength up for tonight," she said with a wink.

You have no idea.

Anytime her aunt looked away, Ashley hid food. Slices of ham in the folds of her napkin, nuts and cheese in her reticule. Too bad there was no way for her to carry some of the delicious soup upstairs, so she ate it. At least she was able to save a buttered roll.

"I have been meaning to ask you something," Aunt said when the footman left the dining room to take away empty dishes.

Ashley's heart pounded. She set her spoon down so it wouldn't rattle against the bowl.

"Are you displeased with the lady's maid I hired for you? Mrs. Gillespie said you engaged another while I was gone, though she seems much too young for the position."

Nearly fainting in relief, Ashley picked up her spoon again. "No, I adore Sally. You made an excellent choice." She ate another spoonful while she considered an acceptable version of events to tell. "I encountered Maggie while we were out for a walk. Her previous ... employer ... was beating her and I could not in good conscience allow it to continue. Sally is training her, and then we'll help her find a suitable position."

Aunt Eunice nodded. "I suspected something like that, after I noticed her bruises."

"I'll pay for her wages."

"Oh, pish. With the amount of Edward's money we're spending for three months in London, another maid is hardly worth noting." Aunt Eunice drank the last of her lemonade. "I think I'll have a lie-down."

"What an excellent notion." Ashley was careful to carry the folded napkin and her bulging reticule on the far side from her aunt as they climbed the stairs.

Her nerves still thrumming from the close call, Ashley closed her door and leaned against it. Claiming to need the ladies' retiring room to escape an awkward social situation was difficult enough. She simply was not cut out for being duplicitous. Ravencroft needed to heal quickly and leave.

A pang of regret filled her at the thought of him leaving. She'd still see him, of course. He was the uncle of her friend. But it would never be the same. He'd call her Miss Hamlin. Not Ashley.

She set the food on the bedside table and checked on her patient. She cocked her head to the side, studying him, trying to figure out what had changed.

"I held the mirror for him," Maggie said, coming to stand beside her. "He wouldn't let me use the razor. Dozed off after shaving only half his face. I kept the water hot, and he finished just a bit ago." She pointed at a spot he'd missed on his neck and another by one ear. "I would have done a neater job."

"I'm sure you would have." His lack of beard stubble made the bruises around his left eye stand out more. At least the edges were fading to green and yellow.

While Sally adjusted the clothing drying on the rack in front of the fire—Ashley refused to blush at the sight of Ravencroft's drawers drying next to her chemise and stockings—she sat down to write the day's note to Westbrook, giving him a more detailed update on Ravencroft's condition.

With her maids off to meet with Gilroy and buy more supplies, Ashley sat on the edge of the bed to change the poultice.

Ravencroft woke up as she was unwinding the bandage.

"Good news!" she quietly said. "With your fever broken, I think it's safe to make this the last poultice. Tonight I can switch to something that smells better."

He drew breath to speak. She shook her head and laid her finger across his lips. "My aunt is in her room just down the hall." He continued to stare at her, and it took her a moment to realize she was still touching his mouth.

She cleared her throat and resumed working on his arm. He gave a mischievous grin as though he were fully awake, but blinked slowly, and kept dropping his hand so she needed to tuck it between her arm and torso. She refused to be distracted by the way he stared at her, watching every movement.

When she finished, she gestured at the food on the bedside table. "Are you hungry?"

His stomach growling was clearly audible, and he gave her a sheepish grin.

"I'll take that as a yes. Table, or a tray across your lap?"

Struggling to sit up had him breathing hard, his face pale. She arranged the pillows behind his back, noting how he closed his eyes in disgust.

"At this stage in recovery from a knife or bayonet injury, Captain Blackthorn said the typical patient response is exhaustion. Your body has been fighting hard to overcome the infection as well as heal an open wound. It's tired. You need food, drink, rest." She brazenly rested her hand on his un-bruised bare shoulder and gave a gentle squeeze. "And time."

He gave a resigned nod, and tucked into the food she'd brought. Eating with his left hand, she noted, trying valiantly not to stare at his face. His handsome, clean-shaven face. Well, mostly clean-shaven. He drank another cup of tea and whisky and settled back on the pillows, seemingly asleep before she even took the dishes away.

Maggie and Sally returned, bringing more food from street vendors as well as a shirt for Ravencroft that Gilroy had sent. Now all he lacked was shoes, coat, and a hat in order for him to be able to leave.

They packed up his shaving accoutrements and other toiletries so that Ashley could sit at the dressing table and let Maggie and Sally experiment with her hairstyle for the evening. The maids good-naturedly argued a bit, each advocating for an entirely different style, until they compromised on a bejeweled upsweep that incorporated elements from both.

"You look stunning, my dear," Uncle Edward said when she descended the staircase.

"The gentlemen won't know what hit them," Aunt Eunice agreed, pulling on her gloves.

Ashley ducked her chin in embarrassment.

Their carriage soon deposited them at their first stop of the evening, a soirée. Knowing she would not encounter the person she most wanted to speak to—because he was asleep in her bed—Ashley listlessly wandered through the crowd, chatting with acquaintances.

"Oh, there you are!" Georgia wrapped her in a quick embrace. "It seems like ages since I've seen you!" She pulled back to study Ashley's face, and her demeanor immediately changed. She tilted her head to one side. "What is wrong?"

"Nothing is wrong." She tried to smile. It probably came across more as just baring her teeth.

Georgia looked unconvinced. Ashley hated to lie to her friend. "I confess I stayed up too late the last few nights. Nothing a good night's rest won't solve." There. Not a lie. Just an incomplete truth.

"Oh, well in that case, come with me. Mr. Huntley is going to sing in the other room. He has a divine voice. If you like tenors."

Ashley chuckled and allowed herself to be towed along through the crowd to a room down the hall where a dozen people had gathered around a pianoforte.

Mr. Huntley was singing and accompanying himself, his playing as excellent as his voice. As the final note died, people called out requests for the next song.

"I'll play, but only if you join me," he said with a flirtatious smile aimed at two of the young women. He began the next tune, and within a few bars most people were singing with him.

Ashley nodded in greeting to Miss Valerie Kenyon, who had detached herself from the crowd to come greet her and Georgia. "I want to run my fingers through his hair," Valerie said with a wistful smile.

Mr. Huntley did indeed have lovely thick auburn hair, with luxurious waves that might make a young woman want to muss them. Not Ashley, of course. She had discovered she was partial to men with long hair. And deep voices.

As if conjured by her thoughts, Lord Fairfax stepped beside Mr. Huntley and lent his voice to the song. Several other singers from groups competing in the Catch Club wended their way into the room, no doubt drawn by the music. When the song ended, Fairfax bumped Mr. Huntley with his hip, and Huntley graciously relinquished the bench at the keyboard.

Fairfax played a tune Ashley didn't recognize, with no music in front of him.

"Tell me, my dear Lord Fairfax," Lady Barbour said when he finished, suggestively running her gloved finger along the open case of the pianoforte. "Do you play by ear?"

"Yes." He quickly played a glissando that included almost every key. "But I find it easier to use my hands."

Lady Barbour looked uncertain if she'd just been the butt of a joke, while Ashley and Georgia stifled a laugh.

Fairfax flashed a charming smile and began playing and singing a familiar tune, in a lower key.

Mr. Huntley shook his head. "Too low for me," Ashley saw him say.

Westbrook joined in, making it a duet, and soon Lord Leighton as well as Lord Sutcliff, a baritone from another quartet, joined in.

Ashley turned to make a comment to Valerie about how the floor seemed to pulsate from the combined deep voices—she could feel the vibrations through her silk slippers all the way up her spine—but Valerie was gone. A moment later she spotted her and Mr. Huntley backing away from the group around the pianoforte, arm in arm.

As the last notes faded away, an older gentleman with a full head of snow-white hair pushed his way through the crowd toward the pianoforte, calling out, "Where are my bassy boys?" When people didn't move quickly enough, he used his walking stick to help clear the path. "Where are my bass—ah, there you are." He laid a hand on Fairfax's shoulder.

Fairfax jumped up and gave the old man a quick embrace. "Mr. Barrett, how delightful to see you," Fairfax said, giving the much shorter man a gentle pat on the back.

Westbrook greeted him next, then Leighton and Sutcliff.

Barrett looked around. "I'm missing one of my bassy boys. Where's Linford?"

"Lord Ravencroft left town to deal with an emergency at his estate," Westbrook said, without looking at Ashley.

Mr. Barrett gave an impatient shake of his head. "Of course. Ravencroft now, not Linford. Terrible tragedy about his father and brother. You'll have to sing without him." He thumped his cane. "Well, don't just stand there." He pushed Fairfax toward the pianoforte. "Play something!"

While Westbrook, Fairfax, and Leighton had a silent argument as to who would play, Sutcliff snuck in behind them to claim the bench, and began to play another familiar tune, again arranged for lower voices. Ashley chuckled, remembering how Georgia had played a similar trick while her father and uncles argued.

Curious as to why gentlemen of the peerage were behaving like schoolboys, obeying a plain Mister, Ashley turned her questioning gaze to Georgia.

"Mr. Barrett was a music instructor for decades," Georgia whispered. "He's been a guest at Linford Hall and Mansfield Grange many times." She spotted Valerie and Mr. Huntley in the far corner of the room, their heads close together in conversation, and blew out an impatient huff. "Well. I'm not sure I'd want to be courted by a man who can sing higher than me, anyway." She shifted to Ashley's other side so the couple was behind her, out of sight.

"And who has prettier hair." They shared a grin.

Word spread that a game of charades was being played in the next room, and several people moved on, making room for others to get close to the pianoforte. Lady Danforth stepped forward, fanning her flushed face as she subtly swayed to the music, her eyes closed.

"She seems to be enjoying herself," Ashley whispered, her chin pointing to the matron.

Georgia hid a smile behind her own fan.

The song ended. "Your entrance was late," Mr. Barrett began. He pointed at Leighton. "You were flat." He turned to Fairfax. "And you had to scoop up to find the right pitch."

"The scoop was a stylistic choice!"

"They could keep this up all night," Georgia said with a shake of her head. "How are you at charades?"

Sally and Maggie had both been on her sofa, nodding off, when Uncle Edward and Aunt Eunice finally called it a night and Ashley escaped to her room. As soon as her maids finished helping her prepare for bed, she dismissed them. She sat on the edge of her bed in her night rail and wrapper, supplies on the bedside table.

One last task to complete.

"As pretty as you were in the green dress and jewels in your hair," Ravencroft softly rumbled, "I like this look even better." He captured her braid and used the tip of it to caress behind her ear, down her neck, and along her collarbone to the drawstring tie of her night rail.

She kept breathing only by conscious effort as she watched him play with her hair, reveling in the sensations he created. "I thought you were asleep when I left."

"Half asleep. Your maids have very firm opinions as to which hairstyle would flatter you most."

"Did their arguing disturb your rest?"

He shook his head. "It's a perspective I don't think I've ever heard before. All I knew is that my sisters take forever to get ready, but not why. Now I have a clue."

"With that clue, you are ahead of most gentlemen." She unwound the bandage on his forearm and gently wiped off the poultice, threw it in the fire, and stirred the preparation in a glass jar that she'd made earlier.

"No moldy bread?"

She sat beside him again. "At the academy, we used this recipe on less serious wounds and cuts. With the infection under control, I feel it's time to switch."

"Smells better."

"Honey, with powdered lavender, marigold, and comfrey. Want to try a taste?" She held up a spoonful, the golden liquid gleaming in the candlelight as it trickled back into the jar.

He grimaced. "I'll rely on your word that it's effective."

He took deep breaths, preparing himself for the discomfort he'd come to expect when she tended his arm. "Drink up." She handed him the cup of tea, heavy on the whisky because according to the sheet, Maggie and Sally had not given him any in all the hours she'd been gone. He was likely thirsty as well as in pain.

He saluted her with the cup before gulping it down.

"I met Mr. Barrett tonight." She glanced to gauge his reaction. He was staring into the bottom of this cup. "He asked about you." Thinking of the elderly gentleman calling out for his 'bassy boys,' she couldn't hold back a grin. "Westbrook told him you were at your estate." Her smile faded. "Barrett said what a tragedy it was about your father and brother."

David continued to stare into his cup as though it held the answers to all the questions in the universe, including those she hadn't dared ask. She proceeded with spreading on the honey preparation and the muslin dressing. When it came time to wind the bandage, David reached his hand between her arm and torso rather than expend the effort to hold up his arm. Without thinking, she tucked her arm close, trapping his hand. Through the loose fabric of her night rail and wrapper, she felt him caress her bicep with his thumb.

"I was at Barrett's house party when they died."

He uttered the words so quietly, she felt them more than heard them.

"He'd invited a dozen of us, some with their wives, to his estate. He and his wife never had children. They invite current and former students to join them every summer, to make music. Put on plays."

His eyes closed while she wound the muslin strip around his arm.

"He retired. This was the first time they'd invited us for Guy Fawkes Day. We wrote music to play during the fireworks display in the village. Liam and I were going to travel back to spend Christmas with our families, but snow kept falling, and we were having fun. Why travel in nasty weather?"

She tied off the bandage and rested his hand on her thigh, covering his fingers with her own. Just to check his temperature. Make sure the bandage wasn't too tight.

"A letter from my mother arrived just after New Year's Day, telling me Father was ill."

She wrapped her fingers around his.

"By the time I reached the house in London, not only had my father died of influenza, so had my elder brother. My mother didn't survive the combined strain of her grief and the illness. Two maids and a footman also succumbed. The butler greeted me at the door as Lord Ravencroft." He squeezed his eyes shut. "While I was off making merry, they were dying."

There was nothing she could say that would take away his grief or guilt, so she did the only thing she could, and held onto his hand. The fire crackled and the clock on the mantel ticked. Her mind raced.

"Was this January, two years ago?"

He nodded, barely moving his head.

"We had an outbreak of influenza at the academy that same winter. The girls were just returning after the holidays for the start of Hilary Term. Captain Blackthorn ended up quarantining with us, when he only intended to drop off his daughter. Our kitchen staff were the first to get sick. By the time it passed, we'd lost our assistant cook and one of our students."

Dark days, indeed. Ashley would never forget the sound of a duke's heart-wrenching sobs when he saw his deceased daughter. She shuddered.

"Did you get sick, too?" he rasped.

"I was the last to succumb. By then most of the staff had recovered or were on the mend. I was bedridden for over a fortnight."

He caressed her knuckles with his thumb. "Worn out from taking care of everyone else."

She ducked her chin. "I just tried to make myself useful."

"I read your journal. Or I should say, journals, plural. You essentially ran the school while Madame Zavrina and other senior staff were ill."

Rising from the bed to hide her discomfort, she fussed with things on the bedside table, tidying her supplies. "I only did what needed to be done, and delegated many of the tasks. Stretched so thin of able bodies, we all had to do things we don't normally do."

Ravencroft rolled out of bed. "Pretty *and* modest." Without bothering to pull on his banyan, he limped to the privacy screen.

Ashley made as much noise as she could to give him at least the illusion of privacy, putting away her containers and finding the food he hadn't eaten yet, and arranging it on a plate.

He returned a few moments later and sat on the edge of the bed before falling backward with a groan, arms flung out to the side. A moment later, he wrinkled his nose and tucked his arms close to his chest. "Eww. I don't think I can stand myself."

"The kitchen staff is asleep. I can heat water for a bath for you."

He scratched his head, his eyes closed. "Not unless you can sneak Gilroy in here. Feel like I just walked ten miles. In deep mud. No way I'd be able to haul my a—, uh, myself in and out of a tub."

Eyeing the full bucket of water still warming on the hearth, she bit her bottom lip. "I'll wash you." Amazed at her own audacity, she cleared her throat and lifted her chin. "I've already done it several times, while you were feverish. And besides, it's time to apply more ointment on your bruises." She gave his leg a gentle nudge.

He scooted onto the bed properly while she filled the ewer with warm water and brought it and the basin to the bed, and quickly collected a towel, soap, and a cloth.

Right. She'd done this several times while he was fighting the fever. No need for her heart to pound or hands to shake just because this time he was awake and alert. Watching her.

"Am I going to smell like rosemary and lavender?"

"This particular bar of Castile soap is unscented. But the ointment I'm going to apply in a few minutes has a strong rosemary scent, with undertones of lavender." She dipped the cloth in the basin of water, wrung it out, and rubbed a little bit of the soap on it. "I'm sorry, I don't have any bay rum on hand."

He watched her hands. "Would be an odd scent to be wafting out of your bedchamber. Someone might get the wrong idea. Like you were hiding a man in here."

A startled bubble of laughter escaped, and she covered her mouth.

He tugged her arm down. "Don't hide from me, Ashley."

Considering how exposed he was, lying on top of the blankets wearing nothing but his drawers, she nodded.

Arms relaxed at his sides, he closed his eyes and let out a little sigh.

Without him looking directly at her, she was able to go about the business of giving him a wash just like she had when he'd been feverish. Only this time she touched him everywhere three times— to wash, to rinse, and then to dry him so he wouldn't get chilled. She tried to keep a cloth between her hand and his naked flesh, but now and then her fingers would slip to the side and she'd find herself stroking him. His soft bare skin, over sleek contoured muscles. Touched the light smattering of crisp, curly hair on his chest, more felt than seen in the soft candlelight.

Having washed everywhere she could reach, she started to rise from the bed. He rolled to his side.

"Don't forget my back."

Looking at his long, strong, naked back, her mouth went dry. She swallowed. "You just want me to look at your bum."

His shoulders shook with laughter. Even though he buried his face in the pillow so the sound wouldn't carry, she felt the rumble.

"Stay here," she said when she'd finished washing and drying his back, and got the tin of ointment.

He let out a slight hiss when she smoothed the ointment on the bruises at his shoulder and upper back, cool at first, quickly warming from the heat of her fingers. When she got to his lower back and dipped her fingers just inside the waist of his drawers to reach the bottom edge of the bruises, he let out a quiet moan.

"Am I hurting you?"

"You have no idea," he muttered, so quietly she barely heard him.

She yanked her hand back, horrified she'd added to his discomfort.

"Got anything else to drink?"

"I set chamomile tea to brew a little while ago. Would you like a cup?"

He nodded and scratched his head.

Without thinking, she patted his upper arm before she rose from the bed. She stirred a spoonful of honey into the cup. "Here."

He slowly rolled over and sat up before he took the proffered cup and sipped. His brows rose and he licked his lips. "Honey?"

Staring at his mouth and thinking about the times she had smoothed healing balm over his split lip with her finger, she barely heard him.

He tilted his head to the side, and his knowing grin told her he probably recognized the lascivious direction of her thoughts.

"Yes. Honey." Spying the still open tin on the table, she cleared her throat. "I need to finish, uh, the rest of you." She gestured vaguely at his chest and grabbed the tin in case he misunderstood.

Watching his Adam's apple bob as he swallowed the rest of the tea, she forced herself to keep breathing. Setting the empty cup on the table gave her a moment to collect her unruly thoughts, so she was all business when she sat on the edge of the bed again, tin in hand.

"Um. This is easier if you lie back."

His smile had a mischievous glint as he sat there, their faces only inches apart. Before her breathing got out of control and she started panting, he finally lay back on the pillows.

As she massaged the ointment into the first bruise, he held up his left hand and examined his nails. "It's been a while since I was dirty with actual dirt." He scratched his head again.

"There was a lot of mud in your hair." Thinking back to his appearance when she'd first seen him after the fight, covered in mud and blood, she shuddered. "I could wash it for you." Confident she had smoothed the ointment on all his bruises—which were beginning to fade nicely—she put the lid on the tin.

He hadn't replied. Was staring at her.

"I often did it for patients in the infirmary. You won't even have to get out of bed. We can do it right here."

He raised one eyebrow and gave her a sly grin, and she realized how her words could be misconstrued.

She felt her face flush, probably to the roots of her hair. She wagged a finger at him and brought out her Teacher voice. "You are being naughty, sir. Do you want your hair washed or not?"

"Yes, ma'am. Please wash my hair." His words and tone were contrite, but his grin was not.

More towels—goodness, the extra laundry they were creating for Sally to wash!—and more warm water in the ewer.

"Scoot over a little, sideways on the bed." As soon as he was in position, she tugged one of the blankets up to his chest so he wouldn't get chilled, and replaced the pillow under his head with a folded towel. She dipped a cup in the water and dribbled it over his hair, making sure the excess fell into the basin on the floor and not the carpet. Using one hand to pour and the other to spread the water through his long strands, she soon had all of it dampened. "Does that hurt?" With her fingers she gently probed the edges of the goose egg on the back of his skull.

"Heavenly," he mumbled, his eyes closed.

Nonplussed, she rubbed her hands on the bar of soap and began to work it through his hair, occasionally lifting his head with one hand. She gently massaged his scalp with her fingertips and carded her fingers through his long hair, paying extra attention to the white streak. All in the name of loosening any dried mud that lingered, of course.

He made a little humming sound when she poured more warm water and continued massaging.

"You stopped singing and writing music after your parents and brother died."

He went silent. He was so still, he might have been holding his breath.

She changed the towel under his neck before water could soak the sheet, and noted the dirty color of the water dripping into the basin. She dribbled more warm water through his hair, then put soap on her hands again and worked it through. "Your mother put you in the music room when your leg was broken. So you could continue to play and compose while you healed."

His eyes flew open. He stared at her.

She slowly poured more water, working it through the silky strands. "It strikes me that music was important to your mother. And that she wanted you to develop your talent. Indeed, you are the most talented singer I've ever heard." Under any other circumstances she would likely never confess something this boldly to a gentleman acquaintance. But in the privacy of her candlelit bedchamber, performing this intimate act of service for a man she was beginning to think of as a friend, someone with whom she wanted to spend more time, she thought it important that he know.

He didn't preen at her compliment. Just continued to stare at her.

"And bear in mind, I have heard many other singers perform, even some who can sing as high and as low as you. Men who also consider the notes of the pianoforte merely a starting point for their range. Heard Lord Fairfax sing just this evening, in fact."

"Pox on Fairfax," he silently mouthed.

Chapter 14

His hair and scalp no longer felt gritty. She poured more water, concentrating on rinsing out all of the soap. Soon she had to empty the basin out the window and refill the ewer from the bucket on the hearth.

"You have any idea what it's like, inheriting a title when you haven't been raised and trained for it? Never wanted it?" he said when she sat on the bed again. "Suddenly being responsible for protecting the lives and livelihood of so many people? Servants, tenants, relatives who I barely knew existed? Taking a seat in the House of Lords? On top of losing three beloved family members at once?" His voice broke on 'beloved.'

She swept water from around his ears in an excuse to cup his cheeks and stare into his troubled hazel gaze. "No, I don't." She had lost both parents in one accident, in one afternoon. Her only immediate family. An orphan because of a broken axle. But she would not make this a competition about who had lost the most or which loss was more painful. "I can't imagine how much your life changed the instant you stepped over the threshold of the Ravencroft townhouse."

A little more rinsing, and the streak at the center of his forehead was white again instead of grey. "I have, however, observed that some gentlemen find a way to balance their responsibilities and their amusements. Find a way to share their talents and not hide their light under a bushel, and still give their title its due."

She dribbled more water, making sure to rinse every strand. Ravencroft continued to watch her. "I don't pretend to know what compromises or sacrifices are required to achieve at least an appearance of balance." She changed the towel under his neck again and poured more warm water, running her fingers through his hair.

"I just know what a pleasure it is to hear you sing and play. What a shame it would be if you didn't continue to perform." Surprised by the lump in her throat, she focused her gaze on his hair. On the water in the basin. Anywhere except his face.

He cleared his throat but didn't speak.

"I'm not the only one. You should have seen Lady Danforth tonight," she said, trying to lighten the mood. "She had to make do with Fairfax and Westbrook's singing."

"A pox on Fairfax," she said in unison with him. They shared a brief grin.

Satisfied the soap was all rinsed out, she wrung the water from his hair with her hands, then got a towel. She was leaning over, squeezing the towel on his long strands, when her stomach let out a growl, unmistakable in the quiet of her room.

Mortified that her body had again betrayed her in front of a gentleman, she refused to meet his gaze.

Fabric rustled, and she was startled to feel his hand on her stomach. No mistake. He definitely had his palm pressed to her abdomen. It felt more intimate than if he cupped her breast. She glanced from his hand to his face.

"Don't suffer on my behalf, Ashley. You haven't been keeping enough food for yourself." He spread his fingers, gently caressing her. "You need to eat more."

It took her a moment to remember to breathe. "The scullery maid is probably asleep by now. After I dry and brush your hair I'll go down and raid the pantry."

"That's my girl." He closed his eyes and dropped his hand ... to her leg.

Her heart hammered in her chest. *My girl* echoed in her mind. She forced her arms back into action, gently drying his hair.

"This part is easier if you can sit up." She guided him into position so he was properly arranged on the bed, pillows bracing him from behind, the blankets pulled up to his lap. She brought his bag of toiletries to the bed and rummaged inside until she found his brush. "Westbrook sent this over."

"If Gilroy packed it, there should be a bottle of hair oil."

She fished out a small, corked bottle.

David nodded. "Gilroy's secret recipe. He negotiated a monthly allowance to buy the ingredients. Apparently he didn't like the way

I cursed at him when he combed out the tangles when I first hired him."

She pulled out the cork and sniffed the bottle—the scent reminded her of the coconuts Uncle Edward had brought back to England—then held it close to David. After he sniffed and nodded approval, she poured a small amount of the liquid onto her palm, rubbed her hands together, and worked it through his hair.

Face-to-face was so much more intimate than sitting at the dressing table while a maid stood behind her to do her hair. She thought about climbing onto the bed to sit behind him, but the idea of her feet and legs on the bed with him somehow seemed even more indecorous. Too brazen, even for her.

Any awkwardness faded when he closed his eyes and leaned into her touch. Too softly for her to hear it, she felt him humming as she gently worked through the knots. This would be much easier if she had thought to brush his hair each day, instead of letting the mud dry on his head and the pillowcase, and then stay messy and damp during his fever.

She tried to brush it into the style she remembered him wearing, using her fingers to lift and separate the chestnut-colored strands and slowly let them fall. To speed the drying process, of course. Not because she was enjoying the freedom of touching his luxurious, almost shoulder length hair. And since he had played with her hair several times, it seemed only fair. Did he feel the same kind of delicious tingles when she touched his hair, as when he toyed with hers?

At last all of the tangles were out. Reluctantly she set the brush on the bedside table and stood, retying the belt on her wrapper. Only then did he open his eyes.

"I'm going on a raid. Any requests?"

"Take no prisoners. Return triumphant."

She smiled as she left. She tiptoed down the stairs, careful of the third one that creaked, and made her way through the dark hallways down to the kitchen, her knitted wool slippers keeping her footsteps silent. She couldn't do any cooking, as the scullery maid was asleep on her pallet before the hearth. What food might Mrs. Gillespie and the cook have in the larder that was ready to eat?

Carrying a wicker basket filled with her bounty, she hurried back upstairs, quietly shut her door ... and swallowed a pang of disappointment when she realized David had covered up and fallen asleep.

She emptied her basket on the table by the window. Though her stomach growled again, none of the food seemed appealing.

"Is there enough to share with the rest of the class, miss?"

Ashley nearly jumped a foot in the air at the low voice just inches from her ear. She whirled and found Ravencroft standing *right there*, even closer than when they had waltzed. She held her hand over her pounding heart, catching her breath.

He arched one eyebrow, his little grin letting her know he'd enjoyed startling her.

She was about to push him away until she realized his chest was naked because he had not put on his banyan. "Wretch."

"Hungry wretch," he agreed good-naturedly, poking through the food on the table. He picked up a tea cake and popped it in his mouth.

She lightly smacked his hand when he reached for another. "Have something of substance before you eat sweets." She pointed at the cold roast beef.

He shivered.

Reflexively she reached up to feel his forehead, and he ducked to make it easier for her to reach. No fever. "Put on your banyan and go sit by the fire, or get back in bed."

"Always ordering me to bed," he muttered as he walked away, "but never comes with me."

Her cheeks heated.

He tied the banyan's belt as he came back to the table, where Ashley was piling food on a plate.

The only plate. She had forgotten to grab another.

"Let's share." He wrapped his left arm around her shoulders and steered her to the sofa, which had been slid back into place in front of the fire after her bath this morning. Sitting side by side, close so they could easily share the food, they ate cold roast beef and ham, walnuts and cheese, tea cakes, scones smeared with clotted cream, and drank wine from the same bottle because she'd remembered the corkscrew but forgot to get any glasses.

Periodically she reached up to play with his hair, lifting the soft strands. Checking to see how well it was drying, of course. Making sure it hadn't gone flat in back when he'd lain down. Had nothing to do with the intimacy of sitting beside a handsome man while they were both clad only in their nightwear, or the amount and type of alcohol she'd consumed.

What she'd thought was claret to go with the beef turned out to be a bottle of port. Heady stuff. She was thirsty so she drank it anyway. He'd drank her chamomile tea and she'd been too distracted to put more on to brew.

Eventually she set the empty plate on the arm of the sofa with a contented sigh, the half-empty bottle at her feet on the floor. They sat together quietly contemplating the glowing coals, and she found herself leaning toward him. It felt natural for him to put his left arm around her shoulders and pull her close, and that spot on his chest just made for resting her cheek.

Beneath the scent of rosemary and lavender ointment, he smelled fresh and clean, of masculine shaving soap and barely-there exotic hair oil, and beneath that something even more elemental, something unique to Ravencroft. She could happily fall asleep right here, with her head on his chest, feeling him breathe, knowing he was healing.

It wouldn't last, though. Snuggling with a man in her life was just a brief interlude. A fantasy, like dreaming while awake. In a few days he'd be strong enough to leave. They'd go back to behaving properly. Follow Society's rules. Address each other formally. "I wonder if this is what husbands and wives do at the end of the day."

"Maybe some of them," he rumbled.

She startled, unaware she'd spoken the words out loud. "Too bad I'll never find out."

"Why? Isn't that your goal in taking part in the Season? To find a husband?"

She shifted, searching for that perfect spot to lay her head on his chest again, and patted his hand where it rested on her shoulder. "My aunt and uncle's goal. I no longer have delusions about finding a match. Before I go back to working at a school I just want to dance. With men." She felt like purring as he stroked her upper arm. "I often helped with dance lessons, taking the man's part so the girls could learn the steps."

"Why is finding a match delusional?"

If her outer ear were stopped up, she could still follow his conversation, just from feeling the words rumbling in his chest.

"Because I'm a bluestocking. Because I'm too old. I'm almost a spinster, you know." Silly man. She traced the outline of the fading bruises on his right hand, so close to her the way he held his injured arm upright, against his chest. Would they hurt when he put on gloves? He'd have to wear gloves when he left, to hide the bruises. The scrapes.

"No, I don't know. Enlighten me."

She let out a sigh. "So far the only men who have shown an interest in me are utterly unsuitable, like Rupert." She shuddered, and went completely still when David gave her a gentle squeeze and kissed the top of her head.

"On behalf of all men, I apologize that you were ever introduced to that bas— blighter."

She patted his left hand again while she attempted to regain her equilibrium. "Or older men, widowers who want a mother figure for their children. Perhaps I've read too many folk tales where the stepmother was not a nice person or was not treated well." Remembering the conversation with Georgia and Clarissa, she quickly added, "It does work out sometimes. Your sister Diana seems happy. But the way my life has gone so far, I would not wager on it."

"What will you do, then? Move to Jamaica with your aunt and uncle rather than go back to your cousin?"

She shook her head, in part to rub her cheek against his chest. "Find work at another school. The positive aspect of being a spinster is that I've reached majority status. If I can support myself, I do not need to rely on a male relative. I've already sent out several letters in response to help wanted advertisements."

Thinking of the three replies she'd received so far, all rejections, perhaps she would have another swig of the port wine to help swallow her disappointment and frustration. But to reach it she'd have to move from her comfy spot on David's chest. This was so nice, leaning against his big strong body. She could go to sleep right here, with his arm wrapped around her. Between his warmth and that of the fire, she didn't even need a blanket. "What about you? Do you think you'll find a match before the end of the Season?"

"No. I'm never going to marry."

She lifted her head to look at his face. "Why? That's—"

He shook his head. "I don't care about passing on the title. My cousin can inherit it."

"But don't you want a wife?" Such a shame. Somebody should have the pleasure of cuddling with him like this. Hear him, no, *feel* him sing.

"And have my bride recoil in horror on our wedding night when she spies these mismatched, deformed pins?" He pointed at his knees. "No, thank you. I decided a long time ago that was an experience I could go my whole life without."

Resting her palm on his chest, she searched his face. He seemed resigned rather than sad or angry. "Wouldn't she know about them beforehand? Even if you two weren't ... intimate ... before the wedding?" She felt her cheeks flush. "It's hard to keep a secret. Even though you think your mother didn't know, there are people who do. Your tailor, cobbler, Gilroy. And Westbrook must know, too. Those men would certainly keep your confidence, but what about the fellows you went to school with? There's precious little privacy in a school dormitory. How can you possibly expect them all to keep quiet?"

"Blackmail."

He said it with such calm conviction, so matter-of-factly, she was startled into letting out a giggle.

"Everyone has secrets, Ashley." With a fingertip he smoothed a loose strand of hair away from her face.

She closed her eyes and leaned into his touch, until she was resting her cheek on his chest again. He slouched into the corner of the sofa, pulling her with him. She snuggled against him and tucked her feet up on the sofa cushion. "I wonder what Lord Fairfax's secret is."

"He's actually a soprano."

Ashley giggled again.

Sally shook her awake. "I'm sorry miss, but you asked me to make sure you were awake by now."

Ashley's eyes flew open. With a guilty start she looked down, relieved there was nothing on the sofa with her except her blanket and pillow. A quick glance confirmed that Ravencroft was asleep in her bed. Apparently he'd slipped out from under her and gone to bed after covering her with the blanket.

She sat up, too quickly, and held her pounding head. Only by great effort did she refrain from groaning. Just how much had she had to drink last night? She held her hands to her flaming cheeks. Had she actually fallen asleep on Ravencroft?

"Do you want me to request a tray be brought up here?"

Ashley stood up. "No, I need to go eat with my aunt. Can't have her coming in here to check on me." The mere idea of food made her stomach roil. Perhaps she could bring most of it upstairs for Ravencroft.

She had dressed and just about ready to go downstairs when Ravencroft rolled over in bed and apparently bumped his arm, as he let out a startled oath and clutched his hand to his chest. He panted, beads of perspiration dotting his forehead, his eyes squeezed shut.

Sally and Maggie had already taken the dirty laundry downstairs, so Ashley gave him a cup of willow bark tea and whisky. "Do you need anything else before I leave?" His hair was mussed and whisker stubble darkened his cheeks again. It took great effort to resist the urge to run her fingers through his hair.

He shook his head and gave her back the empty cup before lying back with a groan.

She considered mixing a cup for herself to help with her headache but decided against it. Leave the whisky for Ravencroft. She updated the paper with the time he'd been given a dose and went down to breakfast.

When she returned, carrying her cup of chocolate in addition to two soft-boiled eggs in her pockets, Maggie and Sally were fussing with garments on the drying rack in front of the fireplace.

"I'm ever so sorry, miss," Maggie said, her voice wavering with misery.

"We've tried and tried," Sally said. "But we just can't get the stains out of the gown you were wearing when you rescued his lordship."

If she were still working at the academy, Ashley would dye the yellow gown to a tan or brown until the stains became invisible. But she didn't have to exercise such strict economies. At least not yet. "Take it with you this afternoon. If you can get anything for it at the linen draper's, put the funds toward buying Maggie a change of uniform. If not, do with it as you please."

"Yes, miss."

"What about his lordship's mud-stained trousers?" Maggie was practically in tears. "And the bloodstains on his waistcoat." She lifted up a corner of the garment in question. "Such beautiful embroidery, and it's ruined. All on account of me."

"I'm sure he has others. We'll simply let Gilroy know to send over replacements for these items as well." She gripped Maggie's shoulders and made sure the young woman was looking at her when she spoke again. "I am confident his lordship does not regret ruining his clothes in order to defend you."

Tears welled in Maggie's eyes, and she sniffed. "Thank you, miss."

"Now help me get changed, please. Aunt wants me to visit the shops on Bond Street with her before her at-home later today."

Ashley sat on the sofa in the front parlour, struggling to keep her eyes open and her attention on possibly the most deadly dull conversation she'd ever heard: decorations for bonnets. Aunt Eunice and her friends had very strong opinions as to the attractiveness of feathers versus wax fruit, while Lady Donkin waxed poetic about silk roses. Ashley's head pounded less and she was finally feeling hungry. Perhaps eating one of the little cakes would help her be more alert.

From the corner of her eye, she saw Sally in the parlour doorway, making a tiny but frantic gesture to catch her attention.

"Excuse me," Ashley murmured as she left the room.

"Beg pardon, miss, you've got to come upstairs," Sally urgently whispered. "We can't get him to be quiet!"

Had Ravencroft injured himself again? Ripped out his stitches and was writhing in agony?

Ashley gathered her skirts, dashed up the stairs, and hurried down the hall. Long before she reached her room, she heard Ravencroft's deep rumbling voice.

Singing.

Maggie stood just outside the closed door, twisting her apron in her hands.

"You two keep an eye out. Distract anyone who might come near."

"Yes, miss," Maggie and Sally replied in unison.

Ashley entered her room and quietly shut the door behind her.

Ravencroft was sitting up in bed, freshly shaved, his hair combed, moving his arm as though conducting an orchestra, his eyes closed. No, the gesture was smaller, as though writing in the air with his finger, his deep voice making sounds as if he played an instrument rather than singing actual words. "*Dum da dum, bum da da dum.*"

She rushed to the bed. "David, you have to be quiet," she pleaded.

He began singing another stanza, finger still writing in the air, his eyes closed as though he could read what he'd written.

She sat on the edge of the bed and grabbed his moving hand, trying not to panic. "Your voice carries. They can hear you out in the hall!"

"Oh, good. An aud'ence." His words seemed slurred as he began singing again, making the same sounds as if he played the viola da gamba.

"You have to be quiet, *now*! You have to—" She let go his hand to cup his cheeks and kissed him.

That shut him up.

After a stunned moment, she pulled back. Her lips tingled. She let her hands slowly fall from grasping his face, tracing down his neck, over the bump of his Adam's apple, and caress his bare chest. He wasn't usually awake when she touched him. It gave her an unaccustomed sense of power to see his eyes widen and his pupils flare. Because of her.

He sat perfectly still, his lips slightly parted, staring at her.

When he drew breath to speak, she leaned forward and dropped another kiss on his mouth. She had wondered what it would be like to kiss him, to touch that full lower lip, the perfect cupid's bow on top, with her lips and not just her finger.

Heavenly.

She sat up straight, her heart pounding at her brazenness, confident she had made her point and that he would not start singing again.

A slow smile spread across his face, lighting up his hazel eyes. He cupped her cheeks and drew her in. "Oh, yes," he murmured. "I knew it'd be like this." He kissed her thoroughly, deeply.

Heedless of potential damage to her reputation, she threaded her fingers through his hair and returned his kiss with reckless abandon, savoring every moment. She might never again kiss a man. Kiss *this* man. He hummed in delight and swept his thumbs across her cheeks as his fingers teased the edge of her hair. Shivers of pleasure followed his touch. She swayed closer, shamelessly wanting more.

He tasted of warm, smoky whisky and something earthy, probably the willow bark tea. His lips were soft and smooth, meeting hers in an age-old dance. He caressed her neck and stroked the hollow of her throat before trailing callused fingertips along her collarbone. How had she lived this long without this man's touch, this tender attention? Her stomach swirled wildly and she held her breath as his fingers dipped lower, down her décolletage, lower still.

His lips left her.

Disappointed the kiss had ended so soon, she opened her eyes.

In time to see his eyes roll back in his head. He toppled backwards, flopping onto the pillows.

She froze, her mouth agape.

She blinked.

He snored.

In disbelief, she plowed her fingers through her hair, heedless of the hairpins she dislodged.

Her first passionate kiss, ever. And he passed out. In the middle of it.

She leaned forward. "David?" she whispered.

The left side of his mouth curved slightly, as though he was having a pleasant dream, but he did not stir.

Now she realized he didn't just taste of whisky, she could smell it on his breath.

She grabbed the paper off the bedside table. No one had given him more whisky since her dose before she went down to breakfast. Actually, now that she studied it more closely, no one else had written on the paper. All of the entries were in her own hand.

She opened the door and gestured for Sally and Maggie to enter. "How did you get him to be quiet, miss?"

Ashley waved her hand holding the sheet of paper. "Neither of you have marked this. Did you give him any whisky today?"

"I gave him a cup when he ate the eggs this morning," Sally said.

"But you didn't note it on the paper?"

Sally looked down at her shoes. "No, miss."

"And you, Maggie? Have you given him any whisky today?"

Maggie also found the toes of her shoes fascinating. "Yes, miss." Her words were so quiet, Ashley had to strain to hear her. "When he was shaving. He wouldn't let me help him 'cuz he sat at the dressing table to see in the mirror, but he let me give him a cup."

"And you also did not note it on this paper. Why?"

Maggie's apron was getting horribly wrinkled with all the twisting in her hands. "I can't," she whispered. "I don't know how."

"And you?"

Sally shook her head. "I can read and write my name, but not much else."

Ashley felt her knees ready to buckle. She sat down hard on the foot of the bed, one arm wrapped around the bedpost for support. "How foolish of me," she muttered to herself. She was about to wad up the useless piece of paper and throw it on the fire, but reconsidered and placed it back on the bedside table. "I owe you both an apology," she said, looking at both maids. "I am accustomed to being at a school for young ladies where we can take it for granted that everyone has already been taught to read and write." She determined to teach Maggie and Sally to read, if they wanted to learn. Then she thought back to the previous few days. "But if you can't read my shopping lists, how did you collect everything?"

"You told me what you needed. What shops to visit," Sally said. "I handed the list to the salesclerks, and they'd gather what things they sold."

Ashley sat at the end of the bed again, absently pushing Ravencroft's foot out of her way. He snored and shifted without waking up. "But what about the hairstyles you copied from *La Belle Assemblée* for me? You replicated them perfectly."

Sally's posture straightened. "Yes, miss. I'm very good at copying."

"Without being able to read the instructions," Ashley said to herself. "Amazing."

Sally and Maggie exchanged glances. "Beg pardon, miss," Maggie said, "what was wrong with his lordship? How did you get him to be quiet?"

Ashley stood and shook out her skirts. "He's cup-shot." She glanced at his face, realized she was touching her fingers to her lips, and clasped her hands at her waist. "He passed out."

Sally's jaw dropped.

Maggie giggled.

"You both gave him a dose, as did I when you were out of the room." She did a swift calculation. "In four hours' time, we collectively gave him what should have been administered over the course of twelve hours." She blew out a deep breath, puffing her cheeks.

"Girls, we got him drunk."

Chapter 15

MAGGIE'S BROW FURROWED. "I ain't never known a gent who could get castaway on the little bit we give him." She picked up the whisky bottle, which was still a quarter full. "Why, some of the men who've tupped me can drink an entire bottle or two and still be wide awake, randy as a stallion."

This time the giggle came from Sally.

Ashley moved farther away from the bed and cleared her throat, desperately trying not to picture Ravencroft awake, sober, and, er, randy.

"He seemed so happy," Maggie continued. "Singing, but I couldn't understand the words. Wonder what language it was." She wrapped an arm around the bedpost and leaned against it, staring at Ravencroft. "Drink don't change a man. Just takes away his mask."

"Reveals who he truly is," Sally quietly agreed.

Ashley stared at the maids, thinking how sheltered her life had been compared to theirs.

"Wish I'd known that the first time Big Bob was drunk and hit me. When he sobered up, he said he was sorry and promised he'd never do it again. But he did." Maggie took a deep breath and shook her whole body, as though dislodging the memory. She pointed at Ravencroft. "Even drunk, he's kind. Hasn't tried to pinch me bottom even once. Speaks to me polite-like, as if I weren't a whore. Even though he wouldn't let me help him spill his seed." She gasped. "Oh! Maybe he likes boys instead of girls?"

Ashley choked.

"His preferences ain't none of our business," Sally said brusquely.

"You are a prostitute no longer," Ashley said. "Unless you want to go back to that work? You don't have to become a maid."

"Oh, no miss! I'm ever so grateful to you! Being a maid is so much better."

"I just want you to have a choice. Sally has enjoyed training you—" she paused to give Sally a chance to respond; she nodded enthusiastically— "and I'm thankful for the extra help these last few days. I'd be in a real pickle if not for both of you."

"I've been *very* happy the last few days," Sally softly said, a dreamy smile lighting her face.

Did her maid harbor feelings for Ravencroft, too?

Ashley checked in the mirror to see what damage she'd done to her hair when she plowed her fingers through it, and replaced pins where curls were coming loose. "I'm going back downstairs. As soon as Aunt's guests leave, I'll write the note for you to deliver to Gilroy."

Restless in her room that afternoon, alone except for the still-sleeping Ravencroft, Ashley gave up trying to nap on the sofa. Every time she closed her eyes, she relived their kiss. *I knew it'd be like this.* He'd thought about kissing her? As often as she'd thought about kissing him?

The wooden case with the lyre caught her eye. She hadn't touched it since Lady Mansfield had sent it over. Eager to distract herself from lascivious thoughts, she selected a sheet of music that looked easy to learn, and sat at her desk to play.

"You're terrible," Ravencroft softly rumbled a while later, so faint she barely heard him. "Worse than I am on mandolin."

She dropped the lyre on her desk, her cheeks flaming.

"Didn't say for you t' stop." He opened his eyes and rolled toward her, his elbow bent, head propped on his hand. "Only way t' get better is practice."

"That was a very blunt statement." She traced her finger over the carved design on the lyre's wood frame. She stopped.

She stared at Ravencroft. "You're still drunk!"

He squinted and held his thumb and forefinger about half an inch apart, and grinned.

She swiveled in her chair so she fully faced him and propped her elbows on her knees, keeping her voice low. "Maggie expressed surprise that you became inebriated on so little alcohol compared to most, er, men of her acquaintance."

"She the one who looks like she should still be in a schoolroom?"

Ashley nodded. "She was disappointed you wouldn't let her shave you."

He tugged the blanket higher. "Stares at me like I'm a buffet and she hasn't eaten in a week."

As she'd probably been guilty of looking at him the same way, Ashley remained silent.

"You found out 'nother secret. Can't hold my liquor." He yawned and rolled onto his back, stretching his arms over his head. It took all of Ashley's self-control to keep her gaze on his face. Thank heavens for peripheral vision, so she didn't completely miss this new view. "Get foxed faster than a twelve-year-old schoolboy. Is why I don't usually drink." He relaxed and let his arms rest on the pillows above his head. "Just a sip here an' there t' not draw 'tention t' fact I'm not drinking."

Ashley frowned. "But you asked for whisky. I offered you the choice of laudanum, and you chose—"

He shuddered and brought his arms back to his chest, and some of Ashley's brain could focus elsewhere again. "Friend broke his arm falling off a horse. Used opium for pain. Two years later, he still can't go without. Needs more all the time." He shuddered again. "Don' wanna be like him."

"Whisky was an acceptable alternative? Even though it meant getting drunk, or at least a bit castaway?"

"My arm hurts like hell, and I'd rather be half-foxed than whimpering." His voice climbed at least an octave with the admission, though still quiet. "Have a care for my manly pride, Miss Hamlin." He rolled toward her again, and his voice dropped to a seductive rumble. "You threatened t' bite me the night we met."

Her jaw dropped. She snapped it closed, as she couldn't deny his accusation because she didn't remember. It did sound like something she might say, though. If she felt threatened. The idea of biting him made her think about flinging back the blankets, climbing atop him, and tasting him. Just little nips with her teeth, on his warm, bare skin. She'd soothe the marks with kisses. And her tongue. She cleared her throat. "I did?"

He must have heard the squeak in her voice, as that slow grin spread across his face again. "I trust you t' stop me if I do an'thing ungen'lemanlike."

Her heart raced, thinking of their kiss. Far from stopping him, she'd encouraged him. All but threw herself into his arms. The fact *she* had been the one to initiate the kiss did not bear thinking on.

She buried her face in her hands. Having him here, right there in her bed, half naked, handsome and flirting—flirting! with *her*!— was becoming a temptation, and she feared she was getting weaker the more he regained his strength. He trusted her, but she didn't trust herself. Not after this afternoon. Not now that she knew how it felt to kiss him, for him to kiss her in return. He had to go. Before she did something beyond foolish and became a cautionary tale.

"Westbrook and I have devised a plan. How you can leave."

He propped his head on his hand again. "Does it involve sneaking out in the dark of night?"

She shook her head. "You're going to walk out the front door in the middle of the afternoon."

His eyebrows rose.

"Tomorrow, you and Mr. Westbrook are going to pay a call on me, to deliver a gift from Lady Mansfield. This lyre." She tapped the instrument. "But inside the package will be Gilroy's coat and hat. Maggie and Sally will help you two switch in the back hallway, and Gilroy will exit through the mews."

David's brow furrowed as he thought through her plan. "How fortuitous I had the foresight to hire a manservant of a similar build as me." He glanced down at his bare chest. "But what will I be wearing besides a coat and hat?"

He was baiting her, and she grinned. "Sally has been meeting Gilroy every day and collecting articles of your clothing from him. They're hidden in my wardrobe."

David glanced over his shoulder, at her dressing room. "Why, Miss Hamlin, how brazen of you, mingling our clothing."

His wicked smile and slow emphasis on the last three words sent tingles down her spine.

Only when Maggie and Sally returned did Ashley trust herself to change the poultice on David's arm. He didn't sit up in bed, but held up his arm without tucking it against her.

If all went according to plan, she would only do this for him one more time. By tomorrow afternoon, his manservant would be the one tending David's wound.

"I sent this recipe to Gilroy today," she said as she spread more of the honey preparation on a dressing. "I'll send a jar of it with your things tomorrow, to give him time to make his own. You should use it for at least another week."

"Honey," David murmured, looking at her through half-lidded eyes.

"Yes, that's the main ingredient." She continued to wind the bandage.

The evening dragged on tortuously slow. Not even spending time with Georgia and Miss Kenyon could shake Ashley's melancholy. Things might have been different if they were attending a ball and she had the chance to dance. Instead Aunt Eunice and Uncle Edward took her to the home of friends for a card party, and then to another rout. Neither Westbrook nor Fairfax, nor any of the other singers she'd come to enjoy hearing, were present at either gathering.

Amidst the noise of conversation and tinkling glassware, Ashley heard David's voice in her head. Singing. Humming. Whatever he'd been doing yesterday afternoon, the sounds he'd been making, before she silenced him with a kiss. She didn't recognize the tune. Had he been creating a new composition? She played it in her head over and over, hoping she remembered the notes correctly. Wondering if she'd ever hear the rest of it.

After Sally and Maggie helped her prepare for bed, she brought out the slates and chalk she'd had them pick up on their errands earlier that day, and gave them their first reading lesson before she dismissed them for the night.

As she put away the chalk, Ashley noticed letters on a silver salver waiting on her desk, next to the papers she had Sally buy that were preprinted with lines for composing music. It had been a gamble that such paper would be available from a stationer rather than needing to go to a shop that catered to musicians. The stack was thinner than she remembered. Perhaps those had indeed been paper ashes she'd noticed in the fireplace. Several sheets on top of the stack were filled with musical notations.

"You've been busy," she said under her breath, trying to hear the notes in her head as she looked over the music. None of it seemed to match the tune he'd been singing when she kissed him.

"Yes, I was." David rolled over and sat up on the side of the bed nearest the desk, swinging his feet to the floor. "My apologies. I didn't intend to use so much of your paper. I'm out of practice."

She held up one of the sheets. "It was purchased for you." She smiled at his expression of surprise. "Is this composition intended for voice, or a particular instrument?"

"Haven't decided yet. Was just trying to get the melody down." In an adorable gesture, he shrugged with one shoulder and gave her a bashful grin. He slipped his arms into his banyan as he rose from the bed and limped to the privacy screen.

Peers of the realm were not adorable, she told herself sternly, even if they were sitting on her bed half naked with mussed hair. To distract herself, she broke open the seal on the top letter. *"Thank you for your inquiry into the vacancy on our staff. We regret to inform you..."* Trying to ignore the sting of rejection, she tossed it aside and opened the next. *"While commendable, we feel your experience is not suitable..."* She tossed that one aside, too, barely resisting the urge to slam her fist on the desk. How in Hades was she going to support herself if she couldn't secure another position?

Tears blurred her vision when she realized the next letter was from Mrs. Rafferty. She hugged it to her chest.

"Bad news, honey?" David stood behind her chair, one hand resting on her shoulder.

Ashley sniffed and composed herself. "Those were." She pointed at the first two letters. "But this is from a former colleague. A teacher who became a dear friend." She cleared her throat. "You would consider her a friend also, as this week I've used much of what she taught me." Briefly, she closed her eyes as she felt him gently squeeze her shoulder. "It is her recipes I've been using for the honey poultice and healing balms." She rose but he did not step away, and without thinking she darted her tongue out to lick her lips, remembering what his felt like on hers. She cleared her throat. "It's time to change your bandage."

As he was wide awake, they sat at the table by the window, her supplies close at hand. David slipped his right arm out of the banyan and rested it on the table, palm up. Ashley struggled to focus her attention on his arm and not his bare shoulder and chest, glowing golden in the candlelight.

"When the school closed, Mrs. Rafferty was kind enough to let me keep her copy of Culpeper's *Complete Herbal*. She knew it so well she could practically recite it. She kept the apothecary chest, though." Ashley removed the old bandage and set it aside.

"The new owners didn't want the chest?"

Ashley flattened her lips at the unpleasant memory. "Madame Zavrina's brother said he had no need for it, as a doctor was among the first clients to sign up for a membership in his new establishment. He calls it a club, but everyone knows it's a brothel."

"He turned the school into a brothel? His sister must be rolling over in her grave."

Ashley stared at him. "You're the first person not to laugh."

"Well, it is funny." He coughed. "Mildly. I was thinking of you and the other staff, the teachers. How hard it must have been to lose someone close to you as well as your employment."

"And my home," she whispered as she applied the poultice. "He gave us a fortnight's notice to pack up and leave. Unless we wanted to stay and work for him. Those he deemed not pretty enough to entertain customers were welcome to work in the kitchen or as maids." She licked some of the honey mixture from her thumb and index fingertip.

As she reached for the strip of muslin, she realized his gaze was fixated on her mouth. Reflexively, she swiped her tongue over her lips, making certain she didn't miss any honey.

David groaned, she'd swear he did, but he shifted in his seat, making his chair creak, so she couldn't be certain. He gestured at the letters on the desk with his free arm. "Are you still in communication with any of your other colleagues?"

"Mrs. Rafferty is the only one so far. I was among the last to leave so I was able to say goodbye to everyone." Ashley began winding the muslin bandage on his arm. "Miss Chase and I would pore over maps while she prepared her geography lessons and talk of traveling to far off places. She especially wanted to visit Spain. I wonder if she's found a way to go there." Ashley gathered up the soiled muslin. "Stay put."

The old bandage sizzling on the coals, she retrieved fresh muslin strips and sat down again to finish. David rested his elbow on the table, his forearm raised. He repeatedly flexed the fingers of his right hand, grimacing as he did so.

"Are you in pain?"

"It itches." He grimaced again and twisted his arm back and forth.

"That's a good sign. It's healing." She grasped his hand. "Don't scratch."

"I know," he gritted out.

After a moment she realized she was still holding his hand. She cleared her throat and let go. "After the academy closed, Miss Blackwell left England to help her uncle with the illustrations for another book on flora. Those are her drawings in the gardening journal, not mine."

"And here I thought you were a talented artist." His low rumble was a soothing caress to her senses, his half-smile melting her insides.

"Sorry to disappoint. My watercolors and sketching are mediocre at best." She lingered with the muslin strips, fussing with how tight to make each wrap. A question she had been wanting to ask was on the tip of her tongue. A very personal question. Impertinent. Miles beyond topics of polite discourse. But the idea had plagued her since she recovered from her initial shock of their kiss. *I knew it would be like this.*

An owl hooted just outside the window, reminding her they were alone, late at night, in a darkened bedchamber.

Tomorrow he was leaving. She may never again find the opportunity to quench her desire to know this one thing.

"The other night, you said you don't intend to marry. You said you didn't want to, ah, watch your bride recoil in horror when she sees that your legs don't match. Sees the scar on your thigh."

His expression became more guarded, but he said nothing.

"Maggie said—" she had to clear her throat— "Maggie said you wouldn't let her, ah, help you ... um, relieve tension."

She wasn't sure whose face was getting redder, hers or David's. The flush on his cheeks spread down his face to his neck and ... oh my, to the top of his bare chest.

In for a penny. He already knew her to be brazen. She had abducted a peer of the realm, stripped him of his clothing, tended his wounds. Bathed his body. Washed his hair. "Does that mean you, ah..." She licked her lips. She definitely had not thought all the way through the phrasing of this question. At least not with words she could bring herself to say out loud. And truly, the answer was none of her affair. She had no right to ask. "That you've never..."

He was so still, she wasn't even sure he was breathing. But he didn't look away. He met her gaze, unblinking. Just stared back at her, his chin slightly lowered so that he peered at her through his thick lashes.

Only the fine tremor in his forearm, which she held, and the fluttering pulse at his throat, betrayed his roiling emotions.

He raised one eyebrow and tilted his head toward her. "No."

No? No, that's not what it meant, or no, he'd never...

"I've never felt ... the need ... strongly enough to want to risk a companion's response."

So quietly did he utter the words, she barely heard them over the pounding of her pulse. Surely it beat so loud he could hear it, too.

She didn't realize she was licking her lips again until his gaze dipped down to her mouth. She tucked her tongue back inside. She wasn't a tease, wasn't trying to lure him into any behavior. She just had an insatiable curiosity to know this one detail about him.

Well, to know *everything* about him, if she were to be honest with herself.

He pulled his arm closer to his chest when she tried to finish tying off the bandage, drawing her with it. "Have you?"

Disconcerted to realize she'd leaned farther across the table, closer to him, she almost missed his quiet question. As impertinent and brazen as her own, yet also fair under the circumstances. She flattened her lips to resist the urge to lick them again. "There has not been anyone for whom I felt strongly enough to risk my reputation, let alone the possibility of conceiving a child outside of wedlock."

"Practical and pragmatic," he softly replied, stretching his arm back to within easier reach for her. He lowered his raised eyebrow to match the other, and then briefly dipped it as he spoke, a gesture she found endearing. "Just as I thought." Not quite a wink. More subtle.

Still did things to her heart rate.

They really needed to stop talking about intimate topics because her mind's eye was providing all sorts of inappropriate images. Not helped by the actual view in front of her of his chest, bare on one side, covered on the other but naked beneath the silk.

She cleared her throat. "A woman has few things that are truly her own. Her reputation is one of them. I couldn't stop it if people were to choose to shred my reputation, but I do what I can to deny them fodder for gossip." She tied off the bandage, reluctantly ending her physical contact with him. For both their sakes. She was quite aware there was a large bed behind her, a comfortable sofa in front of the fire, and a mostly naked man in arm's reach. Her supply of self-discipline was not unlimited.

"Until you decided to hide a man in your bed." He slipped his arm into his banyan sleeve. The garment still gaped open, revealing his chest.

Lest her hands reach over of their own volition to stroke that lovely bare skin, she busied herself putting away her supplies. She knew how it felt beneath her fingers, applying ointment. How would it feel to touch him simply for the sake of caressing him? "I'd do it again." Her voice was barely a whisper. She raised her chin, letting her voice get stronger. "You were hurt and alone. No one else stepped forward. Gilroy and Westbrook weren't around. What else could I do?" *Take him to his sister.* "And at first I thought you'd be able to leave in just a few hours, before the staff returned from their half-day off."

He rose when she did. When she returned from putting things away on the bookcase, he'd taken only a few halting steps toward the bed. Thankfully for the sake of her self-control, he'd closed the banyan and tied the belt.

Without conscious thought, she took his left arm by the elbow and steered him toward the bed.

"I'm glad you were there," he quietly rumbled, accepting her help.

They stopped at the bed. She wasn't going to watch him remove the silk that hid most of his body from view. She wouldn't. She—

He tugged her close, leaned down, and kissed her cheek. "Thank you."

Not trusting her voice or herself, she nodded and scurried to the sofa, blowing out candles as she went.

Ashley's stomach fluttered as a sense of dread filled her. She had double and triple checked all the preparations until she was sure Maggie and Sally were rolling their eyes at her behind her back. David had shaved while she went downstairs to eat with her uncle and aunt, and now he sat at her dressing table, tying the garters on his stockings, wearing nothing else but drawers and the bandage on his arm.

As soon as he finished, she led him to her dressing room.

"You're going to be my valet?" He stroked one fingertip down her cheek.

Ashley already held his shirt bunched up in her hands, ready to slip it over his head, trying not to stare at his neck where he'd missed shaving a spot below his ear. His cravat should conceal it. "You need to conserve your energy." And she certainly wasn't going to delegate this task to Sally or Maggie.

While he buttoned his cuffs and collar, she shook out the trousers Sally had ironed earlier. He stepped into them so quickly she didn't have a chance to turn her back ... had she been inclined to do so ... and didn't look away even while he tucked in his shirt and buttoned his trousers. Feeling especially bold, she helped him tuck it in on the right side when he hesitated to use his arm. Just a few days ago she'd stripped his clothing from him, so it didn't seem at all brazen to assist him in putting clothes on. She helped him into his waistcoat, after retrieving it from where it had been folded in the same drawer with her silk paisley shawl.

He reached into the drawer and traced one of the blue swirls with a fingertip. "I've seen this scarf before."

She glanced from the shawl to his face. "I was wearing it the night we met."

He lifted one corner of the silk between his thumb and forefinger. "I haven't seen you wear it since."

"No." She squeezed her eyes shut against a maelstrom of emotions. "I hate it because Rupert touched it. And I love it because my mysterious rescuer kept it safe for me."

One side of his mouth lifted in acknowledgment of being her rescuer, a mystery no more. He tilted her chin up with one callused knuckle. "We might never have met if not for that blackguard." His tone made it clear his emotions were just as conflicted as hers, being beholden to Rupert.

She had to rest her palm on his chest, over his heart. "I'd already given my handkerchief to Georgia that night."

A slow smile spread across his face as he covered her hand with his own. "So we were destined to meet, one way or another."

They swayed toward each other, David still holding her hand to his chest, Ashley certain they were about to kiss ... when Sally said something to Maggie on the other side of the door.

Muffling a growl of frustration, Ashley dropped her hand and retrieved David's cravat from its hiding place among her shawls. She held it out but he didn't take it.

His hands were at his side, his waistcoat still unbuttoned, as he looked at her expectantly. Was that a light of challenge in his eyes as he raised one eyebrow?

Challenge accepted. He bent his knees long enough for her to loop the cravat around the back of his neck, then held still while she buttoned six of the eight buttons on his waistcoat. Did her hands touching his abdomen feel as intimate to him as when he'd rested his hand on her growling stomach? "I don't know how to tie a cravat," she admitted when she slid home the last button, leaving room for the shirt ruffles and cravat.

"Fortunately, I do." He rested one hand on her shoulder for balance while he stepped into his shoes, bent down to buckle them, and they made their way to her dressing table.

Watching him walk without a limp for the first time in almost a week, thanks to his cleverly made shoes, she swallowed a lump in her throat. "We don't have a stack of cravats, or time to iron this one repeatedly if you make a mistake."

Seated at the dressing table, David looked at her in the mirror as she stood behind him. "Think I can't tie this on the first try?"

"I've heard some gentlemen and their valets require six or seven cravats before they are satisfied with the knot."

"I'm easy to please." He winked at her, and then smiled as they both saw her cheeks pinken.

"Wretch." Fortunately Sally and Maggie were both trying to appear busy, oblivious to their quiet exchange.

True to his word, he tied a credible knot on the first try. His hair still needed combing, but he didn't reach for his brush on the table. He must be tiring and his arm hurting. He had choked down the willow bark tea without whisky this morning so her aunt could not smell alcohol on his breath.

With only a slight hesitation, Ashley picked up his brush. She slowly drew it through the long chestnut strands, reveling in the freedom to run her fingers through his hair again. Had she ever touched another man's hair? She couldn't recall doing so, not even when Captain Blackthorn had been sick in the infirmary, feverish for days.

After all the tangles were out, she set the brush down and used her fingers to adjust the white streak in his hair just so, checking it in the mirror. "This will never do," she said quietly.

He opened his eyes.

"The bruises. The stark white of your shirt and cravat make them stand out." No longer were there any signs of swelling on his face, but the fading bruises were distinctly green and yellow. "They will draw attention. Aunt will ask questions."

"Check my bag."

Sure enough, in the toiletry kit that Gilroy had packed was a compact of white face powder and a small tin of kohl. "Bogeyman?" she silently mouthed.

He nodded.

"We can't use just black and white. Not during the day."

Maggie approached. "If I may be so bold, miss, my lord," she said, "you could use my box of colors. I know how to hide bruises."

Ashley inwardly winced. No one as young as Maggie should have to know how to conceal bruises. "That's very kind of you."

Within a few moments, Maggie had retrieved her cosmetics case.

Ravencroft flinched when Maggie approached him with a brush. She bowed her head and handed the brush to Ashley, who pulled a chair from the table by the window and sat before him, their knees touching. He stayed motionless while Maggie directed and Ashley applied creams and powders that hid the colorful bruises on his face and around his eye, the barest hint of rouge to his cheeks so he didn't look too pale, and a faint smudge of kohl on his lashes.

Ashley sat back and tilted her head, giving her work a critical look. At least from this distance, he didn't look as though he was wearing cosmetics. The shadow of his whiskers was still visible. "One more thing," she said after she realized she had been staring at David's mouth. She didn't like to use any artifice, but after Aunt had repeatedly told her to bite her lips to get some color, she'd made a special batch of lip balm subtly tinted with rose petals. She dipped her fingertip in the tin.

Maggie collected her cosmetics case and left to take it back up to her room. Sally had her back turned, making the bed.

Ashley touched her fingertip to David's full lower lip and swiped on the balm, being especially gentle where the split was almost healed. She dipped her finger again to apply to his upper lip, stroking his perfect Cupid's bow.

Her breath caught as he kissed her fingertip.

She cleared her throat as she put the lid back on the tin. "Here, it's small enough to fit in your waistcoat pocket. Apply more after you eat or drink anything. It will protect the cut while it's healing."

The clock on the mantle struck the hour as he slipped the tin into his pocket.

Her heart pounded. "I have to go downstairs. Aunt's guests will soon arrive for her at-home." Reluctantly she took a step away. "Anything you have to leave behind, Sally will take in the basket to give to Gilroy when she meets with him this afternoon."

With a glance at Sally, still busy at the bed, David rose and tucked Ashley's hand in his, twining their fingers. "One thing we almost forgot," he quietly said as he strode for the dressing room, pulling her along in his wake. As soon as they were inside he shut the door, plunging them in semidarkness. "I've been wanting to do this for days. Dreamed about it."

She got only as far as forming "What—" before he cupped her cheeks, lowered his head, and kissed her.

216

He was fully awake, fully sober, and she was fully in favor of letting him plunder her mouth in a passionate kiss. Oh, my. No wonder girls were willing to toss their skirts and their reputation and elope to Gretna Green if they were subjected to kisses such as this.

He'd dreamed about kissing her?

Which meant he didn't remember their first kiss, or realize it had not been a dream. The kiss *she* had initiated. He trusted her to stop him if he did anything ungentlemanly but he hadn't been able to trust that she'd stop herself.

Before she could feel guilt for her wanton behavior, he slid one hand down her ribs to her hip and pulled her tight against him. She wanted to fist his shirt and yank him closer, to feel his heart beating next hers, but settled for wrapping her arms behind his neck, careful of the bruises she had stroked so often when his skin was naked, laid bare before her gaze, and plunged her fingers in his silky hair.

With a frustrated groan he kissed his way to her neck and held her in a tight embrace. "Honey," he whispered in her ear, his voice as much a caress as his fingers lightly stroking her hair. She felt his pounding heart. Or was that hers?

Much too soon he sighed and took a step back. "Thank you seems woefully inadequate. How can I ever repay you?"

For the kiss? Her dazed mind began to clear. She shook her head. "No repayment is necessary. Mr. Westbrook gave me funds to purchase everything needed for your care." She cleared her throat. "By the way, you should probably move your cash to a new hiding spot."

David let out a strangled laugh. He caressed her shoulders, his thumbs stroking her bare collarbone, then leaned in for a quick kiss before he opened the door.

Following him into the room, she touched her bottom lip and felt the lip balm that had transferred from his lips to hers. He'd need to reapply. "Oh! Your hair!" She pushed him to sit down at the dressing table again and opened the drawer that held her ribbons. "We'll need to tie yours back, since Gilroy has short hair." He held still while she stood behind him and brushed his hair again. Did it give him frissons of pleasure when she touched him like this, as it had when he'd played with her braid? She gathered his hair in her hands, selected a black velvet ribbon, and tied a simple, neat bow at his nape.

Any idea she might have harbored of lingering in this small, intimate space with him was dashed when she faintly heard the front door knocker.

Aunt's first guests had arrived. "Oh dear," she whispered, squelching a sense of panic. How would they make the switch if there were other guests in the parlour? Westbrook and Gilroy were supposed to be the first to arrive, on the quarter hour.

With her hand on the doorknob, Ashley took one last glance to memorize the sight of David sitting at her dressing table, the left side of his mouth tugged up in a smile as he stared back at her. Then she hurried downstairs.

Minutes ticked by. Had Westbrook forgotten what time he and Gilroy were supposed to arrive? Aunt Eunice and Lady Donkin were continuing their debate about fruit, flowers, or feathers as being the best adornment for bonnets, or perhaps a combination. Aunt favored feathers, of course. Ashley wanted to scream.

The front door knocker sounded again just as Lady Donkin and her companion were saying goodbye.

Before Farnham could announce the next guests, there was a commotion in the back hall. A moment later, a servant called for Mrs. Endicott.

Ashley followed Aunt Eunice out into the hall in time to see the ladies exit to the street and Westbrook enter the foyer, Gilroy just behind him carrying the package. Finally.

As soon as Aunt Eunice disappeared around the corner, Ashley gestured for Westbrook to enter the parlour and Gilroy took off, silently running on the balls of his feet, to the back staircase where Sally had poked her head out, waving him on. By the time Ashley joined them, Gilroy had stripped off his coat and was helping Ravencroft shrug into it.

Ashley took the now-empty package and hurried back to the parlour, where she plucked the lyre case from its hiding spot behind the window curtain.

"Anything I can do to help?" Westbrook quietly said.

"Keep an eye in the hall. We might need you to distract my aunt." Ashley resumed trying to fit the lyre in the package and tie the strings, a simple task made difficult by her hands shaking.

While Gilroy buttoned his coat, David put a hat on his head for the first time in nearly a week. He had to adjust it so the brim did not put pressure on the goose egg on the back of his head that was stubbornly slow to recede. Sally gave him an approving nod and gestured with her head that they should move along. Voices coming up from the kitchen indicated Mrs. Endicott was returning.

David had barely sat down in a chair next to Liam, with Ashley and Sally seated on the sofa with the package on Ashley's lap, when Mrs. Endicott entered the room. David and Liam rose and bowed in greeting, their hats in hand.

"My, what a pleasant surprise," Mrs. Endicott said upon seeing the men. She rang the bell and requested refreshments. "I heard you had an emergency at your estate, Lord Ravencroft. I trust everything is now well?"

"As well as can be expected, thank you," David said.

Ashley made a show of opening the package and withdrawing the lyre from its case. She held it up in the light streaming through the window to admire it. "How thoughtful of your sister," she said. "I will pay a call on her to offer my thanks in person."

"And play it for her?" David couldn't resist saying.

"Perhaps in time." Ashley arched an eyebrow at him. "After I've had a chance to practice and become proficient."

He could spend all day looking at her, a halo of sunlight gilding her hair, her expression seeming torn between wanting to kiss him and reprimand him for teasing her.

When the maid brought the tray of refreshments, David's stomach rumbled. Fortunately Liam heard and shuffled his feet and cleared his throat to help disguise the sound. He must not have done it quickly enough, as Ashley ducked her chin to hide her knowing grin.

They ate and chatted, and despite the sustenance, David felt his reserves of energy flagging. Just as he was wondering how long he would have the strength to maintain good posture and keep from letting out a decidedly unmanly whimper at the pain in his arm, Liam rose and wished Mrs. Endicott and her niece a good day.

David bowed and dropped a kiss on Ashley's hand, holding it just a little bit too long, yet not nearly long enough. "I enjoyed my visit," he said, speaking slowly, looking directly into her eyes. So much he wanted to say to her but couldn't, even if he could find the words.

"I as well." He could swear she blinked back tears.

Moments later David climbed into his carriage after Liam. He tossed his hat in the general direction of the opposite bench and slouched against the velvet squabs, utterly exhausted, his right arm cradled against his chest, throbbing with every heartbeat. "Give." He held out his left hand.

Liam retrieved a flask of brandy from his coat pocket, twisted off the cap, and handed it over. "Let me see if I understand the situation correctly," he began after he rapped on the roof and the coach set off for home. David took a long drink and handed back the flask. "You just spent the better part of a week hidden in a lady's bedchamber, mostly naked, at least half-foxed the entire time, while not one or two but *three* women waited on you hand and foot."

Lacking the energy or will to keep his eyes open or hold up his head, David had listed to one side. The window was cold on his cheek, so he leaned to the other side until his head rested against Liam's broad shoulder, clad in a soft wool coat. "Essentially."

"Including the prostitute you got in the fight over."

"Not a pros'tute anymore. Ashley's training her t' be a maid."

"Oh, it's 'Ashley' now?"

David smacked Liam's chest with the back of his left hand. "For a pillow, you talk too much."

"You lead a charmed life, my friend."

The at-home seemed to go on forever. After Westbrook and Ravencroft left, Ashley had zero interest in the conversation. At last Aunt's final guests took their leave and Ashley was able to rush upstairs. Sally had gone up when Aunt Eunice came to the parlour and she was no longer needed as a chaperone. She and Maggie had already packed two shopping baskets with items they needed to return to Gilroy, including Ravencroft's toiletry kit and clothing.

"Everything go according to plan, getting Gilroy out the back?" Ashley asked as she tucked in muslin for bandages that she would no longer need, an extra tin of ointment she'd made, plus a jar of the honey and herb preparation and a letter with instructions on how to use them. She had written out the recipes in case they needed to make more of either. Folded inside that paper, she also returned the coins she hadn't needed to spend. Westbrook had been *very* generous with his friend's money.

"He got out fine," Maggie said. "But Mrs. Gillespie is upset at what I did. She says I'm dismissed."

Ashley looked at Sally, eyebrows raised, silently asking if she wanted to know what Maggie had done to draw Mrs. Gillespie and Aunt Eunice to the kitchen.

Sally shook her head.

"I'll remind Mrs. Gillespie that you work for me, not her or my aunt, and smooth things over."

"Thank you, miss."

With a pang, Ashley realized she hadn't talked to David about when to take out the stitches, eight days from now. Gilroy would probably do that.

Someone else would now be taking care of David.

All of Ashley's energy seemed to depart her at once.

"It's later than you usually meet Gilroy," she said, glancing at the clock. "Do you think he'll still be at the coffeehouse?"

"We worked out a system in case one of us wasn't on time," Sally said, buttoning her cloak. "I'll just send him the signal."

"Do you want me to stay here, miss?" Maggie said, holding her cloak.

Ashley made shooing motions. "Go. Enjoy tea and biscuits. I'm just going to have a lie-down." Up all hours at night tending and talking with David and still keeping to her regular schedule of social engagements with her aunt and uncle, all week she'd had far less than her usual eight hours sleep per night.

"Thank you, miss," they chorused.

As soon as they left, Ashley pulled out the pins in her hair and slipped off her shoes. She eyed the sofa, still with its pillow and neatly folded blanket, then the bed.

Sally hadn't changed the linens yet.

Ashley sat on the edge and hugged the top pillow to her chest. She inhaled rosemary ointment, exotic hair oil, and David.

Now that he was gone, she wouldn't have to worry about treating his injuries, losing sleep, prevaricating with her aunt and uncle, or deceiving her friend Georgia. She could focus more on her employment search. Only six more weeks before her uncle and aunt were scheduled to return to Jamaica.

Ashley touched her lips, remembering her kisses with David. The kiss here on her bed yesterday. In her dressing room a few hours ago. Still hugging the pillow, she lay down, remembering the feel of David in her arms when they embraced. Picturing his lopsided smile. His rumbling voice. His protective nature that saved her from Rupert, Amber from Sir Peyton, and Maggie from her abusive pimp.

He was going to have a long scar on his forearm when his wound healed. Would he still be able to play the viola da gamba? The pianoforte? It would be a crime if he could no longer accompany his singing.

Chapter 16

DAVID SAT DOWN AT THE TABLE across from Liam and poured himself a cup of tea while Gilroy filled a plate for him.

"Beg pardon," Liam said, squinting and leaning toward him. "Do I know you?"

About to drop a lump of sugar in his tea, David lobbed it at him instead.

Laughing, Liam batted it away. "I forgot what you look like fully dressed. And shaved."

David stroked his smooth chin. "Neither seemed worth the effort when I was just going back to sleep in an hour." Since leaving Ashley's bedchamber a week ago, he had spent most of his time sleeping or lounging about like a pampered pet, regaining his strength as the bruises faded, occasionally making use of the instruments in his room. Reliving every moment he could recall with Ashley. Well, at least the moments when he wasn't in excruciating pain.

Gilroy was unfazed about changing David's bandages. Didn't blink when David requested soft-boiled eggs and drinking chocolate several mornings. Yesterday he'd removed the stitches in David's arm. Afterward, David had finished off a partial bottle of whisky and passed out as quickly as he could.

He preferred trying to recall his kiss with Ashley. Kisses. She'd kissed him first, he was fairly sure, though memories of that afternoon were fuzzier than the rest. She couldn't blame him for his licentious behavior while inebriated if she was the one to initiate crossing that particular boundary. Though he couldn't recall why she had done so. What had prompted her to kiss him?

She certainly hadn't objected to the kiss he'd initiated in her dressing room the day he left. Had her maids not been just on the other side of the door, he would have taken more time to truly appreciate having her in his arms, her murmur of pleasure driving him mad. That sound filled his dreams, echoed in his thoughts.

And writing. He'd filled the music composition sheets Ashley had sent over with his other things, and had Gilroy purchase more. Though he'd written several new songs and worked on new arrangements of old pieces, there was one tune in particular he couldn't quite get. The melody teased at the edges of his memory but refused to come out to play.

"Gambling that I can finally stay awake for a few hours, I've asked my steward to meet with me this morning," David said. "Here."

"Didn't go so well last time you went to his lodgings. Or rather, tried to go there."

David tried not to wince. His bruises were mostly gone, he had no broken bones, and his forearm only hurt if he bumped it. Or touched it. Hell, it still ached. But he wouldn't trade those days with Ashley for anything. And he'd protected another woman without dressing up as a character from folklore.

His gut churned, though, almost dreading his appointment with Ogden. It had now been over three weeks since their last meeting. How badly had things gotten out of control, how chaotic? His father had always met with his steward weekly when in London, and at least three times each week when at the estate, scheduling time between rehearsals. After finishing at university, Philip had regularly joined in on those meetings, learning how to manage the estates he would one day inherit. *Should* have inherited.

Instead, David had been thrust into the role of earl, woefully unprepared.

"I have students coming for a voice lesson. You're welcome to stay though you might want to go to the coffeehouse. Mr. Grantham and his son have not a drop of self-consciousness and no trouble with volume, but they have yet to grasp the concept of pitch."

David saluted him with his teacup. "I admire your fortitude in taking on such a challenge."

"Have to do something to afford the coal bill now."

"Still no word from your patron?"

Liam grimaced. "The knocker is still gone from his door."

David closed the accounting book his steward had brought and sat back in his seat, trying to conceal his shock. "Everything looks like it's on schedule and within budget. The planting, everything."

His father, and later Philip, had gone out to the fields to personally oversee the planting every spring and the harvest every fall. Since he had inherited, David had done the same, swinging a scythe with his field hands or filling the seed drill. He had only come to London this spring and missed lambing season and the planting because of a bill in the House of Lords that affected water rights near his estate.

"Thank you, my lord," Ogden said as he raised his cup for a refill. "I was right worried when you missed our last meeting, but Mr. Westbrook explained about your sister's emergency. I hope all is well now?"

Sister's emergency? Oh, right. The other lie Liam had told to cover for David's absence. "Yes, thank you."

Ogden thanked the serving girl and blew on his coffee before taking a sip. "I just kept going as I thought you would want."

"You did exactly as I would have asked." So well, in fact, David wondered why he was even needed. Was it possible he'd been keeping the man on too short a leash the last two years?

Ogden was a few years older than David's father and had overseen Ravencroft holdings for more than two decades. Reference letters from his previous employers that sang his praises were among the documents in Father's library, yellowed and fading. The work Ogden described in the account books spread before David was done just the same as when David had gone out to the fields every day the last two springs, working until he fell into bed at night utterly exhausted, or stayed up all night with the shepherds, checking on the pregnant ewes and helping deliver as needed. "Except for the planting of the north field. Why did you switch crops there, and move the sheep to the east field?"

Ogden's face lit up. "I've been reading journals on farm management and studies about increasing crop yields." He dived deep into a current theory on crop rotation and soil amendments. David was only half-listening, reminded of Ashley's journal documenting her experiments to increase yields for the academy's kitchen.

From the corner of his eye, he noticed a young woman wearing the green uniform and mob cap of a maid had joined Gilroy at his table, her back to David. They sat at adjoining corners of the table rather than across from each other, their heads bowed in close conversation. Gilroy tipped his head back to laugh and rested one hand on the woman's shoulder. Beneath the table, she had one hand on his knee.

"–if it doesn't work, we can always go back to the way your father, God rest his soul, arranged the crops."

David held up a finger as he perused the last column in the accounting ledger again, and compared it to last year at the same time, and then the year before, and the year before that.

Yes. It felt right.

Church bells and a choir of angels should accompany this monumental shift in his mindset.

He flattened his palms on the scarred, scratched tabletop and braced his back against the chair. "Not only do I want you to continue with your current plan, I want you to hire an assistant. Continue to research. Document everything—the yields, the investment of time and materials, all the variables and results." He took a deep breath and released it along with his tight control over the estate that had consumed so much of his time and physical and mental energy since inheriting the title. "Send me updates when you have something to share. We'll meet monthly instead of weekly. Unless you feel the need to meet sooner."

Ogden's eyes grew wide while David spoke. "Yes, my lord. Thank you!" He held his hand over his chest and seemed to blink back tears. "I suggested to your father about changing things around, but every year he said he liked things the way they were."

"Show me it's a good idea or prove that it is not." David tapped the account book. "You'll want a separate journal for your research notes. Make sure the assistant you hire has neat penmanship."

Ogden again expressed his surprise and gratitude, and how much he appreciated Ravencroft's trust in him. With the account books safely tucked in his leather satchel, he whistled as he exited the coffeehouse.

David ate another biscuit, reveling in the feeling of a crushing weight lifted from his shoulders. Midway through another cup of tea, he decided to tackle another task that had seemed insurmountable just a fortnight ago. Back at Liam's apartment, he penned a note, sealed it, and handed it to Gilroy. "You don't have to go. I understand if you don't want to complete this errand."

Gilroy looked at the address and scratched behind his ear. He drew breath to speak, let it out without making a sound, and briefly squeezed his eyes shut. He released another deep breath. "If you can do this, my lord, I can do it."

David squeezed his shoulder. "Good man. We'll get through this together."

Less than an hour later, Gilroy having returned with a positive response, David and Gilroy exited from his carriage in front of a townhouse. A groom sprang to take the horse's head collar, and the butler opened the door before David had even reached the bottom step.

"Welcome home, Lord Ravencroft."

Parker and Deirdre were delighted to host him for a meal while Gilroy went upstairs.

"You don't mind? Be honest," David said as the dishes were cleared by footmen wearing livery with the Ravencroft crest.

"Honestly?" Parker squeezed Deirdre's hand and kissed her knuckles. "We've been hoping you would change your mind and join us."

"Great-Aunt Connie will be delighted as well," Deirdre added.

"I'm not doing this for Aunt Connie," David muttered.

"Do you want to go up by yourself?" Parker offered. "We'll wait down here in the music room." Still holding hands, Parker and Deirdre followed David out of the dining room and kept going past the staircase.

David put one foot on the first riser, his hand on the balustrade, and stared up the grand staircase. Memories assailed him. The keening wail of mourners, from servants in the attic and visitors in the front parlour, come to pay respects. The deathly silence in his parents' bedchambers. Gilroy quietly sobbing in a chair beside Philip's empty bed.

Numb with shock, David had let the butler and housekeeper make most of the funeral arrangements. They had already hung a black wreath on the front door before he arrived. His father's solicitor took care of all the details in the transfer of title, the reading of the wills, and carrying out final wishes.

Liam had been there, too, wrapping David in a bone-crushing hug whenever it all got to be too much. He didn't utter a single teasing remark about David dampening his shirt when he could no longer hold back the tears, and welcomed David to his home when David couldn't bear to stay in the townhouse a moment longer.

That was over two years ago.

It was time. David climbed the stairs.

His bedchamber was exactly as he had left it, kept clean and dusted, ready for his return at any moment. Not a Holland cover in sight.

Parker and Deirdre clearly occupied the room two doors down. Surprising, given that it was one of the smaller guest bedchambers.

At the end of the hall were the adjoining suites his parents had occupied. The rooms were exactly as he remembered them, also kept as though their occupants would return at any moment.

The last room David entered had belonged to his older brother Philip. Gilroy sat in the same chair beside the bed.

"Can we do this?" David quietly said.

Gilroy stood, surreptitiously wiping tears from his cheeks. "Yes, my lord." He cleared his throat and glanced at the empty bed. "It's what he would've wanted." He stood a little taller, his shoulders back.

David nodded. Two years ago he hadn't been sure if hiring his brother's longtime valet was a kindness or cruelty—to himself or Gilroy—but he'd made the offer, Gilroy accepted, and together they'd navigated the aftermath of the influenza that had swept through London and claimed David's parents, brother, and three of the staff.

"Then let's go choose bedchambers."

An hour later, David felt thoroughly disgusted with himself. He and Gilroy had poked around every bedchamber that was not already occupied, including those in the attic. The only bedchamber he could picture himself sleeping in had a dressing room with a ruffled pink dress hanging in it.

Gilroy opened the door to what had been the previous Earl of Ravencroft's suite. "Pardon my impertinence, but this should be your room."

"Technically, yes." David forced himself to walk farther into the room. His father's shaving gear, brush, comb, and half-full bottle of hair tonic still sat on the dressing table. Ignoring the bed, David sat at the writing desk by the window. A quill lay in the tray, sharp and ready to write, though the ink in the pot had dried long ago. Bars of sealing wax nestled in the top drawer along with more quills and a penknife. Reluctantly, David had taken the Ravencroft seal with him.

Idly he opened the middle drawer and shuffled through the papers he found inside. Letters from Ogden, from school headmasters. From committee members in the House of Lords.

And sheet music. David thought all the sheet music was stored in the music room downstairs. He held the papers up to the light from the window.

His father's handwriting. Going by the dedication, lyrics, and the location of the sheets, songs his father had composed to sing privately to his wife. Two were unfinished. Father had scratched out and started rewriting the second verse on one, and the other had an incomplete melody and very little harmony.

When he was growing up, his parents often held hands and regaled their children with the story of how Mother had been courted by no less than two future dukes and a marquess. Her eyes sparkling with mischief, she told how she had chosen a mere earl because he had composed a song for her and she liked his voice the best of all her suitors. They often performed duets, Mother on her harp, Father playing pianoforte, singing together.

David blinked back tears.

Gilroy studied the Gainsborough landscape hung above the fireplace as though he'd never before seen it, utterly entranced, his back to the room.

Clearing his throat, David put the papers away and closed the drawer. "I believe I will take up my old room after all."

Liam sat down hard, almost missing the chair's seat. "You're moving to the townhouse? Today?"

Part of Liam's reaction, David realized, was shock that David was moving to a place he'd refused to even step foot in for over two years. There was also a little melancholy—for both of them—as they'd shared living quarters for those two years whenever David was in London.

David shrugged. "Like swallowing a live toad first thing in the morning. Best to just get it over with." He let out a jaw-cracking yawn. "After my nap, that is." He clapped Liam on the shoulder. "It's a big house. If funds get tight, you can always move in with me."

Liam grinned. "I may just take you up on that."

Two days later, David took a fortifying breath as he exited his coach in front of the Mansfield townhouse, accompanied by Liam, Parker, and Deirdre. They went directly to the music room, where Templeton and Mansfield were warming up.

"There you are!" Diana left her lyre to greet David with a hug before leading him over to get the viola da gamba case from the cupboard. "Everything all right? We haven't had flooding at Linford Hall in at least five years. I didn't think this spring had been particularly wet."

David raised an eyebrow at Liam.

Liam gave a barely perceptible shrug as he took his mandolin out of its case.

"Had more to do with diverting one of the drainage ditches. It's all taken care of now. Mr. Ogden has things well in hand." David took his place, settled the viola da gamba on his calves, and began to warm up.

"Mr. Ogden always has. Father could have played more music if he'd been less of a nuisance tracking his steward's every move." Lydia handed out music. "We only have six days left before the competition. I don't know if you boys can be ready."

Parker stood beside Templeton, both of them looking over Mansfield's shoulders at the music on the pianoforte, while Diana helped Deirdre settle on the sofa with her embroidery. "Then let them get to it, you silly goose," Diana said.

David hadn't touched a bow in over two weeks. He'd played nothing at Liam's but the clavichord while he tried writing music, and the pianoforte at his townhouse when he wrote or rehearsed. As he drew the bow along the strings, the antique wood case of the viola da gamba reverberated with warm tones as though it had missed being played. David allowed himself a few moments to close his eyes and picture his ancestors who had played this instrument before him, see the joy on the face of the audiences who had heard it, going back to King George I. The instrument was a tangible connection between him and his father all the way to the great-great ancestors who had died a century before David was even born.

Ashley loved to hear him play this instrument. He remembered the look of delight on her face, her lips slightly parted. Her utterly distracting mouth. He hadn't been able to look at the audience that first night he'd filled in for Parker. Couldn't risk looking at her and losing his concentration.

At Lydia's command, they began to play and sing *The Last Rose of Summer*, a tune beloved by the public though a bit melancholy for David's taste.

He'd looked at Ashley the last time he sang this. She'd been staring right back at him, her mouth open in a slight "*oh.*" He'd almost forgotten to make the key change, nearly played the wrong chord. He imagined she was in the room now, just out of his sight. Maybe seated behind the sofa, where sometimes Georgia or some of her younger siblings would sit and listen.

They started the next to last phrase when he noticed Lydia had stopped conducting. She simply stood there, arms at her sides. Staring at him, her jaw slack.

She roused herself enough to bring her hand up and cut them off in unison at the end.

As though in a daze, she sauntered toward David. "You've been rehearsing."

He wasn't sure if she was accusing him or was in shock. "You and Mansfield want us to play this for the competition. We've rehearsed it several times."

She put her hands on her hips. "No, I mean *you* have been practicing. By yourself. I can hear it in your voice. It's stronger. Your passaggio, your transitions between octaves, are smoother."

"He did sound as sweet as a twelve-year-old hitting that high C sharp." Diana got up from the sofa and advanced on him. "You *have* been practicing!"

"We always know where he is in the house." Deirdre set a stitch, a smile tugging up the corners of her mouth. "He can't seem to go more than a few minutes without singing."

Startled, David glanced at Parker for confirmation. Did he really make that much noise?

"Or humming," Parker added with a big grin, not the least bit teasing. "Or impersonating a violincello."

Lydia stared at Deirdre. "In the Ravencroft townhouse?"

Deirdre added another stitch. "He moved in when he returned from Surrey."

Lydia let out a tiny squeal and wrapped her arms around David's shoulders in a sideways hug. He tried to return the embrace, awkward with a bow in one hand, steadying the viola da gamba on his legs with the other.

Diana squeezed his shoulder. "Aunt Connie is going to be so happy!"

David dropped his chin to his chest in frustration. He took a fortifying breath as he raised his head. "I didn't do it for Aunt Connie." Even though he knew how much it would please her. He gestured with his bow. "Shall we proceed?" He addressed Parker, Mansfield, and Templeton at the pianoforte. "The Club is not going to admit Lydia. Even if she could get in, we won't earn any marks with the judges having her as our conductor. We should rehearse without her leading."

Diana forcefully cleared her throat, covering whatever indignant sounds Lydia made.

"I'm sorry, darling," Templeton said. "Your brother makes a valid point." Mansfield and Parker murmured agreement. Liam, who Lydia had wrestled to the floor more than once when they were children, suddenly found the fretwork on his mandolin to be utterly fascinating.

Lydia opened her mouth to argue, tilted her head to one side, then puffed out her cheeks as she exhaled. "Agreed." She handed out the sheet music for their original composition, then took a seat on the sofa near Deirdre.

Just as David's arm was tiring, Diana sailed back into the room and announced it was time for them to adjourn to the front parlour before going in to dinner. He hadn't noticed her leave to dress for dinner, or how much time had passed.

Within a few moments he was accepting a tall glass of cool tea with honey and lemon from one footman, while another circulated through the parlour with a tray of aperitifs. Did he dare sit down? In the week before David had moved out, on the occasions he left his bed Liam had teased him about how he'd fall asleep every time he sat on a comfortable piece of furniture. It was happening less often as his strength returned, but still...

"Uncle David!" Georgia hugged his arm. "You're back!"

David resisted the impulse to flinch, and moved her hand to his upper arm, squeezing her hand in greeting. "Scamp. Anything exciting happen while I was away? Any announcements?"

She rested her head against his shoulder, still hugging his arm. "Alas, no. Nothing interesting has happened at *all*. Mother has been busy with Clarissa planning her wedding breakfast. I've hardly even seen Miss Hamlin. How are we supposed to hunt matrimonial prey if we aren't out at every social event?"

Over the buzz of conversation from the dozen or so people already in the parlour, the butler announced the arrival of Mr. and Mrs. Endicott and Miss Hamlin. Georgia quietly squealed in delight and abandoned him to greet her friend.

David tried to slow his breathing. Just his luck that his first time seeing Ashley in over a week would be in front of his very observant, nosy family. He traded his empty glass for a full one from a passing footman and took up his usual stance by the fireplace. Out of habit he started to rest his right arm on the mantel, and barely caught himself in time before he bumped his arm. He switched the glass to his right hand so he wouldn't be stupid enough to do it again.

"You're back."

He'd missed the announcement of Aunt Connie's arrival. He pasted a smile on his face and leaned down to drop a kiss on her cheek. "I'm delighted to see you, as well."

She curled her fingers around his cravat to prevent him from withdrawing very far. "Where have you been?" She lowered her voice. "And don't give me any folderol about dealing with flooding in Surrey. Mr. Ogden is fully capable of handling such an incident even without my brother shadowing his every step."

Aunt Connie was his only surviving parental figure and he'd never been able to lie to her, even as a little boy. He ran his tongue behind his front teeth as he considered what he could say. "I encountered a woman," he quietly said. He bent closer, dropping his voice even lower, keeping his expression neutral. "For the past fortnight, I've barely been out of bed."

Her chin dropped and eyes widened. Then she apparently remembered that gesture gave her a double chin, and she tilted her chin up and to the right as she stared at him, searching his face.

He refused to blink or look away. Hoped to hell he wasn't blushing. From the corner of his eye he saw Ashley's mouth fall open before she quickly turned her back where she was talking with Georgia, her face flushing furiously. A few feet away on his other side, Liam bent over double, ostensibly to adjust his shoe buckle, his shoulders shaking with silent laughter.

"You're telling the truth." Connie let go of his cravat to tap her bottom lip with one beringed finger. "And yet ... not." She tapped his chest with her finger, her large ruby ring sparkling in the light from the chandelier. "I'll have the full story, sooner or later."

He dipped his head in acknowledgment, and was saved having to reply by the butler announcing that dinner was served.

The food was excellent as usual at Diana's home, but once more he was seated too far away to converse with Ashley. The meal seemed to drag on forever. He asked a footman for another glass of honey and lemon tea and rested his voice, not trusting himself to engage in conversation with Aunt Connie, and having zero interest in plans for Clarissa's wedding breakfast other than being glad he had "returned" in time to attend it in two days. Finally they adjourned to the music room.

Still he couldn't speak with Ashley, as Georgia or someone else was always near her. After warming up, Lydia asked him and the other members of the quintet to sing and play their two numbers for the Club competition.

The Last Rose of Summer went well. During Lydia's song, Missy yawned. Everyone applauded politely when they finished and praised Lydia's composition.

This was the largest audience for which they'd performed the original number. Everyone in the room—family and close friends— was inclined to react favorably though honestly. And this tepid response was the reaction?

They weren't going to win anything with it.

Seated on the sofa, Ashley licked her lips as she opened her reticule. Was she going to apply some of her rose-tinted lip balm? He still had the little tin she had given him. He had only applied it at night, though he often opened the container to sniff the contents. He'd continued to apply her rosemary healing ointment until not a hint of bruising was visible, long after he would have stopped bothering to treat bruises before he met her.

The gathering moved on to playing and singing favorite tunes. With everyone shifting about, he didn't get to see what she did with whatever was of interest in her reticule, but she did get up to help Lydia and Diana distribute sheets of music. As Ashley walked past him, the end of her silk shawl brushed against his music stand. Sheets of paper fluttered to the floor.

"Oh, how clumsy of me!" She bent down to gather the papers and handed them to him, still on one knee. And winked at him.

And moved on.

David had trouble catching his breath. He'd never make it as a thespian; he felt his cheeks flush. He desperately wanted to break out in a huge grin. And all from just a hint of a smile and the quickest, most subtle of winks.

To distract himself, he arranged the sheets of music on his stand. Hold on.

One sheet had crease marks. This was a hand printed sheet, but these were not his or Lydia's marks, and it had no title. There was no key signature, no harmony, and barely eight bars of melody, all of it in bass clef.

Under the buzz of conversation, he hummed what few notes were there.

This was it!

The melody that had haunted the fringe of his memory!

He searched the crowded room until he found Ashley, adjusting her shawl as she resumed her seat on the sofa, music sheets in hand. He drew breath to speak to her, then remembered the room full of people, and realized he would have to be patient a little while longer.

Lydia and Diana took turns leading them through one interminable song after another. David hadn't had this much trouble concentrating since his voice started to crack when he was thirteen. Finally the refreshment trays were brought in and he was able to seek out Ashley without being obvious.

"Is that your original composition?" He took a drink of his lemon and honey tea.

Ashley paused with her cup halfway to her mouth. "You do not recognize it?"

"Should I?"

She took a sip, but he could swear she did so only to hide her smile. Unsuccessfully. At last she glanced up at him. "A gentleman acquaintance of mine recently hummed that tune when he was inebriated."

David fought an irrational rush of jealousy. Who the blazes had she been with when the man was inebriated? Didn't she know how dangerous that could be?

She continued to look at him, a hint of a smile tilting her mouth, her eyebrows raised.

He almost smacked his forehead. He winced. No wonder he knew the tune yet had so much trouble recollecting it.

"Just so." She took a bite of a biscuit. "I wrote it down as best I could remember. I trust you can finish it."

He could kiss her. Admired his great restraint in resisting the almost overwhelming urge to do so. He patted his waistcoat pocket, where he had tucked the folded sheet. "At my earliest convenience." They had moved away from the tray as they spoke, and now stood by the pianoforte, as alone as they could be in this room teeming with his relatives. Or soon-to-be relative, glancing at Clarissa and Norcross surreptitiously holding hands. Good thing their wedding was only a couple of days away.

"What did you think of Lydia's composition?"

Ashley took entirely too long to chew and swallow a tiny bite of biscuit. "It's better than the first time I heard it. I like the changes you made."

"Just as I feared. It's bad, isn't it?" He offered his snuffbox to Ashley, who selected a honey and lemon pastille and popped it in her mouth. He selected one for himself and put the snuffbox away.

Ashley shook her head, then shrugged. "I can't really compare as I haven't heard very many original compositions. Songs that aren't already popular." The look of delight that crossed her face when the sweet began to dissolve in her mouth nearly undid his resolve to not kiss her in public.

Now that he was closer and they had good light from the candelabrum on the pianoforte, he noticed the shadows beneath her eyes. Was she still fatigued from the sleepless nights she'd spent taking care of him? He wanted to wrap her in his arms. He settled for tugging her shawl farther up one shoulder. "Is everything all right? You seem troubled."

He saw the denial forming on her lips, but as she looked into his eyes, her shoulders slumped the tiniest bit. "I've had bad news by mail," she quietly admitted. "More people saying no."

Ah, her search for employment. He glanced around to see if anyone within earshot was paying them any attention. "Honey, you're looking for the wrong sort of employment. You're not a teacher."

She inhaled a deep breath to rebut, a flare of anger in her light brown eyes, her bosom heaving in a most distracting way. "How can you say that? How—" She narrowed her eyes at him. "You just called me honey."

With one fingertip, he stroked the tendril of hair that had been allowed to curl beside her face, down to her bare collarbone. "It's the color. I would describe it as old honey, but a lady acquaintance recently advised me it is ungallant to use the word 'old' in any description of a woman."

That teased a ghost of a smile from her.

"How much time did you actually spend in the classroom as a teacher? What percentage of your time at the academy would you estimate you spent teaching?"

Again she opened her mouth in that very distracting way, then closed it without saying anything. He could practically see her doing sums in her head.

"Compared to that, what percentage of time did you spend helping to run the school? Working with the headmistress? Finding ways to make everything run more efficiently? You're not a teacher, Ash—Miss Hamlin." He set his cup down. "I submit that you're an administrator."

She gaped at him. In a move eerily similar to Aunt Connie, she tilted her head up and to the right, deep in thought, as though studying the frieze of cavorting cupids. Over by the fireplace Clarissa laughed with Norcross. Conversation continued to buzz around the room while David studied Ashley's face, watching one thought flit by after another. He could almost hear gears turning in her head as he shifted the pastille dissolving in his mouth from one cheek to the other.

Finally she stared at him, her mouth falling open in shock.

He gently tipped her jaw closed with one fingertip under her chin.

"I'm a fool," she whispered, still dazed.

"Far from it," he whispered back.

"I've wasted so much time and effort," she said, adjusting the other side of her shawl. "Not to mention postage."

He chuckled.

She smiled at him, her expression quickly turning to concern. "Give me your arm."

When he started to offer his right arm out of habit, she took his left arm instead, in a way that felt familiar. Ah, yes, when he barely had the strength to stumble back to bed. He did let himself lean on her, just the tiniest bit, as this was as close to wrapping her in his arms as he was going to get. She led them over to Liam, who was conversing with Parker and Deirdre.

Ashley and Liam exchanged wordless communication, David was sure. He wondered if they had met and talked like this while he lay in her bed, unconscious or asleep.

"I've already taken the liberty of requesting your carriage," Liam said. "I'm sure Parker and Deirdre won't mind heading home."

"No, not at all," Deirdre said. "It's been a full day." She and Parker caught the attention of a footman and requested their wraps.

"Home?" Ashley said, looking between the two men.

"To the Ravencroft townhouse," David confirmed.

Her broad smile and deep inhale, as though she wanted to shout but barely restrained herself, did things to his insides. Warmth spread through his chest. He hadn't moved home for Aunt Connie, nor for Ashley ... but she had certainly played a part in his willingness and ability to finally move in. Move on.

He nodded his head in silent acknowledgment of her unspoken congratulations.

Liam bowed over Ashley's hand and bid her good night, then took David's elbow and steered him out of the room, offering farewell and good night as they went.

David was happy to let his friend speak for him, as his reserves of energy seemed to have forsaken him. Starting with rehearsal several hours ago, this was the longest he had been awake and active since that afternoon in the alley behind the butcher shop.

In the coach they let Parker and Deirdre have the forward-facing seat again. Liam gave David a gentle shove so he could sit on David's left, made a great show of yawning and stretching, then leaned a little toward him. The result was that David, who could now barely hold up his head, rested against Liam with no one the wiser. He almost asked Liam for his flask of brandy but refrained, knowing Gilroy would have willow bark tea and whisky waiting for him.

The sun was high in the sky when David finally opened his eyes the next morning. Afternoon? He was nearly dressed when a footman knocked on his bedchamber door to alert him that he had a visitor downstairs.

Who even knew he was in residence?

Other than his entire extended family. Cousins in the countryside probably knew by now.

With a sigh, David finished dressing and went downstairs. He stopped in the doorway of the front parlour to observe Clarissa's fiancé nervously pacing before the window. "To what do I owe the pleasure, Mr. Norcross?"

Norcross nearly jumped a foot. David graciously pretended not to notice.

"Clarissa said you are the one who arranged the song her father sings to her stepmother."

David nodded.

Norcross reached into a pocket and withdrew a folded sheet of vellum. "I want to sing this for Clarissa at our wedding breakfast tomorrow, but I can't hit some of the notes anymore." He advanced toward David, holding out the paper. "I was hoping you would help me make changes, my lord."

David studied the paper, a song about everlasting love. "When were you last able to sing this as written?"

Norcross seemed to find the pattern in the carpet fascinating. "I was twelve." He looked up, his chin high. "I won a ribbon at the school talent show with it."

David turned so Norcross couldn't see the grin on his face, and headed for the music room, gesturing over his shoulder for the young man to follow. "Let's fit this to the voice you have now instead of the voice you used to have."

Three hours later, Norcross went on his way, still practicing the tune they had generally revised down one octave, and David sat at the pianoforte with papers and pencil, engrossed in trying to finish composing the tune Ashley had written down for him. He paused when a maid carried in a tray with covered dishes and a tea service, gingerly stepping over the wadded-up balls of paper littering the floor on her way to the side table. "I don't recall requesting anything."

"Beg pardon, my lord," the maid said, removing one cover to reveal a plate with beefsteak and diced potatoes, still steaming. "Mr. Gilroy requested it for you." She curtsied and left, passing Liam as he entered the room unannounced.

"It appears I have excellent timing." Liam popped a bite of potato in his mouth. "Mmm, rosemary. Tasty." He ate two more and reached for the knife and fork to cut into the steak.

David looked at him askance.

"What? You said you'd feed me."

"I said you could move in. Said nothing about feeding you," David teased.

"One goes with the other." He moaned in delight as he swallowed a bite of steak.

The maid darted back in, put another place setting on the tray, bobbed a curtsy, and hurried out.

David heaved a dramatic sigh. "Looks like I have to take a break if I want any of my own food." He tucked his pencil behind one ear, straightened the stack of papers on top of the pianoforte so none would slide to the floor, and stepped over to the table. Something about the rosemary-flavored potatoes tickled a memory though he couldn't quite pull it out to look at it.

They ate and drank, tea for David and wine for Liam. "Not that I'm not happy to see you again so soon, but what is the occasion?"

It was Liam's turn to heave a dramatic sigh. "The echoes from Grantham and son's vocal lesson are still rattling around my apartment." He shuddered in mock horror, then tossed off the last of his wine. "What was that I heard you working on when I came in?"

David sat at the pianoforte. "Something I apparently began when I was ... starting to feel better." He played what he had so far, considerably more than what Ashley had written down for him though still far from finished.

Liam gave him a little shove with his hip and sat on the bench beside him. He played it through while David listened with his eyes closed.

"The bridge," they said in unison at the end, and turned to grin at each other. "Needs work."

"What if..."

Chapter 17

ASHLEY RETURNED GEORGIA'S HUG in greeting as soon as she went through the reception line for the wedding breakfast at the Mansfield townhouse. The dividing wall had been drawn back to open the front parlour to the music room. Guests who had already greeted newlyweds Clarissa and Lawrence, who had been married just two hours before, chatted in clusters in the large space. Footmen circulated with trays of champagne and finger foods.

"This is a family event," Ashley said. "I don't know why you invited me."

Georgia looked at her as though Ashley had just declared the sky to be primrose yellow. "Because you *are* family, you silly goose." She hugged her again. "And by extension, that means your aunt and uncle are family, too." Georgia waggled her fingers at Uncle Edward a few feet away, who saluted her with his champagne glass. Aunt Eunice missed the gesture, engrossed in the difficult task of selecting a delicacy from the tray a footman held before her.

Somewhat mollified and feeling slightly less out of place, Ashley accepted a glass of champagne and let Georgia lead her from one group to another, introducing her to more cousins than she could recall names, and catching up on their latest news. Many of the people she already knew from her evenings spent in Georgia's home for dinner and music. There was one guest in particular she kept looking for. She tried not to let her disappointment show when he seemed absent.

Had David overdone things, and was home resting? Had Gilroy removed the stitches? Had the wound become reinfected and he had a relapse? So many questions, impossible to ask when she had seen him last.

"I'm so glad you came," Clarissa said, joining them. She gave Ashley a hug and kissed her on the cheek.

"Wouldn't miss it," Ashley replied, ignoring Georgia's told-you-so grin.

Someone started playing the pianoforte, though the crowd continued chattering.

"This is it," Lawrence said, taking Clarissa by the hand. He led her toward the pianoforte.

Exchanging puzzled looks, Ashley and Georgia followed in their wake.

"Please stay here, my darling." Lawrence kissed Clarissa's hand and walked over to stand beside the pianoforte, where her father had started playing a tune that sounded vaguely familiar but different.

Lord Mansfield turned the page of music and resumed playing. The crowd quieted down and drifted toward the pianoforte. Now they heard a mandolin and the deep tones of the viola da gamba play the opening of the song.

Ashley stood on her tiptoes and was finally able to see Ravencroft and Westbrook seated near the pianoforte, accompanying Mansfield. Her heart pounded.

Lawrence began to sing. Uncertainly at first, until Mansfield, Westbrook, and Ravencroft joined in, and his voice grew stronger. They kept their voices soft and their instruments barely above pianissimo, a supportive foundation to let Lawrence shine as he sang directly to Clarissa, lyrics of undying love, his devotion evident in his animated expression and gestures.

Clarissa had one hand over her mouth, tears glistening in her eyes, and blindly reached for her mother's hand. Lady Mansfield held on, and barely glanced at the now-silent crowd that had gathered to listen before turning back to watch her husband and new son-in-law, a dazzling smile on her face.

At the end of the song, Lawrence bowed to hearty applause, a few polite *Huzzahs*, and a shouted "Bravo, boy!" from Lady Bedford. Clarissa rushed to Lawrence and they stepped aside, hand in hand, trying for a moment of privacy. Lady Mansfield likewise took her husband by the hand and led him from the room.

Ashley hoped for a chance to converse with Ravencroft but he set aside the viola da gamba and immediately sat at the pianoforte and began to play a scale. Westbrook exchanged his mandolin for a violin and joined him in warming up.

Some of the crowd dispersed. Ashley and Georgia stayed, now with a clear view.

Ravencroft and Westbrook began to play. Chills chased up Ashley's spine as she recognized the tune. The same tune Ravencroft had been humming just before she kissed him the first time. The notes she had tried to transcribe for him.

Now there was melody and harmony. Westbrook stood just behind Ravencroft's right shoulder, playing from the same sheets of music. What she had transcribed as the barest charcoal sketch he had transformed into an oil painting.

Lady Templeton came to stand beside them, clutching her shawl, barely breathing as she stared at her brother and his friend.

Parker and Deirdre joined them. "It's come a long way," he said softly.

"Come what?" Lady Templeton stared at him.

"Yesterday afternoon and evening," Deirdre said. "We heard them working on this."

"They must have stayed up half the night," Parker said. "Rewriting passages, playing it on every instrument in the house. Even heard them on the shawm and sackbut. They were still working on it when I went down to the kitchen to fetch a snack for Clarissa. I'm surprised Uncle David didn't send for his viola da gamba."

Lady Bedford had one hand on Deirdre's shoulder. "At the Ravencroft townhouse?"

"Didn't even come to dinner," Deirdre said. "Ravencroft's valet had the staff serve them food in the music room."

"At the Ravencroft townhouse?" Lady Bedford repeated, giving Deirdre's shoulder a gentle shake.

Deirdre nodded. "Moved in when he returned from Surrey. Said he didn't want to overstay his welcome at Mr. Westbrook's."

Lady Bedford turned her stare on Ravencroft, a slow smile spreading across her face, the dazzling expression lighting up her hazel eyes, so much like her nephew's. "Balderdash. Those two have lived in each other's pocket practically since they were let off leading strings. If one eats beans, the other breaks wind."

Ashley and Georgia both stifled a chuckle.

"David wrote this." Lady Templeton sounded as though she didn't dare believe it. "Or did Liam compose it?"

Even without lyrics, the pianoforte and violin together expressed yearning and an invitation to play and frolic, a call and response. To desire, and have desires fulfilled. Or perhaps Ashley was projecting her own wants and needs onto a charming melody that had no deeper meaning than to sound pleasing to the ear. "Ravencroft created it," she whispered.

"Really? Oh, thank God," Lady Templeton softly said, glancing heavenward.

Lady Bedford looked sharply at Ashley.

"I heard him humming it," she offered, hoping her face and voice gave nothing away.

Concentrating on reading the music, Ravencroft and Westbrook paid no attention to their audience, and when they finished, looked pleasantly surprised by the applause.

Lady Templeton rushed over to talk with them, Lady Bedford following at a more sedate pace. When Melissa gestured that she wanted the bench, the group stepped away from the pianoforte and continued their conversation by the cupboards.

The crowd resumed chattering, and Melissa began playing a Vivaldi sonata. With so many musicians in the family eager for an audience, Lord and Lady Mansfield had not hired anyone to entertain for the event. Another cousin stood beside Melissa, music in hand, waiting his turn.

Ashley strained but couldn't hear a word of the conversation with Ravencroft. "Your aunt seemed shocked that Ravencroft composed something."

Georgia's brows were furrowed as she stared at her uncle. "He used to arrange music to suit his voice or someone else's, or other instrumentation. And he'd often compose something entirely new. He wrote a song for each of us—my cousins, siblings, and I—for our birthdays." She folded her arms across her chest. "But I can't remember him doing any composing or arranging since my grandparents and Uncle Philip died." Her head tilted, she turned to stare at Ashley. "I wonder what changed."

Ashley resisted the urge to squirm. "Yes. I wonder."

Before the moment became too awkward, cousins came to ask Georgia to clarify a childhood memory. As Ashley debated what to do with herself, Mr. Westbrook appeared at her side, offering a glass of lemonade. "Did you enjoy it?" He took a sip from his own glass.

Ashley accepted the drink. "It's lovely. Quite took Lady Templeton and Lady Bedford by surprise."

Westbrook grinned. "Me as well." He glanced around, confirming no one nearby seemed interested in their conversation, and lowered his voice. "Whatever you did to him, I like it."

Ashley felt her cheeks heat. "I- I don't know what you mean."

"He's singing again. Of his own volition. Before he moved out, when he was awake he'd walk around dropping bass notes like a mad gardener sowing seeds." He smiled again. "Working on that piece with him last night was the most fun I've had in years."

"Truly?" Ashley looked over her shoulder, but no one was by the cupboards now except Lord Templeton going through a music folder. She took a sip to conceal her disappointment.

"He had to leave," Westbrook said, following her gaze. "Has a committee meeting. Said he felt obligated to attend today since he didn't make it to the last one two weeks ago. The one he missed because of ... his emergency in Surrey."

That night Uncle Edward and Aunt Eunice escorted Ashley to a ball. According to the note Georgia sent over, she and her family would not be in attendance as they were still entertaining a houseful of relatives celebrating Clarissa's wedding.

Sally and Maggie had assured Ashley that she was turned out in the first stare of fashion, wearing a taffeta and lace confection from Madame Chantel in sea green, topped with a sapphire blue silk shawl. Strands of seed pearls adorned her hair, and a pearl necklace circled her throat. She tried to project an aura of calm assurance without being arrogant, carefully following every rule of society. Not too bold, not too shy.

Yet she still sat out most of the dances with the wallflowers, spinsters, and chaperones. Lacking invitations, she watched the younger women like Miss Kenyon be invited onto the floor time after time. The only ball where Ashley had been in high demand as a dance partner was when her face had been disguised by a half-mask at the masquerade.

Her prospects were so dismal, she gladly accepted Lord Grantham's invitation to waltz.

"Enjoying yourself, Miss Hamlin?" Without waiting for her response, he began to hum along with the musicians. Off-key.

It took all her training not to roll her eyes and to keep her expression polite, to give him a politely bland and appropriate reply. Even when he stepped on her toes. Twice.

To distract herself, she again replayed in her mind the conversation she'd had with Ravencroft, when he'd shocked her by saying she was an administrator rather than a teacher. She had considered it over and over, especially when perusing the Help Wanted advertisements. And the calendar, as the date of Uncle Edward and Aunt Eunice's departure for Jamaica loomed ever closer. She fought off a growing sense of desperation at the lack of matrimonial or employment prospects.

Lord Grantham led her back to her seat where she sat out the next two songs. Too bad she couldn't take the initiative and ask gentlemen to dance. At the assemblies in Torquay, when she wore the sash indicating she could dance the man's part, she had become comfortable inviting girls from the academy to dance. If all the students had partners, she'd seek out a wallflower, someone tapping her toe in time with the music, so they both could have the pleasure of dancing.

Could she somehow take the initiative in her employment search? Beyond responding to advertisements someone else had placed?

"I wonder how we could summon the Bogeyman."

Ashley froze. She had retreated to the ladies' retiring room to repair the hem on her dress after realizing Lord Grantham had stepped on it. Still sitting on a stool in a curtained alcove, needle and hem in hand, she peeked around the velvet drape.

"I haven't heard of him appearing to anyone since Amber Barrow-Smith." Miss Kenyon stood before the mirror, fussing with a curl that had come undone.

Ashley didn't recognize her companion, who held a comb and hairpins, handing them to Miss Kenyon as needed.

"My sister thinks our dancing master is going to marry her. While Mr. Giovanni is handsome and charming, he hasn't a feather to fly with. He's still wearing the same coat from last year. I recognize the brass buttons." She handed Miss Kenyon a pin. "I've tried to speak sense to her, but you know how silly and stubborn girls of only seventeen can be."

Considering the speaker barely looked to be nineteen, Ashley held back a snort.

"And you think the Bogeyman would get through to her?" Miss Kenyon successfully pinned up one curl, only to watch another fall down. She grimaced at her reflection.

"He certainly made an impression with Amber."

Ashley set the last stitch, bit the thread, and let her skirt down. She cleared her throat as she pushed back the curtain. "I couldn't help overhearing," she said as she stepped from the alcove.

"Miss Hamlin!" Miss Kenyon squeezed her hands in greeting. "Allow me to introduce my friend, Miss Bettencourt."

Greetings exchanged, Ashley asked the other two to help check her hem in the back. Once assured there was no further damage to her dress, Ashley slipped her tiny sewing kit into her reticule. "I have an idea that might help with your sister," she began.

"About how to summon the Bogeyman?"

Ashley felt barely a pang of conscience as she shook her head. "Have you talked with your sister about what it would be like to live as Mr. Giovanni's wife if he truly hasn't a feather to fly with?" She pinned up Miss Kenyon's recalcitrant curl as she spoke. "Can she sew her own wardrobe? Because she wouldn't be able to afford a modiste. Does she know how to prepare meals? They probably couldn't afford to pay a cook, either."

Miss Kenyon grinned. Miss Bettencourt looked thoughtful.

"They wouldn't have many servants to help with the housekeeping at all. Perhaps none." With satisfaction, Ashley watched the swift play of emotions on Miss Bettencourt's face. During her time at the academy she had successfully convinced several girls not to elope. She glanced from side to side and leaned in. The other two checked that they were still alone and leaned close as well. "She might even," she lowered her voice as though imparting a great secret, "have to empty and clean their chamber pots herself."

Miss Bettencourt gasped, then laughed. "My sister would *never* want to do such a thing!"

They straightened as two ladies entered and nodded to them in greeting.

"Thank you so much, Miss Hamlin," Miss Bettencourt said as the trio exited the room. "I'll have another talk with her tonight."

Before bed, Ashley gave Maggie and Sally their usual reading lesson. Both had made marvelous progress. Neither of them said a word about her not letting them change the pillowcases on her bed. The afternoon Ravencroft left, she'd lain down on her bed clutching one of the pillows that smelled faintly of him, and slept straight through to the next morning.

She clutched a pillow now. The other scents were fading, only the rosemary still distinguishable. After allowing herself to wallow a minute longer, she set the pillow aside.

Sitting at her desk, she took out a sheet of paper and drew a line down the middle. On one side she wrote down all the men she had danced with or otherwise been introduced to who could remotely be considered matrimonial prospects.

Lord Ravencroft—had decreed he would never marry. Ignoring the stab of pain in her chest that made breathing difficult, she crossed his name out.

Lord Fairfax—an incorrigible flirt who showed no interest in pinning his attentions on only one woman. Listening to his deep voice would continually remind her of Ravencroft. Crossed him off.

Mr. Westbrook—handsome, humorous, and musically talented, she could be friends with him. But she could not marry a close friend of Ravencroft. Even the idea made her heart ache. Crossed him off.

Lord Grantham—ugh. At least twice her age, and he sang off-key.

Hmm. Perhaps she had requirements for her suitor after all, like the Linford family, in needing him to have at least a modicum of musical skill.

Mr. Huntley—definitely had musical talent. He was also prettier than she, could sing higher, and had nicer hair. Shallow of her, she admitted, but she crossed him off, too.

The widower with eight children ... what was his name? She wrote *Widower w8* and crossed him off.

She stared at her paper, cudgeling her brain, trying to think if there was anyone else whose name she could add.

While she tried to come up with someone, *anyone*, else, she turned to the other side of the paper and listed all the positions she'd applied for, consulting her journal to remember which potential employers had already replied and which she still waited to hear from. The only posting for an administrative position she'd been able to find was in Berwick. Located just a few miles south of the Scottish border, Berwick was so far away that visits with Mrs. Rafferty and other friends from the academy would be out of the question. Letters would take weeks to reach each other. She'd hope to make new friends, of course, but she'd be isolated from her current circle of acquaintances.

She browsed through her other journals, skimming the meticulous notes she'd kept as she assisted Madame Zavrina in operating the academy. Bartering with local farmer's wives for hand cream the students made in exchange for manure for the academy's garden had increased their crop yields and cut their food expenses, and gave them a more varied diet. Changing the wording and placement of advertisements had increased enrollment while spending less. Efficiencies in the kitchen had allowed the scullery maid to attend classes part time.

She slammed the journal shut and stared at it. Ravencroft was right. She *was* an administrator. Someone who could teach as needed, but her specialty had developed into helping the school run cost effectively and efficiently while still giving the students an excellent education.

Georgia was not the only girl she had rescued from a too-ardent suitor. She'd persuaded several others not to run off with their groom, footman, or other person their family deemed unsuitable, and had taught many of them the judicious use of a knee, elbow, or teeth if a man was too forward in his attentions.

Her mind racing, she got a fresh sheet and started making notes.

Near dawn, she finally fell into an exhausted sleep, clutching a pillow to her chest. When she awoke, she knew exactly what she needed to do.

"Come in," Uncle Edward called.

Ashley stepped inside his study. "I wish to discuss a business proposition with you," she said, sitting in the chair across from him and setting several of her journals on the desk as well as pages of notes.

He pushed aside his account book and set the quill pen in its holder. "I'm listening, my dear."

Dear, sweet Uncle Edward. "You have been most kind and generous to me this Season. However, even with the dowry you bestowed, I have been unable to find a suitable match, and given my experiences of late, that's not likely to change." She tapped the top journal. "I've been trying to secure another position at a school, as I do not want to live with Cousin Niles after you return to Jamaica. That's not going well, either."

"Idiots, the lot of them," Uncle Edward muttered.

"I beg your pardon?"

"I am so sorry, my dear. When we arrived in London, I had the highest hopes that you would find a match. Someone who would recognize your stellar qualities, who would hold you in esteem and affection. I am sorely disappointed in the gentlemen of the *ton*."

Ashley felt her throat constrict. He wasn't the only one disappointed.

Uncle Edward interlaced his fingers on the ink blotter. "What third option have you devised?"

Ashley took a deep breath and let it out slowly. "I wish to open my own school."

She waited for his gasp of shock, for him to tell her what a crazy idea it was.

He leaned toward her. "Tell me more."

251

Lovely, dear, open-minded Uncle Edward. "Let me invest the money set aside for my dowry to instead set up the school. Procure a location, furnish the facility, advertise to attract students, and hire staff. Mrs. Rafferty and some of the other staff from Madame Zavrina's academy are not happy where they ended up or have not yet managed to secure a new position." Ashley patted her stack of journals. "I spent most of my time at the school helping to run it. I took extensive notes. And Madame Zavrina was younger than I am now when she first opened the academy." She folded her hands in her lap. "I was able to save much of my wages and have that money to invest."

Uncle Edward listened without interrupting. What she proposed might seem unorthodox, but she was pitching her business idea to the man who had freed the slaves on his newly inherited sugar plantation and then offered them paid employment. 'Unconventional' seemed to run in the family. Even if Edward wasn't actually a blood relative.

"These are your plans?" He pointed at the loose papers on top of her journal.

She nodded and slid them across to him. He rang the bell, requested tea and biscuits, and they spent the afternoon discussing the school.

"Eunice will not be happy about your decision, at least not at first. However, I think we can bring her round to our way of thinking." Uncle Edward refilled his teacup. "I'll have my solicitor meet with us tomorrow. If you haven't changed your mind—"

"I won't."

"—we'll get him to draw up documents that will protect you, and me, and keep your cousin Niles or any other man from interfering in your business venture."

Excitement bubbling up within her, they clinked teacups in a toast.

That night's entertainment was a soirée at the home of Lord and Lady Oswego. As excited as Ashley was about her school and plans for it, she decided not to share the news just yet with Georgia or anyone else. Aunt Eunice had seemed near tears when she found out, though she admitted to the logic of the plan. She had also cast an aspersion or two upon the bachelors of the *ton*.

At least two hundred people filled the ballroom. The floor was alternating black and white marble tiles, in squares large enough Lord Oswego was known to have his servants stand in costume so he could play life-size chess matches. Lady Oswego had hired musicians to play in the background as everyone circulated, chatting and drinking, while a group near the terrace doors indulged in country dances led by Lord and Lady Oswego themselves. Here and there around the perimeter, couches and chairs were arranged in cozy conversational nooks.

"Let me know if you would like any introductions, my dear," Uncle Edward said as they entered the ballroom. For the past six weeks this phrase had been his way to help her find a match. Tonight they were also looking for anyone who could help with making her school a reality. Especially those with daughters or nieces who would be of an age to benefit from a ladies' academy.

Aunt Eunice's gasp caught them both by surprise. "What is it, my dear?" Uncle Edward said.

Aunt Eunice snapped open her fan to cover the bottom half of her face as she turned her head and lowered her voice. "Don't look now, but over by the pianoforte, isn't that Alvanley and Pierrepoint?"

"How do you expect me to tell if you don't want me to look?" Uncle Edward groused good-naturedly. He leaned to the right to see around some people, and quickly straightened. "By Jove, I think you're right!"

Ashley popped up on her tiptoes to see over shoulders, hoping for a glimpse of Prinny's famous friends.

"Do you think Alvanley's fat friend is in attendance tonight?" Uncle Edward whispered with a broad grin.

Aunt Eunice smacked him with her fan. "Lady Oswego would be over the moon at such an exalted guest."

"As crowded as it is, it would be easy for him to sneak in. But he doesn't seem the type to 'sneak' anywhere. I think we would all be well aware if he were here."

Giving up on trying to see the prince's friends—or the prince himself—Ashley kissed Uncle Edward on the cheek and tilted her head in the direction of Georgia, who she saw chatting with Mr. Westbrook. "I'm just going to visit with my friend," she said.

"Have fun, dear," Aunt Eunice said.

As Ashley got closer to Georgia, through the crowd she saw Lord Fairfax seated nearby in one of the conversation circles, chatting with Leighton and Sutcliff.

Her heart caught in her chest when she spotted Ravencroft giving Mr. Barrett a hug. As he straightened he gave his head a slight shake to flip his long hair out of his eyes. Even through the buzz of conversation, she heard his deep rumble of laughter, felt it right down to her toes.

Before she got close enough to speak to him, the retired music teacher took Ravencroft and Fairfax by the hand as though they were small children and led them right past her, exclaiming, "Mrs. Barrett will be so happy to see you both!"

Mr. Barrett was oblivious to her, Fairfax acknowledged Ashley with a nod, and Ravencroft gave her a self-deprecating shrug and half-smile at being led like a child.

They didn't have far to go, as Mrs. Barrett was seated in the next cluster of couches. Ashley debated moving away so as not to eavesdrop on the reunion, while Mrs. Barrett declared she hadn't seen 'young Mr. Linford' in over two years.

"Amazing, isn't it?" Georgia said, suddenly at Ashley's side. "No matter how old one gets, the teacher always sees you as a student."

"That is true, miss," Ashley said, affecting a stern voice. "And what do you have to say for yourself?"

They bent their heads together, laughing. They quieted just in time to hear Mrs. Barrett request they sing the "Switch Song."

"Do you still remember it?" Mrs. Barrett said, addressing both Fairfax and Ravencroft. "You came up with it when Mr. Barrett insisted you practice your upper ranges and you were bored."

"Ooh!" Georgia clutched Ashley's arm. "I've heard about the Switch Song, but never heard it performed," she whispered. "I remember Mother and Aunt Lydia talking about it. Uncle David and his friends won a school talent show with it, more than once."

After Fairfax beckoned them over, Westbrook, Leighton, and Sutcliff joined Ravencroft and Fairfax in a tight circle, speaking so quietly their voices were indistinguishable. After a moment they broke apart.

"Your wish is our command, madam," Lord Sutcliff said, bowing over Mrs. Barrett's hand. He was as tall as Fairfax yet stouter than his companions, with short brown hair, and crinkles at the corners of his brown eyes from smiling.

"Oh, la, Lord Sutcliff," Mrs. Barrett said, fanning her cheeks with her hand. "Go on with you!"

The five gentlemen trooped out of the room.

"I have to tell Mother!" Georgia grabbed Ashley's hand and they worked their way through the crowd searching for Lady Mansfield.

"He's going to do what?" Lady Mansfield said a few moments later. "Lydia needs to hear this!"

They found Lady Templeton, had a similar conversation as with Lady Mansfield, who then tasked them to seek out Lady Bedford.

"He's what?" Lady Bedford quickly made her way over to chat with Mr. and Mrs. Barrett.

While the musicians on the far side of the room continued to play for the dancers near the terrace doors, Mr. Barrett had apparently spoken to Lord Oswego. Footmen rearranged several of the conversation circles to make a small stage area and moved the couches and chairs into rows.

Butterflies of anticipation danced in Ashley's stomach, for no logical reason. She'd heard all five men sing before, though not together. This would be her first time hearing Lord Sutcliff in a formal performance. Certainly that was no cause for excitement; Ashley would not be adding Sutcliff's name to her list of potential suitors, no matter how attractive his face or beautiful his voice, after she heard Mrs. Barrett greet another woman as Lady Sutcliff and invite her to sit on the couch beside her.

The five men returned and wended their way through the clusters of people to the cleared makeshift stage area. Lord Oswego gave the signal for the musicians to take a break, and more of the crowd drifted over to watch whatever was about to happen, whispering and wondering aloud. The few couches and chairs filled up quickly, leaving most of the crowd standing.

The men lined up arm's width apart, each standing in the center of a tile, with Leighton on the far left, Ravencroft next to him, and Westbrook on the far right.

Leighton began singing, higher than she'd ever heard him before, while the other four provided harmony. Ravencroft took up the melody, singing in a low tenor voice. They all began to exchange puzzled glances as they performed. Fairfax sang the next stanza, in a high baritone range she would not have thought possible for him. They went down the line, each man singing lower than the one before, until Westbrook ended the first verse in a bass voice.

As the crowd began to applaud, each man held up a finger, silently asking the crowd to wait. They gathered in a tight circle, heads together, and engaged in an exaggerated yet silent argument. They quickly moved back out into a straight line, each centered in a different marble tile, this time with Ravencroft on the far left singing high tenor, down the line until Leighton on the far right sang bass. Again they each looked perplexed while they sang, sometimes tapping their throat as though the wrong sound was coming out.

With scattered laughter and applause, the crowd began to catch on. Ashley recognized several of the matrons who edged their way to the front for a better view as those who'd been in attendance at previous performances. Lady Danforth already fanned her flushed cheeks.

At the end of each verse they lined up in a different order, seeming still perplexed. Whoever was on the far left sang high tenor, and their voices descended until the man on the far right sang bass.

They began switching places and parts while they sang, their register seemingly dictated by which tile they stood on, the audience laughing in all the appropriate places. Their transitions were seamless, each man perfectly suiting his voice to his position in the lineup, almost dancing as they gracefully swapped tiles. Previous expressions of confusion were replaced with delight as they gave in to the magic ability of the tiles to change their voices. Fairfax flirted with the audience, winking at several women. Leighton was equally charming. Sutcliff saved his smiles and a wink for his wife.

Ashley and Georgia exchanged glances now and then, utterly captivated by the performance. She imagined them as young men still in university, how much time they must have spent in rehearsal not just to learn this skit but also to be able to sing in each range. A way to practice their upper ranges, Mrs. Barrett had said, while their voices deepened as they matured into grown men. The lyrics would have been easy to memorize as this was a popular tune. Ashley had sung it herself and heard it in numerous evening entertainments, though this arrangement was a little different, heavily weighted toward the bass clef. She wouldn't be surprised if Ravencroft had made the changes.

Her face almost hurting from smiling so much, Ashley leaned around Georgia to check Lady Mansfield and Lady Templeton's response. They were holding each other by the arm, tears of joy rolling unchecked down Lady Templeton's cheek as she watched her brother sing and perform as though he had not a care in the world, with not a hint of self-consciousness. Lady Bedford stepped closer, and Lady Mansfield rested her head on her aunt's shoulder as Lady Bedford put her arm around her.

"Disgraceful, if you ask me," Lady Bigglesworth said with a snort of derision, the ostrich feather in her green turban trembling in her outrage. "Peers of the realm, acting like common minstrels."

"No one asked you," Lady Danforth muttered, quickly turning her attention back to the performance.

"Hush," Lady Barbour said beside her, shooing away Lady Bigglesworth, before giving her full attention once more to the performance.

The men settled on a spot for the final verse, each singing impossibly better than before in what she thought was his most natural tone—Sutcliff as low tenor, Leighton as baritone/tenor, Westbrook as baritone, Ravencroft in a mellow baritone/bass range, and Fairfax's rich bass sometimes dropping down to a bone-rattling basso profundo. Despite no instruments, the combined melody and harmonies from their voices wove a tapestry of sound.

Stunning.

Delicious chills chased up Ashley's spine. Little hairs on the back of her neck and her forearms stood on end. She felt the reverberations from this chamber choir of five, each a master of his voice as an instrument, all the way through her core, deep into her bones.

As much as Ashley was enjoying the performance, Ravencroft seemed relaxed and content, at peace with himself in a way she had never before seen.

He radiated joy. He sounded divine.

Occasionally the left side of his mouth would quirk with a half-smile as the audience reacted to the group's antics or showed their appreciation for a particularly fine solo, whether his or from one of the others.

Ashley spared a quick glance to see how the crowd was responding. Most of the women were unabashedly as enthralled as she, as well as quite a few of the men. Over at the edge of the crowd she noticed two gentlemen, their heads bowed in close conversation, one writing with a pencil in a small notebook.

"Oh dear lord, is that Alvanley taking notes?" Lady Mansfield whispered, glancing at the same two men.

"Prinny's friend?" Lady Templeton's eyes grew wide.

"With Henry Pierrepoint," Lady Bedford said with a slow nod. "Company must be thin at their club tonight."

The singers were almost at the end of the song. In the front row, Lady Sutcliff was smiling, Mrs. Barrett was beaming, and the buttons were in danger of popping off Mr. Barrett's waistcoat he looked so proud of his 'bassy boys.' If they all sounded this good, how in the world would judges be able to determine a winner at the Catch Club competition?

The men ended the song in a sustained, perfectly harmonized four-octave chord, a small hand gesture from Ravencroft cutting them off in unison.

The delighted audience erupted in applause and cheers.

"You know, it hasn't been that long since a Ravencroft entertained at the court of the Hanover king," Lady Bedford said when the applause began to die down.

"I recall that Father was gone for several months once," Lady Mansfield said. "David hadn't been born yet. Mother told us Father had been summoned to entertain King George at Windsor Castle."

"His Majesty was bereft at losing the American colonies," Lady Bedford said, nodding. "Not sure he's ever fully recovered from it."

Ashley wanted nothing more than to speak with Ravencroft, to congratulate him on such a crowd-pleasing performance, but the throng of well-wishers that surged forward at the conclusion made it impossible for her to even see the singers. She didn't know where Georgia had got to. A footman bearing a tray of drinks paused before her, and she selected a glass of champagne.

"You look happy."

Ashley almost choked on her drink at the rich masculine voice speaking so close to her ear. If she tilted her head back, she could rest it on Ravencroft's shoulder. "I could say the same of you." She turned so she could see his face, look deep into those gorgeous hazel eyes. "Mr. and Mrs. Barrett certainly seemed to appreciate it, as did the crowd." Recalling Lady Bigglesworth, she added, "Well, the majority. Some thought it was undignified."

Ravencroft grinned. "Of course it's undignified. That's why it's fun." He tossed back the last of his drink and beckoned to a footman.

"More tea with honey, my lord?" he said, taking the empty glass.

"Good man." Ravencroft waited until the footman had moved away. "Seriously. You look happy. Have you had good news?"

Indecision gripped her for a moment. But only for a moment. She strolled over to one of the conversation nooks that were currently unoccupied. Ravencroft sat beside her on the sofa, far enough away that no one could construe it as improper. "I have made my own good news."

Chapter 18

RAVENCROFT RAISED ONE EYEBROW. "I am utterly intrigued by your phrasing."

"You were right. I am an administrator, not a teacher. As there is a shortage of headmistress or assistant headmistress positions open, I have decided to open my own school."

Ravencroft blinked a few times, apparently processing her statement, but otherwise did not immediately react.

Normally she would not be this frank with a gentleman acquaintance. However, given the somewhat intimate nature of their friendship—having stitched his arm, bathed him, and washed his hair, after all—she plunged ahead. "It appears that no suitable gentleman is going to offer matrimony or even court me in the time available before my aunt and uncle leave for Jamaica."

She paused, giving him a chance to disagree. To announce he'd changed his mind about never marrying and he wanted to court her. Or at least assure her that some worthy gentleman would come up to scratch.

He made no such protest or proclamation.

"Therefore, I have persuaded Uncle Edward to allow me to invest the money he set aside for my dowry into opening a school. Isn't that marvelous?"

The footman returned with Ravencroft's tea. He took a long drink, then another. As though he were stalling.

She searched his expression, unable to identify any single emotion as a series of them seemed to flit across his face in rapid succession. Did he think her idea absurd?

"That's fabulous, honey," he finally said. "Where will it be?"

She exhaled, a mix of relief and disappointment. "Uncle's solicitor is meeting with us tomorrow. Among other things, he should have recommendations of agents to help me find the best location for the school. Location is very important."

"Your uncle is bringing in his solicitor? He's quite serious about this project."

"We have a great deal to do and not much time before he sails for Jamaica."

She would have liked to continue conversing with him, if for no other reason than for the physical pleasure of his deep voice washing over her like a warm bath, as it always did. Discuss the Switch Song, or plans for the school, or anything, really. Just to keep spending time with him. But another gentleman approached him, soliciting his opinion on a matter that was soon due for a vote in the House of Lords, and Miss Kenyon wanted to introduce Ashley to another friend.

Giving each other a rueful shrug, they departed in separate directions.

"This wasn't expressly on the list of your requests." Reginald Chadburn, Esquire, slid a portfolio across Uncle Edward's desk the next afternoon, halfway between Ashley and her uncle. "But I took the liberty of collecting other information I thought you might find useful." A stout man in his fifties, he sat back in his chair and pulled several more portfolios out of his leather satchel. "I have information on three properties so far that would be suitable for converting into a school." He indicated the folios in his hand. "While I was researching real estate information for another client, I happened across two schools where the owners are planning to retire and quietly wish to sell." He indicated the folio on the desk.

Ashley and her uncle exchanged surprised glances.

"Your name as an investor in this enterprise, Mr. Endicott, will help attract some families who are abolitionists such as yourself. However, Miss Hamlin, you should know your uncle's views will also prove a detraction to some prospective clients who do not share his beliefs."

"I'm not sure I'd want to attract those sorts of clients." Ashley tapped her bottom lip. "However, there could be the opportunity to allow the girls to form their own opinions if they are exposed to views different from that of their parents."

"Quite so." Uncle Edward opened the folio and turned it so Ashley could read the papers at the same time.

"You face many challenges in your endeavor, Miss Hamlin, as I'm sure you're already aware. It is a conundrum of our society that your relatively advanced age made it difficult for you to secure a suitable match in the Marriage Mart, while your relative youth may cause some to question if you are mature enough to head up a school for young ladies."

Ashley barely resisted the urge to swear. "Yes, I am painfully aware of society's contradictions."

"Assuming ownership of a school that is already established would greatly simplify things compared to starting from the ground up, as it were," Mr. Chadburn continued. "I am, however, employed at your leisure. I will pursue whichever path you wish in order to procure information so you may select a suitable property."

Ashley was gratified that Mr. Chadburn included her in the last statement, given that Uncle Edward paid his fees, not her. "I honestly hadn't considered taking over an existing school would even be a possibility," she said. "I just want to follow the same path as Madame Zavrina."

"Ah, yes, Miss Penelope Smythe." Mr. Chadburn shuffled through the papers in a folio and pulled out one sheet.

At Ashley's confused expression, Mr. Chadburn handed her the paper with details of the exchange of property in Torquay to Miss Penelope Smythe. "You knew her better as Madame Zavrina."

Ashley gasped. "I once heard her brother refer to her as Penny. I thought the difference in their last name was because she was widowed at a young age."

Mr. Chadburn shook his head. "I've done only a cursory search so far, but I found no evidence that she ever married. There may have been a broken betrothal. That would require more research, and I wanted to know how you wish to proceed before I invest more time in any particular line of exploration."

Ashley took a moment to ponder the information that changed her view, however slightly, of Madame Zavrina. She'd never been married. If Ashley went forward with her plan to run her own school, would that also doom her to never marry? Never be at the mercy of a husband's whims. But also never cuddle on the sofa before the fire after a late-night snack. Fall asleep with her head pillowed on her loved one's chest, his arm around her.

Mr. Chadburn brought her back to the present. "Mr. Smythe has already established a new, *ahem*, business enterprise on the academy's property."

Ashley waved her hand dismissively. "Yes, we knew he was turning it into a brothel. That's why we all left."

Uncle Edward sputtered. "Good heavens, no, you don't want to go anywhere near that property."

"I did, however, enjoy being able to walk along the seashore in Torquay when I had free time," Ashley continued. "Perhaps we can find something suitable between Plymouth and Dover?" Many of the former students as well as teachers from the academy were from towns near Torquay. Maybe she'd be able to visit with old friends now and then after all. New friends like Georgia were wonderful, but she also treasured long-term relationships. Mrs. Rafferty, for example, had been one of her instructors when Ashley attended as a student, before becoming a colleague and friend. And a school in a picturesque location should make it easier to attract and retain staff.

"I will have my associates help me look into it. The two we found by happenstance are in Manchester and Lancaster. We can try to locate something near the southern coast." Mr. Chadburn retrieved another document from his portfolio and slid it across the desk. "I did as you requested, Mr. Endicott, and transferred the funds you intended for Miss Hamlin's dowry into her account earlier today. We should have no difficulty finding a suitable property with this much of an initial investment available."

Ashley reached for the document and scanned the numbers.

Stunned, she dropped the paper as though it had bitten her, her heart pounding. She knew how much Uncle Edward was gifting her. She also knew how much she had managed to save over the years, and the paltry amount of interest those funds had earned.

This figure was too high. *Much* too high.

She quickly did the math in her head. The amount was ... ten thousand pounds too high. Exactly. To the penny.

Uncle Edward picked up the statement. His eyes widened as he looked over the numbers and he let out a low whistle. "Madame

Zavrina must have paid a much more generous salary than I thought possible."

"Are you certain this is the correct amount?" Ashley swallowed hard. "Certain this is for *my* account?"

Mr. Chadburn consulted a small notebook he retrieved from his coat pocket and compared it to the bank statement. "Yes, I am certain this matches the account information you gave me. Is something wrong?"

Her mind raced. Where could the money have come from? A bank error?

A memory teased.

"Yesterday, in trying to rescue you, it seems I inadvertently abducted you."

"What are you asking for ransom?"

She folded her arms and tapped one finger on her chin. "I think a peer of the realm should be worth at least ten thousand pounds, don't you?" She grinned at her silliness.

Ransom.

Ashley stared out the window, trying to get her racing heart and erratic breathing under control.

Ravencroft had paid her a ransom.

Never mind how he'd found which bank she kept her account, or that the bank had allowed him or his representative to make a deposit into an account that wasn't his.

Did he actually consider it ransom? Or had he made this deposit after she told him about opening a school? Did he wish to be an investor? If that were the case, why hadn't he spoken with her first?

What conditions were tied to this money?

"My dear, is everything all right?" Uncle Edward reached across to pat her hand.

She shook herself. "Fine, uncle. I simply earned more interest income than I anticipated."

"Ah, yes," Mr. Chadburn said with a broad grin. "The power of compound interest!"

"She's going to do what?" Liam set down his violin and bow while they were taking a break during rehearsal at Mansfield's townhouse.

The Catch Club competition was tomorrow night. Lydia had stayed home today, Templeton said, because she didn't trust herself not to interfere. Which gave David the perfect opportunity to have everyone try out the new song he had written, thanks to Ashley's help in transcribing the melody he'd started while drunk.

"Open her own school. Got tired of receiving letters rejecting her application for employment." David set down his bow and viola da gamba to pour a glass of honey and lemon tea. "Doesn't want to rely on her cousin's hospitality or go back to Jamaica with her aunt and uncle at the end of the month. No gentleman has come up to scratch whom she wants to marry, so she's forging her own path."

By now his solicitor should have deposited money in her account. It wasn't ransom, though he'd chuckled at that memory. Nor was it payment. A gift, he considered it, to help her on her path to independence. A shawl or fan would have been a proper gift, whispered a little voice in his head that sounded suspiciously like Aunt Connie. But their relationship had been improper since their very first meeting, and what was the point of taking on the burden of a title and being wealthy if one couldn't help a friend realize her dream?

"And you've accepted this? Where will the school be located?"

David shrugged. "I doubt even she knows yet."

He tried to take a sip but Liam took his glass and set it down, rested his hands on David's shoulders, and marched him backwards until his spine bumped up against the shelves.

"Are you truly this oblivious?" There was no hint of humor in Liam's voice or face.

David tried to step forward.

Liam held him in place and leaned in closer, lowering his voice. "I'd wager a year's rent there is a gentleman whom she would accept if he would just get his head out of his arse, open his mouth, and speak the words she longs to hear."

David furrowed his brow, wracked his brain. Tamped down an unexpected surge of jealousy that constricted his chest. "Who?"

Fairfax? No, the viscount was an incorrigible flirt. Couldn't be Huntley, could it? The cub was barely out of university. Sutcliff was already married. Leighton? Who else had she met?

Looking deeply frustrated, Liam briefly covered his face with one hand, shook his head, then gave David a not-so-subtle shake. "It's you, you bacon-brained idiot."

"Me?" The floor seemed to drop out from under David. Good thing he was leaning against the shelves. Only them at his back and Liam holding his shoulders seemed to be keeping him upright. "But... but she knows I have no intention of ever marrying." He barely got the words past his closed-off throat.

"Does she know why you think that?"

Mutely, David nodded.

"While you were recuperating, hidden in her bedchamber, did she ever have occasion to observe you walk barefoot?" David nodded again, and Liam continued. "Does she know why you limp?" Liam tightened his grip, digging his fingertips into David's shoulders. "Did she see your legs?"

Again David nodded, not trusting his voice.

"And what was her reaction? Did she run away screaming in horror? Make a derogatory comment? Look upon you with pity?"

David stood tall. "Of course not!" He slumped a little. "She was..."

"Yes?"

"Concerned their difference caused me pain." His voice was barely a whisper.

Liam patted David's cheek. "I should show you the letters she wrote me each day while you were in her care."

Jealousy flared in David's chest again. "Letters? To you?"

"Updating me on her patient's progress." A sparkle of mischief lit Liam's eyes. "After she confessed that you were in her bed, unconscious, I asked her to take good care of you. Her maid met with Gilroy every day to bring me a letter and get your clothes from your valet, piece by piece."

A surge of emotion swept through him, stealing his breath. David's mind raced, trying to remember the days he spent in Ashley's care. So much of it, especially the first few days, was fuzzy. She wrote to Liam? Every day? He narrowed his eyes.

Liam gave David's chest a double pat and dropped his hands. "Yes, I think I could easily fall in love with her. But because of my friendship with you I doubt she would accept my suit. And if you don't get your head out of your—"

"You made your point," David growled.

"—I won't even be able to remain friends with her. She's a bluestocking, and brazen, and she laughs at my stories in all the right places." Liam walked back to his chair. "I quite like her for it," he tossed over his shoulder.

David quite liked her, too. Did he love her? He certainly enjoyed the time he spent in her company, even if much of the time he had been in pain or half-foxed. Or both. She kept her head in a volatile situation. Possibly saved his life, or at least his arm. Upon learning his deepest, darkest, most closely guarded secret, she had responded with compassion and concern, not revulsion, pity, or contempt.

Though not a trained musician, she'd done her best to save the composition he'd been creating while drunk but promptly forgot when he sobered up. She had pushed him to make changes in his life though in such a gentle way he hadn't even realized what she was doing, her words kind and thoughtful, helping him heal emotional wounds while she ministered to his physical needs.

And her kisses...

Enthusiastic. She made his blood boil, his heart pound, in a way no one else ever had. Even when he smelled of flash powder and had barely altered his costume from the Bogeyman by flipping over his cape and adding a red mask so he could attend the masquerade ball, he'd risked discovery ... just so he could waltz with her. Hold her close.

She knew all his secrets. About his short leg. That he'd been the one to rescue her from being ruined by Rupert. That he'd dressed up as the Bogeyman to protect two women and been injured in a fight protecting yet another. And he hadn't suffered a moment's worry that she would betray his confidence. Instinctively he knew he could trust her. Georgia's three-legged pup had trusted Ashley right from the start. Dogs had excellent instincts about people. She'd invited the battle-scarred dog onto her lap and called him a handsome fellow.

That pause when she told him about the school... Had she been waiting for him to declare himself? The sudden stab of pain at the idea of her leaving London to open her own school had startled him. Did that mean he'd never see her again?

Another stab of pain shot through his chest, stealing his breath.

He slapped his forehead. "I'm an idiot," he muttered.

"Glad we're in agreement." Liam grinned.

David slammed back his honey tea and set the glass on the table with a thud. He needed to have a conversation with Ashley, urgently. He'd walk out right now, go directly to her uncle's townhouse.

The other men in the room looked at him expectantly.

With a mental sigh, he weighed his responsibilities and desires. Once more, duty took precedence over his personal wishes.

He'd talk with her tonight. He had to see his family and friend through the competition, help Liam win his needed share of the prize money. And they weren't going to win any prizes with what they'd done in the last hour.

"Mansfield, you missed the key change," David said, striding to the pianoforte. "That's an E flat, not an E natural."

Mansfield squinted at the sheet of music where David stabbed his finger. "Bugger," he muttered.

"Did you lose count?" David asked Parker as he straightened. "You were late coming in on the second verse."

"Um..."

This wasn't going to work. Not in time for the competition. David rubbed his temples.

"I think we can learn to play the music," Liam said. "Or sing the lyrics. But not both. Not in time for tomorrow night."

"You two obviously can play and sing it well," Templeton said. "The rest of us simply need more rehearsal time to become as proficient. You've composed a beautiful song. I want to do it justice."

David locked gazes with Liam.

Liam nodded.

"Shove over," David said, giving Mansfield a slight push.

Mansfield rose from the pianoforte bench and shook out his coattails. "I yield. With gratitude."

David flipped his coattails back and sat on the bench, and confirmed the other men had abandoned their instruments and gathered around the pianoforte, sheet music in hand.

"Let's try it this way, shall we?" David played the opening chords.

Ashley paced in front of the fireplace at the Mansfield townhouse music room. Except for the children, all of the Templeton and Mansfield ladies were present.

All of the men were gone. Tonight was the big night. The annual competition at the Noblemen and Gentlemen's Catch Club.

Georgia pleaded with Ashley to stay long past when she and her aunt would have gone home after a musical evening at the Mansfield townhouse. Parker's wife Deirdre dozed on the sofa, using Lady Bedford's shoulder for a pillow. Lawrence was not competing but had gone as part of the audience, as had Uncle Edward. Clarissa repeatedly threw a child's stocking stuffed with wool scraps for Tuffy, who would retrieve it and sit at her feet, panting and wagging his tail until she threw the toy again.

Lady Mansfield and Lady Templeton had faced each other over a chessboard for more than an hour yet hadn't progressed much beyond opening moves with the pawns. Georgia sat at the harp, listlessly plucking a tune.

Last night, Aunt Eunice had pleaded a headache, so Ashley and Uncle Edward had stayed home, poring over real estate listings and working on plans for the school. She wished she'd had a chance to see Ravencroft before the competition. To wish him luck, of course. Not because it was almost physically painful if she did not see him each day, talk to him each evening. Late at night in her room, alone, she heard the echo of his uneven footsteps, remembered his rumbling chuckle. How he'd toy with her hair. Their intimate conversations.

Ashley tugged her silk shawl higher up on her shoulders. Despite feeling silly, as she was not generally a superstitious person, tonight she had worn her pink dress with ruffles at the bottom that Ravencroft had noticed hanging in her dressing room, and topped it with the cream, red, and blue paisley silk shawl she'd worn the night he rescued her.

Just as Ashley worried she was going to wear a path in the carpet and must choose another route, they heard a commotion at the front door. Many footsteps and men's voices filled the foyer and spilled down the hall. The women jumped up, practically pushing each other in their eagerness to see the cause of the commotion.

Lord Mansfield, Templeton, and Parker froze as they saw the women, their expressions carefully blank. The door to the street remained wide open. More men were visible behind them, waiting to enter.

"Well?" Lady Templeton tapped the toe of one silk-slippered foot.

No one moved or seemed to breathe.

Mansfield and Templeton exchanged glances, then shouted in unison, "We won!"

At least two dozen men cheered, and moved farther into the entry, making room for even more to file in. Men with boisterous voices raised in conversation spilled into the entryway, in a trail leading down the steps all the way out to the street. Parker and Lawrence came in, followed by Lord Bristol and the other four in his group, wearing matching red neckcloths, then Mr. Barrett, and dozens more men.

"Make way for the champion!" boomed a familiar bass voice, though Ashley had never heard it raised that loud before.

The crowd parted, revealing Ravencroft carried aloft on the shoulders of Fairfax and Westbrook, with Sutcliff and Huntley holding his legs. Ravencroft ducked his chin, his cheeks flushed almost as pink as his neckcloth as he held onto Westbrook and Fairfax to keep from falling from his precarious perch.

"Make way, I said, make way!" Fairfax gestured with his free hand, and those who had drifted into their path stepped aside. The procession went straight to the music room, followed by more and more people until it seemed every gentleman in London was trooping into the house, all of them talking at once.

Lord Mansfield must have spoken to the footmen, because the wall separating the front parlour from the music room suddenly swept back. Within moments, even the enlarged space felt crowded with so many people continuing to pour in.

Lady Templeton stood with her back against the wall, watching the river of masculine humanity, her jaw slack. Lady Mansfield directed the servants to bring in more chairs, though most guests seemed inclined to stand and circulate, analyzing tonight's competitive performances. Two maids rolled trays with glasses and pitchers of lemonade into the hallway, and confirmed that tea would be ready shortly.

Ashley stood on her tiptoes, trying to see over shoulders and between bodies, searching for a glimpse of Ravencroft.

There. By the pianoforte, receiving so many pats on his back and shoulders and handshakes, jovially shoved back and forth, it was a wonder he was still on his feet. Someone grabbed him by his right arm. Ashley winced in sympathy as she watched him quickly retrieve his arm and hold it close to his torso, only the slight tightening at his eyes betraying his discomfort from the jostling of the barely healed wound.

"Sing!" called an unfamiliar voice over the din of dozens of conversations. "Sing the winning songs!"

"Sing! Sing! Sing!" The chant was taken up until almost every man present joined in. "Sing! Sing! Sing!"

"It's tradition," Lady Mansfield told Ashley amidst the shouting. "Lydia was at home in the country about to give birth the last time a Ravencroft group won, but it's tradition for all the men of the Catch Club to gather at the home of the winner to celebrate."

Now as Ashley looked over the crowd, she noticed that instead of plain white cravats as at typical society functions, most of the men wore neckcloths or cravats in a variety of colors and prints. Fairfax and the others in his group wore dark green, as usual. Four men she'd never seen before wore matching floral print cravats, and another quintet wore blue and green paisley. Hardly anyone, come to think on it, was wearing a white cravat.

Someone played a few notes, and Ashley found herself ushered to the sofa on the far side from the pianoforte, seated between Lady Bedford and Lady Mansfield. Georgia perched on one arm of the sofa. Lady Templeton and Deirdre shared the overstuffed armchair immediately to their left, and Aunt Eunice and Uncle Edward shared the other sofa with Mr. Barret. The rest of the men sorted themselves out until they either sat on the remaining furniture or stood around the edges of the room, allowing Ashley to see Ravencroft seated at the pianoforte, with Mansfield and Westbrook standing just behind him on one side, Parker and Lord Templeton on the other.

They launched into *The Last Rose of Summer*. David must have changed the arrangement, as it was now in a lower key perfectly suited for five male voices and only one instrument. The room quieted as they sang the first phrase, and the audience had gone utterly still by the time they reached *All her lovely companions are faded and gone.*

Ashley felt and heard David's sisters gasp.

While the song had a pretty melody, the lyrics had always struck Ashley as being too melancholy. She disliked the image of picking the last surviving rose of the summer and scattering its petals on the ground. Several girls at the academy had rehearsed this song, and they'd just been singing words about a flower, with no deeper meaning. After her parents died, Ashley stopped seeing the appeal of songs that could make one cry.

Until now. The men imbued such emotion into the lyrics as they told the story of the song, they each had to be thinking of a lost loved one. Now the song was about a shared experience of loss to which everyone could relate.

She'd heard David sing before, but this... this performance was magical, an entirely different level of talent than he'd previously displayed. His voice was an exquisite instrument as much as the pianoforte he played with such skill, far beyond technical proficiency.

'Tis the last rose of summer, Left blooming alone;

They were alternating who sang lead on each phrase, the others providing a soft background harmony. David looked up from the music, his gaze darting around the room, settling on Ashley in time for his line: *I'll not leave thee, thou lone one!*

Though there must be over a hundred people in the room, it felt as though he sang directly to her.

Her heart thumped as she remembered the first time she'd heard him sing that line. How he'd spoken those words to her just before he lost consciousness in the alley, still bleeding. Words that had made her think of taking care of him, seeing to his injuries, with not a thought for her reputation or other consequences until much, much later.

Ashley swallowed hard, willing herself to not tremble.

She felt Lady Bedford hold her left hand and Lady Mansfield squeeze her right, but she couldn't take her eyes off David.

The next phrase went to Mr. Westbrook, and David glanced down at his music and the keys. Only now did Ashley realize Lord Mansfield's quintet was not wearing the blue neckcloths they had in previous performances. Tonight they each wore a pink cravat.

The same shade of pink as the gown Ashley currently wore, a shade found in the dawn sky for only a few fleeting moments.

Don't think I've ever worn pink, he'd said. From what little she could see of it, David's waistcoat was also pink, embroidered with roses and leaves.

Her heart began to pound. It could mean nothing. Mere coincidence.

But he had to know she'd be here tonight, keeping Georgia company, waiting with his family for the men to return from the competition.

Parker sang, then Templeton. Mansfield did not solo but kept the bass line going in the vocal tapestry the men were weaving. And he did not sound the least bit like a bullfrog.

Ravencroft sang two phrases together:

When true hearts lie wither'd and fond ones are gone, Oh, who would inhabit this bleak world alone?

There was such sorrow in his beautiful voice, she wondered how he could sing at all, let alone with such a clear, gentle baritone. Lady Mansfield sniffed. Lady Bedford surreptitiously dabbed at her eyes with a lace handkerchief. Undoubtedly they were thinking of the previous Lady Ravencroft, who had been unable to bear the grief of losing her husband and eldest son in the span of a few days, and succumbed to the same illness that had claimed them.

Refusing to think about her own losses and to keep herself from bawling like a baby, Ashley glanced at the other audience members. Everyone sat motionless, their attention riveted on the performers, no affectation of ennui from any of them. Mr. Barrett dabbed at his eyes with a snowy white handkerchief that matched his hair before blowing his nose, sounding like a goose honking. Behind her, she heard more than one man sniff back tears.

The singers repeated the final stanza in perfect harmony, their voices blending so well covering four octaves, the little hairs on Ashley's arms stood on end. After a stunned silence while the last chord faded away, the room erupted in wild applause and hearty shouts of *huzzah!*

Georgia leaned over her mother to address Ashley. "I don't think I've ever seen Uncle David wear pink before." She gave a significant glance at Ashley's dress.

"He requested the change for tonight," Lady Mansfield said, gesturing at her throat.

Ashley felt Lady Bedford's stare upon her, though the elegant matron said nothing. Ashley shrugged one shoulder. "I've never worn this gown before." Madame Chantel had made it in the first weeks of the Season, in fabric Aunt Eunice had picked out. Ashley had preferred to dress mostly in light blues and greens that complemented her coloring, while the pink had struck her as too youthful, perhaps even immature, for someone nearly on the shelf.

As the applause died down, the crowd shifted to allow more people into the room. Now a pair of military officers in full uniform joined the gentlemen, standing out in their bright red coats with gold epaulets and braid.

The room quieted as Ravencroft began to play again. Ashley recognized the tune as the one he and Westbrook had played at Clarissa's wedding breakfast. The tune he'd begun composing when he was drunk in her bedchamber, when she'd kissed him to stop him from singing. The tune she had transcribed as best she could so he wouldn't forget it.

Instead of the call and response between the pianoforte and violin, now the call was from tenor voices and answered by the baritone and bass. It was indeed an invitation to play, as she had thought. The lighter voices beckoned one to frolic in the innocence of childhood, to explore, to satisfy one's desires. The deeper voices sang of duty, responsibility, and sacrifices that come with maturity and leaving childhood behind.

After Ravencroft played an intricate passage, Parker and Templeton sang of the blush of youth and innocence, of falling in love. Finding one's true love. Parker's voice faltered on that line as he locked gazes with Deirdre, adoration shining in his eyes. Ravencroft smoothly covered Parker's tenor part, before going back down to low baritone with Westbrook and Mansfield, singing of the need to be practical. The risk of pain and loss, of not wanting to be a fool.

"Damn," Fairfax rumbled from behind her. "I forgot just how good he is when he lets loose."

Ravencroft played the interlude again, giving his head that little toss she found so endearing to flip the hair from his eyes as he glanced up at the audience and locked gazes with her, before once again looking at his hands on the keyboard.

"My bassy boys," Mr. Barrett quietly said, a beatific smile erasing a decade from his face.

All five voices sang the third verse together, about finding the balance between duty and play. How one must dare being foolish in order to win the heart of one's true love. As painful as it could be to lose a loved one, the risk was worth the reward. Nothing compared to the joy of finding true love and knowing one's affection was returned in equal measure.

Ashley could barely draw breath. Ravencroft looked directly at her when he sang of love and joy, as if she and he were the only people in the room. She hoped he read her smile and slow nod as the answer to his barely disguised question; she could no longer see him clearly through the unshed tears blurring her vision.

The last chords played out. Applause erupted. Men jumped up from their seats and where they'd stood lounging on the sides of the room, once more the buzz of conversation filling the air about the song that won tonight's prize for best original composition.

"Boy's got it bad," Lady Bedford softly said, turning to smile at Ashley.

Georgia leaned across her mother to squeeze Ashley's shoulder and whisper in her ear, "Aunt Ashley."

As Georgia straightened, Lady Mansfield squeezed Ashley's hand and raised it to give a quick kiss to the back of her hand. "Aunt Connie, Georgia, perhaps we should go find ourselves a cup of tea," Lady Mansfield said. "I think Ashley and David will need a moment without us." As she rose, she gestured for Lady Templeton and Clarissa to come with them.

Ashley twined her fingers together on her lap, trying not to wrinkle her gown or bite her nails while she waited. Should she rise and try to make her way through the mass of men clustered around the pianoforte? On the other hand, David knew where she was sitting. Surely he would soon get through the crowd that kept stopping him to congratulate him, and join her on the sofa.

Perhaps he'd take her by the hand and lead her to a quiet corner where he could tell her how he had changed his mind about never marrying. Ask her the question she thought she'd never hear. Had all but given up hope of hearing from him yet thought she'd heard in the song he wrote.

Minutes dragged by. Still no David.

To see better through the crowd, Ashley stood. Dozens of men still swarmed the room, now holding cups of tea, lemonade, wineglasses, or tumblers of amber liquid, the din of conversation getting impossibly louder. No sign of David.

Had she misunderstood? Had his pink cravat merely been a coincidence? The song meant nothing more than any other composition, just a pleasant combination of lyrics and music?

As more doubts assailed her, Ashley frantically dove into the crowd, searching each masculine face, looking for the beloved long chestnut hair with a streak of white. She looked at each man in the front parlour and the music room.

No David.

Chapter 19

PERPHAPS HE WAS IN THE CRUSH in the hallway around the refreshment trays.

"My dear, congrat—" Aunt Eunice cut herself off as she searched Ashley's face, her smile fading to an expression of worry. "What is wrong?"

Lady Templeton's joyful expression swiftly changed to concern. "Miss Hamlin?"

"Where is that boy?" Lady Bedford demanded, setting down her cup of tea.

Too choked up to speak, Ashley could only give a bewildered shrug and shake of her head.

In short order the women began a methodical search of the ground floor, enlisting Clarissa and Georgia. Lady Mansfield even went upstairs to look in the nursery. In a particularly deep knot of men conversing near the pianoforte, they found Lords Mansfield and Templeton.

"He's right—" Lord Mansfield cut himself off, looking around him. "He was here..." he consulted his pocket watch... "a few minutes ago."

"Where's Westbrook?" said Lord Templeton. "He'll know."

Come to think on it, Ashley hadn't seen Westbrook, either.

The search was easier and faster this time, as guests had begun to drift away to other entertainments. Even the officers in their bright red coats were gone.

No Ravencroft. No Westbrook.

Deirdre, bless her, persuaded Parker to leave his friends and congratulatory conversations, analyzing every group's performance at the Club tonight and why theirs was so much better, and go home. Perhaps David had some reason to return to the Ravencroft townhouse without speaking to Ashley.

Feeling as deflated as a hot air balloon upon landing in Hyde Park, Ashley gratefully leaned on Aunt Eunice's arm as they walked to Uncle Edward's carriage and went home.

She was half tempted to have Sally take the pink gown and dispose of it, but decided to wait. Surely there was a good explanation for what had happened tonight. Or rather, what had *not* happened. She wrapped the paisley shawl in tissue paper and tucked it back in its drawer.

While she was trying to choke down breakfast after a sleepless night, Farnham entered the dining room with a silver salver holding a note from Georgia.

Deirdre said Uncle David's valet is gone. The other servants said no one has seen either of them since David left for the Catch Club. Father says no one is home at Uncle Liam's rooms at the Albany. Wherever could they have gone? And why?

Where, indeed.

Not trusting her voice, she let Aunt Eunice read the note, then passed it to Uncle Edward.

They kept her busy, with a shopping trip to Bond Street and working on plans for the school, and attending the ball hosted by Lord and Lady Bigglesworth that evening, just as they had planned to do for weeks.

Georgia greeted her with a fierce hug. "I can't imagine how you're feeling," she said, tears shining in her eyes. "But I'm here with you. Ask of me whatever you need."

Ashley sniffed back tears. "Thank you," she whispered. She plucked a tiny feather from Georgia's shoulder. "Is Robin all right?"

"Oh, he's fine, though he had a bit of a scare." Georgia brushed her other shoulder, dislodging another tiny feather. "I dropped the worm for his dinner and it wiggled away. By the time I retrieved it from under my bed, Smokey had jumped up onto the stool and was hanging from the open cage door. He was quite miffed when I dropped him to the floor. Robin scolded Smokey the entire time I was getting ready."

"Naughty kitty." Ashley cleared her throat and squared her shoulders. "You look stunning in this gown. Let's go find an eligible *parti* for you to stun."

Georgia giggled, as Ashley intended. They linked arms and set off.

A little while later, they heard music coming from a side room—a pianoforte and a male soloist. They exchanged glances, then headed directly for the music.

The singer was a gentleman they'd never heard before, someone who was at least forty and had curly black hair with a hint of grey at his temples.

"That reminds me. I haven't seen Lord Leighton tonight," Georgia said slowly, repeatedly opening then folding her fan.

"I was hoping to speak with Lord Fairfax, but I haven't seen him either." Or heard him, as she often heard his deep voice cutting beneath the chatter long before she saw him, just as Ravencroft's voice did. She frowned. "Have you seen Lord Sutcliff?"

Georgia's eyes widened. "Let's see if we can find any of them."

Within the hour they shared their concerns with Lady Mansfield and Aunt Eunice. "Are you saying all five gentlemen who sang The Switch Song are missing?" Aunt Eunice began plying her fan.

"I haven't seen Mr. Barrett," Lady Mansfield said slowly. "But that's not entirely surprising. He is getting on in years. After the excitement of the last few days, he's probably at home tonight with his wife, resting."

"I'll ask Edward to make a few discreet inquiries," Aunt Eunice said, snapping shut her fan.

Lady Mansfield pursed her lips. "I'll ask my husband to do the same." She glanced at Ashley and Georgia. "In the meantime, say nothing to no one until we get to the bottom of this. I'm sure everything is fine and there is a logical explanation. There are at least a dozen different entertainments they could have attended tonight. Or they could have simply gone to their club. Or even stayed home."

That there might indeed be a logical explanation didn't keep Ashley from worrying. One explanation could be that David had run afoul of Big Bob and Little Lenny. Maggie was still careful to wear a bonnet with a wide brim when she went out on errands with Sally, to help keep from being recognized should anyone from her old life see her.

Another explanation could be that Mr. Barrett was hosting another house party for his former music students. Now that David was indulging in his musical side once more, he would want to attend. She could never resent him developing his incredible talents even further ... but couldn't he have at least said goodbye if he was leaving town for a house party?

Her emotions swung from one extreme to another.

Anger that he could abandon her so blithely.

Heartbreak at missing someone she loved and considered a friend, someone she'd thought she would spend her life with, if she'd correctly understood the song he performed.

Fear that something dreadful had befallen him. That something dreadful had happened and she wasn't there to help him this time. She couldn't confide her fears to Westbrook as she had during David's fever, since he too was missing.

It took everything she had to maintain a polite, cheerful façade for the world as time passed with no word from David. She poured herself into plans for the school. There were only a few weeks before Uncle Edward and Aunt Eunice would set sail for Jamaica again. Rather than try to hide her preoccupation, Ashley decided to let Sally and Maggie in on her plans during their nightly reading lesson.

"You're opening a school of your own?" Sally's eyebrows shot up to her hairline before she quickly reverted to an expression of polite interest.

"And you want us to work for you there?" Maggie glanced around the room. "Away from London?"

"Only if you want. If you wish to stay in London, I will write you a sterling reference and help you find a suitable position. If you decide to come with me, your duties will change. I won't be attending a lot of balls and other entertainments, and naturally will dress very simply as a headmistress. I'm hoping to find a location near the seashore."

"So far away?" Sally looked downcast.

"I've never been to the sea," Maggie said slowly. "Does it smell like the Thames at low tide?"

"It can smell fishy." Ashley thought back to the evenings and her days off when she would walk along the shore at Torquay. She loved to slip off her shoes and stockings and curl her toes into the warm sand. Hike up her skirts in the summer if no one was around, and let the waves tickle her bare ankles. "Naturally the school will need to be a little farther inland, not right on the waterfront. But we'll have lots of fresh air. The fog won't be yellow from burning coal."

"No yellow fog? Count me in!" Maggie clapped her hands twice, then with a guilty expression clasped her hands together at her waist and cast her eyes down.

Sally kept her lips pursed, deep in thought.

"You're going where?" Georgia looked as horrified as if Ashley had just kicked Tuffy, though they were sitting on a sofa at Lady Hartwell's soirée the next night. There still had been no word from Ravencroft, Westbrook, or the other three men. They had simply vanished.

"My uncle's solicitor found three properties that look promising, in Dorset and on the border with Devon. I wanted you to know why I'm leaving tomorrow. I haven't told anyone else outside of our household about the school yet." She had a flashback to her conversation with David. "Well, I did mention it to Ravencroft when he inquired about my search for employment."

"Uncle David knows that you're leaving London?"

"He knows about the idea of the school. I had not yet narrowed my search to any particular properties when we discussed it."

Georgia heaved a great sigh and looked down at her skirt. She absently picked at a few stray hairs that could belong to either Smokey or Tuffy. "You will be sure to write and let me know where you are going? And that you have arrived safely?"

Ashley rested her hand on Georgia's forearm. "I'm not going alone. In fact we are taking two carriages, as Aunt Eunice insists on accompanying Uncle Edward and me, and of course that entails maids and his valet. I will be quite safe."

"But so far away." Ashley barely heard her soft-spoken words.

"Hastings isn't that far, nor is Bognor. Even Lyme Regis is only a journey of two or three days."

"I just wish..." Georgia blinked back tears. "I was so sure."

Me too, Ashley thought as she embraced her friend, her own throat clogged and aching.

Ashley and her party left London at dawn, making sure one of their stops for a meal and to change horses was in Tunbridge Wells. They strolled along the famous Walk to a coffeehouse where they could partake of the famed chalybeate spring water, before climbing back into the carriage and continuing on.

Before Ashley changed for dinner at the inn in Hastings, she kept her promise to Georgia and penned a short note letting her friend know they had arrived safely, expressed hope that Bognor— their next stop—would turn out to be better than its name might imply, and dropped the letter in the outgoing post.

Dinner at the inn could have been cooked by the finest French chef or a child throwing ingredients together at random, for all Ashley could taste. Aunt Eunice had insisted on bringing their own linens so the beds were warm and dry if a little lumpy. Ashley had resisted bringing the pillowcase that still bore Ravencroft's faint scent. Barely.

"What do you think?" Mr. Chadburn said early the next morning. The solicitor had arrived in Hastings in his own carriage, and now rode with them to the estate that was available for lease.

The two-hundred-year-old manor house sat on a bluff, high enough to command a view of the Channel in the distance, and had access to its own private, sandy beach.

"It would do just fine," Ashley said without enthusiasm. Instead of a well-to-do family living here and everyone having private bedchambers, there was plenty of space for classrooms and dormitories. The house had sat vacant through the winter, though a kitchen garden had been planted last year, and the stables were close enough to be convenient but not so close as to smell them in the summer. Madame Zavrina had kept several horses, for pulling the carriage as well as saddle horses to encourage the girls to spend time outdoors and make sure they could ride competently while being courted.

Courting. The process of finding a husband.

Refusing to let herself sigh, Ashley resigned herself to permanently being the headmistress and not the one being courted. Madame Zavrina had done it. She could, too.

Uncle Edward and Mr. Chadburn discussed the property in greater detail and made notes.

"It's close enough to town that you won't feel isolated, and it has adequate fields that you could be almost self-sustaining were you to hire an estate manager," Mr. Chadburn pointed out.

"The landmarks nearby will make teaching history easier," Aunt Eunice added. "Won't your students be excited to visit historic sites?"

"England is such an old country," Ashley muttered, "where *aren't* there historic sites nearby?"

They spent another hour examining the property and making notes before heading back to the inn.

"Perhaps Bognor will be more to your liking," Mr. Chadburn said. "Mrs. Platt's school has an excellent reputation and has been operating for more than a quarter century. Many of the students currently enrolled are the daughters of previous graduates. "

"Taking over an existing school will certainly be simpler than starting one from scratch," Aunt Eunice reminded her.

At the inn, they consulted a map. "My parents may have considered sending me here rather than Torquay," Ashley said. "I vaguely recall not liking the name of the town."

Aunt Eunice smiled at her. Ashley tried to respond in kind but couldn't get the corners of her mouth to lift.

That night, as Ashley was going to her room where Sally and Maggie awaited her, Aunt Eunice tugged her aside.

"Things will get better," she said softly, embracing Ashley. "You just need time."

Ashley nodded, too choked up to speak.

They set out early the next morning. One of their stops for a meal and to change horses was in Brighton.

"If you choose the school in Bognor," Aunt Eunice said, "you'll be able to visit Brighton often and get more than just a glimpse of the Royal Pavilion from a distance. Perhaps even see His Highness!"

Ashley did not comment, as all she could think of was a grumpy *harrumpf.*

They reached Bognor in good time. Late afternoon sunlight glistened on the waves, sparkling like diamonds. Bathing machines on the beaches would enable her to swim in the ocean, not just get her ankles wet. Quaint shops and coffeehouses lined the streets, enticing visitors to linger, and numerous inns offered lodging for those on holiday.

The inn they had chosen for the night was not far from the school, so they decided to drive past the school for a cursory look.

Several young women were out in front of a modest manor house, tending flowerbeds, supervised by a fashionable matron with white hair who vaguely reminded Ashley of Lady Bedford. The matron smiled and waved at the passing carriage. Ashley impulsively rapped on the roof and asked the driver to stop.

"I couldn't help noticing that you're planting marigolds," Ashley said, striding up the front walk from the street. Two of the young women stood up, dusting dirt from their hands. Their hair in long braids, they couldn't be more than fourteen or fifteen. "And that you have beds with lavender and rosemary." The other two girls stood up, shaking dirt from their skirts.

"You are interested in horticulture?" the matron said.

"One of my favorite healing balms uses marigold, lavender, and comfrey."

"I am Mrs. Platt," the matron said, tugging off her gardening gloves. "I am the headmistress here." She tilted her head. "*One* of your favorite balms?"

Ashley introduced herself as well as Aunt Eunice, who had descended from the carriage and joined her.

"Oh, Miss Hamlin!" Mrs. Platt said with a welcoming smile. "We weren't expecting you until tomorrow."

"I didn't mean to intrude." Ashley gestured at the flowerbeds that were being planted. "I just..."

"What if Wendy, Susan, Alice, and Carol here give you a little tour, and we see how much they remember of their lessons?"

The girls curtsied and took turns pointing out each of the plants they were growing, between the four of them listing the medicinal and culinary uses, along with giving the Latin and common names. In the distance Ashley heard the peaceful, muted roar of the surf as the tide came in. More girls came out onto the steps of the *port cochere* to watch the proceedings. By the time they got all the way around the front garden, the sun was beginning to set.

"I don't wish to keep you any longer," Ashley said, raising her voice to be heard above the sound of thundering hooves. Goodness, was this noise something they routinely had to deal with, located so close to an inn? "Tomorrow we can—" She broke off as a coach and six came to an abrupt stop in front of the school, harnesses jangling, blocking the street.

And not just any coach and six. The most elegant coach she had ever clapped eyes on, with so much gilt trim glinting in the setting sun she was almost blinded. Each horse was more stunning than the last, with not one but three men riding postilion.

Two grooms occupied the jump seat at the back. Four riders in full military uniform halted just behind the coach, the horses stamping their hooves.

Aunt Eunice gasped. "Is that the royal crest on the door?"

"Are you expecting visitors?" Ashley said faintly.

Mrs. Platt shook her head.

Behind them the girls were chattering, wondering who could possibly be in such a fancy coach. Could it be the king himself? Perhaps the prince was on his way from one pleasure house to another, but what could possibly bring His Majesty or His Highness to Bognor? And stop at the school?

One of the grooms jumped down. Before he could reach the coach door, it flew open and the occupant stepped out.

Ashley held her hand over her heart that threatened to pound right out of her chest. "David?

Chapter 20

RAVENCROFT GOT HIS BEARINGS on the ground, tugged his waistcoat into place, and gave his head a little toss to flip his hair out of his eyes as he looked around.

Aunt Eunice gasped again.

Ashley was incapable of gasping, as she couldn't draw air. Couldn't move a muscle if her life depended on it.

David spotted her. He broke into a huge grin and strode toward her.

His smile faltered as he got closer, perhaps uncertain of his welcome. He stopped directly in front of Ashley, giving a nod of acknowledgment that included Aunt Eunice, Mrs. Platt, and all the girls avidly watching. His tongue darted out to lick his lips before he drew breath to speak. "His Highness extends his apologies and hopes you'll forgive him."

Of all the words she'd been waiting and hoping to hear from David, these weren't them. "I beg your pardon? The prince asks *my* forgiveness?" She blinked. "The prince."

David nodded.

Ashley looked beyond David to the coach. Definitely looked like it belonged to the royal family. Each of the smartly uniformed outriders, grooms, and postilions looked back at her.

She stared at David. "Why?" So many questions swirled through her brain, she couldn't string together more than one syllable.

David's cheeks flushed pink though he didn't break eye contact with her. "For abducting me when I was about to propose to you."

Beside her, Aunt Eunice muffled a startled exclamation, her hand over her mouth.

David noted their audience, everyone unabashedly eavesdropping, and held out his left arm. "Walk with me?"

Ashley glanced at Aunt Eunice, who made shooing motions. Ashley tucked her arm through David's and they strolled to a row of mulberry bushes on the far side of the garden.

Moving her feet apparently freed her tongue. "I've been worried about you. And angry. And worried."

"I'm so sorry, honey." He held both of her hands in his. "The prince sent his equerries, a lieutenant colonel and a major, to summon me for a command performance. I didn't have a chance to speak to anyone before they practically carried me out of Mansfield's townhouse."

She remembered how he'd arrived that night. "The way Fairfax and Westbrook carried you in?"

He growled. "One of these days I'm going to strangle them both." He ducked his chin and looked at her through his long eyelashes. "I sent a note as soon as I could. It must have arrived after you'd already left London."

"Was Westbrook with you? He's been missing, too."

David nodded. "Along with Fairfax, Sutcliff, and Leighton. We've all been in Brighton, at the Royal Pavilion, entertaining the prince and his guests. They're still there, eating and drinking. And singing."

Ashley felt a bubble of hysterical laughter rise up. "We just passed through Brighton this afternoon."

"While I made a mad dash up to London and then down to Bognor." He squeezed one of her hands. "Georgia thanks you for your note. As do I. I wouldn't have been able to find you so quickly otherwise."

"It looks like you had a comfortable ride." As she watched, Gilroy stepped out of the gilt-encrusted carriage and stretched his legs, walking along the street.

"I have been in agony." David let go one hand to cup her cheek. "I composed that song for you. I sang it for you. *To* you." He caressed her cheek with one thumb. "I'd barely played the last note when I was practically dragged away from you."

He looked at the street for a moment, where Sally was climbing out of Ashley's hired carriage. "Lord Alvanley saw our schoolboy skit and thought the prince would enjoy it. His Highness remembered that his ancestor granted my ancestor the Ravencroft earldom for performing before the court, and decided it was time for another command performance. He even remembered my father entertaining at court when His Highness was a child."

"But how..." Ashley gestured at the royal carriage. She dropped her arm when she noticed Sally and Gilroy holding hands, their heads bowed in close conversation.

"It was several days before I could convince the courtiers to give me a private audience with His Highness. Turns out Prinny is a romantic. When I explained what he'd interrupted, he sent me packing. With an escort. And his apology for you."

Ashley's heart, which had settled down to its usual pace while they talked, began to pound again. "About that interruption..."

David held her hands and raised them in turn to kiss her knuckles, his lips soft and warm. He cleared his throat, his eyes searching her own. "Ashley, I love you beyond distraction. Will you do me the honor of being my wife?"

For a moment she froze, absorbing his words and their meaning, words she'd given up hope of hearing from him. Then she gulped in a deep breath and nodded. Suddenly tears were streaming unchecked down her cheeks. She reached up to grasp his face with both hands, bringing him close. "Yes!"

He claimed her lips in a kiss, tender at first, but they both quickly let loose the emotions they'd been holding so tight. All the fear and worry, gone, replaced by love that had blossomed from their unconventional friendship and scandalous first meeting.

She could have happily gone on kissing him, until the sound of cheers, whoops, and a few whistles brought her crashing back to the present. To where they stood in the front garden of a school for young ladies, with many of the students gawking and cheering. Uncle Edward had left the carriage and stood on the front walk with his arm around Aunt Eunice, who rested her head on his shoulder, both of them beaming at David and Ashley. Maggie was half-hanging out of one carriage window, cheering, while Mr. Chadburn, alone in the other coach, just looked confused. The grooms, outriders, and postilions cheered and whistled.

They quickly sorted things out, with Mrs. Platt and the students going indoors, everyone else taking Uncle Edward's coaches to the inn, and David asking the royal postilions to also take them to the inn, just, "Take the long way around."

"Your carriage awaits, milady," David said with an elegant bow and sweep of his arm.

Ashley accepted his hand as he helped her into the coach.

She barely spared a glance for the opulent interior, with its gold lanterns and sparkling glass chimneys, crimson velvet curtains, and had no idea how comfortable the dark red velvet squabs were, because as soon as David sat on the bench, he pulled her sideways onto his lap. She wrapped one arm around his neck.

"This seems vaguely familiar," he murmured, nuzzling her neck.

She tilted her head back to give him better access, then twined her fingers in his hair and pushed aside his neckcloth so she could rest her head against his chest long enough to hear his heartbeat racing just as fast as hers. She inhaled his honey lemon scent. "No one is being abducted this time."

"I didn't abduct you that first night," he said between kisses along her jaw. "It was a rescue."

Coherent thought was becoming difficult as he nibbled the sensitive skin below her ear. "Just as I rescued you from the alley after the fight."

"No, you kidnapped me."

She pulled back far enough to see his face. "Speaking of ransom... We need to talk about the extra money in my bank account."

He shook his head. "It's a gift. Consider it an anonymous donation for your school. Teach girls to be like you."

She gazed into his beautiful hazel eyes. "To be a bluestocking?"

"Resilient." He gently bit her left ear lobe. "Resourceful." He kissed below her right ear. "Compassionate."

Before he could aim somewhere else, she cupped his cheeks and held him still so she could kiss his mouth. His deep rumble of approval went right through her, making her stomach flutter. Desire stirred low in her belly, shocking her with its intensity. She turned more fully toward him, running her fingers through his thick hair, letting the kiss go on and on.

He broke it off, his warm breath stirring the fine hairs beside her cheek.

Startled, she opened her eyes. "What's wrong?"

"There's something..." He licked his lips. His red, kiss-swollen lips.

Her own must be equally red and swollen. Good. She raised her eyebrows in silent query.

"You didn't... Um." He glanced out the window. His cheeks flushed pink again. "I said... but you didn't... Never mind." He reached to kiss her again.

Understanding dawned. She shifted, hiking up her skirts so she could straddle him, her knees bracketing his hips. She cupped his face. "I love you." She kissed his forehead. "I think I have loved you since I first heard you sing, helping your niece learn an aria." She dropped a kiss on his right cheek. "I've loved you since I heard you entertain children with a scary story." She kissed his cheek just below his left eye, where his face had recently been black and blue. "I have definitely loved you since you fought two bullies to defend a woman most men wouldn't give a second thought to, unless they wanted to toss her skirts."

She leaned back in his embrace and took a fortifying breath. "I haven't had much experience saying those three words the last few years. No one to say them to." Her voice broke. "Until now."

"Honey." The endearment, rumbled in his deep voice, was as much a caress as his hand cupping her cheek.

She sniffed back tears. "I will happily say those words to you. Every day. For the next sixty or seventy years." She shifted, letting more of her weight rest on his lap, and smoothed hair back from his face, stroking the long, silky strands.

He groaned and pulled her toward him for another bone-melting, toe-curling kiss. She shivered with delight as his hands skimmed down her shoulders, along her ribs, around to her hips, and cupped her backside.

She wrapped one hand around the back of his neck and rested one palm over his chest, delighting in the feel of his pounding heart. She tilted her hips, needing to be even closer to him, and gasped when she felt the evidence of his desire. She moaned and parted her lips when his tongue sought entry, and rocked her hips in time with their deep kiss.

"Honey," came his ragged groan minutes or hours later. "We're not going to make it three weeks for the banns to be read if we keep this up."

"I don't care," she whispered, gleefully tossing years of protecting her reputation out the window. "I want to touch you. All of you. And I want you to touch me." She could untie his cravat so she could kiss his neck, but that would require letting go of his face, withdrawing her fingers from his hair. Perhaps she could use her teeth...

He moaned, pulling her tight against him.

The horses slowed and came to a gentle halt. Shouts from ostlers made it clear they had reached the inn yard.

She swore in frustration, a very unladylike oath, and dropped her forehead to his shoulder.

He chuckled, and she felt the delicious vibration through her whole body as he wrapped his arms around her and held her in his snug embrace. "Gilroy can ride in the other carriage with Sally tomorrow," he murmured in her ear.

She sat up a little, her brows raised.

"That means we'll have this coach to ourselves." He tugged her sleeve back up on one shoulder and tucked a loose tendril of hair behind her ear, trailing his fingertip down her neck. "All the way back to London."

Her breath caught at the mischievous glint in his eyes.

Hearing the groom's footsteps drawing near, she sat on the opposite bench and straightened her skirts just before the door opened. "I like your plan."

Epilogue

London
Four weeks later

THE RECEPTION LINE FOR THEIR WEDDING BREAKFAST dealt with, David took his bride by the hand and strolled through the swirling crowds of well-wishers that filled the public rooms of the Ravencroft townhouse, aiming for the dining room. Thanks to planning from Aunt Connie and Mrs. Endicott, who had asked him to call her Aunt Eunice, the table and sideboards groaned beneath platters of delicacies and different kinds of punch. One pitcher, Ashley discreetly pointed out to him, did not contain any alcohol.

He'd been too anxious to eat anything this morning. Not that he worried his bride would leave him at the altar. But they'd hardly seen each other since the first reading of the banns, what with her inspecting properties, selecting the one to be her school, and getting ready to take over as headmistress at Mrs. Platt's school, while he'd needed to visit his estate. Spring had been colder than typical, and summer was still nowhere in sight other than the almanac, and as a result this year's crops were not growing the way they should. Mr. Ogden had been concerned it was due to his experimental changes. David reassured him it was not; he had talked with enough landowners in Parliament to know the unusually cool weather was adversely affecting everyone.

Notes from a Vivaldi sonata on the pianoforte drifted out from the music room. Sounded like Missy was getting better. David raised Ashley's hand for another kiss, and was rewarded with her smile that still made his heart beat double-time.

The smile fell from her face and she let go of him to plant her fists on her hips. "No," she said in what he'd come to think of as her Headmistress voice, standing tall and fierce as she addressed the two army officers who had just stepped foot inside. "You are not taking him again." She put her body in front of his, her chin raised to a mutinous angle. "Not today."

The colonel shook his head. "I would not dream of it, Lady Ravencroft."

Feeling a rush of emotion at the reminder this fabulous, fierce woman was now his countess, David rested a possessive hand on her shoulder and caressed her bare nape with his thumb.

"We ask only for a moment of your time," said the other officer, a major. "Outside."

As Ashley drew breath to protest, the colonel added, "Both of you."

He and Ashley exchanged puzzled glances, then followed the officers out the front door and down the steps. An elegant black carriage waited in the street, with a uniformed postilion instead of a coachman, plus two grooms, and two outriders on horseback. Though the door displayed no crest, David suspected he knew the occupant's identity.

The major strode forward to open the carriage door and beckoned David and Ashley closer.

Holding hands, they cautiously approached and peered inside.

Ashley gasped and dropped into a deep curtsy.

"My felicitations on your wedding, my boy," came a familiar voice from the interior.

David bowed. "Thank you, sir."

Ashley squeezed his hand until her knuckles were white but displayed no other reaction.

"I would have abandoned me for her, too." He chuckled and extended a beringed hand.

David nudged Ashley, who gave herself a slight shake and reached up so that her hand could be kissed.

"I'm having another gathering of friends in a few weeks and I would like you to attend." He cleared his throat. "Both of you."

"That's very generous of you, sir."

"Uh, yes, thank you ... sir."

"My secretary will contact your secretary." After a subtle signal from the occupant, the major and colonel both climbed into the carriage, shut the door, and the carriage set off. The outriders nodded as they rode past. One of them, whom David recognized from his mad dash a few weeks ago, gave them a broad wink.

"Well." Ashley stared after the carriage as it merged with traffic and gradually disappeared from sight.

"Nonplussed, honey? You?"

She tore herself away from the view of the street to gift him with the same dazzling smile that had made him weak in the knees when they'd exchanged vows just hours ago. "No, I just—"

"Whatever are you two doing out here?" Aunt Connie called from the top step.

"Receiving felicitations from an acquaintance who didn't want to disembark from his coach." Taking Ashley's hand once more, they climbed the steps and back into the hallway.

"His laziness is no excuse for you to neglect your guests," Aunt Connie said with a knowing grin.

When David tried to go left to the dining room before his stomach betrayed him with a growl, Ashley spotted her cousin Niles and his wife making serious inroads on the amount of food on the sideboard. She tugged David the other way, then suddenly let go of him to greet the three women who had just arrived.

After muffled squeals of delight and exuberant hugs, Ashley quickly made the introductions of former colleagues of hers—two women about Ashley's age, Miss Chase and Miss Chetwynn; and a gray-haired matron with work-roughened hands, Mrs. Rafferty.

He gave appropriate greetings to the former teachers, then addressed Mrs. Rafferty. "I've heard excellent reports about your honey and comfrey healing poultice."

"Have you now, my lord?" She stood a little taller.

"I say, Ravencroft," Fairfax said, steering him by the elbow toward the sideboard with the wine, champagne, and punch bowls.

Ashley wiggled her fingers farewell at him before she delved deep into conversation with friends she hadn't seen in months.

"What?" David barely resisted it coming out as a growl.

"I heard your wife is going to be headmistress of a school. That can't possibly be true, now that she's a countess. Can it?"

Liam, who was already at the sideboard, handed David the glass he'd just filled from the pitcher of apple cider, then filled a glass with rum punch for himself. "Why not?"

Fairfax looked between the two of them, obviously uncertain if they were serious. "Your wife is planning to work? Are you going to allow that?"

David shrugged one shoulder. "She's going to help shape impressionable young minds." He looked over to where she was in animated conversation with her friends. "I've offered to help her provide the girls a curriculum with a little more focus on music."

"That will certainly improve the quality of misses coming into the Marriage Mart," Liam said.

"I'm glad you agree." David wrapped an arm around Liam's shoulders. "You can help create the music lessons."

"No, no, no. I have my own music students and need to prepare lessons for them."

"I thought—"

Liam shook his head. "My primary student returned to town a few days ago and requested we resume his lessons." He dipped his chin. "*Just* lessons. Apparently there is a widow he wishes to impress with his musical ability."

David thought that was suspiciously convenient, considering Liam had practically twisted David's arm to participate in the Catch Club competition so Liam could get a share of the prize money. Liam had worried he'd offended his patron and in doing so, cut off a large portion of his income. "Everything is well between you two?"

Liam grinned. "He has a new grandson. There were delays in getting the letter from his son in Northumberland, so he barely arrived in time for the birth even though he left London abruptly."

Aunt Connie tucked her arm through David's. "Excuse me, gentlemen. I'd like to borrow my nephew for a moment."

David barely had a chance to swallow a mouthful of cider and set down his cup before Connie began walking. They strolled through the hall, nodding as they passed Templeton and Mansfield. Lydia and Diana beamed at him. If he were a suspicious person, he'd wonder what they were up to.

Connie led him all the way to the terrace in the small back garden. Birds chirped from their perch in the apple trees. Instead of heading to a bench in the dappled sunlight beneath the trees,

Connie paused at the railing and rested both hands on his forearm. He was surprised to note a slight tremble in her hands.

"Your parents aren't here so I'll do my best to fill in." She looked up at him, anxiously searching his face. "I'm not sure how much attention Sebastian gave you, what with teaching Philip to follow in his footsteps."

"I never felt neglected. Father needed to train his heir."

"Did he... That is..." Connie cleared her throat, then looked him straight in the eye. "Did he tell you what you need to know to take good care of your bride on your wedding night?"

David choked.

"Since Ashley's parents are gone," Aunt Connie blithely continued, "I hope her aunt is making sure she knows what to expect." She tapped her chin with one finger, her ruby ring flashing in the sunlight.

David wasn't sure if he should laugh, and hoped his cheeks weren't blushing bright red. "I'm sure Aunt Eunice feels Ashley is adequately educated for her role as my countess." He turned back toward the door. "Was there anything else?"

Connie tugged on his arm to hold him in place. "My father, your grandfather, was a good man, but he spent too much time with his music, in here," she tapped her temple. "So much so, the estate was almost bankrupt by the time Sebastian inherited. Your father worked hard to restore the family funds and keep the tenants fed. He squeezed every penny before he spent it, kept everyone on a strict budget. Hired good people like Mr. Ogden. Still stuck his nose in every move they made. Practically every time a lamb took its first breath or a seed sprouted, he knew about it."

She reached up to pat David's cheek. "When Philip reached twenty-one and showed an aptitude for taking care of the earldom, Sebastian finally began to relax a bit. Played music. Composed new pieces again."

David thought back to the pages of unfinished music he'd found in his father's bedchamber.

"I trust that you will not be like your grandfather, living for his music to the detriment of all else. Nor should you be like your father, waiting decades before indulging your talent."

"Who do you think I should be like?"

"You." She patted his arm. "Forge your own path."

Seeing Ashley through the open doorway, still animatedly speaking with her friends, he took one step toward the house. "That's exactly what I planned."

Aunt Connie tugged on his arm again. "You didn't answer my first question."

David thought through their conversation, and felt his cheeks heat. "Yes." He cleared his throat. "I know how to take care of my bride. Every day and night for the rest of our lives."

"Good boy." Still holding his arm, she headed for the door. "I wasn't looking forward to continuing that particular conversation," she muttered.

Me, neither.

Connie drifted into the crowd. David retrieved his cup of cider from the sideboard.

Liam spoke quietly, tilting his head toward Connie. "Need something a little stronger after that?"

David scrubbed his face with his hands, then glanced at where Connie was gliding into the music room. "No, I think we'll both survive."

Ashley walked up to them just then and tucked her arm through David's. After Fairfax and Liam acknowledged her, she gave David's arm a squeeze. "Mrs. Rafferty has just agreed to be my assistant headmistress. That means she'll handle the day-to-day operations of the school."

David glanced over to where Mrs. Rafferty was now conversing with Aunt Eunice. "That's fabulous, honey."

"Gentlemen, if I may, I'm going to steal my husband."

Several steps away, David steered Ashley into an alcove behind a statue. "You may steal me anytime you wish," he murmured, nuzzling beneath her ear.

"You're trying to distract me," she replied, tilting her head back.

Smugly, he noted she was quickly becoming breathless. "Mm-hm."

She tugged his watch out of his waistcoat pocket. "Save it for—" she consulted the watch, then tucked it back in his pocket, intimately pressing her palm to his abdomen as she did so "—about four hours from now."

He groaned in frustration when she took his hand to pull him along. "That's an eternity."

"Clarissa and Georgia told me about the Linford family tradition regarding spouses," Ashley quietly said as they stepped through the music room doorway. "I want to play for you."

He drew breath to assure her she'd passed the Linford test long before she transcribed his composition for him, but got distracted when she nervously licked her lips. "Anything you want, honey," he murmured, resisting the urge to kiss her only because of the numerous friends and family still circulating around them, wanting a hug or handshake or to pat him on the back.

He let her position him beside the pianoforte, standing close to the keys, before she settled on the bench and made sure the sheet music was in order. Within moments he went perfectly still, chills coursing down his spine, as she played the opening bars of Pachelbel's *Canon in D Major*.

Of all the music he'd ever played, composed, or arranged, this was still one of his favorites. It always brought him peace. Made him feel tranquil no matter how much his life might be in turmoil.

How did she know?

He hadn't played it since that night in Liam's music room when he'd lain awake, worried about Ashley learning his secret. And earlier that same evening, when he'd played it as a warmup at Diana's house, horribly botching it without sheet music after not playing it for so long. Had Ashley been listening to him?

About five measures in, the deep strains of the violoncello joined the pianoforte.

Diana spared him only a brief smile before she returned her attention to her instrument and sheet music.

A few moments later, Clarissa began playing the viola. Then Deirdre on her violin, and Lydia joined on her lyre. The music continued to swell as Missy played her flute and Georgia plucked the harp, everyone coming in after a specific interval. Lydia's arrangement.

Dear Lord, even Aunt Connie was playing her soprano viola da gamba.

All the women in his life, it seemed, had come together to practice and play.

For him.

Between planning the wedding breakfast and all the preparations for her school, when had Ashley possibly made time to rehearse?

He considered getting his viola da gamba and joining them, until he realized Ashley was playing for the same reason Norcross had wanted to sing to Clarissa at their wedding breakfast.

An expression of her love.

He basked in it, resting his hands on the pianoforte, reveling in the sensations, the subtle vibrations in the wood frame, as his wife played. For him. Peace radiated from his chest and spread warmth through his body.

For once he was able to ignore imperfections like someone playing the wrong note or coming in late, and focus on the gesture of love being offered to him.

Ashley glanced up at him when she turned the page. At her tender, vulnerable expression, his breath caught and his throat closed up. Distantly he registered the room filling with sound and people. His nieces and nephews, brothers-in-law, Liam who was like a brother, his friends, her friends, his new in-laws.

Though they'd both lost their parents, this room was filled with family. With love.

With the woman who was now his wife. His life. A drastically different life than the one he'd envisioned before he reluctantly became the earl. Not the carefree life he'd planned to live as the second son, but not the life of unrelenting duty and soul-crushing responsibility that he thought he'd inherited with the title, either. Ashley had helped him see that. He had carried her on a dark garden path the night they met, and in return she'd helped him find his path.

His heart felt full to bursting.

As soon as Ashley played the last notes and dropped her hands to her lap, David sat beside her on the bench and slid one arm around her waist. "Beautiful, honey," he said in her ear. Too choked up to utter another syllable or be more eloquent, he buried his face against her neck, inhaling her faint rose scent.

She wrapped her arms around him, burrowing under his coat. "You truly liked it?"

He pulled back far enough to give her a kiss, uncaring of their audience. "You were magnificent." He pushed a loose tendril of hair over her shoulder, an excuse to caress her bare skin. "I'm so glad you abducted ... my heart."

When he paused on the *m* in 'my', her eyes widened in panic. She looked to see if anyone was close enough to hear, then quickly narrowed them in mock anger. "Wretch," she whispered.

"Happy wretch," he whispered back.

With a mischievous grin, she clutched his cravat and tugged him close for a kiss.

Thank you for reading David and Ashley's story! I hope you enjoyed it as much as I did writing it. The next book in the Brazen Bluestockings series, *My Devoted Viscount*, features the other bass singer we spent time with: Vincent, Viscount Fairfax.

Vincent's secret is *not* that he's a soprano, as David teased. Can't wait for you to meet his heroine, Sophia, a music teacher, and read their adventure in an old manor by the sea that may or may not be haunted. Keep reading for a sneak peek at their story.

My Devoted Viscount sneak peek:

"Where the devil did they move the bootjack?"

The irritated voice Sophia heard was so deep it was more of a growl than speech. While she pondered why an unknown man had entered her dreams, the mattress dipped, rolling her over onto her back.

A curse, but in a foreign language. Italian? Something thumped on the floor, and Sophia's eyes flew open.

Not dreaming.

Sitting on the edge of her bed, his white shirtsleeves and dangling ends of a cravat luminous in the midnight gloom, a man she'd never before seen raised his right foot, trying to pull off his boot.

How had she been so careless as to forget to wedge the chair under the doorknob?

She grabbed the candelabra from under her pillow as she sat up and held it with both hands like a cricket bat. "Get out." Not wanting to draw attention to her predicament from other members of the household unless it became necessary, she kept her voice quiet and confident, proud it didn't quaver despite her pounding heart.

The man's booted foot thumped to the floor as he stared at her, his face in shadow, his voice low. "What are you doing in my room?"

His speech wasn't slurred, and she didn't smell any alcohol emanating from him. Just horse and leather and fresh ocean air.

Two years ago, one of the uncles dropping off a student at the academy had to stay the night when the roads became impassable following a torrential rainstorm. After drinking more wine at dinner than all the staff combined, he had entered Sophia's room after midnight, claiming he had mistaken it for his own.

"I've been staying in this room for the past fortnight, at Mrs. Digby's request." Sophia tightened her grip on the candlestick to keep her hands from trembling. "Get out, now. Or you won't be the first unconscious man I've removed from my bedchamber."

He uttered a low sound, one that could have been a chuckle. Abruptly he walked unerringly, albeit unevenly—one boot on, one boot off—to grab a candle from the writing desk, lit it from the coals in the fireplace, then lit another candle on the mantel.

He turned to stare at her, arms folded in front of his broad chest, feet planted wide and confident. His gaze traveled from the top of her hair in twin braids, down her face, over her flannel night rail, and to her legs under the blanket, which she'd crossed tailor-style in preparation for leaping at her attacker.

"Tiny thing like you? You wouldn't be able to budge me." Not only was he more than a foot taller than her, he had to outweigh her by at least six stone. He seemed amused and spoke as though they were bantering in a crowded ballroom.

Two other teachers had helped her drag the unconscious uncle by his ankles to his room, but she was confident she could complete the task tonight on her own if necessary. "I might drop you on the floor a time or two. You'll have bruises as well as a bump on your head."

He made another rumbling sound that might be a chuckle.

In one fluid movement, she stood up, candelabra at her shoulder as though ready to swing a bat, just as the groundskeeper at the academy had taught her. She drew breath to threaten the intruder again.

"Why do you sleep with a candlestick under your pillow?" He tilted his head as he blatantly looked her up and down, his long hair brushing one shoulder.

"Takes up less space than a cricket bat." She returned his stare just as boldly. How rarely had she seen a man undressed to his shirtsleeves, his cravat untied and shirt unbuttoned, exposing a vee of naked skin at the base of his throat? No grey strands marred his black hair, worn roguishly long and loose. He was too far away and the shadows too deep to see if his face had wrinkles. His smooth voice held a flirtatious tone rather than malice. But she had been fooled before.

"Of course. How silly of me."

She adjusted her stance, debating. Should she get down from the wobbly mattress, or stay where she had the advantage of the high ground?

"A fortnight, you say?" He scratched his jaw. "You don't look like a ghost."

She almost dropped the candelabra. "I beg your pardon?"

"Aunt Gertrude wrote that a ghost other than the Grey Lady has been fluttering about the grounds. If you're not the ghost, then you must be the scribe she wanted paper and ink for." With his chin, he indicated a satchel on the dressing table chair, almost buried beneath a greatcoat.

Aunt Gertrude? Understanding dawned, filling her with a different kind of dread. "You're Vincent. Mrs. Digby's nephew."

She heard the smug smile in his deep, rumbling voice. "You've heard of me?"

"Only that it's been so long since you last visited, the pianoforte and harpsichord were out of tune."

"Ah, dear Aunt Gert. I've been busy. I promise I will attend to her pianoforte in the morning."

Which still left him standing in her room. "Clearly I am not a ghost. Nor am I yielding this bedchamber in the middle of the night." She frowned as a glance confirmed that the chair she'd wedged under the doorknob, blocking access from the hall, was still in place. "How did you get in? Who else knows you're here?"

"Didn't want to wake the staff, so I used the hidden passageway." He dropped his arms to his side and lowered his chin, his voice impossibly deeper. "No one knows I'm here except you, *cara*. That's a big, comfortable bed. We could share."

Despite the Italian endearment, his cultured accent was entirely British. The tone of his outrageous suggestion was lighthearted rather than lascivious. She'd had to share a room with a stranger on her journey here. But inns always paired travelers of the same gender. She adjusted her grip on the candelabra and bluffed. "The last man I hit lost two teeth."

His bared teeth gleamed in the candlelight, and he made that quiet rumbling sound again that made her insides quiver. "I confess, I prefer my teeth just the way they are." He bowed. "You win. Tonight." He strode confidently toward the bed despite his uneven gait from wearing only one boot.

"What-" She cleared her throat to get rid of the squeak. "What do you think you're doing?"

He was tall enough that he sat on the edge of the bed without needing the steps. She bent her knees to keep from falling as the mattress shifted under his weight. "Putting my boot back on. I'll sleep downstairs, on the sofa in the library." He picked up his boot. "What was Aunt Gert thinking, giving my room to someone else," he muttered.

"Perhaps if you visited dear Aunt Gert more often, she would also think of it as your room."

Vincent paused in pulling on his boot to cock his head to the side and look up at her from beneath what she could now see were long, dark lashes. "Touché," he said, a smile tilting the corner of his mouth.

Her breath hitched. Dear lord, he was handsome. She coughed. "Shouldn't you leave it off? And remove the other one? Someone will hear your footsteps!" Now that she felt sure the intruder didn't plan to ravish her, years of carefully protecting her reputation flashed before her. Would Mrs. Digby toss her out if she thought Sophia had been improper with her nephew? Even if Mrs. Digby let Sophia finish the task for which she'd been hired, she'd never find another job at a ladies' academy if her reputation was tarnished. And she couldn't let this job end prematurely. Too much was at stake.

When Vincent stood, his gaze was level with Sophia's chest. "I have never ... enjoyed a woman's company ... with my boots on." He raised his gaze to her face, winked at her, and gathered his coat from the foot of the bed. "Do not fret. No one is going to hear me." He collected his greatcoat and satchel, then touched one of the wallpaper ivy leaves beside the fireplace. With a soft click and puff of chilled air, a section of the wall swung outward.

Sophia's mouth fell open. How could she have been so careless? Knowing about the secret passageway that connected the library, kitchen, and tunnel to the beach, why hadn't she checked her own room more thoroughly? It was only logical that someone needing a secret passageway to the beach or stables may need to evacuate from an upper floor. A chair wedging the door closed from the hall was of no use if someone could merely walk through the wall.

"Your virtue is unchanged and my teeth are intact. Shall we agree that tonight's misunderstanding will remain our secret?" Standing beside the mantel, a candle close by, she saw a faint smile still lifting one corner of his mouth. As she stared, he lifted one eyebrow.

She gulped. "Yes. That's for the best."

"I look forward to meeting you in the morning, *cara*."

She snorted. He probably addressed every female–except his aunt–as *cara*.

With another elegant bow, he ducked into the opening and pulled the door—wall?—shut.

I hope you enjoyed reading this excerpt from *My Devoted Viscount!* To keep reading, visit the Books page on my website: ShirleyKarrAuthor.com or your favorite book retailer. Newsletter subscribers can also download my free book, *Regency Phrasebook: A Compendium of Slang, Idioms, and Curious Phrases Commonly Found in Historic Fiction.*

Author's Notes

While I was finishing up my previous series, Scandalous Ladies, I started thinking about what I would write next. I had just taken up writing again after a 14-year break. My "Story Ideas" folder was sadly out of date.

A friend on social media shared a link to a new YouTube video by a singer I'd never heard of before, Geoff Castellucci, doing his low bass singer cover of *Monster Mash*. Ninety seconds in, I was a fan. The harmonies! The humor! In addition to his solo work, Geoff is the co-founder and bass singer of the a cappella group VoicePlay. When the first video finished, YouTube took me to Geoff's cover of *Headless Horseman*, then VoicePlay's version of *Oogie Boogie's Song* and *This is Halloween*, both from *The Nightmare Before Christmas*. (To get the full experience, headphones or earbuds strongly recommended.) Geoff quickly became my favorite bass, baritone, and tenor singer. But I needed story ideas, not to spend hours listening to music ... no matter how entertaining.

Apparently inspired by the spooky songs, a few days later I woke up wondering, what if the Boogeyman—or someone pretending to be the British equivalent—was a member of London society? What would motivate a Regency gentleman to adopt the persona of a scary character from folklore? A week later I had answers that became the plot of this book, and a week after that started writing it as part of NaNoWriMo ... the fastest I have ever gone from random plot bunny to Chapter One.

Music plays a huge role in this story, and I went down some really fun rabbit holes in my research. Let me give you a tour of the burrow.

For a previous project, I had found references to The Noblemen and Gentlemen's Catch Club. Founded in London in 1761, it was active for over 200 years. (For a long time, "catch" was interchangeable with "round." Many of us learned *Row, Row, Row Your Boat* as our first catch.) Membership in the prestigious Catch

Club was highly sought after, as were its annual prizes awarded for best performance, best original composition, and so on. Membership was capped at a relatively low number. If you missed too many meetings, your membership was forfeit and a singer from the waiting list was allowed to take your place. Many other glee and catch clubs formed, filled with men waiting for a chance to get into the original Catch Club.

I'd heard that when Francis Scott Key put his poem *Defense of Fort McHenry* to music he used an old drinking song, *To Anacreon in Heaven*. The combination became known as *The Star Spangled Banner*. No way I believed a bunch of drunk guys could sing that tune. Turns out The Anacreontic Society, a London gentlemen's club for singers from about 1766 to 1792, would sing it at the beginning of their meetings ... when everyone was still sober. Anacreon (uh-NACK-ree-uhn) was an ancient Greek poet known for his love poems and drinking songs, and the Society met to eat, drink, and sing catches and glees (relatively short songs written for three or more voices).

Okay, so my hero likes to sing, has an awesome voice, and is probably a member of a club of like-minded gentlemen. Then what?

My friend Helen, who's been a fan of a cappella music for years, clued me into the group Home Free. Knowing I liked Geoff's multi-octave voice (basso profundo up to tenor), she was correct that I'd appreciate Home Free's bass singer, Tim Foust, who is also known to have a range of five octaves. (Apparently the same physiology that allows someone to sing low bass also allows them to continue to sing baritone and into tenor range, without going into Frankie Valli-style falsetto, if they keep practicing the upper ranges, though it does take a lot of work.)

She pointed out that Home Free and VoicePlay had competed on season four of *The Sing-Off*, that ran 2009-2013. I had watched the show during an earlier season when Peter Hollens performed with On the Rocks from the University of Oregon, but lost interest after our "local guys" were eliminated. All the episodes are available on YouTube. I quickly realized the show could be a musical version of a Fantasy Football League, jumping-off points for creating characters. So now it was easy to figure out who my hero sang with and competed against.

David's title, Ravencroft, is an homage to Thurl Ravenscroft (1914-2005). He stood 6'5" and his career as a bass singer and voice actor spanned 65 years though he is probably best remembered for singing *You're A Mean One, Mr. Grinch*, and being the voice of Tony the Tiger, mascot of Kellogg's Frosted Flakes cereal, for 50 years. *("They'rrre grrreat!")*

My high regard for low voices is not new. While my high school classmates were rocking out to Van Halen, I cranked the bass on my boombox until Richard Sterban of The Oak Ridge Boys rattled the windows on the "*oom poppa mow mow*" lines in *Elvira*. Instead of power ballads from Journey, I sang along with The Statler Brothers (*Flowers On the Wall; You Can't Have Your Kate and Edith Too*), a group known for their comedy almost as much as their gospel and country music. Lead singer Don Reid's baritone is smooth as butter but it's his brother, Harold Reid, whose bass voice called to me.

Harold was the class clown of the quartet. My Switch Song skit was inspired by a comedy bit Harold did when the Statlers performed with legendary bass singer J.D. Sumner (1924-1998) and his group at the time, Masters V. Harold did a sound check with the mic from different singers, "proving" that it was the mic that dictated each singer's range, not his voice. An imposing gent who stood 6'5", J.D. joined in the silliness. Harold was a solid bass but J.D. could drop into the cellar at will with a bone-rattling basso profundo.

A giant in southern gospel music, J.D. Sumner composed over 700 songs in a career that lasted 60 years. One of his early fans was then-teenager Elvis Presley, and the two formed a lifelong friendship. In the 1970s, J.D. and his group toured with Elvis as his opening act, then joined him on stage as part of the backing vocalists. In what turned out to be Elvis's last song to hit #1, *Way Down*, you can hear J.D. in the backing vocals, including a C1 at the very end. That note is just three white keys from the end of the 88-key piano keyboard.

By the way, Steinway created the piano with 88 keys in the 1880s—for a total of seven octaves—which then became and remains the standard. That's pretty much the limit of frequencies the human ear can hear.

Bach, Handel, and other Baroque composers wrote for the harpsichord, which has been around since the middle ages and was the gold standard for centuries. But it has a range of only five octaves

308

and uses a mechanism to pluck the strings, so no matter how hard or soft you press the key, the volume produced is the same. Since it can't get very loud, it was great for playing in the family parlour in the evening. As advancements were made with other instruments and music venues got larger, it began to fall out of favor.

Bartolomeo Cristofori (1655-1731) improved on the harpsichord's limitations by building an instrument that uses a hammer mechanism to strike the strings instead of plucking them. Because a player can change the dynamics (soft, medium, and loud) he named it the pianoforte—which literally translates to "soft loud" in Italian. During the Regency era both instruments had 60 keys, but the increased flexibility of the pianoforte made it the new standard, and Beethoven and others began composing music specifically for it.

Flute, harp, and violin were common instruments for ordinary folk to play in the days before any form of recorded entertainment was available. What other instruments might my characters play?

The Orchestra of the Age of Enlightenment (OAE) plays instruments similar to those that existed when Bach, Mozart, and Vivaldi were composing, in the style of playing that was popular at that time, so we can hear their music as the composers intended it to be heard. The ancestor of my favorite instrument, the trombone, did exist in the Regency but it was known as the sackbut. Its name is derived from two French verbs meaning push and pull, which is what you do with the slide. Call me juvenile but I just could not write that word without giggling. Sorry. And I wanted my hero to sing to his heroine while he played, so that eliminated all wind instruments.

The OAE introduced me to the viola da gamba, aka the bass viol. It can be strung with five, six, or seven strings. The seventh string gives it access to a deeper range than a bass, while the upper strings can still play the range of a violin, and everything in between. For a hero with a singing range of almost five octaves, what else would he play but the viola da gamba? It was a popular solo instrument that allowed people to provide their own entertainment and accompaniment, and reportedly was a favorite of King Louis XIV.

I decided Liam plays the mandolin because its light tone suits his personality and provides a pleasant contrast to the viola da gamba. And because two of my favorite composers, Mozart and Vivaldi, wrote awesome concertos featuring the mandolin. If you don't know Vivaldi beyond *The Four Seasons*, you're missing out on a lot of splendid music. Bugs Bunny cartoons and eight years of playing the trombone in concert band gave me a lifelong love of classical music, even if I played with more enthusiasm than actual skill. I often have it playing in the background while writing, to help evoke the era my characters inhabit.

What did my hero sing with his magnificent voice? I was surprised to learn that there was almost no singing by congregants in church during the Regency era, so hymns were out. Songs from operas were popular. Irish poet Thomas Moore (1779-1852) was a prolific lyricist, and at the request of publishers, wrote lyrics to traditional Irish tunes. *The Irish Melodies* were released in ten volumes over a span of 26 years. They proved to be immensely popular and were translated into several languages. Over 200 years later, many are still regularly performed, including *The Last Rose of Summer:*

> 'Tis the last rose of summer,
> Left blooming alone;
> All her lovely companions
> Are faded and gone;
> No flower of her kindred,
> No rose-bud is nigh,
> To reflect back her blushes
> Or give sigh for sigh!
> I'll not leave thee, thou lone one.
> To pine on the stem;
> Since the lovely are sleeping,
> Go, sleep thou with them;
> Thus kindly I scatter
> Thy leaves o'er the bed,
> Where thy mates of the garden
> Lie scentless and dead.
> So soon may I follow,
> When friendships decay,
> And from love's shining circle
> The gems drop away!
> When true hearts lie withered,
> And fond ones are flown,

Oh! who would inhabit
This bleak world alone?

Like David and Ashley, I find it melancholy, but who am I to question something that's been popular since 1813?

Henry Purcell (1659-1695) started writing music as early as age 11 and was a prolific composer, including what is arguably England's first opera, *Dido and Aeneas,* in 1688. Purcell wrote dozens of operas, hymns, instrumental works, and music for plays ... but is most remembered by non-scholars for his catches with suggestive lyrics and double entendres. Shakespeare had nothing on Purcell when it came to entertaining the masses with bawdy content. Playing on his popularity with working-class men, Purcell's songs were often about women, drinking, and sex. He's heavily featured on *The Art of the Bawdy Song*. I still have that cassette tape, a relic of the 1990s, complete with liner notes and lyrics.

I'm going to indulge my fondness for bass singers at least once more. The hero of *My Devoted Viscount,* the next book in the Brazen Bluestockings series, is Viscount Fairfax. There's an excerpt from his book at the end of the Epilogue.

Also by Shirley Karr:

Brazen Bluestockings
My Reluctant Earl
My Devoted Viscount (spring 2024)

Scandalous Ladies
What An Earl Wants
Kiss From A Rogue
Confessions of A Viscount
The Viscount's Hidden Treasure

ABOUT THE AUTHOR

Shirley Karr's love of all things Regency began in childhood, when her father's Air Force career took the family to England for four years. Not only did they visit historic houses, museums, and castles galore, they lived in centuries-old housing.

She currently resides in the Pacific Northwest with her husband (whom she met on a blind date and married five months later), son, and multiple four-legged family members. To unwind, she loves to make jewelry with gemstones and pearls, grow tomatoes, and go tent camping at the Oregon coast.

She's back after a fourteen-year break from writing, telling lighthearted stories of adventure and romance with a dash of spice, set in Regency England.

I love to hear from readers! Drop me a line at:
Shirley@ShirleyKarrAuthor.com
Visit me on the web:www.ShirleyKarrAuthor.com

Follow me on social media:
Facebook: Shirley Karr Author
Pinterest: Shirley Karr Author
BookBub: Shirley Karr
Goodreads: Shirley Karr